First Abigail Drake grabs you with her fresh writing, then she keeps you in the throes of her story with an incredible voice and a gifted talent for spinning tales that will amaze and delight. I am stunned. Tiger Lily will consume you, and before you know it you are fighting for air yet begging for more. You've been warned!

— - NY TIMES BESTSELLING AUTHOR
DARYNDA JONES

This is one of those hidden gems that you long to come across. It has a little bit of everything in it; romance, paranormal, mystery and lots of action. There are so many twists and turns. A book that packs a punch you'll never see coming.

Absolute perfection!

— DARK RAVEN REVIEWS

THE HOCUS POCUS MAGIC SHOP

ABIGAIL DRAKE

Cover Art by Najla Qamber

Developmental Edits by Ramona DeFelice Long

Line Edits by Lara Parker

In loving memory of my own nunny, Florence Lonnett Riddel, and with appreciation to my amazing great-aunt, Alvida Pisani Lonnett, for all the lessons you have taught me and all the laughter we have shared. Ti amo.

CHAPTER 1

NEVER TRUST AN ATOM. THEY MAKE UP EVERYTHING.

Dr. Lewis, head of the chemistry department at the University of Pennsylvania, sat stiffly at his large, imposing desk. The sun made the wood in his office take on a honeyed glow, and it illuminated the words etched in the stained-glass window behind him.

Sapientia et Veritas. Knowledge and Truth.

They seemed like very important words all of a sudden.

"Do you have anything you'd like to share with me, Ms. O'Leary?" he asked.

My heart pounded as I struggled to figure out where this was leading. I'd worked as his teaching assistant for the last two years, but he'd never once looked at me with such animosity in his expression, and I'd never heard such an undercurrent of fury in his voice.

"No. Is there a problem?"

He slid a manila envelope across the desk, avoiding direct contact with my hands, like he couldn't bear to get too close to me. Frowning, I opened the envelope, revealing the answer key to the test I'd given in my organic chemistry class yesterday. My initials clearly marked the bottom of the page, and my full name, Grace O'Leary, stood out in large block letters across the top. This looked like my copy, but I knew with absolute certainty I'd tucked my answer key into my briefcase last night, putting it, as always, in the spot right next to my laptop.

I lifted my briefcase onto my lap and rummaged through it, growing more panicked by the minute. When my long red hair fell forward, blocking my face like a curtain, I shoved it behind my ears and resumed my search, but the answer key wasn't there.

My gaze shot to Dr. Lewis, but he refused to meet my eyes. "Where did you get that answer key?" I asked.

"A student found it on the floor of the classroom following the exam yesterday afternoon. According to him, you gave it to several of your students prior to the test to ensure they passed. Additional evidence, acquired during confidential discussions, supported this accusation."

"Confidential discussions with whom?" I asked. My throat tightened, but I needed to remain calm. Getting upset would only make the situation worse.

Dr. Lewis's expression grew even more shuttered. "I'm not at liberty to divulge such information, but I can tell you the student who found your key is the son of one of our wealthiest contributors."

"You're talking about Seth Billings, aren't you?"

Seth's father, a famous chemist and a prominent Penn alumnus, donated millions of dollars every year to the school. He had even more power than Dr. Lewis, and Dr. Lewis was like a god on campus.

"Yes, Seth Billings," he said. "He demonstrated great bravery by stepping forward with this information. I commend him for it, in fact."

"He's lying."

Dr. Lewis's eyes narrowed. "It's your word against his."

I knew one way to be certain this was the answer key I brought home with me last night. I opened it to the third page, fumbling in my haste.

"I always review the key before grading the tests. Yesterday, I found a mistake, two transposed numbers, and I corrected them at my apartment last night. If Seth found this key right after the test, it wouldn't have these corrections on it."

He glanced at the answer key and then waved his hand dismissively. "Did anyone actually see you make those corrections?"

I shook my head, numb. My boyfriend Jonathan Gottfried, a TA in the same department, hadn't been around when I looked over the answer key. I'd eaten a quick dinner and left for the lab soon afterward. Most evenings followed the same schedule. As I worked on the final stages of my PhD thesis, I spent a great deal of my time at the lab. I got home later than usual yesterday, after Jonathan had already fallen asleep, so no one could corroborate any part of my story.

"Well, I guess we're done here. Good day, Ms. O'Leary. Leave your security fob with my secretary on your way out."

I clenched my hands into fists. "This isn't fair. You've reached a preconceived conclusion without studying the evidence, the opposite of everything you've taught me, Dr. Lewis. You're ignoring half the variables in this equation."

"Untrue, Ms. O'Leary. I'm following procedure, and I am always fair. A review board made up of your peers will make a decision on this matter in two months' time. Until then you are persona non grata, suspended both academically and as an employee of this university. Roger will take over your classes."

"But I'm only months away from finishing my PhD..."

"You should have thought of that before handing out

answer keys." Dr. Lewis stood and packed up his briefcase, his tone hard and unyielding. "I repeat, good day, Ms. O'Leary."

I managed to rise to my feet and stumble out the door. Roger, another TA in the chemistry department and Jonathan's best friend, waited outside, a cruel smirk on his face. I ignored him. I walked home in a fog, hardly registering the brisk chill in the air or the colorful leaves crunching under my feet.

Two months signaled a death knell for my PhD work, but this encompassed more than my studies and my reputation. It unjustly sullied my character as well. I'd never cheated in my entire life. Raised by my detective father and teacher mom with a firm hand and a healthy dose of Irish Catholic guilt, I followed the rules, respected authority, and kept my nose clean. This made no logical sense. Someone had obviously set me up, but who could have done this...and why?

When I got back to our apartment, Jonathan stood next to an open suitcase on our bed. His blond hair stuck up in a disheveled mess, and a muscle worked in his jaw.

"Where are you going?" I asked.

He'd emptied his side of our closet and now dug through the chest of drawers, his movements erratic and angry. Twin spots of color bloomed on his pale cheeks.

"How could you, Grace?" he asked, his voice dripping with disgust.

I sank onto the chair in the corner of our room. Normally, Jonathan covered it with his laundry, but today he'd thrown the whole pile into his suitcase. One positive aspect to the fact that he appeared to be leaving me. At least I wouldn't have to yell at him to pick up his laundry anymore.

"I assume Roger told you what happened." My voice sounded tight and strange, even to my own ears. He responded with a curt nod. A giant lump formed in my throat, making it hard to swallow. "And you believed it?"

"Dr. Lewis thinks you did it, which is all I need to know." He slammed his suitcase shut. "This is terrible. Did you ever once consider how your actions affected me?"

I stared at him, dumbfounded. "No, I did not. Please enlighten me."

Jonathan hefted the suitcase off the bed and carried it to the front door. I followed him. "Unlike you, I'm not the darling of the department, but I am on track for a permanent teaching position. My thesis is nearly done, and I have to present it soon. How would it look if they knew about my association with you? It's not worth the risk."

We'd lived together for six months, and dated for several years, but right now a complete stranger stood in front of me. "You mean I'm not worth the risk."

His expression softened, and for a second, I saw the man I'd fallen for more than two years ago. "I care about you, but this job is my life. I'm in a vulnerable position. I can't risk it for anything, not even you. I hope you understand."

In a funny way, I did understand, but I needed his support right now, both as a boyfriend and a colleague. "Maybe if you stood up for me—"

He interrupted me. "You know I can't play Russian roulette with my career. I'm moving in with Roger for now. They gave him all your classes, by the way. If that isn't the biggest slap in the face..."

I never realized what a selfish and weak human being Jonathan was until those words came out of his mouth. I wanted to throw something at him, but composed myself, donning a mask of cool, politeness.

"I'm so sorry to inconvenience you."

Jonathan missed the sarcasm in my words. He ran a hand through his thinning hair. His premature balding brought me an absurd amount of satisfaction at the moment.

"If the charges are dismissed in November, maybe we can resume our relationship."

My temper flared. "Get out. I never want to see you again. You are such a..." I paused, the words hovering on my tongue.

"A what, Grace? What am I?" Now he sounded angry, too, and his anger pushed me to respond, to tell him what I honestly thought of him.

"A scyphozoan."

He blinked. "A jellyfish?"

"Exactly. Totally spineless. No brain. No heart. And since they have no excretory system, they use their mouths for the expulsion of waste. Remind you of anyone?"

He had the nerve to look stricken, which I found hilarious. "We're reduced to this, are we? Oh, how the mighty have fallen. But I won't allow you to bring me down with you."

His words cut like a knife to my already wounded heart. "Goodbye, Jonathan. And good riddance," I said, sounding braver than I actually felt.

When he left, slamming the door behind him, I stood frozen in the middle of our living room, my briefcase clutched in my hand. I still wore my jacket, and I looked around in a daze, not sure what to do next. I always knew what to do next. I'd spent my life knowing what to do next.

For a week, I went through the motions, falling into a black pit of self-pity and despair. I ignored worried phone calls from friends, ate way too much Ben & Jerry's, wallowed in my sorrow, and obsessed over how my copy of the key ended up in Seth's hands.

Fact: I updated the answer key at home the night after the test. Fact: I put it directly into my bag. Query: Who could have taken it?

Not Jonathan. Sabotaging me reflected poorly on him, and Jonathan cared only about protecting Jonathan. But who else could have done it?

Considering the possibilities sent my logical brain into a tizzy. I couldn't figure it out.

Exactly seven days after I became persona non grata, I stumbled into the library to pay a fine on overdue books. Although I knew I shouldn't even be in the library, I snuck into the stacks, grabbed some books, and carried them to my favorite table in the back.

I opened one of the books and immersed myself in learning an exciting new theory about biosensors. I needed this. Sitting alone in my tiny apartment only made everything worse. After a few hours of reading, the words blurred on the page. I put my head down on the pile of books planning to rest my eyes, but when sleep overtook me, I didn't fight it. I was so tired of fighting...everything.

CHAPTER 2

I READ A BOOK ON HELIUM ONCE. I COULDN'T PUT IT DOWN.

"Grace O'Leary, you have a call at the front desk."

I lifted my head and gazed up at the stern face of Ms. Felicity Younger, Head Librarian. Straightening my reading glasses, I noticed a large, damp spot on the book I'd been resting on. I just drooled all over a new copy of *Perspectives on Structure and Mechanism in Organic Chemistry*. Not cool.

I tried to cover the drool with my hand, hoping Ms. Younger wouldn't notice, but nothing escaped those hawk-like eyes. She stared at the book, and at me, with disgust.

"We normally don't accept personal calls on the library phone, especially for someone no longer entitled to library privileges, but it sounded like an emergency."

Clearing my throat, I said a quick, "Thank you," and followed her to the front desk. She kept her back ramrod straight, like my very existence offended her. She wasn't the only person on campus treating me this way, but her reaction stung. She'd always liked me, or so I thought, but I couldn't be sure about my relationships with anyone at this point;

friends, acquaintances, boyfriends, librarians. Even the barista at the coffee shop had turned on me. She no longer surprised me with little smiley faces in the foam on my lattes. I got angry faces now, another cruel blow.

I put the phone to my ear. "Hello?"

"Gracie?" When I heard my mother's voice on the line, my heart stopped.

"Is everything okay? Is it Mary?"

My oldest sister, six months pregnant with her first child, suffered from serious complications and needed total bed rest. Since Mary's husband travelled a great deal for work, Mom went to stay with her in upstate New York until the baby came.

"Mary's fine. I'm calling about Aunt Lucy. She fell, and she's in the hospital."

"Oh, no."

Lucy Trabuski, my grandmother's flamboyant youngest sister, called herself Madame Lucinda. She owned the Hocus Pocus Magic Shop in the South Side area of Pittsburgh. I adored every crazy, gaudy bit of her.

"I'm so worried about her," she said. "But I can't leave your sister right now."

I pictured my mother with her faded red hair in a halo of curls around her head and worried brown eyes, the same color as Mary's. Mary got our mother's petite stature, too. I towered over both of them.

As the middle child in a family with five redheaded girls, I'd always been the anomaly. The only one with green eyes that made me look like a cat, the only one taller than our police officer dad, and the only one who never got into any trouble. Ever. Until recently. Not that my mother knew anything about that, since I hadn't quite told her yet, and planned not to do it any time soon.

"I'll go," I said. "I have some free time right now."

She paused as she processed what I said, because I never had free time. Normally, she'd ask me a million questions, but today I got off easy due to her preoccupation with poor Mary.

"Are you sure?" she asked. "I know how busy you are."

I held the phone closer, turning my back on Ms. Younger's judgmental stare. "I can work on my thesis as easily from Pittsburgh as I can from here. It's no trouble at all."

She let out a sigh of relief. "What wonderful news. I know I tell you this all the time, but I'm proud of you, Grace. You work so hard, and now all of your dreams are about to come true."

I squished up my face, the kindness in her words almost my undoing. "Thanks, Mom."

"Your father and I will pay your gas money." I protested, but she shushed me. "We insist. You're doing us a huge favor. How's Jonathan, by the way?"

"He's fine," I said. I hadn't spoken with Jonathan since the day he moved out.

Hanging up the phone, I thanked Ms. Younger, who responded with a grunt. I left the library, my heart a tiny bit lighter. Although worried about Aunt Lucy, her injury gave me a chance to briefly escape this whole horrible situation.

Back at my apartment, I took a much-needed shower, slipped into my coziest PJs, and packed my things. As I shoved clothing into my dilapidated old suitcase, I called my best friend, Laura Fienberg. She answered on the first ring.

"It's about time. I was so worried about you."

I met Laura freshman year of college, and we'd been roommates until I moved in with Jonathan a few months ago. She worked as a nurse at the Children's Hospital of Philadelphia, just around the corner from Penn.

"Sorry. I wasn't ready to talk about it yet," I said.

"Are you ready now?"

Twenty minutes later, Laura stood at the door of my apartment with a bottle of wine in one hand and Chinese take-out in the other. Tiny, with delicate features and short platinum blond hair, Laura took care of everyone she knew, including me.

We talked and drank, and I ate the first real meal I'd consumed in a week. Afterward, feeling much better, I told Laura all about Dr. Lewis and Jonathan, and filled her in on Aunt Lucy. She offered to check on the apartment for me and water my plants, since I couldn't determine how long I'd have to stay in Pittsburgh.

"You do know Jonathan's being a total dick, right?" she asked, her normally sweet face set in an angry scowl.

I let out a wry laugh. "I called him a scyphozoan."

"A jellyfish?" She snorted. "More like a loser. He was always so jealous of you."

I froze, my chopsticks halfway to my mouth. "Jealous?"

Laura rolled her eyes. She sat Indian style next to me on the couch. "Do you remember the chemistry class we all took together freshman year?"

"Of course, I do. That's where we met."

Laura took a long sip of wine. "I realized something in that class. We all did."

"What?" I'd gone through an emotionally exhausting week, and my head felt fuzzy from the wine, so I couldn't figure out what she meant.

Laura leaned close to me. "You're special, Gracie. The way you're able to understand chemistry, the way things work for you in class, it's like you're in charge, like you control the outcome. It's...magic."

I snorted. "It's called 'studying,' and I've done very little else for the last seven and a half years. I see nothing magical about it."

She shook her head, her blue eyes serious. "No. You have a gift. It goes beyond simply studying."

I struggled to find a way to respond to her absolute support and sincerity. "Thank you, Laura. That means a lot."

She patted my hand and got up to throw away the food boxes. When she saw the empty ice cream containers in the garbage can, she raised an eyebrow at me. "Have we been drowning our sorrows in a sea of Cherry Garcia?"

I winced. "Yes, but I'm done with ice cream therapy now."

Laura gave me a tight hug. "You don't deserve any of this, but I'm almost glad it happened. Otherwise, you may have spent years with Jonathan, and you deserve better."

With a tummy full of Chinese food and a happy buzz from the wine, I agreed with her. I did deserve better, and I couldn't wait to get away from this big, ugly mess. I'd miss my students, my heart stung from Jonathan's betrayal, and my professional life remained in a shambles, but for the first time since this whole thing started, I saw the tiniest glimmer of hope on the horizon.

I put on some upbeat music I knew Jonathan hated, and carefully organized all my beloved chemistry books on the shelf in my bedroom. It almost hurt to part with them, but I'd compiled most of my thesis work on my laptop and planned to finish it using all the free time I'd have in Pittsburgh.

No classes to teach. No professor to please. No boyfriend to cater to. Laura's words suddenly rang true. This might be a good thing.

I nearly drunk dialed Jonathan to give him a piece of my mind but decided against it when I remembered Jonathan's words. *Oh, how the mighty have fallen.* Such a typical Jonathan Gottfried reaction. Because I'd always been Dr. Lewis's favorite, his golden girl, it filled Jonathan and all the other TAs with envy. Competition at any Ivy League school often bordered on cutthroat and being the top student in my class simply meant more people hoped I'd fail.

Jonathan expressed his annoyance about this many times. "According to Lewis, you can do no wrong."

He tried to make it sound like a joke, but I knew it irked him. Dr. Lewis gave me an organic chemistry class of my own to teach, while he and Roger trudged on covering the weekly study sessions.

Roger agreed with him. "I wish I had boobs. If I did, I'd be his favorite."

I'd seethed over his remark but forced myself to ignore it. Roger spent more time at our apartment than he did at his own, and we shared the same tiny office in the chemistry building. I needed to maintain a professional demeanor whether he did or not, since Dr. Lewis never tolerated squabbles among his staff.

I didn't have to deal with Roger and his misogynistic comments anymore. I didn't have to play nice with him, or coddle Jonathan's fragile ego, or stay one step ahead of Dr. Lewis's rigorous demands. The golden girl of the chemistry department? Ha. More like Dr. Lewis's bonded and indentured servant.

Through the worst possible set of circumstances, I was finally free...at least until the review board hearing took place.

The thought of the review board made my stomach clench in an uncomfortable knot. Later, alone in my big bed, it all came rushing back to me. The look of betrayal on Dr. Lewis's face, the way Jonathan slammed the door on his way out, the smug satisfaction in Roger's eyes. Suddenly, it didn't seem like such a good thing at all.

I wrapped my arms around my pillow and held on tight.

In a chemical equation, each side balanced, the reactant and the product, but no balance existed here. I realized something with sickening clarity.

For the first time in my life, I'd encountered a problem I didn't know how to solve.

CHAPTER 3

IF YOU'RE NOT PART OF THE SOLUTION, YOU'RE PART OF THE PRECIPITATE.

I visited Aunt Lucy in the hospital when I arrived in Pittsburgh. She opened her eyes as soon as I tiptoed into her room and gave me a loopy smile.

"It's so nice to see you, Gracie. What on earth are you doing here?"

In spite of her pallor, and grogginess from the pain medication, she looked better than I'd expected. I brushed her hair back from her forehead with my hand. "I'm here for a visit, Aunt Lucy. I'm staying until you get better."

"You can't stay *here*," she whispered. "Get the keys to my apartment out of my purse. You should stay there, silly girl."

"Good thinking."

I found her purse, a gigantic, heavy thing in a leopard skin pattern with red leather accents, next to the bed. It took me a while, and a lot of digging, to locate her keys. At last, I pulled them out triumphantly and sat next to her on the edge of the bed.

"What happened?" I asked. "How did you fall?"

She reached for my hand. Hers felt icy cold, the purple

veins clearly visible through her fragile skin. "I didn't fall. Someone pushed me."

"What are you talking about?"

Her eyes met mine, and in spite of the drugs she took for pain, she seemed perfectly lucid. "It wasn't an accident. Anton's ghost tried to kill me."

"Your husband Anton?" I waited for her to laugh, but she didn't. She looked frightened.

"He asked me for the Dragon Rouge. I had no idea what he meant. He said something else to me, about Mama Regina. His mother's name was Olga. Isn't that odd?"

I felt a headache coming on. "Odd doesn't cover it."

"Now I know I've heard the name Mama Regina before, but when I try to remember, it slips away." She held her hands, palms up, like imagining those elusive bits of memory slipping through her fingers like sand. It broke my heart.

"Why would Uncle Anton ask you for a red dragon?" I asked, trying to inject some logic into the conversation.

"I don't know," she said, utterly perplexed. "That's odd, too."

Pity and weariness consumed me, but I didn't want to upset her. I patted her hand. "We'll figure it out."

"Thank you. It's a real mystery. When I didn't understand, he got angry. I've never seen my darling Anton look so angry, and he pushed me right down the stairs."

I studied her face. "You must have hit your head when you fell, Aunt Lucy. Did they check you for a concussion?"

"I'm not crazy," she huffed. "I know what I saw. The ghost of Anton Trabuski is not going to rest until he finds what he's looking for."

I did my best to calm her, and soon her eyes grew heavy. She fell, once again, into a deep sleep with her leg elevated to reduce swelling. She looked so tiny, like a baby bird with a broken wing. I tucked the blankets carefully around her, kissed her on the forehead, and went to find her doctor.

It didn't take long. The nurses directed me to a man about my height and age with hazel eyes and dark blond hair. His nametag read "Dr. Ryan Mallinger."

He led me to a quiet corner of the family waiting room so we could talk. I sat in one of the hard, plastic chairs. "Has my aunt spoken with you about what happened, Dr. Mallinger?"

"She has, but I'd like to ask you a question before we discuss it further. Has she been acting strangely lately?"

"Define 'strange.'"

He smiled. "Out of the ordinary? For her, I mean."

I folded my arms over my chest, thinking about it. "Aunt Lucy has always been eccentric, but I've never seen her so confused and agitated."

"I noticed the same thing. We checked her for a concussion, and she doesn't have one, which is good news. I'm concerned about her, though, and I'd like to get her evaluated." His hazel eyes were gentle. "I want to rule other things out. Like dementia, Alzheimer's—"

"Oh, no. Do you really think that's what this is?"

"I'm not sure." Dr. Mallinger glanced around the waiting room to make sure no one eavesdropped on our conversation and kept his voice soft. "She said some troubling things about someone wanting to hurt her, but it didn't make any sense."

I winced. "The ghost of her husband Anton, right?"

"Yes," he said, double checking his chart. "Has your aunt demonstrated any odd or delusional tendencies before?"

I sighed, remembering the many times my Nan referred to Aunt Lucy as being "off with the fairies." It was part of her charm, but how could I explain this to her doctor?

"Well, she's never accused poor dead Uncle Anton of hurting her before." I shook my head, wondering if we'd missed something. "But I only see her once a year or so when she comes to Philadelphia to visit."

He leaned back in his chair, his expression somber. "Maybe she's confused after her accident. Let's give her a few days to recover and try more testing. Does that work for you?"

I agreed, but on the way to the shop I couldn't stop thinking about it. Could I attribute the whole ghost thing to Aunt Lucy being Aunt Lucy, or was it a sign of something more serious?

I called my mom to give her an update, and she promised to let my sisters know, too. "How long will you stay?" she asked.

"I'm not sure. I only planned to visit for the weekend, but I think I'd better hang out longer, just to be certain she's okay."

A pause ensued, one even more pregnant than my sister Mary. "You can stay longer?"

I cleared my throat, glad she couldn't see my face. My mother always knew as soon as one of us shied away from the truth. My father called her the "Human Lie Detector." Even my older sister Blythe, a trained detective, couldn't get anything past her, but I'd never lied to her about anything important...until now.

"Another student took over my class for the last half of the semester so I could finish my thesis. Being here will give me some quiet time to work."

"If you say so," she said, and I heard the doubt in her voice. "Life with your Aunt Lucy is never particularly quiet."

"It'll be fine," I said, infusing some false brightness in my voice. "How are the twins? They have a lot going on this semester, right?"

"They do. With you getting your PhD soon, and Ava and

Aishling graduating in May, it'll be the first time in years one of the O'Leary girls hasn't been in college."

"What about Blythe? And Mary?"

My multi-question distraction technique worked effectively. We continued chatting about my sisters, and she didn't mention my sudden and unexpected wealth of free time again. I said goodbye just as I pulled up in front of the Hocus Pocus Magic Shop. What I saw filled me with a sense of dread.

I hadn't visited the shop in years, not since the summer before my senior year of high school, and I nearly didn't recognize it. Contrasted with the bright new shops popping up all over the South Side, it seemed old and rundown, its purple and green façade weathered and faded. I couldn't tell if the shop truly looked worse, or if my memory claimed a vision kinder than reality. Either way, it appeared sad and neglected.

During my childhood years, the shop was sandwiched between a used bookstore called Librarie Antique, and Yonky's Candy Emporium. For a little bookworm with a sweet tooth like mine, visiting Aunt Lucy felt like a glimpse of heaven. I also loved staying in her apartment upstairs. I'd spent many a summer vacation sitting behind the counter of her shop with a book resting on my knobby knees and a giant lollipop in my mouth.

Now something called Party Ark replaced Yonky's. A rainbow rose above a sign showing an ark full of happy animals wearing party hats. New and annoyingly cheerful, a large poster on the door read "Let our Ark Angels help you find what you need for fall!" and displayed pumpkins and cheery scarecrows.

"Yeah, no thanks," I said under my breath. It made me depressed. How could Aunt Lucy compete with a place like

Party Ark? Instead of being as spooky and fun as I remembered, the Hocus Pocus Magic Shop looked positively dreary.

I put my suitcase on the sidewalk and dug through my backpack for the keys to the shop. At least twenty keys hung on Aunt Lucy's keychain. As I worked my way through them, one stood out right away. Ancient and kind of rusty, I stared at it, my curiosity piqued, as I tried to figure out what a key like this could possibly open. A treasure chest? A closet with skeletons inside? Whatever it was, it wouldn't open the front door, so I pushed it aside. I assumed most of Aunt Lucy's keys opened locks that no longer existed.

I heard a cheery voice behind me. "Hi, there."

Two college-aged girls in Party Ark T-shirts stood behind me, smiling. I did a double take. In addition to the matching T-shirts (pink), matching hair color (blond), similar eye color (blue), and the same hairstyles (perky ponytails), they even clasped matching cell phones in their identically well-manicured hands.

"Uh, hello."

"I'm Missy," said one of the girls. "And this is Sissy." She held up a hand to indicate her friend. Apart from having one different letter on her nametag, Sissy looked like a clone of Missy. There could only be one possible explanation.

"Are you twins?"

They giggled. "Oh, my. No," said Sissy. "We're not even related."

As I considered the likelihood of such similarities existing between unrelated subjects, I noticed the conversation stalled, and realized it must be my turn to speak. "Oh, hello. I'm Grace."

"We know," said Missy. "We wanted to stop by and see how your aunt is doing. We heard she fell. That's so terrible."

"So terrible," echoed Sissy.

"And we brought her flowers," said Missy.

Sissy handed me a bouquet of cheery fall blooms. "For your aunt Lucy. We hope she gets better soon."

"Very soon," said Missy. "Is there anything she needs? We'd love to help."

"It's the neighborly thing to do," said Sissy.

Missy nodded. "Neighbors always help neighbors."

Watching them speak reminded me of viewing a tennis match with the ball going back and forth and back and forth. I shook my head to clear it. "Uh, no. We don't need any help, but, thank you, and I'll be sure to give Aunt Lucy the flowers."

They gave me finger waves. "Don't forget our offer," said Missy.

"We're here to help," said Sissy.

"Great," I said, choosing a random key and shoving it into the lock. To my great surprise, I picked the right one.

I pushed open the door of Aunt Lucy's shop and stepped inside. What I saw made the breath catch in my throat. The rows of potions, labeled with a calligraphy pen in Aunt Lucy's elegant handwriting, still lined the shelves, but they seemed dusty and disorganized. Charms hung on faded ribbons near the cash register, and jewelry rested in a large glass display, but a long crack ran across the front of the case and the entire display teetered precariously on uneven legs.

I let out a sigh. What had happened here?

To a child's eyes, Aunt Lucy personified everything magical. With her colorful clothes, flaming red hair, and flamboyant personality, she behaved so differently from my nan or my mom. She'd married Anton Lupei Trabuski in her late twenties and travelled the world with her gypsy husband. They never had any children, and he died long before my birth, but she kept a photo of him in a silver frame behind the counter. A handsome man with dark hair and a significant moustache, time could not erase the twinkle in his eye or the mischievous tilt to his lips. His middle name, Lupei, meant "wolf," and there was definitely something wolfish about Uncle Anton.

I sighed and sat at the ornate table in the center of the shop, my backpack still hanging on my shoulder, over-whelmed by the task in front of me. With odd items strewn over every surface, and unopened boxes of inventory filling the room and covering the floor, the shop didn't seem very magical at all.

I should have checked on Aunt Lucy more. I should have known. I leaned back in my chair and plopped my backpack on the floor. A crooked sign with the words "A Witch Lives Here" hung above the door, bringing a nostalgic smile to my lips.

No witch actually lived here, but many shopped here, and Aunt Lucy's store served as a sort of hub for the local Wiccan community. Bursting with brooms, pentagrams, tarot cards, and crystal balls, posters on her windows advertised palm readings and Samhain celebrations. Books on potions, witch-craft, and magic spells dotted the shelves.

Aunt Lucy herself never practiced these arts. A bit of a pagan, she liked hanging out with Wiccans, but had never been much of a joiner. A coven required too much of a commitment for her.

I approached the steep, wooden staircase leading up to the small loft on the second floor of the shop and paused as I tried to imagine my aunt tumbling down those rickety steps and landing on the cold, hard stone below. Picturing her lying on the floor all alone, calling out for help, made me shudder.

The finial at the bottom, created from a repurposed crystal ball, wobbled when I touched it. The newel post did the same, and several rails were missing. The entire place felt like a death trap, an accident just waiting to happen.

I jogged up the steps to the open loft area overlooking the

rest of the shop. Bookshelves lined both sides, and assorted costumes hung on a long rod across the back wall. A full-length antique mahogany mirror stood in the corner, its claw feet and beveled edges covered in grime. A door in the back led up the short flight of stairs to Aunt Lucy's apartment.

I went to the edge of the loft and tested the balustrade. It swayed, indicating yet another issue. The ornate black chandelier hung unevenly from the ceiling, also a potential risk. Covered in cobwebs, half the lights appeared to be broken or missing. Disconnected wires stuck out from the top in a tangled mess. The whole thing screamed fire hazard...if it didn't fall first and kill someone walking beneath it.

I sank onto the faded velvet sofa, a cloud of dust filling the air around me in a puff. Aunt Lucy always garnered a steady business within the local Wiccan community, but most of her sales came from Halloween. That wouldn't happen this year, not with Party Ark right next door. How could Aunt Lucy compete with them? Her shop looked like such a quirky mess of a place in comparison to their bright, flashy, ultra-modern storefront.

I sat up straight. Could the negatives, things like the eclectic nature of the shop and its unusual offerings, be turned into positives? It happened in chemical equations. Why couldn't it happen in retail as well?

I checked the date on the calendar hanging on the wall. With October only a week away, the busiest time of year for Aunt Lucy loomed on the horizon like a dark cloud. If she couldn't work this month, it would mean the end of her shop.

I took a deep breath, considering my options. I knew very well I didn't have time for this sort of undertaking. I had a thesis to finish, and a case to defend in front of the review board. My professional life and all my dreams were in jeopardy, but even the thought of turning on my laptop and reading over my work made me physically ill. Maybe helping

Aunt Lucy revitalize the shop for a few days would take my slightly obsessive-compulsive mind off my own problems and allow me to focus on someone else's instead.

I jumped off the couch and ran down the steps, full of resolve. Aunt Lucy kept her cleaning supplies in a storage room in the back. Grabbing some rags, I filled a bucket with warm soapy water and decided to clean the lower floor first.

I slipped into Aunt Lucy's Irish knit wool cardigan because the temperature in the shop ranged somewhere between freezing and sub-arctic. The soft sweater, in a beautiful shade of heather green, surrounded me in warmth, like a hug from my aunt. I wore old jeans, a pair of beaten up Tom's, and a long-sleeved T-shirt one of my students gave me for Christmas last year. On the front, chemical symbols spelled out the word "Chocolate."

I pulled my hair into a ponytail and surveyed the room. I'd left my glasses in the car, but they weren't necessary. I only used them for reading, driving, or trying to look smarter and more professional than my twenty-four years allowed.

I dusted off the bottles of potions and reorganized them on the shelves. I washed the front windows and the glass on the door using a bottle of window cleaner and some paper towels I'd found in the back. The autumn air smelled fresh and lovely, so I decided to leave the front door open as I worked, singing a song to myself. The labor felt good, like I'd accomplished something.

As I knelt behind the counter, organizing the mess beneath the cash register, a deep voice boomed right above me. "How's it going?"

I jumped, banging my head on an open drawer. Stars flashed in front of my eyes, and I sank back to the floor.

"Ow, ow, ow."

"Are you okay?"

A giant, hulking shape filled the space behind the counter,

almost blocking out the light from the front window. It took me a second to realize that instead of a giant, a large and extremely handsome man stood in front of me.

"We're closed." Wincing, I grabbed the edge of the counter to pull myself up. Strong hands reached out to help me, but I brushed them off.

He backed away, his dark eyes concerned. "You hit your head pretty hard. Don't you think you should sit for a minute?"

I glared at him, but even glaring hurt. "Don't you think you should stay out of shops that are closed?"

He waved a hand toward the entrance. "But you propped the door open."

"Because I'm cleaning. You can leave now."

He grinned, his teeth a flash of white. He had a square jaw, chiseled cheekbones, and a slightly scruffy and yet appealing five o'clock shadow. His dark hair curled away from his face in waves, except for one errant lock falling onto his forehead. Enormous and muscular, he reminded me of all the handsome jocks I'd carefully and selectively avoided in high school. His "South Side Community College Hockey" shirt confirmed this initial assessment. Definitely a jock. I'd nailed it.

"Are you always so prickly?" He led me to one of the chairs surrounding the ornate table in the middle of the shop and bent down on one knee, his eyes level with mine. I detected a faint whiff of soap and manliness coming from his body. I probably smelled like the French fry laden Primanti's sandwich I'd eaten for lunch, and dirt. I didn't necessarily mind smelling like Primanti's, those sandwiches had always been one of my favorite things about Pittsburgh, but the dirt? Not as appealing.

"Who are you?" I asked, rubbing my sore head.

"Dario Fontana. You must be Madame Lucinda's niece."

His large hand engulfed mine when I shook it. I'd never been a tiny girl, but Dario Fontana made me feel positively dainty.

"I'm Grace O'Leary. Why are you here?"

He studied my face. "Are you sure you're okay?"

I nodded, which made my head throb. "I'm fine."

"In that case, do you mind if I ask you some questions? I write for the *Post-Gazette*." He pulled a notepad and pen out of his back pocket.

I frowned, confused. "Why interview me?"

"I'd like to talk to you about your aunt's accident. Is it true someone pushed her down the staircase?" His gaze went to the loft.

Standing up caused fresh pain to thrum through my head. "Mr. Fontana, I'd like for you to leave."

Dario towered over me, but I didn't find him the least bit intimidating. Growing up with big, burly policemen constantly stopping by our house, I'd grown accustomed to large men, and experienced at reading people. A valuable skill, one learned from my detective dad, it served me well...until Jonathan at least. I hadn't seen that one coming at all.

I took Dario by his muscular arm and led him to the door, practically pushing him out. "I have nothing to say to you because I don't know what happened."

He stood in the doorway, blocking it and refusing to budge any further. "Can I come back tomorrow? I just have a few questions. Honestly. I've known your aunt for years. My grandma goes to her tarot card readings."

I tried to push him, but it felt like shoving a brick wall, and the effort amplified the ache in my sore head. "Fine. Come back tomorrow. But I'll only talk with you if it's okay with Aunt Lucy."

He flashed me a grin, making my insides go weak. The

man was sex on two legs, and he knew it. "How about tomorrow morning at nine? I'll bring coffee. And donuts."

The donuts won me over. I nodded and he backed away. A beautiful blonde came up to him and laced her arm in his. "Dario, I've been waiting forever. Are you almost done?"

The blonde gave me a dirty look, and I closed the door, locking it. Dario ignored the woman next to him and stood on the other side, smiling at me. I tried to pull down the blinds, but they got stuck and fell crookedly to one side. His smile broadened.

I stomped away and took the staircase back up to Aunt Lucy's apartment, furious at myself for letting Dario Fontana unnerve me. I'd tell Aunt Lucy about him but would not be at the door waiting for him and his stinking donuts the next morning.

CHAPTER 4

HE WAS HOTTER THAN A BUNSEN BURNER SET TO FULL POWER.

T he next morning, I stood at the front door promptly at nine, unlocking it and letting Dario Fontana into the shop. Aunt Lucy normally opened the shop on Saturdays, but I needed another day to clean and get organized, so I planned to keep it closed.

I wore a conservative wool skirt and sweater, and I'd pulled my hair back. Reading glasses with heavy, dark frames perched on my nose. They made me look serious and provided me with a sort of armor. People treated me differently when I looked this way, and it made me more confident. I needed all the confidence I could muster to face Mr. Fontana of South Side Community College.

I went to the hospital, certain Aunt Lucy would agree I shouldn't talk to him, but instead she'd insisted I do it. "Dario's a nice boy," she said. "If he wants to talk with you, I'm sure he has good reason."

"I'm not going to tell him you think Uncle Anton's ghost pushed you down the steps."

"But that's what happened."

She looked better today, and Dr. Mallinger said he'd

release her in another day or two, but she couldn't stay at the apartment with a broken leg. Because of the steep steps, she'd never be able to make it up to her cozy place above the shop. Instead, she planned to stay with her friend Mags, a sweet older lady who worked at a nearby coffee shop called the Enchanted Garden Café. Mags owned a big house with a bedroom on the ground floor and said Aunt Lucy could stay with her as long as she liked.

I reached for Aunt Lucy's hand. Maybe she didn't know how she sounded, so I gave her my most serious look. "If you say stuff like that, people will think you're crazy."

She frowned. "People always think I'm crazy, but I'm telling the truth."

I decided lying was the best option at the moment. "I believe you, but we have to keep this a secret, okay?"

"Fine, but do you promise to help me find the Dragon Rouge? It's the only way Anton's ghost will be satisfied."

"I promise," I said without hesitation. An easy promise to make since I doubted it even existed.

She seemed mollified. "I give you permission to tell Dario whatever you want, but I hate lying to such a nice young man. Be gentle, Gracie. You can be so intimidating." The idea made me laugh, but I agreed to do what Aunt Lucy asked.

He came into the shop with a box of donuts in one hand and a carrier with two coffees in the other. I took the box from him and put it on the table in the center of the shop, surprised by the weight.

"How many donuts did you buy exactly?"

He grinned, opening the box and showing me a dozen enormous donuts. "One is never enough. These are from Oram's, the best donuts around."

"I remember Oram's from when I stayed here as a child. They made cinnamon rolls as big as my head."

He lifted one and held it next to me. "They still do," he

said and took a big bite. Like an overgrown St. Bernard puppy, if he'd had a tail, it would have been wagging right now.

I chose a cream filled donut with thick chocolate frosting; glad I didn't know the fat content or calories. It certainly exceeded what most people required for a week.

"What did you want to talk about, Mr. Fontana?"

He wiped his mouth with a napkin. "Please call me Dario. I see you want to get right to business. The outfit should have been my first clue."

I'd searched long and hard at discount stores to find this tweed skirt and brown cashmere sweater, as well as the pieces that made up the rest of my wardrobe. Most of the people I went to school with came from money. I didn't, so I studied them and learned how to dress the part. I wanted to be taken seriously, and for someone with my curves, my height, and my coloring, it meant high quality clothes in conservative styles, and nothing too tight. Otherwise, people stared at my breasts and nothing else.

"What do you mean?" I asked.

He waved his hand, indicating my hair, glasses, and clothing. "You wore a nerdy T-shirt and jeans when I first met you, but you look very serious and grown up today."

"Is that a bad thing?"

"No." He indicated his faded jeans and untucked oxford shirt and grinned. "And I'm not one to talk. This was all I had clean. I'm behind on my laundry at the moment."

"You look...fine." He looked more than fine, but rather than flatter him, I took a sip of coffee and tried to seem nonchalant. Not an easy task, especially when he gave me a smile that made me go all tingly inside.

"Why, thank you." He reached into the leather commuter bag he wore across his body and pulled out a notebook and a pen. "I guess I should start asking questions before I irritate

THE HOCUS POCUS MAGIC SHOP

you even more, so let's get to work. Can you tell me about the night your aunt fell?"

"She doesn't remember anything."

The falsehood slid off my tongue so readily I kind of impressed myself. Normally, I choked on lies, getting all flustered and embarrassed, but not today.

Dario studied me with his warm, brown eyes. I didn't look away, and to my great surprise, a strange and unexpected heat built between us. It reminded me of the single flame of a Bunsen burner. On low, it didn't present much of a problem, but increasing the flame to high brought on a whole world of worry. All chemists knew an uncontrolled open flame in a lab was a scary thing, and Dario turned my internal Bunsen burner up to a dangerous notch with a single look. I tore my gaze away, not able to handle the heat. When I reached for my coffee again, I almost knocked it over.

I took a deep breath, going over the periodic table of elements in my head, my way of composing myself. By the time I got to boron, I regained my composure.

"Do you take cream?" he asked.

"No. I take it black and bitter. Like my soul."

He laughed, showing those perfect teeth and a dimple in his cheek. Adorable, and likely not above using his manly wiles to get what he wanted from plain, boring, unsuspecting women like me.

"You're wasting your time here, Mr. Fontana." He frowned at me and I rolled my eyes. "I mean, Dario. There is nothing to tell. Aunt Lucy fell down the steps and broke her leg. End of story."

He swished around the contents of his coffee cup. "Why did she tell my grandmother someone tried to kill her?"

I took off my glasses and put my head in my hands. "Her medication, and the trauma from the accident, made her confused. Please don't print what she said."

He pulled my hands from my face. "I'd never do that to Mrs. Trabuski. I want to find out what happened. If someone is trying to hurt her, isn't it better to know the truth?"

"No one is trying to hurt her. It's all in her head." I fiddled with the edge of my empty coffee cup. I'd eaten my entire donut, and Dario currently munched on his third.

He put away his notebook. "Can we talk about this? Off the record?"

I hesitated, only for a moment. "I guess."

"What happened? I'm asking as a friend."

I gave him a steady look, trying to assess whether I should believe him or not. "Do you swear you won't tell anyone?"

He lifted his right hand, like a boy scout giving an oath. "I do."

I caved. Aunt Lucy had already told half of the South Side her story about what happened anyway. It was only a matter of time before Dario heard it from someone else.

"She says the ghost of her dead husband pushed her." My cheeks burned thinking about how the whole thing sounded, how it made Aunt Lucy seem. "She's not well. They're running tests and hoping it isn't the start of something serious. Which is why I have to ask you not to spread this around."

He reached out and covered my hand with his. "I'm sorry. That's tough."

"It might be nothing, but..." I tilted my head to indicate the chaos surrounding us. "Something is not right here."

He glanced around the shop. "I came here thinking this was about her business."

"What do you mean?"

"Well, the South Side is becoming more gentrified, and some of the newer residents and business owners want to turn it into a homogenized, sanitized, prettier version of itself. Mostly by getting rid of the older shops and replacing them with newer chain stores."

"Like Party Ark?"

"Yes." He looked at his hand, which still covered mine, and I pulled it away self-consciously. "I'm not an investigative reporter. I normally write for the sports section. But I've paid attention, and I've noticed some disturbing trends. A pattern is emerging."

I frowned. "In my work, I look for patterns, too. What do you mean?"

He leaned close, his voice low. "When Party Ark moves into a neighborhood, odd things happen. I checked the openings of the last five Party Ark stores in Pennsylvania. Each time, a sudden rise in vandalism and petty crime occurred, and then many of the smaller shops in the area closed."

"Shops close all the time, and more people coming to an area could explain the rise in crime, couldn't it?"

"It could, but I interviewed a few of the shop owners. They refused to go on record, but they felt Party Ark carefully and methodically pushed them out because their businesses didn't fit the right image. One man, an artist who specialized in nudes, told me some Party Ark employees visited his studio and called his work 'pornographic.' A few days later, online trolls accused him of doing some pretty horrific things. None of it was true, but it didn't matter. His reputation was ruined, so eventually he just closed his studio and left. That's just an example."

My heart sank. "And I guess a little old lady who reads tarot cards and sells smudging sticks doesn't fit their image either?"

He lowered his voice. "Your aunt's shop isn't the only one in trouble."

"Who else?"

His dark eyes grew hard. "Second-Hand Sally's."

I shook my head sadly. "Because Sally is transgender? How awful."

Sally worked as a professional football player until she got tired of living a lie and started dressing as her true self. She replaced her football helmets with vintage pillbox hats, and her cleats with elegant pumps. She was a 6 foot 5-inch pastel covered goddess, and one of the nicest people I'd ever known. I hadn't seen her in years, but she'd made quite the impression on me as a child.

"No one ever said it's because she's transgender. They insist a second-hand clothing store doesn't match the new vibe they're trying to create here, but we all know what it's about. And they also seem to dislike the tattoo shop, the Black Lotus."

"It must be new. I've never heard of it."

"They opened last year, around the same time I started working at the paper. Supposedly a tattoo parlor brings the wrong sort of crowd into the South Side."

"Do you honestly think this has anything to do with what happened to Aunt Lucy?"

He considered it for a moment. "It very well may."

I closed my eyes. "Great. Lovely. It's the busiest time of year for her with Halloween just around the corner..." I paused. "This couldn't have happened at a worse moment, but I'm going to get this place cleaned up and running as soon as possible. I'm not sure if your conclusions are fact-based or pure conjecture, but I can't afford to take any chances, and I won't let them do this to my aunt."

"I won't let them do this to her either." He looked around at the dusty interior of the shop. Even with the hours I put into it yesterday, I'd barely made a dent. "But it looks like you could use some help."

"Aunt Lucy said her assistant, Will, should be in right after lunch. He's been off the last few months, travelling with his band, but he's back. He agreed to lend a hand, especially with the heavy lifting."

He grinned at me. "Have you met Will? Trust me. You'll need some additional help." He looked at his watch. "I can stay until noon. Let's get to work."

I tried to protest, but he refused to hear any of it. He stood up and stretched, giving me a brief glimpse of his bare belly. In spite of his obvious fondness for donuts, Mr. Dario Fontana had a six-pack...maybe even an eight-pack. Not wanting to get caught staring, I hopped to my feet and turned my back to him, reciting the names of several elements under my breath. This time I got to chlorine before I spoke to him.

"Do you honestly intend to stay?"

"I said I wanted to help, and I meant it. Also, I need more information for my article. Hanging around here and talking to you will be research."

I gulped. He filled up the shop with his presence, and not only because he was huge. He distracted me, making it hard for me to concentrate, but I knew I couldn't do the lifting on my own. If he insisted on helping, I planned to take full advantage of it.

"Fine. I'll change my clothes and we'll get to work."

I ran up the stairs wondering how I ended up in this situation. I'd avoided men like Dario my whole life. I knew his type, and they weren't interested in boring, scholarly, wool-covered, intellectual women like me.

When Aunt Lucy said I could be intimidating, she'd been right. Not many men could handle a woman with brains, and usually the large, handsome, athletic ones saw me as the biggest threat. My intelligence made them feel less powerful, less manly, and sometimes they got mean about it. Although not as bad in college as in high school, I'd learned to stick with men like Jonathan and stay away from men like Dario at all costs.

I'd calmed significantly by the time I slipped into my jeans and a faded T-shirt and went back downstairs. I watched as Dario removed the boxes of inventory blocking the front entrance and piled them neatly in a corner. He smiled when he saw me.

"Where do you want to begin?"

We went up to the loft and dug through the costumes. Because of his height, he easily removed the items from even the top shelf without a stool. We took everything down, thoroughly cleaned the shelves, and then started on the books. As we went through them, I checked each of the titles and rummaged through the drawers. I found nothing about a red dragon anywhere. Not in the books, not on the costumes, and not on any of the shelves.

"Are you looking for something in particular?" he asked.

I sighed. "You'll think I'm crazy."

"I know you're crazy. I could tell as soon as I met you."

"Be serious for a moment. Please."

"Fine. What is it?"

"This is still off the record, right?" I asked, and he nodded. "Well, according to Aunt Lucy, the ghost who pushed her down the stairs wanted something called the Dragon Rouge. I promised her I'd help her find it because she thinks it's the only way to get rid of the ghost." I shook my head in disbelief. "I can't believe those words just came out of my mouth."

He laughed. "We're looking for a red dragon? Did she give any details?"

"No, but I promised her I'd try to find it to make her settle down." I chewed my lower lip because saying those words seemed like a betrayal to Aunt Lucy. "We should focus on the task at hand. I'm going to clean this place from top to bottom. If a red dragon magically appears, good. If not, I'll deal with that as well."

"Sounds like a plan. How do you want these books arranged? Alphabetically or by subject? The current method seems haphazard."

I laughed. "Uh, a little." I turned, surprised to find him staring at me, and immediately felt self-conscious. "What? Is there dirt on my face?" I wiped my cheeks and he smiled.

"No. It's...well, you have a nice laugh."

As I stared at his bemused face, the hot energy sparked between us again. I jumped away so fast I tripped over a pile of books sitting on the floor. He grabbed my hand to keep me from falling, and I ended up plastered against his chest.

He let go immediately, but even the slight contact with his body set my pulse racing. Chiding myself silently for my ridiculous behavior, I picked up the pile of books I'd tripped over, and started to ramble, something I always did when a situation made me uncomfortable.

"These are about fairies. Those cover Wiccan holidays and ceremonies. Let's do it both alphabetically and by subject, otherwise I'll never be able to figure this out. Or we could do it by author name, but it might get confusing. I think Aunt Lucy sorted by color or something. It made no sense at all."

As I put the books about fairies on one section of the shelf, and the books about Wiccans on another, my heart pounded in my chest, and my cheeks burned with embarrassment. Dario watched me closely, his calm energy like a soothing balm.

"I'm sorry. I didn't mean to make you uncomfortable. It surprised me...your laugh...and everything else."

"I'm not uncomfortable." I handed him the Wiccan books, unable to look him in the eye. "I saw a labeler downstairs. Let me get it. It'll be easier for customers to find the books if the shelves are marked."

I ran down the steps, trying to stop my hands from shaking. My reaction to Dario surprised and terrified me. I'd never experienced anything close to the surge of pure desire I felt for him. It defied all logic and common sense, but in the brief moment I'd come into contact with Dario's body, I'd wanted him. Badly. Like, in a biblical sense.

What the heck?

When I got back to the loft, labeler in hand, Dario had already organized several of the categories. Together we labeled the shelves, put the books in alphabetical order, and sorted through the costumes. He asked me questions without being too nosy, and I answered him as honestly as I could. He didn't push or pry. A perfect gentleman, every so often I caught him looking at me with a puzzled frown, like he was trying to figure me out. As much as I appreciated his help in the shop and his concern for Aunt Lucy, I didn't want to let him get too close, or tell him about the current chaos in my personal life. I had good reason to keep it secret, and the less he knew, the better.

CHAPTER 5

Dario insisted on picking up lunch from Emiliano's, my favorite Mexican restaurant, and Will came in as we finished eating. Tiny, dark, and very Goth, his eyes lit up when he saw Dario.

"Fontana. Always good to see you."

He shook Dario's hand, the top of his spiky, black hair barely reaching Dario's chest. Piercings lined his brows and large gauges made his earlobes hang so low they nearly touched his narrow shoulders. His beard consisted of intricate braids tied together with a small, leather string. And his eyes, fringed with long eyelashes and accented with black eyeliner, were a startling pale blue.

"Have you met Grace?"

He shook my hand firmly, his grip surprisingly strong, as he held my gaze. I felt like he stared into my soul and I found it kind of unsettling.

"My grandmother had a sister named Grace. She's dead."

He let go of my hand and wandered to the back room of the shop. Dario chuckled at the expression on my face. "He's odd, but he grows on you."

"Like a fungus?"

He snorted. "Your aunt says he's from another dimension. She might be right. He's in a band and performs most nights, so this job suits him. He doesn't start until after lunch."

"Good to know."

Dario packed up his bag. "Time to get back to work." He nodded at Will who'd meandered back into the room. "I think you can handle things from here, buddy."

Realization hit me and I narrowed my eyes at him. "You didn't want me to be alone, did you?"

Will answered for him. "It's a good idea to be careful. Tat Cat's coming over later to talk to you about it."

"Tat Cat?"

Dario's lips twitched. "The tattoo artist from the Black Lotus. You'll like her. She's cool."

All these South Side characters took a little getting used to, especially the names, nicknames, and aliases. I could imagine Tat Cat already, and presumed we'd have nothing in common. The truth, however, surprised me.

Cat came into the shop as Will and I dusted off bottles stored on a back shelf. Labeled things like "Eye of Newt," "Tail of Dragon," and other such nonsense, it didn't take a chemist to know most of the bottles contained nothing but bits of tree bark and some dried leaves. As I argued with Will, trying to convince him we should throw all of it away, the bell above the door jingled and Cat walked in. Will's face lit up and he handed me the bottles we'd been arguing over as his entire focus shifted to the tiny girl who'd come into the shop.

"Tat Cat."

"Will Wax."

She gave him a wave. In her short floral skirt, dark tights, and baggy sweater, she was the antithesis of everything I expected from a tattoo artist. Her thick, long, hair; dyed very black, hung to her shoulders. A heavy set of bangs framed her face. Her dark eyes, behind sooty lashes, contained a twinkle in their depths, and a dusting of freckles covered her nose. Her lips, painted a bright, fire engine red, curved into a smile as she extended her hand. "I'm Cat. Catherine Simon. I work across the street at the Black Lotus."

I towered over her like a big, Irish Amazon. "Dario told me."

"Oh, you've met Dario Fontana," she said with a mischievous smile. "Now that's a canvas I'd love to ink."

Will shot her a look that spoke volumes, but Cat didn't seem to notice. I wondered if she knew Will Wax carried a torch for her. Her body language told me she did not.

We both spent a moment silently picturing Dario naked and tattooed. Will made a sound of disgust and slammed a cabinet door before stomping to the back room of the shop.

I watched him go, sorry for poor Will. "Is his name really Will Wax or is that another South Side thing?"

"Nope, that's his actual name."

A door slammed and I jumped. "Is he okay?"

"He has an issue with tall people," she said. "It makes him peevish, but it's part of his charm. He's like a brother to me. I've known him forever."

It wasn't my place to tell Cat about what appeared to be an un-brotherly attraction on Will's part. Although I could easily comprehend chemistry in a laboratory, the chemistry between people remained a mystery. It often made no sense at all. Will looked at Cat with something akin to adoration. Jonathan, in all the time we'd been together, never once looked at me with such passion.

I changed the subject. "You're a tattoo artist."

"Guilty as charged."

I looked at her bare forearms and pale neck. Not a tat in sight. "But you don't have any tats."

She winked at me. "Oh, I've got tats, but I hide them well."

"Why?"

She nibbled on her ruby red lip. "Tattoos are personal. They express who I am and what I'm about. I don't get them for show, or to impress other people. It isn't about them at all. It's about me."

"I never thought of it like that."

"Do you have a tat?"

"Uh, no."

She giggled at the expression on my face. "We'll have to remedy that. If you ever want to get inked, come to the Black Lotus. I'll figure out exactly which one you need." She studied me, looking deep into my eyes, like searching for something. "If we manage to stay open, that is."

"Let's talk."

I cleared off the table in the middle of the shop. I'd been working on ideas for a display to put there but hadn't yet decided what should be front and center. I grabbed a cup of tea for each of us from the kitchen and we sipped it as Cat looked around the shop.

"You've already made such a difference."

It did look less dusty and slightly better organized, but I had a long way to go. "How did it get so bad?"

Cat stirred her tea. "Your aunt is getting older, and the pressure has been pretty intense here lately."

"Because of those people who want to change the South Side?"

She laughed, but it held no humor. "Yep. There's an online forum called SSI. South Side Improvements. All names are confidential, of course, and they say they love the South Side, but only their version of it. They see an opportunity to make it better by filling it with ritzy little shops and exclusive boutiques. Did you know the Beehive is closing?"

"No," I said, shocked. "That's one of my all-time favorite coffee shops."

"Mine, too."

"What happened?"

She sipped her tea. "They couldn't compete with the chain coffee shop that opened right across the street. The entire South Side is changing, and the first goal seems to be to make it more family friendly. It's not a bad thing, but..." She hesitated.

"But I guess tattoo parlors don't fit into their plan."

"Nope. Nor do witches, like your aunt."

I almost choked on my tea. "Excuse me?"

She leaned forward. "It's what some of the trolls are calling her online."

The idea struck me as ridiculous. I picked up a deck of tarot cards and leafed through it with an irritated flick of my hand. "She's a sweet little old lady who likes ghost stories and makes a fuss about Halloween." I stopped on the card depicting the devil, a chill going over my skin. "Do you think someone honestly may have pushed her down those stairs?"

Cat sighed. "I don't know."

I drummed my fingers on the table as my blood boiled. My temper, something I'd spent years learning to control, nearly got the best of me. In the past few weeks, my boss accused me of cheating, and Jonathan abandoned me when I needed him most, but I'd remained relatively calm throughout it all. Maybe too calm. The idea of someone hurting poor Aunt Lucy made everything come to the surface in a rush of fury.

I stopped drumming my fingers and frowned. "Dario hesitated to leave me alone this morning. Am I in danger, too?"

Cat shook her head. "He probably didn't want anyone to bother you."

I pretended to be interested in my tea all of a sudden. "Do

you know him well?"

"Well enough." She lowered her voice. "And I'm not dating him either, by the way, so he's free game."

"Oh, I'm not interested. I learned a long time ago to avoid men like Dario Fontana. I like to stick to men who are less..." I couldn't come up with the right word. "Overwhelming."

Her eyes sparkled over the top of her cup as she held it in her hands and soaked in the warmth. "And how has it worked out for you so far?"

I thought about Jonathan. Safe, steady, academic, non-athletic, balding Jonathan, and my heart clenched in my chest. "Not well, actually."

"Then it's good you're here. It's time for a new beginning. Funny how life works out, isn't it? I never planned to come back and work at my dad's shop, but..." Her eyes clouded over. "Here I am."

"Your dad owns the Black Lotus?"

"Yes. My parents invested their life savings into it." Her sweet face tightened with pain and grief. "About six months ago, they were in a motorcycle accident. Mom died instantly, and Dad got badly hurt. He has lingering nerve damage and it's hard for him to do the detailed line work. I'm here to help, until he gets better."

I squeezed her arm. "I'm so sorry."

"Thanks. I'm happy to work with my dad, but this whole thing with those stupid people..." She blinked away tears. "If he loses this shop, he'll have nothing left."

I'd just met Cat, but I liked her. I wanted to help her, and I knew where we could start.

"In the lab, we follow strict protocols, but no matter how careful you are, sometimes accidents happen. The key to a successful outcome is to control all possible variables. Controlling the variables means controlling the outcome, or at least pushing the outcome toward the desired results."

Cat paused, her teacup halfway to her mouth. "What are you talking about?"

"The variables. We can't control what others say or do, but we can control what we say and do. We can also use the tools at hand to sway other variables in our favor."

"Please stop talking scientist. We have tools?"

"Yes, we do, and one of them is big with lots of muscles."

"Dario?"

"He wants to report about what's going on here. The key is to make sure he tells our side of the story."

"You're a lot more devious than you look, Miss O'Leary."

"It's an acquired skill."

The bell above the door jangled and a familiar face greeted me, one I hadn't seen in a long time. I jumped out of my seat and greeted her.

"Fiona Campbell. It's been ages." Blonde and beautiful, she stood taller than Cat, but I still dwarfed her. I pulled her into a big hug.

"You know each other?" asked Cat.

Fiona grinned. "Grace made my summers bearable as a little girl when she came to stay with her aunt."

Fiona's mom owned the Enchanted Garden Café, a wonderful place full of the aromas of warm coffee, spices, and freshly baked cookies. Her mom, Claire, a hippie chick, possessed the ability to make even the most boring things fun and exciting. Fiona and I spent entire summers building fairy forts in their back garden, chasing lightning bugs, and whispering late into the night during sleepovers under the stars.

Cat looked at her watch. "I'd better get to work. I have an early appointment. Another tramp stamp for a soccer mom." She rolled her eyes. "I don't know what it is with suburban housewives, but they are all about the ink these days."

Fiona glanced at her watch. "Sorry to just pop in and leave, but I have to go, too. I promised Mom I'd work today.

I'm so excited you're here, Grace. I wish I could stay and help you."

"Me, too," said Cat. "The Black Lotus is closed on Wednesdays. Do you want to have a girls' night?"

"Yes," said Fiona. "We could bring take out and help you get this place organized."

I blinked, touched by their generosity. "That would be great."

They left and Will went home a few hours later, leaving me alone in the shop for the first time all day. I worked in the back room, organizing Aunt Lucy's files and sorting through the pile of bills mounting on her desk. When I finally finished, I turned off the lights and trudged up to the apartment. Opening a bottle of wine, I took off my clothes and drew a bath, adding bubbles from a bottle I found next to the tub. Pulling my hair up, I sank into the warm, soothing water with a satisfied sigh.

If downstairs looked like a witch's shop, upstairs appeared to be the opposite. White walls, lace curtains, and doilies covering every conceivable surface. Statues of angels stood on each table, and paintings of angels hung on nearly every wall. Even the bathroom included golden cherubs frolicking in a painting hung above the toilet.

I took another long swig of wine, set the glass on a table next to the tub, and sank into the water until I was submerged up to my chin and the bubbles tickled my ears. If people took one look at Aunt Lucy's apartment, they'd never call her a witch. Witches didn't knit doilies. But the magic shop on the other hand...

I frowned, refusing to doubt Aunt Lucy for a minute. The cherubs above the toilet gave me an accusing look. Or at least it seemed accusing. I'd skipped dinner and the wine went straight to my head. I needed to get out of the tub and go to bed.

As I slipped into my robe, I heard a crash downstairs. My heart hammered in my chest, and I pulled my belt tight around my waist. Unsure about what to do, I stepped into my slippers and stomped down the steps. I hoped the stomping sounded threatening enough to scare any thieves or miscreants away, but fuzzy slippers and a pink bathrobe could hardly be considered intimidating, so I grabbed Aunt Lucy's broom on the way, just in case.

"I'm coming down, and I'm armed," I announced, looking at the broom.

Clutching the broom in one hand and my phone in the other, I turned on all the lights in the shop, scared to death, until I found the source of the noise. A shelf full of empty potion bottles had crashed to the floor, littering the whole area with broken glass.

I groaned, studying the carnage. "For Pete's sake. This place is a magical minefield."

After making sure all the doors and windows remained securely locked, I swept up the mess. It didn't take long. I put away the broom and headed back upstairs, planning to finish the entire bottle of wine and fall into a deep and dreamless sleep.

As I shut off the lights, I heard a muffled sound and saw a pair of ghostly eyes staring back at me from one of the shelves. Letting out a squeal, I took the stairs back to the apartment two at a time. Upon reaching the angel-filled safety of Aunt Lucy's abode, I locked the door, jumped into bed, and pulled the covers up to my neck. I kept the lights on, knowing I was being completely nonsensical, but it took a long time to slow my racing heart. Hours later, I finally fell into a restless sleep, but throughout the long night, my head remained filled with visions of shattered glass, dark shadows, angels floating on clouds, and eyes watching my every move.

CHAPTER 6
YOU CAN'T FORCE CHEMISTRY TO EXIST WHEN IT DOESN'T,

A unt Lucy's homecoming turned into quite the event. As I wheeled her up Mags' sidewalk, she waved like a queen. All her friends from the South Side came to see her, and one person stood head and shoulders above the rest. Dario waited next to the front door, a grin on his face and a tiny white-haired lady by his side. He juggled a giant platter with a white frosted cake on it and several bags of groceries. Everyone carried something, either plates of food or bouquets of flowers, and Aunt Lucy enjoyed the attention.

"Hello, everyone!" she said as she blew kisses to the crowd.

She wore a red dress and a wide-brimmed purple hat. Pinned together with a brooch depicting a witch flying up to the moon on her broomstick, her purple cape covered her like a warm, velvet blanket. On first glance, I'd mistaken the brooch for something normal, like a bouquet of flowers, but Aunt Lucy didn't do normal.

Her broken leg stuck out straight, supported by the footrest of the wheelchair. She'd chosen bright neon orange for her cast which clashed not only with her hair, but the rest of her outfit. When I'd asked her about it, she'd simply replied, "What other color could I possibly choose? It's nearly October."

Mags led us to a wheelchair accessible ramp. "We installed this after my mother suffered a stroke, God rest her soul."

Her spacious Victorian home, painted soft beige with brown and burgundy touches, consisted of a hodgepodge of shapes and colors with unexpected curves and angles. A turret on the left side, topped with a roof resembling a chocolate kiss, stood more than three stories high. The ramp, placed to the side of the main staircase, curved gently up to the wide veranda.

"Your home is beautiful."

The veranda spanned two sides of the house. I pushed Aunt Lucy past some comfy looking rocking chairs and a porch swing. When I got to the door, Dario put the cake on a table and helped me maneuver the chair through the doorway. Aunt Lucy beamed up at him, patting his muscular forearm and almost purring.

"You're handy to have around, big guy," she said with a saucy wink.

Dario ate it up. "You're a flirt, Mrs. Trabuski."

He gave her a smile that made Aunt Lucy giggle and did funny things to my heart. As Aunt Lucy chatted with one of her neighbors, Dario's dark eyes met mine. His smile morphed into something that did funny things to other parts of my body as well. The tiny old lady standing next to him interrupted our moment by whacking him in the arm with her purse.

"Dario Fontana. Stop making googly eyes at Lucy's niece and get the cake."

He ducked his head. "Yes, Nunny."

He went back out to the porch, and she assessed me with

her piercing dark eyes. The top of her head barely reached my chest, but I recognized a family matriarch when I saw one, thanks to a lifetime of experience with my nan. This woman reminded me of her; a petite powerhouse in pumps who'd threaten even her adult grandchildren with a wooden spoon to keep them in line. She had white curls, deep dimples in her cheeks, and a twinkle in her eyes. She wore black dress pants, a soft leather jacket that hung past her hips, a silk blouse, and a leopard print scarf. She reached for my hand, her grip strong for someone at least eighty years old.

"I'm Alvida Fontana. Dario's grandmother."

"Nice to meet you, Mrs. Fontana."

Her eyes scanned my face, missing nothing, but she seemed satisfied with whatever she saw there. "Call me Nunny. Everyone else does."

"Except Uncle Tony. He calls you the Hammer of Thor." Dario stood behind her, the cake in his hands and a cheeky grin on his face. His grin disappeared immediately when Alvida shot him a withering glance.

"Do something useful, please. Put the cake on the table in the dining room."

"Yes, Nunny." He walked away, but not before giving me one last glance over his shoulder. He looked so nervous about leaving me with his grandmother I almost laughed.

"Where did 'Nunny' come from?" I asked.

"Most Italians use Nonna, but not in the part of Calabria we're from. I called my grandmother Nunny, too."

"My grandmother is 'Nanny,' so it's close."

"Maybe you're part Italian." She laughed at the whole idea. With my red hair and pale skin, I could have been the poster child for the Irish tourism bureau. Dario came back to join us, and Alvida nudged him with her elbow. "I like this one, Dario, and look at her red hair. Gorgeous. She's like an Irish Sophia Loren."

As the two Fontanas inspected me from head to toe, my cheeks burned. I adjusted my glasses and straightened my wool skirt. "Sophia Loren?"

Alvida leaned close to whisper to me. "You've got her body, honey, even if you try to hide it under all those clothes."

Dario took pity on me. "Stop torturing her, Nunny. You're making her blush."

She waved away his comments. "I tell it like it is. And I'm always right." She gave my arm a gentle pat, her nails bright red against my charcoal grey sweater. "It's a nice thing you're doing, coming to take care of your aunt. She thinks the world of you."

Suddenly, a lump in my throat the size of a watermelon formed. "I think the world of her, too."

Fiona and her mother, Claire, stopped by, carrying a big pot of soup and a box full of cookies. I got to meet Fiona's boyfriend, Matthew, and her long-lost father Simon, too. He and Claire met in India years ago and were recently reunited. Fiona told me the story over a bowl of soup.

"He never knew about you?" I asked.

She shook her head. "They didn't see each other for twenty-five years, but Frankie Quattrone ran into my dad in a café in India one day, and the rest is history."

"I remember Frankie," I said with a laugh. "He taught us how to play poker."

"Me, too," said Matthew with a grin. He gave Fiona a peck on the cheek and shook my hand. "I have to get back to work. It was nice meeting you, Grace."

Matthew and Fiona were two of the best-looking people I'd ever seen up close. Matthew's silky, dark hair skimmed his shoulders and he wore an expensive looking suit that seemed tailor made for him. Fiona, her blond hair in a bun and her blue dress in a vintage style, was adorable. Although very different, they fit together perfectly. Matthew leaned forward to whisper in Fiona's ear, and the way he looked at her, and the way she looked at him, spoke volumes. They enjoyed a special bond. A unique kind of...well, chemistry.

My heart fluttered as I wondered if I'd ever be lucky enough to experience the same connection with another person. I'd never even come close.

I turned my head and saw Dario standing in the corner of the room, surrounded by little old ladies. His gaze rested on me, so intense and focused it was almost like a physical caress. I dropped my spoon, breaking the spell. Unsettled, I picked it up and carried it into the kitchen. As soon as I got there, I patted my cheeks with cool water. What Dario and I had might be chemistry, but it reminded me of the danger- ous, volatile, scary kind of chemistry that resulted in burns, pain, and life-threatening injuries. I knew better than to even get close to him. In the lab, the danger was losing an eye. With Dario Fontana, I could lose my heart.

I went back out to find Aunt Lucy, and when she saw me, she grabbed my hand. "Gracie, I want to introduce you to someone. This is Matilda Periwinkle. She used to help me in the shop until she retired last year."

Matilda Periwinkle, the tiniest person I'd ever seen, stood even shorter than Dario's grandmother. Her silver curls sat in a loose bun on top of her head and she dressed entirely in blue, from her lacy dress to the shoes on her impossibly tiny feet. She reminded me of a blueberry with her rounded shape, and as soon as her bright blue eyes met mine, I knew we'd be friends.

"I've heard all about you, dearie." A hint of brogue tinged her voice, reminding me of my great grandmother.

"Matilda offered to help out in the shop until I get back on my feet. Will can't come in until after lunch most days, so Matilda will be there in the morning."

Mrs. Periwinkle patted Aunt Lucy's hand. "Your auntie

wanted to rush back in, but I told her to take a few more days and rest up. It's hard for her to get around, even in a wheelchair."

"Thank you, Mrs. Periwinkle. I'd appreciate your help." It might give me time to clean up the mess in the shop and get things organized for Halloween. I may also have time to work on my thesis, even though the thought of it made my stomach tighten in a panicked knot. I'd only planned to stay a few days, but clearly Aunt Lucy needed me longer. I couldn't afford to get too far behind on my own work, and Mrs. Periwinkle's offer provided the answer to my problems. The relief on my face must have been apparent.

"I'll be there as long as you need my help." She looked at Aunt Lucy and gave her a wink. "Think of me as your fairy godmother."

Aunt Lucy covered her mouth with her hand and giggled. Mrs. Periwinkle did the same. The more I stared at them, the more they laughed. It must have been an inside joke, but I wondered if someone spiked their tea.

Aunt Lucy looked up at me apologetically. "Sorry, Gracie. We haven't seen each other in a long time, and it's so nice to be together again."

Mrs. Periwinkle put her hand on Aunt Lucy's shoulder. "It is indeed."

After a wonderful, noisy, boisterous lunch followed by Alvida's fantastic Italian cream cake and Claire's cookies, we finally got Aunt Lucy settled into her room. Spacious and comfortable, it faced the back garden of the house.

"Thank you for letting her stay here. She couldn't have managed the stairs at the shop."

Mags gave me a hug, a big smile lighting up her face. Nearly as tall as me, but wider and softer, she had dark skin, a head full of salt and pepper curls, and an aura about her radiating calm and goodness. Although she helped out part time

ABIGAIL DRAKE

at the Enchanted Garden Café, she mainly worked as a Reiki therapist.

"It's a joy to have her here. Since my kids have all grown and flown the coop, it's awfully quiet and lonely in this big old house. I appreciate the company."

I thanked Mags again and stepped into Aunt Lucy's room to kiss her goodbye. "Did you find the Dragon Rouge yet?" she asked, her blue eyes worried. "The more I think about it, the more I'm certain I've heard of it before."

"Any idea what it looks like? Big, small…fire breathing?"

"Oh, no, not fire breathing." She frowned. "I can't remember. Getting old sucks."

I kissed her forehead. "It's better than the alternative."

"Definitely." She smiled and settled back onto her cozy nest of pillows. Her hat hung on a clothes tree in the corner of the room with her glorious purple cape. I put some pillows under her leg, and she sighed. "And I passed all of Dr. Mallinger's tests."

"I'm still worried about you. But I trust you to tell me if you notice a problem."

"Thank you. Between you and me, I'm glad you came to help instead of your mom."

"Why?"

"Well, you know I love your mother, but she could not have handled the ghost. Have you seen him yet?"

I remembered the eyes staring at me from the shelf, but decided it came from my overactive imagination. "No, but if I do, I plan to give him a piece of my mind for scaring you and making you fall."

I tried to make light of the whole thing, but Aunt Lucy grabbed my hand, her face serious. "I know you don't believe in this stuff, but you mustn't tease. If he doesn't get what he wants, I'm afraid someone else might get hurt, and it could be you."

54

Her words stayed with me as I checked all the doors and windows and locked up the shop for the night. A truck rumbled past, making glass jars rattle on the shelves. One of them nearly fell, and I pushed it away from the edge.

"Aha," I murmured to myself. "Not a ghost or a monster or a demon. A truck and an old, loose shelf."

I slept better than I had all week and woke to bright autumn sunlight streaming through the windows. My eyes widened when I heard a noise in the shop. It sounded like singing.

I jumped out of bed, put on jeans and a sweater, and ran downstairs. Matilda Periwinkle, dressed all in blue once again, held a duster in her hand and cleaned one of the shelves. For a second, I thought she floated on air, but she simply stood on her tiptoes in a pair of ridiculously high blue pumps. She gave me a cheerful smile.

"Good morning. There's coffee ready in the back room. It's going to be a lovely day, isn't it?"

"Thank you, Mrs. Periwinkle."

I grabbed my coffee and pored through a list of inventory while a few customers trickled in. Most wanted Halloween decorations and costumes, but a Wiccan came in needing smudging supplies. Mrs. Periwinkle took care of her, a good thing, since I didn't know where to find many of the items. I needed to adjust to the rhythm of working in the shop, and Mrs. Periwinkle helped enormously. She left before lunch, pulling on a blue boiled wool cardigan with ornate brass buttons, and promising to return first thing in the morning.

I went outside to sweep the sidewalk just as a gust of wind blew out of nowhere. My hair flew around my face and I stumbled, knocking right into someone.

"Sorry." I looked up and realized I'd bumped into a blond Viking, one of the most beautiful men I'd ever seen.

The broom slipped out of my grasp, clattering to the sidewalk. We both reached for it at the same time, and when my hand accidentally brushed his, an odd tingle passed over my skin.

"It is I who should apologize," he said. "I nearly knocked you to the ground."

His bright blue eyes twinkled, and his fair hair hung to his shoulders, sparkling in the autumn sunlight. He had dimples in his cheeks, a cleft in his chin, and an extremely sexy accent. Judging by his tan skin and the gold and white highlights in his hair, he probably spent a lot of time outdoors. Like a Norse god would do anything less.

Something struck me as familiar about him, but I couldn't place it. I figured he must be famous, an actor or an athlete. Maybe even a model, like the ones on the covers of romance novels.

As he stared at me, I realized I should probably say something. "Oh. I'm fine. No harm, no foul. Rushing around as usual. Not looking where I'm going. You know." I waved my hands awkwardly, swinging the broom and nearly hitting an innocent bystander. The woman sidestepped me, giving me a dirty look. "Oops. My bad."

I'd lost the ability to finish a cohesive sentence. Better to get back to my sweeping and stop talking altogether.

The Viking peeked into the window of the store. "The Hocus Pocus Magic Shop. This looks like a delightful place. Do you work here?"

"It belongs to my aunt, Lucinda Trabuski. I'm Grace O'Leary." I pushed my hair behind my ears and extended my hand.

"Ivan Rochat. I'm pleased to meet you, Miss O'Leary."

He took my hand and the same strange jolt occurred again when he touched me. It started at my fingertips and raced all the way up my arm. I'd never experienced anything like it except when one of my sisters tricked me into using an electrified pen as a joke.

Ivan must have felt it, too. "How odd," he said, wiggling his fingers, before lifting his azure eyes to my face. "I apologize for staring, but you truly are lovely."

I nearly said, *"You, too,"* but this whole encounter made me uncomfortable. I never received this sort of attention from giant, gorgeous men, or got an electric shock when I touched someone. Ivan summed it up with one concise and very accurate word. Odd.

"Um, I'd better get back to work."

"Adieu, Miss O'Leary."

Adieu. I almost fanned myself but cringed when I noticed the dust all over my shirt and hands. Ivan likely assumed I worked at the shop as a scullery maid and felt bad for me.

Will Wax walked up as Ivan strolled away, his blond hair billowing in the wind and the fabric of his expensive suit outlining the firm muscles of his body. I let out a sigh. Ivan had an extremely nice ass. It figured. Will didn't look quite as impressed.

"Great. Now there's a Viking in the South Side. Are there any normal-sized people in this freaking town? I need to move. I'm sick of this place."

I couldn't tell if he meant it as a joke or not. We walked into the shop together, and Will put the mail on the table, but it took a while before I found the time to sort through it. Mostly it consisted of bills, but one envelope caught my eye. It didn't have a return address or a stamp. Someone put it directly into our mailbox, and it must have been recently because I'd seen the mailman walk by before Mrs. Periwinkle left.

I frowned and opened the envelope slowly, pulling out a single sheet of paper covered in large, block letters. *"NXT*

TIME I'LL THROW HER OFF THE ROOF INSTED OF DOWN THE STAIRS. U HAVE BEEN WARNED."

After reading it a few times to get through the misspellings, I pictured a dark hooded figure carrying poor Aunt Lucy up to the roof, the cast still on her broken leg, and tossing her over the side. A strange rushing sound filled my ears. I stood up, thinking I might get sick, but couldn't seem to get my feet to move. I heard the bell above the door to the shop ring but wasn't able to turn and see who'd entered. Will came out of the storage room, took one look at my face, and lowered the boxes he carried.

"Are you okay, Grace?"

"A reduction in blood flow to the brain. Dizziness. Nausea. Tingling in my fingertips. Strong emotional reaction to outside stimuli. Typical warning signs." The room swam before my eyes as my bones turned to jelly and everything started going black. "I'm going to faint now."

CHAPTER 7

WHAT DID THE THERMOMETER SAY TO THE GRADUATED CYLINDER? AT LEAST I HAVE A DEGREE.

I regained consciousness in Dario Fontana's arms with Will hovering over us like a worried little emo hen. "She stood there, reading the mail, then she mumbled absolute gibberish and fell over like a giant, ginger-headed redwood."

I frowned. "Did you insult my height, my intelligence, and my hair color in one sentence?"

Dario put an arm around me. "Take it slow. You fainted."

"I noticed."

"Does it happen often?"

"Never. I saw the letter..." I closed my eyes as the image of Aunt Lucy falling from the roof came into my mind again. "Hydrogen, helium, lithium, beryllium, boron, carbon, nitrogen, oxygen."

"Uh, oh. Is she going to pass out again?" asked Will.

"She's trying to calm herself. Get her a glass of water."

I heard Will scamper to the back of the shop and opened my eyes. Dario's face loomed above me, full of concern. "Are you okay now?" he asked softly.

I nodded. "How did you know I recite the periodic table to calm down?"

"I do the same thing, but with the Fibonacci sequence."

"Oh. Good idea. 1, 1, 2, 3, 5, 8, 13..."

Will came back with the water and came to a stop when he heard me. "She's doing it again."

Dario laughed. "She'll be fine. What letter are you talking about, Grace?"

I pointed to the table. He forced me to sit in the chair, and picked up the letter, a scowl darkening his handsome face as he read it. "This isn't funny anymore. We need to call the police."

He handed the letter to Will. Will scanned the page quickly, looking even paler than usual. "And we should tell Cat and Sally about this, too. They need to know, even if the threat is directed at Madame Lucinda."

The door opened, and the blonde from before hovered near the entrance of the shop, a sour expression on her face. "Are you almost done, Dario?"

Not a fan of the Hocus Pocus Magic Shop, and likely not a fan of mine, either. Dario fueled her irritation by responding without even glancing her way. "Sorry, Tiffany. I'll be a while. You should head back to work on your own."

She turned with a huff and a swish of her hair. Tiny and pretty, she boasted the bone structure of a ballerina and the attitude of an angry Chihuahua. I strongly suspected she'd nip at my heels if she could.

Dario watched my face as she left. "She's not my girl-friend, if that's what you're thinking," he said softly. "She lives in the apartment building across the street. She wanted to lend me a book, and we came here so she could pick it up. We work together. She writes for the paper."

"Let me guess...the society pages?"

He snorted. "The obituaries."

I looked at him in surprise. "You're kidding. She's so tiny. And blonde."

"She has a dark side. Most blondes do. That's why I prefer redheads."

I pushed my hair self-consciously behind my ears. "I'm not looking for a boyfriend."

His eyes met mine and my heart literally skipped a beat. I put a hand to my chest in surprise. It had never done such a thing before.

"Good," he said, his voice husky. "Because I'm not looking for a girlfriend, either."

As I tried to figure out what he meant by his words, Sally Stein burst into the shop in a swirl of vintage pink satin and tulle. Perfectly coiffed as always, with bright red hair, hot pink lips, and eyes shadowed in blue, she was a vibrant explosion of color and the dearest and kindest person I'd ever known. I met her years ago when I visited Aunt Lucy during summer vacations. Fiona and I used to spend hours in Second-Hand Sally's, trying on dresses and learning about fashion. Sally taught me how to buy nice clothes on a tight budget, and she helped me appreciate the importance of quality instead of quantity.

"Oh, poor, sweet, little Gracie. Will called me. He said someone sent you a threatening note. What happened?"

Only Sally could call me "little" and get away with it. In heels, she stood close to seven feet tall.

Dario handed her the letter and she sank onto the chair next to me as she read it. "This is terrible. Cat has faced some problems, too, mostly vandalism and the like. We should tell her about this."

"I called her right before I called you," said Will.

"She's coming over on Wednesday to help me organize." I shook my head in confusion. "Why would anyone threaten Aunt Lucy like this, or someone as nice as Cat? And I can't imagine anyone ever having a problem with you, Sally. You're an angel."

She fluffed her hair. "Not even close, but you may have given me an idea for my Halloween costume this year."

Will tilted his head to one side, his light eyes even lighter in the bright autumn sunshine. "Are you going to host the party?"

"The party?" My head felt fuzzy.

"Your aunt always hosts the after-party for the Wiccans on Samhain. It's sort of a tradition," he said.

"Your aunt is the organizer, and it's held here, but we all pitch in to help," said Sally.

"Grace has enough on her plate right now." Dario interceded, going straight into protective mode, which I found extremely irritating. I hadn't formed my own thoughts on this issue yet, and certainly didn't need for him to step in and decide things for me.

"I need to think about it," I said, shooting Dario a hostile glare. "And then I'll decide."

"Of course, dearie." Sally patted my cheek. "No one expects you to do it this year, especially under the circumstances."

"It may be a good idea, though," said Will. "Show them you aren't afraid."

"But I *am* afraid." I chewed on my lip as I considered it. "Not for myself. For Aunt Lucy."

"Which is why you shouldn't do it," said Dario.

I narrowed my eyes at him. "It's my decision, and I didn't say I wouldn't do it. I agree with Will. I won't let them bully me, and it might be good for the shop if it looked like business as usual."

He shook his head. "It's a huge undertaking, and your aunt is still in a wheelchair."

"It isn't up to you," I said. "So I suggest you stay out of it."

"Fine," he said, raising his hands in defeat. "I give up. I'm going back to work."

"Have fun with the obituary writer." The words left my mouth before I could stop them. Sally and Will chatted about something on the other side of the room, their heads bent close together, so thankfully they hadn't heard me.

Dario came close, so close I caught a faint whiff of soap and sensed the heat radiating from his body. "I told you once already. She isn't my girlfriend."

I folded my arms across my chest and tapped my foot. "It's none of my concern either way."

"It's none of mine, either." His brows drew together, a storm brewing in his eyes, but as he took in my stubborn pose and aggressively tapping foot, he let out a long breath and his expression softened. "What is my concern, however, is keeping you, your aunt, and all the people I care about *out* of those obituary pages."

"Do you honestly think we're in any real danger?" I asked, almost afraid to hear his answer.

He put a hand on my shoulder and lowered his head until his eyes were even with mine. "We'll figure this out, but that letter sounded like a threat. Be careful, okay?"

"Caution is my middle name."

He snorted. "I highly doubt it."

As soon as he left, I called my sister, Blythe, and told her about the note. I heard the sounds of traffic around her, and she raised her voice to be heard above the melee.

"You think someone actually pushed Aunt Lucy down the steps? Are you serious?"

I chewed on my nail. "I don't know, B. Aunt Lucy says it's true, but she also thinks Uncle Anton did it."

She paused. "*Dead* Uncle Anton?"

"Yep. She says he's looking for something he brought with him from Romania, and he won't rest until she finds it."

Blythe laughed, and I pictured her tossing back her head of auburn curls. "Well, this sounds like a typical Aunt Lucy situation," she said. "Except for one thing. The note. It makes alarm bells go off in my head for sure."

"Me, too."

Blythe let out a sigh. "I wish I could come and help you right now, but I'm stuck, Grace. I'm working undercover, and if I leave, the whole operation will be compromised."

"I get it, Blythe. It's fine. Please don't worry."

"If anything else happens, call me, okay?"

I promised I would. On Wednesday, when Fiona and Cat came over, we talked about the note as we ate Chinese food.

"I think they're blowing smoke," said Cat.

I toyed with my chopsticks, pushing the noodles around my plate. "I called the police and spoke with Officer Belfiore on the phone. He said the same thing, but he wants to come over and talk in person." I took a long sip of the tea Fiona brought over, green with a hint of floral and citrus. Her mother mixed all the teas sold in the shop herself. "Your mother's teas are always so delicious. How does she do it?"

Fiona's cheeks got pink. "I'll let you in on her secret, but you can't tell anyone. She uses the water from the fountain out in our back garden."

I frowned, looking into my cup. "For the teas?"

"And the coffee. I have no doubt she uses it for other things, too. She says the water has magical properties, and it comes from a secret underground river." She rolled her eyes. "I know it's nonsense, but I got the water tested and at least it's safe to drink. The odd thing is..."

"What?"

Fiona pushed a lock of hair out of her eyes and got even pinker. "There *is* something special about the fountain. I don't know what it is exactly, though. Is there any way you could test the water for me and see what you come up with? You'd be more thorough than the local water authority."

"I'd love to, but I don't have access to a lab right now."

Cat poured herself another cup of tea. "You could use the lab at the community college. My friend works there. I'll hook you up."

I doubted they'd have the equipment I needed, but I didn't want to seem ungrateful. "That might work."

We finished our meal and discussed ideas for organizing the shop. I pulled out a bottle of wine, and we sipped on it as we worked. Fiona came up with a great display of Halloween items for the front table, and Cat helped me decorate the windows. Soon it looked like a different shop. The windows glowed with orange twinkle lights and a fun and spooky assortment of black cats, haunted houses, and pretty, sparkling witches' hats.

We were about to go up to the apartment for dessert and more drinks, when I heard a scratching noise coming from one of the bookshelves. Peering into a space between two books, I gasped as a pair of glowing eyes stared back at me. A fuzzy black shape jumped out and I screamed, flying backward and knocking the loose crystal ball finial right off the post at the bottom of the staircase. Fiona and Cat screamed, too, even louder than me. The crystal ball landed with a thud on a pile of costumes I'd placed next to the steps. I nearly landed in the costumes, too, but managed to catch myself right before I fell.

"Did you see that?" I asked as my panicked gaze flew around the shop.

Cat scrambled up onto a chair. "Was that a rat?"

"It seemed bigger than a rat."

Fiona looked around nervously. "Bigger than a *rat*?" She climbed up on the chair, too.

I grabbed a broomstick and held it over my shoulder as I

tiptoed around the room. Everything, even the sounds of traffic outside, made me jump, which made Cat and Fiona squeal. My heart pounded in my chest and my hands shook as I looked under the jewelry display cabinet near the cash register. Two bright eyes peered back at me.

"Meow."

My entire body sagged in relief. "It's a cat...well, more like a kitten."

Cat and Fiona got off the chair and came to kneel beside me. "Awwwww," said Fiona. "It's so cute."

"And so scared," said Cat.

The kitten pushed itself back against the wall. I could barely see it, but I agreed with Cat. It looked terrified.

I ran upstairs to the apartment, opened a can of tuna, and put some in a saucer. I carried it downstairs and placed the saucer in front of the cabinet. The kitten eyed it with interest, but still seemed hesitant. We sat back and waited quietly for it to build up enough courage to come out. It didn't take long. Hunger won out. A fluffy ball of pure black fur with huge green eyes, it took a few tentative bites of the tuna, before hunkering down and gobbling up the rest.

"I wonder how it got in here," said Fiona, reaching out to give the kitten a tentative pat as it curled up in my lap for a snooze. I stroked its soft fur and the tiny creature purred so loudly we giggled.

"I think you have a pet," said Cat.

"And it's a boy kitty cat," said Fiona, after a quick examination. "What are you going to name him?"

"Jinx. It suits him."

Cat gave me a smile. "How perfect. You've got a black cat *and* a broomstick." She pointed to the broomstick on the floor, the one I'd planned to use as a weapon. "You've reached full witch status now."

Fiona patted Jinx on his head, and he rubbed against her

sleepily. "Thank goodness you found him, Grace. It's dangerous for black cats this time of year. People can be so superstitious, especially around Halloween, and there are creeps who like to hurt helpless creatures for the sake of hurting them."

Jinx opened one eye and stretched. Small and so sweet, the idea of anyone trying to hurt him sickened me. "I think he found me."

I located a plastic container I could use as a litter box, and, oddly enough, found some kitty litter in Aunt Lucy's storage closet. "She puts it on the sidewalk when it's icy," said Cat.

Jinx promptly used the litter box, so at least that gave me one less thing to worry about. I picked up the crystal ball finial and tried to put it back in place. I wiggled it around, turning it back and forth, but I couldn't get it back on properly. Finally, I pushed it hard, twisting it, and heard a popping sound as a drawer slid open from under the bottom step.

"A hidden compartment." Fiona clasped her hands together.

Dusty, old, and filled with papers, the drawer probably hadn't been opened in a long time. "It's most likely garbage," I said. "But you never know."

Cat's eyes twinkled. "Let's bring it upstairs and find out."

We went up to Aunt Lucy's apartment and lit a cozy fire. She had a gorgeous fireplace with a marble hearth. Jinx curled up in front of it and promptly fell asleep. We poured more wine and sifted through the contents of the drawer.

Fiona picked up a piece of paper and frowned. "These look like legal documents, but none of them are in English."

"Aunt Lucy's husband came from Europe. These may have belonged to him."

Cat looked at me over the edge of her wine glass. "You mean the ghost?"

I rolled my eyes. "She told you the story, too?"

Fiona nodded. "Yep. She told everyone. She believes it's true."

"Who's to say it isn't?" asked Cat. I gave her a dirty look and she giggled. "Okay. Fine. But you never know."

"I know. I'm a scientist. I deal in facts. Aunt Lucy fell and hit her head. She thinks she saw the ghost of her long dead husband, and he pushed her down the stairs because he's looking for a red dragon, but it isn't real. There is no ghost. No one pushed her and there is no dragon. There is also nothing truly magical or mysterious about anything in this shop."

"Are you sure?" asked Fiona. She lifted an old leather-bound book out of the drawer with the word "Grammar" burned into the cover.

"A book on grammar. So what?"

"Grammar is an old way to say 'grimoire.' It's a witch's spell book."

A chill went up my spine. "Seriously?"

"Yes. Growing up with my crazy mother has made me the queen of useless and obscure trivia."

"Your mom isn't crazy," said Cat, studying the contents of her wine glass in the glow of the fire. "She's unique."

Fiona snorted. "Another name for crazy." She handed the book to me. "It's not in English anyway."

I opened it, marveling at the pages inked by hand hundreds of years ago. "No, but I can read it."

Fiona's eyes lit up. "Seriously?"

"It's Latin. I learned it at Catholic school, and it's a necessary evil for science."

"Aren't you young to be finishing your PhD?" asked Cat.

Fiona raised her glass to me. "Grace is a genius. She skipped like five years of school."

"Two." I hated talking about this because it always

sounded like bragging. In truth, high school was a nightmare for me, so graduating early provided a means of escape. When I went to college things changed for the better, but some of those old wounds never completely healed.

"Another reason you should date Dario," said Cat. "He's smart, too. He went to college on a full scholarship."

"Academic?" I asked.

"I'm not sure," said Fiona, "but I know he played a lot of hockey."

"Oh. Sports. It figures." I tried to keep the disappointment out of my voice.

Cat pointed to the book. "Tell us about the grimoire. What does it say? Is it magic?"

I turned the delicate pages, reading the spidery handwriting. "It's a book of spells, but it isn't magic." A bubble of excitement built in my chest, the way it always did when I hovered on the verge of figuring out something new and exciting. "It's science."

CHAPTER 8

CHEMISTRY IS LIKE COOKING, BUT DON'T LICK THE SPOON.

We ran back downstairs, grimoire in hand. Cat carried Jinx, and he seemed to be having as much fun as we were. We went to the room in the back of the shop where Aunt Lucy set up a large table she used for mixing potions, assembling magic kits, and making nut rolls at Christmas. The walls of the room were lined with old bottles and jars and lots of other supplies.

I studied the grimoire. All the spells seemed to follow a logical progression. I didn't think they carried any special power, but hundreds of years ago they may have seemed miraculous.

"Which one should we do first? Here's one to relieve constipation. It's mostly cod liver oil. I can't imagine it's pleasant."

Cat wrinkled her dainty nose. "Ew."

"Here's one for a hangover. We may need this tomorrow."

Fiona raised her glass. "Cheers."

I leafed through the book until I found something I knew they'd both enjoy. "Ladies, this is it. We're going to make a love potion."

"A love potion," said Cat, her voice a whisper.

"Will it work?" asked Fiona.

Cat swatted her arm. "Like you need it. You have Matthew, Mr. Perfect Man."

Fiona's eyes grew dreamy. "Yes. I do."

I laughed at the expression on her face. "Well, I can't promise any magical love eruptions, but it looks harmless enough. Shall we try it?"

We assembled the ingredients. I held up an elegant glass bottle. "First on the list is rose water from the East. This rose extract came from Istanbul. That's east enough, I guess."

I measured carefully and poured it into a marble bowl, as per the instructions. "Honey gold on a silver spoon."

Aunt Lucy kept a pot of honey near her teacups. I dug a silver spoon out of the drawer near the sink and carefully added the honey to the rose extract.

"Yummy," said Cat.

"It gets even better. I need brandy wine and know right where to find some. Aunt Lucy keeps a bottle around 'for medicinal purposes.' I don't think she'd mind if we used a wee bit." I reached under the sink and took out the bottle, dusting it off. Opening it, I took a sniff and cringed. "Yep. This will be strong enough."

I added the brandy wine and found the next ingredient in the back of the fridge. Holding it under Fiona's nose, I let her smell it.

"Cherry juice?" she asked.

"Yes. Aunt Lucy uses it for her joints. It's good for inflammation."

I added a few drops of the tart cherry juice. Only one ingredient remained.

"Water from a sacred pool. Hmmm."

Fiona almost fell off her chair. "Our fountain. In the back garden. We can get the water there."

We grabbed sweaters and a few large pitchers and ran all the way to the Enchanted Garden Café, giggling the whole time. Claire and Simon were having a glass of wine in the kitchen.

"Hello, you two," said Fiona, giving them each a kiss on the cheek. "We have to get some water from the fountain."

Claire looked at our faces in confusion. "Why?"

Fiona opened the door to the garden. "We're mixing magic potions."

"It's fun," said Cat, and let out a hiccup.

"I found a book," I said. "We need water from a sacred pool."

For all intents and purposes, we looked like high school kids planning some sort of juvenile prank, but Claire smiled. "You're in the right place. Our fountain is connected to a secret underground river. You can't get more sacred than that."

I nodded like it made perfect sense. "Right. Thank you."

We ran back to the Hocus Pocus Magic Shop, water sloshing around in the pitchers we carried. When I stirred the ingredients together, Fiona gasped. "It's so pretty."

The purple potion danced and glowed. It exhibited a mesmerizing and unexpected pearlescent quality.

"No matter how well you know each element, no matter how much you think you can predict the outcome, something mysterious can happen and it changes everything, even in the most basic experiments," I said.

"We need to bottle this shit," said Cat.

It sounded like a good idea. I found small glass bottles, which we capped with corks. Not wanting to cover up the pretty potion with a label, we decided on a better idea. Fiona wrote instructions in her neat, elegant handwriting. We copied those instructions on Aunt Lucy's ancient copier, using an unopened package of what looked like parchment paper the size of postcards. I found it ironic that Aunt Lucy purchased the paper at Party Ark.

Cat took the first sheet off the copier. "*Magical Love Elixir. Give a few drops to the object of your desire, dance naked under the light of the moon. In the morning, your true love will be yours.*" Cat's lips twitched as she read the words. "It never mentioned anything about naked dancing in the grimoire, Fi."

Fiona held up her hands in surrender. "I just thought it sounded like fun. Little known fact, dancing naked is an older tradition than Wicca. They called it being 'skyclad.' I kind of like the sound of that."

"And you also know this because of Claire, right?" I asked.

"Oh, yes," she said. "I'm a veritable fountain of useless knowledge."

We rolled up the instructions and tied them onto the bottles with slender lavender ribbons. As soon as I placed all the bottles on a shelf, lining them up neatly near the teapot, Cat rubbed her hands together. "Let's make some more."

Together we mixed up several batches of the love potion. Oddly enough, it felt like being back in the lab again. Mixing up those silly potions, even if only for a laugh, made me happier than I'd been in a long time.

Fiona crashed on Aunt Lucy's sofa, and Cat curled up on some cushions on the floor. For the first time since I'd come to the South Side, I felt relaxed and calm. Things finally headed in a more positive direction and finding Jinx in the shop probably explained some of the recent weirdness. Maybe Aunt Lucy glimpsed the kitten's glowing eyes in the dark, and thought she saw the ghost of poor, dead Uncle Anton.

Strange to think my life involved dealing with ghosts and potions and black cats on a daily basis. The university and all my problems there seemed so far away and thinking about Jonathan's betrayal only gave me the slightest twinge of sadness at this point. I'd found friends in Fiona, Cat, and also Dario. He confused me and set me off kilter, but somehow I knew I could count on him.

And now I had Jinx. He climbed into bed with me, and I didn't have the heart to make him stay on the floor. He fell asleep instantly, his warm body curled up next to mine. His soft purring made me smile as I drifted into a deep and restful, albeit slightly drunken, sleep.

I woke up to bright sunshine streaming through the windows and Jinx sitting on my chest, staring at me. "Good morning, little guy."

He rubbed against my hand, purring in appreciation. I took a look at the clock and blinked in surprise. I'd slept later than I had in years.

Fiona and Cat left before I awoke, their blankets folded neatly and placed in a pile. They'd put a note on the fridge thanking me for a fun evening and promising to stop by again as soon as possible. My head ached, but I chuckled at the memory of mixing potions with the girls.

I fed Jinx and drank a big glass of water. The grimoire sat on the coffee table. Silly, superstitious nonsense, but it appealed to me in a strangely visceral way. I stroked the book again, outlining the world *Grammar* with my fingertips. Oddly enough, it seemed warm to my touch, like a living, breathing thing.

I shook my head at my own imagination, making my brain swish and bang around in my skull. Judging by the occasional jingle of the bell above the door, the smell of coffee wafting up the stairs, and the soft murmur of voices, Mrs. Periwinkle had already opened up shop for the day. Mornings always kicked off at a snail's pace in the South Side, so I decided to pop a few painkillers and take a long, soothing shower before heading down to work.

I let the hot water run over my skin, enjoying the way it

relaxed my aching muscles and cleared my sore head. The potion making had stained my fingers, so I scrubbed them clean.

Dr. Lewis once called me one of the greatest scientific minds of my generation, a comment that made Jonathan furious at the time. Imagining how my colleagues at the university would have reacted if they'd seen me mixing potions in the back room of a magic shop, brought on a fit of giggles, especially when I pictured Jonathan's smug and superior countenance. What an arrogant ass. How could I not have noticed it before?

I called Laura after I'd pulled my hair into a bun and dressed in a simple wool skirt, tights, and a sweater. She answered on the first ring, sounding groggy.

I winced. "Sorry. Did you work the night shift?"

"Yes, but it's okay. I just got home. How are you doing?"

I sat on the couch and Jinx hopped onto my lap. "Fine. Aunt Lucy is getting better, and I adopted a kitten. Well, he adopted me, I guess. I found him in the shop last night."

"How nice." Her voice sounded odd.

"Are you okay?"

"I saw Megan yesterday." Megan, another TA in the chemistry department, worked under a different professor. "She wanted me to warn you. She thinks Jonathan and Roger are up to something."

My heart pounded in my chest. "What did she say?"

Laura let out a sigh. I sensed her worry over the phone, like a palpable thing. "She thinks they want to get you fired. She said Roger has tried to convince all the other TAs to testify against you...and Jonathan is part of it, too."

It stung. I expected such things from Roger but hearing of Jonathan's involvement hurt me more than I anticipated.

"The university is keeping things hush-hush," she continued. "They won't even announce who is on the review board, but Roger is seriously out to get you."

"He wants my job and sees this as the easiest way to acquire it."

I patted Jinx on the head. He closed his eyes and leaned into me, kneading my thigh with his tiny feet. Having him around made everything so much better. I didn't even have to list the periodic table to calm down this time.

"What are you going to do about it?" asked Laura.

"Nothing."

"You can't give up, Gracie. Don't let them win."

"I'm not. I'm going to work on my thesis from here and tell the board the truth when I face them. I didn't do anything wrong. The data is there, Laura. It'll prove my innocence conclusively. We're dealing in facts and logic. Common sense alone dictates I'd never jeopardize my position at the university or my reputation by doing anything so ridiculous."

Laura remained unconvinced. "You're thinking like a scientist, sweetie, but this isn't a lab. It's real life. People lie."

I snorted. "People lie in the lab, too, Laura. They fudge results and choose selectively to make the outcome of experiments point to what they want to happen instead of the truth. They skew statistics to support desired results. But I'm not that kind of scientist. I'm not that kind of person, either, and the people I worked with know it's the absolute truth."

Even as I said those words, I understood absolutes did not exist. Those were things people told themselves so they could sleep better at night. As much as I worried about my future, it seemed out of my hands at this point. I needed to face the board, tell the truth, stand on my record, and let the chips fall where they may. The entire incident blindsided me, and I still reeled from the shock, but making Laura fret wouldn't solve anything.

"It'll be okay," I said, lying through my teeth. "Please don't worry."

"You're right," she said, and I knew she lied for my sake as well. "I'll shut up now. Tell me more about the shop."

I told her about the state I found the shop in when I first arrived. "But now it's slowly getting better. I'm still worried about Aunt Lucy, though. She's loopier than usual, and her memory is slipping."

"Don't jump to the worst-case scenario. Look for the most likely thing first. She hit her head, right? She may have a concussion, but there are lots of other possible causes of memory loss."

"Like what?"

"Vitamin deficiency, taking the wrong prescription meds, brain tumor, black mold, thyroid problems..."

"Wait...*brain tumor*?"

"Whoa, Nelly. I'm not saying it's a brain tumor. I'm saying there are other possibilities."

I put a hand over my chest. "Thanks, Laura. How are you doing, by the way?"

"I'm fine. The important question is, how are you? Are you bored and lonely yet? I know what you're like away from that lab of yours. It gets ugly quickly."

I laughed, mostly because she spoke the truth. "Actually, I'm doing okay. I mean I miss you, but the shop has kept me busy, and I've made some new friends."

"Guy friends or girlfriends?"

"Both."

I talked about Fiona and Cat, and all the other people I'd met. I may have put more detail into describing Dario than necessary, and Laura picked up on it right away.

"He sounds like he has potential."

"No way. He's too..." I struggled again to find the right word. "He's not my type."

Laura laughed. "Well, if Jonathan is your type, maybe you need to change types, Miss Gracie Ann."

"Maybe I do."

Laura promised she'd come to the Halloween Ball, which made me very happy. When I hung up the phone, I considered what she'd said about changing the type of man I dated. I'd automatically been cautious with Dario, and not only because I'd recently broken up with Jonathan. I also avoided him because he reminded me so much of the kind of boys who'd teased me my whole life, the athletic, popular, handsome ones.

I understood they experienced a primal need to be more manly and dominant, but it hurt nonetheless when they called me names in high school and made fun of my height and red hair. They even instigated something called "Kick a Ginger Day" and celebrated by torturing me.

"I'm one of Pavlov's dogs," I said softly to myself. Classically conditioned. But instead of salivating when a bell rang, I reacted with immediate distrust of Dario purely because of unrelated past experiences. I never allowed biases while working in a lab. Why permit my own against Dario?

I glanced out the window to the street below and saw Tiffany leaving her building. South Side Flats, it was a new apartment complex, and it boasted a host of luxurious amenities, including a spa on the first floor. It seemed like exactly the sort of place Tiffany would frequent. Expensive and exclusive. Not my style at all, and perhaps not Dario's either. I couldn't picture him in a spa.

I put Jinx on the couch. He'd fallen asleep while I spoke on the phone with Laura, and looked so sweet, curled up in a black ball on the sofa. I gave him another pat and went downstairs to the shop.

When I got to the landing at the top of the steps, I froze. The entire shop bustled with people. Customers streamed in and out, and an actual line formed at the register. Mrs. Periwinkle, a bright smile on her face as she worked, didn't seem at all overwhelmed by the crowded store. I scrambled down the steps and jogged to her side.

"Mrs. Periwinkle, I didn't know we were this busy. You should have called me."

Will, who'd fortunately come in early today, scurried around restocking shelves and helping customers. I never should have slept so late. I couldn't believe I'd been having a relaxing shower and chatting with Laura while all hell broke loose down here.

"Oh, tut, tut, dearie. This is nothing I can't handle. We're always busy around Samhain."

"Samhain?"

"Halloween," piped in Will, looking more cheerful than I'd ever seen him. "The best time of the year."

"I know what Samhain is, but I don't understand why all these people showed up here today." I looked around as even more people poured into the shop. "How can I help?"

She pointed to a pile of brown craft paper shopping bags with twine handles. They were stamped in black with the words "Hocus Pocus Magic Shop" and the outline of a witch flying on a broomstick toward a full moon.

"You can bag for me, if you'd like."

I opened a bag and filled it for the customer, a girl around my age dressed in a business suit. She nearly bubbled over with excitement. Her mousy brown hair slipped out of her French braid as she spoke. She pushed it away from her face and adjusted her glasses.

"My coworker told me all about this. I took an early lunch so I could get here before you ran out."

"Ran out?"

I looked at the bottle in my hand. Seeing one of the love potions we'd made last night, a wave of nausea came over me.

I put the bottle into the bag, not sure what to do or how to react.

Mrs. Periwinkle introduced us. "This is Candace Rosenthal. She works at the bank. She's a lovely girl. Always so kind." She turned back to Candace. "Remember my instructions, dearie."

"I will," said Candace, beaming.

"Thank you," said Mrs. Periwinkle. "Have a magical day, and good luck with your special someone."

She gave Candace a saucy wink, making the girl blush all the way to the tips of her ears. "Thank you, Mrs. Periwinkle. You're the best."

After she left, I pulled Mrs. Periwinkle aside. "You put those things on the shelves? But we made them as a joke."

"Joke or not, they seem to be popular."

I put a hand to my head. "None of this makes any sense. How could people know about the love potions so soon? We opened only a few hours ago."

"When you use magic, the word gets around." She smiled at me, a twinkle in her bright blue eyes. "You must have found the long-lost grimoire of Maeve McAlroy. Well done, Gracie."

CHAPTER 9

KEEP CALM AND PUT YOUR LAB COAT ON.

"Who the heck is Maeve McAlroy?"

"One of your ancestors, a powerful witch and very famous. People wrote books about her. And you're one of her direct descendants. It's obvious."

"Why?"

My brain moved in slow motion. I'd never heard of Maeve McAlroy. I came from sturdy, Irish farming stock. Not witches. Not magical. Not famous.

Mrs. Periwinkle touched a lock of my hair. "Alroy means 'red-headed.' You have her hair. And her magic, too."

She went back to ringing up customers, and after a moment of hesitation, I joined her. "Look, Mrs. Periwinkle, you're a nice lady. I don't want to insult you, but this is a load of nonsense. I don't believe in magic spell books."

She giggled, a sound so contagious the customer she waited on giggled, too. "I'm not insulted, and it isn't nonsense." She continued waiting on customers as they bought my faux love potions, never once losing the sweet smile on her lips. "And a grimoire is not a spell book. It contains instructions for things like making amulets and summoning spirits as well as casting spells. It's more like..." She considered it a second before raising one delicate and well-manicured finger. "A textbook. A scientific journal, but more personal."

"Love potions would never be found in a scientific journal." I folded my arms across my chest and glared at her.

"Are you sure?"

I frowned, thinking about how the items listed for the potion made sense. How they felt so right when I combined them, so logical, like experiments done in a lab. Of course, this particular experiment took place in the back room of a magic shop, and the results, from the swirling purple color to the way they seemed to be selling, were completely unexpected.

"And another thing about the grimoire," continued Mrs. Periwinkle, as if discussing the weather. "Spell books are... well...books. Grimoires, on the other hand, are more. They aren't about magic. They *are* magic."

I narrowed my eyes at her. "Let's say for the sake of argument the grimoire I found did come from my red-headed ancestor. Let's also say, for the sake of argument, she may have been a witch. If both of those things are true, why didn't I know about Maeve McAlroy before, and why would Aunt Lucy hide such a valuable heirloom in a secret compartment under the stairs?"

She pondered my question. "Perhaps as a precaution? A grimoire isn't something evil, but it can be dangerous. You should be careful. Magic is not to be taken lightly. In any form."

Mrs. Periwinkle left at lunchtime, but she got me set up at the cash register first, and the afternoon flew by. She'd made the price abnormally high for the potions I'd created, but it didn't seem to bother our customers one bit. We sold out in no time.

I ran upstairs periodically to check on Jinx. He'd adjusted well and hadn't destroyed anything. Not yet, at least. And every time I opened the door, he ran to greet me, purring and rubbing against my legs. Definitely the cutest kitty cat ever.

As the late afternoon sun burst through the newly cleaned windows of the shop, Aunt Lucy rolled in for a visit. Still in a wheelchair, she'd been to the doctor and no longer needed to keep her leg extended. She sat in the chair with her knee bent and her foot in the footrest, looking much more comfortable. Mags pushed her through the door and they both stared around in amazement.

"Gracie," she said in a hushed voice. "What have you done? This is wonderful. And there is no one shopping in Party Ark right now. They all came here."

I leaned forward to give her a kiss, taking the opportunity to whisper in her ear. "We need to talk, but I'm with a customer right now. Give me a couple of minutes."

As soon as I finished, Will took over the register, and I pushed her into the back room. Mags slipped outside to run some errands. I turned Aunt Lucy around to face me and leaned back against the table.

"Aunt Lucy, I've done something possibly bad and potentially dangerous."

"Oh, how fun," she said, her eyes twinkling. "Whatever can it be?"

"I'm not sure where to begin."

"The beginning is usually a good place." She fluttered her eyelashes when I scowled at her. "Just pointing out the obvious, my dear."

"Wow. Thank you." It seemed appropriate we were having this discussion in the back room, the place where I'd drunkenly mixed up fake magic potions only hours before. "Okay. Here goes. Last night, Fiona and Cat came over to help me organize the shop, and I found this."

At the sight of the grimoire, her face lit up. She reached for it, stroking it and flipping through the pages. "Maeve's grimoire. I haven't seen this in ages. Where did you find it?" I told her about the drawer in the stairs and she laughed. "I'd forgotten all about that. Silly me."

"Some documents were stored in there as well, but I couldn't read them. They weren't in English."

"Those aren't terribly important. Most are deeds to some property Anton owned in Romania, but when he died, he left it all to one of his nephews. We'd planned it that way, especially once we knew we couldn't have children of our own. I'd kept copies for my records, but only as a backup. And our marriage certificate would have been with them, too, if I'm not mistaken."

I looked at her in surprise. "You can remember the contents of a drawer you haven't opened in decades?"

"Of course, sweetie. I'm not as dotty as I seem." She gave me a wry smile. "Don't respond, please."

She sounded so much like herself I got emotional. "You scared me, you know."

"I scared myself," she said with a laugh. "But I'm better now. For the last few months, I've been so foggy, but I'm finally normal again. Or as close to normal as I get."

I snorted. "And to think you made me search for a dragon..."

Aunt Lucy gave me a steady look. "I still need to find the Dragon Rouge. The ghost won't rest without it."

All my hopes Aunt Lucy might not be losing her mind faded away like the morning mist. "You still believe you were pushed down the steps by Uncle Anton's ghost?"

"Yes, because it's the truth. I've been in a muddle lately, but I'm not out of touch with reality. And now I have a way to help us find it."

Arguing with Aunt Lucy never got me anywhere, so I played along. "And what would that be?"

"We'll use this." She handed me the grimoire. "It'll guide you to the red dragon. Magic calls to magic."

I took the grimoire from her hands and as soon as I made contact with it, I got the same strange sensation again. Like I touched a living thing.

Aunt Lucy and her friends had definitely gotten to me. I needed to get back in a lab. I missed white coats and safety goggles more than I could express at this point.

"Don't make that face, Gracie Ann."

She shook her head, her long, dangly earrings brushing against her cheeks. Today she dressed in emerald green, and wore a purple scarf covered in pentagrams. It took me a second to see her earring were pentagrams as well, with chains of glittery stars twinkling down from them. I recognized them because I sold two pairs this afternoon to an elderly woman in a witch's hat.

"What face?"

"That scientist face. You've used it on me since you were a little girl, and it's only gotten worse with time. Sometimes you have to let go of all you know and believe in the unknown. The ghost will return. He said he'd be back again before the night of the full moon, and it's just a few weeks away. I don't know what he'll do if you don't have it."

She looked so distraught I gave her a hug. "I'll find it. Don't worry. And I already found one thing I think you're going to love." I ran upstairs to get Jinx, and she cooed in delight when she saw him.

"Who is this?"

"His name is Jinx. I discovered him hiding in the shop last night."

I put him on her lap, and he rubbed against her, enjoying the attention. "He was in my shop? How did he get in?"

I scratched him under the chin. "I have no idea, but I'm glad he did."

"So am I, but I don't understand. You said you'd done something bad. I half expected you to tell me you'd cheated on your Jonathan with Alvida's handsome grandson."

"Dario?" I asked, huffing in exasperation. "First of all, Jonathan and I broke up before I came here, so it wouldn't be cheating. Secondly, there is nothing between Dario and me. Nothing at all."

"Whatever you say, dear." She winked at me and I clenched my teeth, resisting the urge to say something I'd later regret. "So what is your deep, dark secret if it isn't sleeping with Dario Fontana?"

"It has nothing to do with men," I said, "It has to do with public safety. I not only found the grimoire last night...I, uh, used it."

She froze. "What do you mean?"

"I mixed up a love potion, as a joke, with Cat and Fiona. We were goofing around."

"Magic is not a joking matter," she said as she went back to petting Jinx. She gave me a thoughtful look. "Which one did you make?"

I pointed out the spell I'd used in the book. "I woke up late today, and by the time I came downstairs, Mrs. Periwinkle had already stocked them on the shelves and was selling them for an outrageous amount. There is nothing harmful in the potions, but of course they won't work. I'm afraid people will give you a hard time and ask for their money back."

She stared at the words in the book. "Wait a second. You can read this?"

"It's Latin. Of course, I can read it."

"Amazing. I studied Latin years ago, but I could never..." She shook her head. "Matilda would never put anything on the shelves that might harm a customer. Why are you so certain the spell won't work?"

I folded my arms across my chest and glared at her. "I don't believe in magic potions."

"And yet you created one." She tapped her chin with one bejeweled finger. She loved rings. She wore at least five on each hand. "I'm curious. Did you sell very many of them?"

A sick knot formed in my stomach. "We sold all of them. The word spread like wildfire. Like people knew the potions were here before the shop even opened."

"Magic can be like that, although I have no actual experience with it myself. I'll tell you a secret and you can't share this with anyone." I leaned close so she could whisper in my ear. "I don't have the gift. I've known it my whole life. My mother had it. My sister Betty, too, but not me. And your mother is as magical as a doorknob, as is your nan. It apparently skipped a generation and went straight to you, lucky girl. I suspect the twins have it, too, which is not a good thing. Those imps would use it for something ridiculous. You, on the other hand, have a more practical nature, and that's a useful attribute for any witch."

"Why open a shop like this if you aren't magic?" I couldn't believe I even asked that question, but Aunt Lucy didn't seem to find it odd.

"I married into it. My husband possessed his own special kind of magic, and the things that man could do in bed..." Her eyes grew misty at the memory. I winced, not wanting to hear any more about Uncle Anton's sexual prowess.

"But you read tarot cards..."

"I took a class online."

I rolled my eyes. "Great. Back to the potions, Mrs. Periwinkle sold every single bottle in just a few hours. There's no way we can get them back, or even figure out who bought them. What should we do?""

She gave me a bewildered smile. "Well, isn't it obvious, dearie? You have to make more."

"No, I can't. I won't. It's ridiculous."

She looked at Jinx. "But you must. Otherwise..." She let out a shaky sigh. "Well, I guess the shop will have to close."

I knew manipulation when I saw it, but the hint of tears in her voice did me in. She sat there, a tiny, old lady in a wheelchair with a kitten curled up on her lap. Even Jinx looked at me accusingly with his green eyes. Aunt Lucy's business teetered on the brink of ruin. If some fake magic potions helped her keep her shop, we both knew I'd make them.

I let out an exasperated sigh. "Fine, but if we get in trouble for this, it's on you."

She looked up at me, no trace of tears in her eyes at all. "Of course, dearest."

She tricked me, the minx, but she seemed so genuinely happy about it I couldn't get angry. We went back into the shop where Aunt Lucy sat with Jinx on her lap, smiling and greeting the customers. Mags came back with a giant picnic basket in her arms.

"From Claire at the Enchanted Garden Café. She made her famous chili, and Fiona sent over some cornbread and cookies. She said you ladies enjoyed quite the party last night."

"We did."

We cleared the table in the back room and enjoyed a delicious meal as soon as I closed the shop for the day. Will had a gig, so he couldn't stay and eat with us. Afterward, I made a pot of tea and we nibbled on Fiona's cookies.

I sighed. "She's a cookie genius."

Aunt Lucy and Mags agreed. "She said she'd make cookies for the Halloween party again this year," said Mags. "If you plan on having it."

Aunt Lucy grew pensive. "It draws a lot of business into

the shop, but it's so much work. Fiona and Claire handle the Samhain celebration itself. We host the after party in the event room out back, but I don't think I'm up to it this year and I can't ask you to do it. You've done so much already, dearie."

I took a long sip of the tea Claire sent over. She called this mix Sweet Serenity, and it fit. I hadn't been so calm or relaxed in ages, the reason I said something I'd probably live to regret. "I think I want to do it."

Aunt Lucy and Mags exchanged a worried glance. "Are you sure? We'll all pitch in, but it's a big event," said Mags.

"It'll be fun."

Halloween fell on a Saturday, which gave me just over four weeks to prepare. We discussed how to decorate the large event room, and I loved seeing the spark come back into Aunt Lucy's eyes.

"I'll work on the invitations tonight," she said, her face glowing with excitement. She clapped her hands. "This will be wonderful. We have a lovely community of Wiccans in the area. Eliza Dragonsong is their high priestess. I'll contact her right away."

"Eliza is a lawyer by day," said Mags. "She's quite the character."

"I'm sure she is." This sounded like more work than I'd anticipated already. "Wait. Are we having a bonfire here?"

Aunt Lucy laughed. "Of course not. It'll be at the Enchanted Garden." She grabbed my hand, giving it a heartfelt squeeze. "Thank you. For everything."

After they left, I cleaned up the remnants of the meal, fed Jinx, and planned to go upstairs. I should have been working on my thesis, but instead found myself back at the table with the grimoire open, mixing more potions. This time I made four batches of the love potion. By the time I'd finished bottling them and placing them on the shelves, the pitchers of water we'd gotten at the Enchanted Garden were empty. My muscles ached with fatigue, but I felt oddly satisfied and content.

A drop of the love potion sat in the mixing bowl, in all its purple glory. I stared at it a moment before wiping it up with my finger and taking a sniff. It seemed innocuous enough, which made me decide to break one of the cardinal rules of chemistry.

Don't taste anything in the lab.

As soon as the sweet, thick liquid hit my tongue, something strange happened. An odd, tingling warmth spread throughout my belly and my appendages, disappearing almost as quickly as it came. I wiggled my fingers, studying them, and shook my head.

"It must be the damned tea," I muttered to myself. I suspected it contained caffeine because I felt wide awake and jittery.

I grabbed a pile of books from the shelves in Aunt Lucy's kitchen and went upstairs. After taking a long, hot bath, I put on my pajamas and peeked out the window. The street below looked quiet and deserted. About to close the curtain, I noticed a light on in one of the apartments in the South Side Flats. A woman stood at the window, staring down at the dark street.

Tiffany. I moved quickly to the side, hoping she wouldn't notice me. Her apartment, located on the second floor, sat only one story below mine. When she didn't glance up, I relaxed. She sipped from a mug she held tightly clenched in her hands. Her gaze remained fixed on the street below, like she waited for something...or someone. Her expression contemplative, she reached out and pressed a hand against the glass. She seemed lonely, and kind of sad.

She wore a pink robe (of course), and she looked a lot younger and more vulnerable than in person. It seemed strange to study her like this, but I couldn't tear my gaze away. Who did she wait for? Could it be Dario?

When she glanced up, as if she sensed being watched, I closed the curtains with a swish. I felt like I'd done something wrong. "Fiddlesticks," I said, stealing one of Aunt Lucy's favorite expressions. I could look out my window if I wanted to, and I wasn't spying on her or anything.

Was I?

I poured a glass of wine and curled up by the fire with the books I'd brought up from downstairs. The books were a mix of the odd and the fascinating, but none were as old or as interesting as my grimoire.

I chastised myself for imagining it as my property, but I'd grown possessive of the stupid little book. I even brought it upstairs with me because I didn't want to leave it downstairs alone. Yes, I'd turned into a total nut case.

Jinx played with a ball of string he found in Aunt Lucy's sewing kit, until he wore himself out and fell into an exhausted heap near my feet. I picked up the grimoire and stroked its worn leather cover. Although not magical exactly, it did give off a sort of unusual energy, perhaps from all the people who'd passed it down generation to generation for so many years. And all those generations appeared to believe in the magic of the grimoire, even Aunt Lucy.

It will guide us to the red dragon. Magic calls to magic.

I frowned, looking through the pile of books I'd collected from Aunt Lucy's stash. Most of the other books I'd found were nonsense, filled with incantations and spells involving imaginary ingredients like wolf's breath and ogre tongue.

Ogre tongue? Seriously? Who came up with these things?

I didn't believe in magical powers, but at least the grimoire seemed practical. It also utilized ingredients that actually existed.

I stood and scanned the bookshelf by the fireplace, my

gaze immediately drawn to a well-worn copy of *Dracula*. I pulled it out and read it as I sipped wine, thinking about vampires and castles and things that go bump in the night, until finally my eyelids got heavy and I let out a yawn.

When I tried to return the book to its spot on the shelf, something jammed up the space and I couldn't slide it back in. Removing all the books from the shelf, I stared in shock at what I'd uncovered. Pushed deep into the back corner of the bookshelf was an old wooden box, decorated with a beautiful painting of a red dragon. Fire spewed from the dragon's mouth, and the flames mingled and intertwined with the words Dragon Rouge written in fine gold leaf across the top.

"Holy guacamole," I said, reaching for it.

Larger than the palm of my hand, it measured about three inches deep. I tried to take the lid off, but it refused to budge. I inspected the keyhole and grabbed Aunt Lucy's key ring from the table. I chose the oldest, rustiest key, the same one I'd noticed the first day I arrived at the shop. The box opened with a loud click, and inside, resting on a bed of black velvet, sat a giant blood-colored stone. Lumpy and strange, it looked like a ruby, but I'd never seen one so big, and the shape reminded me of something else as well.

"A dragon," I said, softly. Rather than being the box, the Dragon Rouge was what the box contained.

I lifted a finger, about to touch the stone, mesmerized by the way it glowed in the light of the fire, when Jinx woke up and arched his back, his eyes on the box. He let out a hiss, making the hair stand up on my arms.

"Jinxie. What is it?"

A gust of wind caused the flames in the fireplace to dance and the windows to rattle, but Jinx's attention never left the Dragon Rouge. A clap of thunder sounded outside as rain hit the roof, pounding so hard I thought it could be hail. When a log fell in the fireplace, and it let off a shower of sparks, Jinx flew straight into my arms, his gaze darting frantically around the room, nearly knocking the box out of my hands.

"It's okay, buddy."

I sat him gently on a cushion, locked up the box with the ancient key, and put it back where I'd found it on the shelf, hiding it behind a row of books. I sank onto the couch, trying to slow my beating heart.

What had just happened?

I decided to analyze it rationally. It probably had nothing at all to do with the dragon box, or the blood-colored stone. In Aunt Lucy's poor befuddled state, she'd remembered the box, and, for some reason, came to the conclusion the ghost wanted it. The subconscious mind often put things together that did not connect at all. It even happened to me, since I saw a connection between holding the grimoire and finding the dragon box, when none existed.

I gave myself a mental shake, knowing this place always got to me. Jinx had obviously woken up from a dream, and the rain frightened him, but his reaction scared me. Fear could sometimes be contagious.

"Fear is contagious," I said softly to myself. Jinx sat next to me, wide-awake and alert. I gave him a pat on the head. "Oh, Jinx. I know what I have to do."

Only one person could help me contain this particular contagion, and I needed his help. I scrolled through my contacts until I found Dario's number and sent him a quick text asking him if he could meet me the next morning. He texted me back right away and said he could.

I tried to ignore the flip-flop my heart did at the thought of seeing him again. A purely physical reaction caused by the excessive amounts of tea I'd consumed earlier. It had nothing to do with Dario. Nothing at all.

I looked at Jinx and spoke in a serious, no nonsense voice. "What's the protocol for dealing with a contagion? It's

QIVC. Quarantine. Investigate. Vaccinate. Cure. I can't quarantine stupid people, but maybe we can educate others enough to eradicate this particular strain of stupidity once and for all. Knowledge is key, Jinxer. Ignorance is the disease, and the people harassing Aunt Lucy, Cat, and Sally are ignorant. We have to find a cure, and Dr. Dario might be the right person to help us."

CHAPTER 10

YOU MUST BE A CARBON SAMPLE, BECAUSE I REALLY WANT TO DATE YOU.

I spent far too much time getting ready the next morning. Knowing I'd soon see Dario made my heart race and my skin get hot and tight, a strange reaction to mere mental stimuli. This never happened to me before. Maybe the others knew what they were talking about. Maybe I had been dating the wrong sort of men. Maybe I should give Dario a chance.

Not that any conclusive evidence existed he'd actually be interested in dating me. I winced, wanting to smack myself on the head for my own stupidity. My aunt teetered on the verge of losing her business, and I still faced the investigation at Penn. I'd finished zero work on my thesis and couldn't even look at my laptop without my belly clenching in panic. I knew I should be working, and I'd been certain about the quality of my research, but now I felt lost. The last thing I needed to worry about right now was a darkly handsome man with twinkling eyes and a wolfish grin. But my body, in the powerful throes of a chemical reaction and taken over by hormones, rebelled against such logic. As a scientist, I acknowledged the truth. I wanted Dario Fontana. Not convenient, and certainly not wise, but I did.

I put on a white blouse with a brown herringbone skirt and a tan cardigan. I buttoned up my blouse, then changed my mind and undid a few to reveal more cleavage. I never ran short on cleavage, but normally tried to disguise my figure and minimize my curves. Calling me voluptuous could technically be classified as an understatement.

Brushing my hair until it shone, I pulled it up, allowing tendrils to slip out and fall around my face. I added a touch of mascara to my lashes and eyeliner on my lids to enhance the already cat-like shape of my green eyes. I fluttered my eyelashes at Jinx.

"Do you like it?"

He seemed less than impressed and went right back to licking his balls. In other words, Jinx reacted like any male would under the same circumstances.

I picked up my phone and called Aunt Lucy. Dario was due to arrive shortly, but first I had to tell her about finding the Dragon Rouge.

When I gave her the news, she gasped, sounding both surprised and delighted. "I remember it now. The box is made of alder wood from a sacred tree, right?"

I stared skyward, trying to remain patient. "Well, it's definitely wooden."

"And you found it on my bookshelf?"

"Right behind your copy of *Dracula*."

"Oh," she said. "That makes sense."

I didn't ask her why. I knew it would be something convoluted and borderline ridiculous. "I'm meeting Dario in a few minutes, so I'd better go. Are you coming into the shop today?"

"I can't," she said. "I have an appointment. But promise me something, Gracie, and this is important. Whatever you do, be a good girl and do not touch that stone. Don't take it out of the box or even lay a single finger on it. I'm serious. It's dangerous."

I promised her not to play with the Dragon Rouge and hung up the phone. In Aunt Lucy's mind, I still wore pigtails and braces on my teeth. She didn't see me as an adult, not really, but something in her voice worried me. She acted more lucid than she had when I first arrived, but she continued to have an oddly fearful obsession with that silly box. I just couldn't understand why.

I stuck on a pair of nude heels, popped my glasses onto my nose, and marched down the stairs to the shop. Dario waited at the door, a box of donuts in his hands and a smile on his face. The smile widened when he caught a glimpse of me. Unlocking the door, I pulled my sweater around my body self-consciously. Last night this seemed like such a good idea, but now, as Dario stood in front of me, all rippling muscles and hotness, my confidence evaporated quicker than a beaker of water left next to a sunny window on a hot day.

"I brought gifts," he said, handing me the box of donuts with a flourish. Mrs. Periwinkle hadn't arrived yet, so I put on a pot of coffee, and we sat on the soft velvet chairs near one of the bookshelves.

Dario looked around the shop as I served the coffee. "I like what you've done with the place," he said.

Sunlight streamed in through the window making the crystals near the cash register sparkle and sending rainbows dancing around the room. The shelves were tidy and well organized. The charming window displays made pedestrians pause on the sidewalk and stare. The items inside the shop, grouped to draw the eye, created focal points and interest. Fiona and Cat had helped me a great deal, but it turns out I exhibited a knack for this sort of thing myself. I'd never been much of a shopper, so this ability came as a surprise.

"Thanks. I've had fun."

He raised a finger. "Before I forget, Nunny wants you to come over for dinner tonight. I have to warn you, though. It's a set-up. She wants us to go out, and this is her way of arranging it."

"I'd love to come," I said, as shyness washed over me. I'd resisted his outrageous attractiveness quite capably before, but something had definitely changed. Not able to come up with a better explanation, I blamed the donuts.

He paused, one of those donuts halfway to his mouth. "Are you serious?"

"I like your grandmother," I said, unable to meet his eyes.

"And you are okay with this being a date? Because that's how she'll see it."

I worked up the courage to look at him. "Yes."

His jaw dropped. "Wait. I thought you didn't like me."

"Not true."

My cheeks grew hotter than a Bunsen burner, and he grinned, his teeth a flash of white. "Good to know."

Holy hemlock, no man should be this ridiculously attractive. If I could bottle him the way I bottled my fake love potions, I could make some significant bank for Aunt Lucy.

I paused as an odd thought occurred to me. I'd taken one taste of the swirly purple glop of the love potion last night, and now I flirted shamelessly with Dario Fontana as I unbuttoned my blouse and seduced him with my eyes. Well, not the last part, but the rest actually happened. Could there be a connection?

A less logical person might think so, but I viewed the changes in my behavior as a normal progression. Why wouldn't I be attracted to him? Everything about him, from his face to his body to his mind drew me like polar molecules attract nonpolar molecules due to momentary dipoles. They normally didn't mix, like oil and water, but if one fluctuation occurred...boom. Instant attraction. Oddly enough, a momentary dipole must have occurred for Dario, too, because he seemed attracted to me as well.

A niggling doubt persisted as I recalled the odd tingling sensation I'd experienced right after tasting the love potion. Could a component in that potion be the impetus for me changing my mind about Dario? I'd contacted him right after I sampled it. But I didn't believe in coincidences. I believed in facts. This seemed too freaky to be factual, and Dario seemed too hot to be ignored.

"Are you still willing to write an article about us?" I asked.

"Of course," he said, pulling out his notebook. "What do you have in mind?"

"Well, I don't want to say anything about the threats. It'll give fuel to their fire."

"I agree." He twirled his pencil between his fingers. "I normally write about sports, as you know, but I contribute a few freelance articles now and again for the community pages. Maybe I could write about the upcoming Samhain celebration, since you seem dead set on hosting the after party."

"I know you don't approve, but I have to do it...for Aunt Lucy."

"I get it, and I don't like it, but I guess I'd do the same." He tapped his pencil on his notebook. "Is there anything in particular you want me to cover?"

I sipped my coffee. "I'll leave it up to you. I trust your judgment."

Taking a bite of my donut, I groaned as the rich taste of sugar and cream hit my tongue. Dario watched me closely, especially when I licked cream off the corner of my lip. His eyes followed the movement of my tongue, an interesting response. I tried it again to see if I'd get the same result, and

I did. As he shifted in his chair, I suppressed a smile. Looking puzzled, he set down his notebook.

"You're different," he said, taking in the makeup, the looser bun, and the exposed cleavage. I cleared my throat, and his gaze shot guiltily back to my face.

"Is that a criticism?" I asked.

"No. An observation."

I waved my hand to indicate the entire shop. "This place has always produced a weird effect on me, even as a little girl. I don't know what it is or how to explain it but being here is good for me. Especially this time."

"What do you mean?"

I weighed my options, trying to decide if I wanted to tell him the details about my personal problems or not. "Did you ever hear the analogy about the frog in hot water?"

He picked up his coffee. "I don't think I have."

I wiped my mouth with a napkin, setting my plate aside. "If you put a frog into boiling water, it'll jump out right away. But if you put a frog in room temperature water, and heat the water slowly until it boils, the frog will never leave. He'll sit in that water as it gets hotter and hotter and not even notice it until it's too late."

"And you are the frog?"

"Well, I used to be."

"Can you tell me about it?"

I leaned back in my chair, my hands folded neatly on my lap. "It's a long, boring story."

"I'm a good listener."

I smiled. "I noticed."

He looked into my eyes. "I mean it. I'm curious." His sincerity did funny things to my heart.

"Well, if you really want to know..."

The words poured out of me as I told him about what happened at the university with Dr. Lewis, Jonathan, Roger and even Seth Billings. It felt good to open up about it, and Dario didn't exaggerate. He was a good listener.

When I finished, finally, he got right to the point. "Well, it's obvious you were framed, and your ex is a jerk, but do you know what's wrong with that whole story?"

I frowned at him, nonplussed. "No."

"Why *you*?"

"What do you mean?"

"Whoever did this could have set up Jonathan or Roger or one of the other TAs. Why did they choose you?"

I twisted the edge of my cardigan with my hands, my eyes downcast. "I don't know."

He tilted his head, so I'd meet his eyes. "Well, then you need to start asking the right questions. They'll lead you to the right answers."

"But there is no way I could have foreseen the allegations..."

"Of course not, but think carefully about what happened. If you remove all the emotion from the issue, the hurt and betrayal, you may be able to see something previously undistinguishable."

I pondered this. Had there been warning signs I'd ignored? Professionally, I couldn't be sure, but there were with Jonathan. I made excuses about his behavior over and over again, chalking up all of his eccentricities to his brilliance and his extremely busy schedule. Well, I happened to be more brilliant, and even busier, but I didn't possess those same selfish quirks.

As far as seeing something I'd missed at work, I doubted it existed. I'd been over and over it in my head, and simply didn't have enough data to solve the problem. Dario had good intentions, but his suggestion didn't really help.

"Anything I could come up with would be pure conjecture. A hypothesis not based on any concrete facts."

"Great discoveries come from pure conjecture, don't they?"

"Yes, but that doesn't necessarily apply here. This isn't an experiment. It's my life. My future."

"Which is why it's so important. I'm certain you follow your intuition all the time in the lab. It's the mark of a great scientist. And you need to listen to it to solve this puzzle, too."

"Do you honestly think so?" I highly doubted it, and I guess my expression conveyed as much.

He laughed and leaned closer, so close I caught a whiff of the soapy, spicy scent of his skin and felt his body heat. My own temperature went up a few notches. This man should come with a warning label. When his gaze locked on mine, I couldn't look away.

"What's your intuition telling you now, Gracie Ann?"

I opened my mouth, about to speak, but Mrs. Periwinkle burst into the shop in a flurry of blue wool and sparkles. The sparkles came from the blue scarf around her neck and the blue felted wool hat on her head. The hat contained threads of pink, purple, and green in it as well.

"Good morning, lovelies. I see you are both up and eager early this morning."

Dario sat back, his eyes still smoldering. I placed a cool hand on my hot cheek. "Is it warm in here or is it just me?"

Mrs. Periwinkle hung up her coat and hat and breezed back into the main room of the shop. "It's you, dear. And if you get any hotter, you'll spontaneously combust."

She gave me a wink, and I cringed, mortified at her insinuation. I jumped to my feet and made a show of tidying up, hoping Dario missed the meaning behind Mrs. Periwinkle's words. Thankfully, he seemed oblivious as he jotted notes in his little book, his eyebrows drawn together in concentration.

"Hey, Grace. I have one more question," he said.

I paused mid-step, worried about what he may ask. "Sure."

"Not about the article. About you. Will you tell me about your PhD work?"

I sat back in the chair. I doubted he'd understand any of it, but I planned to explain it as simply as I could. "Have you ever heard of molecular dynamics?"

"It's a computer simulation, right?"

"Yes," I said, impressed. "It simulates the physical movements of atoms and molecules. I'm studying molecular dynamics for my thesis, but in the context of N-body simulation. The atoms and molecules are allowed to interact, but only for a period of time. It gives us a view of the motion of the atoms. It's fascinating. I only need my laptop at this point to complete my project. No lab necessary. For most of it, at least."

I'd planned to involve my students in the final stages of my thesis, but that changed because of my current academic status. I'd looked forward to defending my thesis since I'd gotten my first chemistry set in sixth grade, and the work itself brought me the most joy. I wanted to finish it, whether I could present it or not. Doing it for my own gratification and not for another person's validation felt sort of...good.

Dario reached for my hand and gave it a squeeze. "It'll be brilliant. I'm sure of it."

He didn't know me well, and probably knew even less about molecular dynamics, but his faith made me oddly emotional. He leaned closer and I hoped he'd kiss me, but Mrs. Periwinkle bustled back into the room, destroying the mood.

"Oh, I see you've made more potions. It's a good thing. I imagine we'll sell out of these before lunch time."

"Potions?" asked Dario, fighting back a grin. "You made potions?"

I shot a glance at my watch. "Look at the time." I jumped to my feet and tidied up again, hoping to distract him, but no such luck.

"What kind of potions?"

Mrs. Periwinkle answered for me. "Love potions, of course. Grace is a master. She has the gift."

I stood behind her, shaking my head and mouthing the words, "*No, I don't.*"

He bit his lip to keep from smiling, and Mrs. Periwinkle continued, oblivious. "She found the old grimoire of Maeve McAlroy. Truth be told, it found her. Which is how magic works, you know."

A tension headache started coming on. "You and Aunt Lucy have worked in this shop so long you actually believe what you're selling."

Dario chuckled, but Mrs. Periwinkle remained unfazed. "I've always believed in magic. If you opened your scientific mind a crack, you'd believe in it, too."

Dario watched my reaction, his face glowing with amusement. "May I see the grimoire?"

I narrowed my eyes at him. "Why? What do you plan to do with it?"

"Well, I'm not going to cast any spells." It looked like he bit the inside of his cheek to keep from laughing. "I'm just curious."

"You won't put it in your article?"

He raised his hand. "Scout's honor."

I brought the grimoire to him and he studied it carefully. I held Jinx in my arms and watched Dario flip through the pages, his dark head bent over it and his brows furrowed.

"Oh. Here's your love potion. It doesn't look too complicated."

I blinked. "You can read Latin?"

"Twelve years at St. Alphonse," he said, giving me a crooked smile.

He made it sound like a prison sentence. "I did my stint at St. Cecilia's."

"It comes in handy sometimes. It helped with my SATs." He turned the book over, looking for any markings on the back. "But the Latin in this book is strange. Nothing I've ever seen before. I can only make out bits and pieces of it."

I frowned. "It doesn't seem weird to me."

"And that itself strikes me as odd." He stroked the cover with his finger. "I think you should take this next door."

"To the bookstore?"

"Yes. Maybe they can give you an idea about its history."

"Does Mr. Sebastian still own it?" A kindred spirit, I remembered him fondly.

"No, he retired and moved closer to his daughter in Florida. A new guy bought it a few months ago. His name is Constantine Dalca, I believe."

Dario got up to leave, handing me the book. Once again it shocked me how warm and alive it seemed. "Does the book feel strange to you? Kind of...hot?"

He touched a deliciously cool hand to my cheek. I resisted the urge to lean into it. "You're the one who's hot." He winked at the double entendre. "I'll pick you up at seven. Is that okay?"

If possible, my cheeks got even warmer. "It's a date."

"It is," he said, a million promises of naughty, lovely things in his eyes.

After he left, I sighed. Mrs. Periwinkle sighed as well. "He is a beautiful man," she said.

I agreed with her. "Definitely very easy to look at."

We watched him cross the street, and Mrs. Periwinkle nudged my arm. "I bet he's amazing in the sack."

My mouth dropped open in shock. "Mrs. Periwinkle..."

She shrugged, a delicate lift of her dainty shoulders. "I know about things like this. Trust me. You're in for a real treat."

I spluttered out a response, but she ignored me, her gaze going to the sidewalk. "Look, Grace. The word has gotten around. They're lining up for your potions already."

She didn't lie. At least ten people stood outside waiting for the shop to open, and more joined them by the minute. I snuck a glance at my watch. "It's 9:58. Shall we let them in two minutes early?"

She tilted her head and considered it a second, like a tiny blue bird.

"Let the games begin."

CHAPTER 11

DO THESE PROTONS MAKE MY MASS LOOK BIG?

Mrs. Periwinkle's estimation proved correct, and we sold out right before lunch. I went to the back room to mix more, but something strange happened. The love potions didn't turn the same oddly pearlescent purple this time.

"What could be wrong?" asked Mrs. Periwinkle. She'd stayed late to help me as Will minded the shop.

"I don't know." I read over the ingredients again and again, checking my notes. "The only thing I didn't do..." I shook my head. It couldn't be.

"What is it, dearie?"

"It says we need water from a sacred pool, but water is a non-reactive agent so it shouldn't make any difference at all where the water came from."

"Where did you get it last time?"

"The Enchanted Garden Café. In the back they have a fountain, but water is water."

Mrs. Periwinkle tilted her head to one side. "Is it really?"

I frowned. "Yes, it is."

She handed me an empty pitcher. "Prove it. Go back to

the Enchanted Garden and collect more water from the fountain. Mix your potion again, and let's see what happens."

I gave her a dirty look but did as she asked. To my great surprise, this time the formula worked, and the potion turned a lovely, pearly, swirly purple.

"It's not possible."

"The proof is in the pudding. Or in the potion, rather," she said with a giggle.

I studied the liquid in the vial. "It must have to do with the water. Maybe there's a high sodium content, or iron, or some sort of mold on the fountain's surface affecting the chemical composition of the formula."

"Or maybe it's from a sacred pool, which makes it magical."

I ignored her but decided to take Cat up on her offer to use the lab at the community college. I itched to get a sample of this water under a microscope and figure out what made it different from tap water.

Mags had stopped by earlier to drop off the invitations for the Halloween party. They sat in a shoebox in the corner of the room. Looking at them made me more and more nervous about my decision to host such a large event. I had no experience with this sort of thing. Some of the invitations were labeled and alphabetized. Others were left blank to invite people not on Aunt Lucy's initial list. All in all, close to one hundred filled the box.

Officer Belfiore came in as we filled vials with the love potion. He took off his hat and held it in the crook of his arm. "I'm Anthony Belfiore. We spoke on the phone. I'm Dario's cousin."

"Oh." I wiped my hands on my apron before reaching to shake his. "I didn't realize you were cousins."

He took out a notebook and the resemblance to Dario became more obvious. Same dark hair, same good looks, but

Anthony was leaner and more compact. He lacked Dario's giant, muscular frame. I sighed thinking about it. I liked Dario's giant, muscular frame. I liked Dario's giant, muscular everything.

I touched a hand to my cheek. "Is it hot in here?"

Mrs. Periwinkle looked skyward. "No. It's you. Again."

I shushed her, embarrassed, but Anthony didn't seem to notice. "Can I see the note you received?"

I brought him the message and he read it carefully, shaking his head in disgust. "Do you mind if I take this as evidence?"

"Not at all," I said, grateful to be rid of it.

He put it in his pocket. "Until we figure this out, be careful. Check your doors. Lock your windows. Keep an eye out for any suspicious behavior. Call me if you have a problem."

He handed me a card. I took it and put it in the pocket of my apron. "Thank you."

Mrs. Periwinkle dug through the box of invitations. "Here's one for you, an invitation to our Halloween party. You're welcome to bring a guest. Maybe that lovely dark-haired nurse. Isn't her name Brenda?"

He blushed this time. "Thank you." He put on his hat and gave me a nod. "I'll see you at Nunny's tonight."

I gulped. "You're going, too? Is it going to be a big group?"

"It's always a big group." He laughed. "I have to run. A group of women were caught dancing naked last night in Riverfront Park. Thanks to them I have loads of paperwork to fill out before my shift ends."

As soon as he left, I looked at Mrs. Periwinkle. "You don't think..."

She gave me an innocent blue-eyed stare. "What, dearest?"

I shook my head. No way the naked dancing women had anything to do with my potions. That would be crazy. The potions were for fun. No one could possibly take the instructions seriously.

I frowned. If a connection existed, it would be more ammunition for anyone who wanted to hurt us. At this rate, we basically handed the opportunity to them with a big sign saying, *Here you go. Feel free to put us out of business.*

Mrs. Periwinkle studied me over her glasses. "What will you wear on your date?"

"I don't know. I didn't bring anything dressy, only this sort of thing."

I motioned to my clothes, and she made a tsking sound. "You're as sexy as a nun."

"Hey." I glanced at my cleavage. "I even unbuttoned an extra button."

She patted my arm. "I admire the effort, but why don't you run over to Sally's and look around? I'll finish bottling these, and Will can handle the store. Bring her some of the invitations as well. She promised to pass them around for us. You can kill two birds with one stone."

"Are you sure?"

She handed me a pile of invitations and practically pushed me out the door. "Go."

Always one of my favorite places to visit growing up, Second-Hand Sally's invoked the exhilaration of a treasure hunt, and always involved the discovery of many wonderful surprises. Sally, a treasure herself, wore red from head to toe today. A tiny crimson hat perched daintily on her head, and long crimson gloves made of satin stretched up to her elbows.

"Grace. I heard you'd be stopping by."

"You did?"

"Mrs. Periwinkle called."

"She's on the ball," I said. "As always."

I kissed Sally on the cheek and handed her the invitations. Only she and Dario towered over me like two gigantic redwoods. She and Dario shared another thing in common as well, since they'd both been professional athletes. Sally played football, not hockey, but close enough.

I took a moment to imagine Dario on the ice, ramming and slamming people, or whatever they did while playing hockey. I'd never seen a game, but the idea of Dario all sweaty and sporty did something to me. I fanned my face.

"Is it hot in here?"

"I don't think so, honey, but I run hot." Sally gave me a saucy wink. "It must be a red-head thing."

A pale, slim woman entered from the back of the shop. With her faded red hair pulled into a conservative chignon at the nape of her neck, and her plain grey cardigan, she looked more subdued than the usual visitors to Sally's shop.

Sally motioned for her to join us, putting a gentle arm around her shoulders. "Grace, this is my baby sister, Agatha. She's here for a visit, and I'm so delighted about it."

Agatha extended her hand. "Agatha Stein. Please call me Aggie," she said, her voice soft. She seemed as delicate and fragile as a porcelain vase.

"Nice to meet you. I didn't know Sally had a sister."

"She's much younger than me," said Sally. "My parents always called her their happiest accident. Isn't it lovely? Aggie lives a few hours away, I almost never get to see her. She's a professor, like you."

"What do you teach?" I asked.

"Applied mathematics," she said. "At Grovetown College."

"They have a fantastic math department. Do you know Sheila Winters? She's a good friend of mine."

"Yes," said Aggie. "Not well, but I know who she is."

"We lived next door to each other while undergrads," I said. "She's amazing."

Aggie nodded but her manner grew suddenly stiff and uncomfortable. I wondered if it related in any way with

Sheila. I'd worried about how my tattooed and pierced friend would fit in at such a conservative campus, but she said she'd adjusted easily. She loved the students, even if they were a bit "white bread," as she called them, and she'd made friends amongst the staff. A math genius, she'd gotten tons of attention for her various publications in prestigious academic journals, so it probably helped ease the way for her.

"Sheila loves Grovetown," I said, hoping to find some common ground with Aggie again.

"It's a beautiful school," she said. "And you're a chemistry professor?"

"Well, not yet. I'm a PhD candidate..." My voice trailed off. I could never figure out how to explain my current predicament. I came to the conclusion the less I said, the better.

"I remember those days," said Aggie. "Hectic, exhilarating, and completely terrifying." She gave me a shy smile, likely recognizing a kindred spirit when she saw one. "How is your aunt doing?"

"She's much better, thank you."

Sally gave Aggie a squeeze. "Aggie took quite a shine to your Aunt Lucy. She visits her every day and brings her smoothies. She mixes them up herself."

"What kind of smoothies?" I asked.

"Fruits mostly, with the occasional vegetable," said Aggie. "I'm worried about her. She doesn't seem to be eating right. At the grocery store, she fills her cart with chocolate and cookies."

I laughed. "Sounds accurate. Aunt Lucy always had a sweet tooth. Thanks for thinking of her. You're so kind."

"I got very upset when I heard about her fall. Have they figured out who pushed her?" asked Aggie.

I bit my lip. "Well, we aren't certain anyone actually

pushed her. Some of the details are fuzzy, and there is still a bit of confusion on Aunt Lucy's part."

"Poor Lucy," said Sally, shaking her head.

"I'll come and visit her soon," said Aggie. "Nice meeting you, Grace."

"You, too."

As Aggie went to the back of the shop and closed the door behind her. Sally shook her head sadly. "Dear, sweet Aggie. She's going through a bad spell at the moment. She had an issue with one of her fellow professors. He acted inappropriately, and when she complained about it, the department head took his side. She's been staying with me for a few months now."

My heart went out to Aggie. Even though the circumstances differed, it reminded me of my own plight. "Is she filing a lawsuit?"

"She should," said Sally. "But you can't force a person to make that sort of decision. It's a private and personal thing. All we can do is support her and love her and help her get through this."

"Harassment is more common in the world of academia than people like to admit, and fighting it is risky. It can get ugly."

"And I'm not certain Aggie would be up for any sort of battle," said Sally. "But let's talk about something happier. I take it you're looking for a dress. What can I help you with?"

The shop, with its rows of vintage clothing and hats in all shapes and sizes, contained everything I could imagine, but suddenly, I felt unsure about this whole thing. "I don't know. I sort of have a date."

Sally linked her arm with mine. "Do tell. Who's the lucky guy?"

"Well..." I cringed, my bubble of happiness gone. Could this be classified as an official date? If not, I worried about it getting around. I'd feel like a total fool. Sally seemed to immediately understand.

"Don't worry, sweet pea. What happens at Sally's stays at Sally's. This is between us."

Suddenly, I was ten years old again, and sharing all my secrets with her. "Dario Fontana."

"I won't tell a soul," she said, pretending to zip her lips and throw away the key.

"I don't want to make a fuss about it, but I need something new to wear."

She looked at my outfit. "You certainly do."

I put my hands on my hips. "Hey."

She waved my protests aside. "You always look lovely, but you have been known to hide your light under a basket, haven't you?"

Ignoring my protests, she swished around the shop in a blaze of red satin and tulle, grabbing things from around the room and draping them one by one over her arm. I eyed her with concern. "Don't go crazy, Sally. It's only dinner at his grandmother's house."

She paused, considering the items in her arms. "But I'm sure there will be many dates to follow, dear."

"I can't afford a new wardrobe. Not right now."

She put a red-gloved hand on my arm. "Your Aunt Lucy wants to get you a few things as a way to repay you for coming to help her. Mrs. Periwinkle took care of everything when she called."

"That's very kind, but I shouldn't."

"You should," she said. "Your aunt is delighted to do this for you, and it's only a few dresses. But I have another surprise, too."

She pulled a beautiful green satin evening gown out of a garment bag, and I took a step backward in shock. "No. Absolutely not. Aunt Lucy is being far too generous."

"These are from your aunt Lucy." Sally lifted the arm with the dresses on it. Then she pointed to the evening gown. "This one is from Mrs. Periwinkle."

I frowned in confusion. "Mrs. Periwinkle?"

"Of course. All fairy godmothers want Cinderella to have a dress for the ball, right? Or the Halloween party, as the case may be."

"Fairy godmother...?"

"Oh, hush, Grace. Don't be shy. She insists, and Mrs. Periwinkle is a force to be reckoned with. She won't take no for an answer."

I reached out to touch the soft emerald-hued satin. "Well, I guess I could try it on."

Sally smiled. "I guess you could."

I went into the dressing room, yanked off my clothing in record speed, and let the satin dress slide over my skin. Sumptuous, sexy, and decadent, it elicited an immediate physical response; an unexpected moment of purely sensual contentment.

Off the shoulder, it exposed an expanse of creamy white skin and a whole lot of cleavage, much more than opening one button. Even more than my tiniest bathing suit. I tried pulling it up, but that just made my breasts stand out even more.

"Sally. We have a problem. It's too small. It doesn't cover my chest."

"It isn't supposed to cover your chest. It's supposed to enhance it."

My boobs almost popped out of the top. "Oh, it's enhancing it all right. I'm not sure if this much enhancement is legal." I stuck my head out the door of the dressing room, keeping my body hidden. "I look like a porn star."

Sally lost patience with me, demanding I stop acting like a

prude. "For heaven's sake," she said. "Get out of that dressing room and show me your dress. Now."

I stepped out, not sure how to act or stand or move. This dress made me feel different, sexy and beautiful, but I couldn't call it a comfortable sensation, or one I'd ever experienced before.

Sally gasped when she saw me. "Oh, you are a vision. An absolute vision. That dress isn't too small. It fits you perfectly."

She showed me to a full-length mirror and made me turn around. I couldn't help but admire my reflection. She unpinned my hair and let the tendrils cascade to my shoulders. The color of the dress matched my eyes and contrasted nicely with my hair.

"Wow."

"Wow is right," said Sally.

The dress hugged my curves. It emphasized my bust, but also my tiny waist, the shape of my hips, and the creamy color of my skin.

"Fine. I give up. You're right. It's perfect for Samhain. But what about my date tonight? If I'm going to Alvida's house, I need to wear something that covers my bust."

Sally tilted her head and pretended to ponder it. "I don't know. It's a lot of bust to cover."

I gave her a playful punch on the arm. Even though she hadn't played football in years, her biceps were still rock hard. "Ouch."

She laughed. "Which is what you get for resorting to physical violence. Now back into the changing room."

I tried on a dress with a nude shell covered in a sheer, black, polka-dotted fabric. It hit above the knee and covered my chest completely. A black grosgrain ribbon encircled my waist, tying neatly in the front.

I spun around in a slow circle, and as the full skirt fluttered around my legs, it looked sexy and yet still proper. "This is it, Sally. Perfect for a dinner with someone's grandmother."

"Exactly," she said, immediately handing me another dress. "And this is for your second date. One not involving his grandmother."

The midnight blue cocktail dress covered my bust, but it left my back and the sides of my waist exposed and showed off the curve of my hips. In some ways it made me feel even more bare than the green satin gown.

I stuck my head out of the dressing room. "Sally. Parts of this dress are missing."

She rolled her eyes and hauled me out of the dressing room, leading me back to the large mirror. "It is vintage Yves Saint Laurent. A masterpiece. Many women have tried to wear it, but they did not have the body for it. You, my dear, have the body."

I turned and looked over my shoulder. The fabric, covered in sparkling beads, glowed in the light of the shop. I ran my hands over it. Although short and tight, the dress did kind of suit me. "I don't have the right shoes..."

Sally cut me off. "Your aunt Lucy insisted on getting those, too. And she told me to pick out some undergarments. You can't wear white cotton under something like this. That's sacrilege."

I gaped at her. "I like white cotton. And wool. And plaid skirts. And covering my chest and my back and all my other bits and pieces."

Sally spun me around to face the mirror again. Putting her hands on my shoulders, she rested her cheek against mine as she regarded my reflection. "You're a young, beautiful, sexy girl. Embrace it. Celebrate it. Enjoy it."

"Enjoy it?" I frowned, thinking about my colleagues back at the university. "But if I wear something like this, I won't be taken seriously."

"Did people take Madame Curie seriously?"

"Of course," I said, confused.

"Because of her clothing?"

"No. She wore black dresses with giant puffy sleeves. Her genius had nothing to do with her fashion sense."

"That's my point. Who you are as a scientist has nothing to do with what you wear on your body. Now, I'm not suggesting you wear this to the lab." She giggled, covering her mouth with her hand. "You might cause a fire. But I'd hate to see you go through life thinking you have to look a certain way. Wear what you want. Be who you are. Make them take you seriously. Not because of your clothing, but because of what you can do."

I watched as she smoothed the fabric of her red dress over her hips and experienced a sharp pang of pity for her. "It must have been hard for you, Sally."

She spread out her arms, showing off her dress, resplendent in red. "This is who I am. I tried to dress like a man. I truly did. I wore T-shirts and jeans and even owned flannel shirts." She shuddered at the memory.

"When did you decide to change?"

"When I accepted that I was wasting my life by living a lie. I knew I was gay. I'd known since high school when I developed a terrible crush on one of the running backs. Toby Thomas. A beautiful boy. Straight as an arrow, mind you, but glorious to look at." She sighed at the memory, shaking her head. "But I hid it. Things weren't like they are now. People are so much more accepting. Well, some people, at least."

A shadow passed over her face. "Are you thinking about the people who sent the letter to the shop?"

"Yes. Those cowards. They don't show their faces, but they make a lot of noise. It's not my first time dealing with people like this, but it's never easy."

"The idea that they may try to harm you or Aunt Lucy or

Cat..." I couldn't control the catch in my voice. "None of you deserve to be treated this way."

Sally took my hands. "Which is why we have to stand together and work as a team. Hut, hut and all that stuff."

I laughed. "Do you miss football?"

"I loved it, and once it occupied a big role in my life. I'm grateful for it. A football scholarship paid for my college education and playing professionally gave me enough money to buy this shop. For a while, I missed the excitement of it, but now I watch it on TV. Sometimes I wish I could have coached children, but can you imagine me on a football field? It would outrage all the parents completely."

She smiled, but I glimpsed the sadness in her eyes. "You'd be a great coach, Sally."

"Well, we can't have it all, but now I have this shop and my friends and Ralphie and life is pretty good." She picked up a photo in a silver frame of a balding man in a bow tie and showed it to me. He wore tortoise shell glasses and sported a sizable moustache. "We have nothing in common, but it works. It's funny how love sort of creeps up on you when you least expect it. People always say when you stop looking for love, you'll find it. People are right, I guess. I'd about given up when Ralphie came along and swept me right off my feet. The most important lesson I learned is this; to be lovable, you have to love yourself."

She blew a kiss at the photo before putting it back on the shelf next to her cash register. I returned to the dressing room thinking about what she'd said as I put on my white blouse and cardigan sweater and tweed skirt. When I looked in the mirror, I liked the person staring back at me, but I'd trained myself so long to fit a certain mold, I'd lost track of who I truly was.

Rather than being a setback, this felt more like an opportunity. No longer Jonathan's supportive girlfriend, or Dr.

Lewis's golden girl, or the head TA in the chemistry department, this gave me a chance to step back, take stock, and reexamine everything. And once I did that, the truth hit me like a zap from an electrical current.

Maybe I didn't have to act and dress a certain way to be taken seriously. Maybe I didn't have to squeeze into a narrow, restrictive box. Maybe, just maybe, I could simply be...myself.

CHAPTER 12

FLUORINE, URANIUM, CARBON, POTASSIUM.

Dario arrived promptly at seven, smiling at me as I unlocked the door to the shop. In jeans, he'd been hot, but in a suit, he took my breath away. Although relieved I'd taken time with my appearance and gotten the dress from Sally, I still clasped my hands self-consciously behind my back. Dario had made a mistake, a terrible miscalculation. In no possible universe could a man as handsome, charming, and all around glorious as him be interested in a shy, abnormally tall, redheaded bookworm like me.

"Grace," he said. "You look...beautiful."

The way he stumbled over his words made my heart do a flip-flop in my chest. Not a cardiac emergency flip-flop, the kind that would require medical intervention and the use of a defibrillator. This was a good kind of flip-flop. A sweet tightening because of happiness and excitement and nervousness all at the same time.

"Thank you."

"Oh. I brought you flowers."

He handed me a bouquet of peach-colored roses, my favorite. Another flip-flop. If someone attached me to an

EKG machine right now, the results may have seriously concerned a cardiologist.

"They're lovely."

He smiled. "They made me think of you."

I stuck the flowers in a vase, and he helped me put on my coat. I had my hair down, parted on the side, and I wore dangly, sparkling earrings I'd found at Sally's. They were the only things I'd purchased myself. Aunt Lucy and Mrs. Periwinkle paid for every other item, right down to the sexy black lingerie hidden beneath my gorgeous dress. Sally told me nothing makes a girl feel prettier than beautiful lingerie, and she'd been absolutely right.

We decided to walk to Alvida's house and enjoy the unusually mild autumn weather. Leaves rustled under our feet, and a soft breeze lifted my hair away from my neck. We chatted as we walked, and it seemed so...comfortable. Like I'd known Dario forever. I trusted him, too, a rare thing for a person as naturally cautious as me, but Dario somehow seemed instantly trustworthy. I couldn't explain it but knew it instinctively.

Dario told me to follow my intuition when it came to the debacle back at school, and maybe he had a point. Perhaps I needed to listen to the voice inside my head more often.

Alvida's house, a large Victorian on a block full of large Victorians, teemed with people. Anthony told me to expect a big group, but it still caught me by surprise, and I tripped over a loose brick in the sidewalk. Unable to stop my momentum, I stumbled right into Dario.

"Oops," I said. "Sorry."

"Don't apologize." His voice turned husky as he pulled me closer. I sighed and closed my eyes, waiting for his kiss.

It never happened. We were interrupted by a sound from Alvida's house. The front door opened and an entire herd of dark-haired Fontanas watched us from the porch. Alvida stood next to them, a wooden spoon in her hand and a white "Kiss the Cook" apron over her dress. I jumped away from Dario so fast I almost tripped again.

"For the love of God and all things holy, Dario Fontana. Bring the poor girl inside the house, before she freezes to death, and stop trying to catch some nookie on the sidewalk."

He put a protective arm around my shoulder. "She tripped. I caught her."

"Is that what they're calling it these days?" Alvida rolled her eyes as the other Fontanas laughed and filed back into the house.

"Sorry," he said, his voice a soft whisper in my ear.

"It's fine." I snuggled closer to him, and he gave me a squeeze.

"Maybe I shouldn't have done this to you on a first date," he said with a frown. "When Nunny suggested I ask you, it seemed like a good chance to get you to go out with me. It isn't fair to you, though. These people are ruthless."

I reached up to touch his cheek. "I have four crazy sisters and so many aunts, uncles, and cousins I sometimes lose count. It'll be okay."

"Are you sure?"

"Yes, but you could have simply asked me out. I would have said yes. Maybe we should try that for our next date."

He grinned. "As long as you still want to go out with me after this."

"I will."

Lifting my hand, he brought it to his lips, causing a million happy little nerve endings to rejoice all at once. "Then I'm a very lucky man."

As soon as we entered the house, someone grabbed my coat and Dario introduced me to his family, sticking close the whole time. I counted at least three Anthonys and five Marias, and I quickly lost track of the Joeys.

"You're the only Dario," I said.

"My parents named me after my late grandfather," he said.

"Were you close?"

"Yes," he said, his eyes growing sad. "My parents were killed in a car accident just after I turned three. He and Nunny raised us. He was a great man."

"I'm so sorry. I didn't know."

"It happened a long time ago," he said. "And having such a big family meant my sister and I never lacked for love and attention. We faced some hard times, of course, but we got through them together."

I saw what he meant about the love and attention. His family welcomed me warmly and took turns winking at Dario and elbowing him. He gave me a look of long suffering.

"They're always like this," he said, putting his hand on the small of my back to steer me through the crowded dining room. "Actually, I take it back. Usually, they're much worse."

Dario's older sister, Angie, lived in Boston, but the rest of his family appeared to be in attendance. I met a whole plethora of uncles, aunts, and cousins.

"We usually do this on Sundays, but today would have been my grandfather's ninetieth birthday. We celebrate each year with a party."

"How nice."

A long table took up most of the dining room, with folding chairs added to accommodate all the guests. We sat down to lasagna, salad, homemade bread, and a variety of delicious side dishes. The conversation, loud and raucous, soon turned serious as they discussed the threats against Aunt Lucy.

"It's a disgrace," said Alvida, turning to Dario. "And you should write about it, young man. You're the finest reporter this paper has ever hired."

"Thanks, Nunny, but I mostly cover football games."

Some of Dario's cousins sang, "Here we go, Steelers. Here we go." Alvida shushed them, and pinched Dario's cheek as she got up to refill a bowl of green beans. "You're still the best writer they have, but don't let it go to your head, *nipote*."

"You'd never let it, Nunny."

Dario's aunt Florence sat across the table from us. "I hear you're planning to be a college professor, Grace. What will you teach?" she asked.

"Chemistry," I said, hoping this discussion did not lead to my current academic status.

"She's a genius," said Alvida. "Like our Dario. You know where he went to school, don't you, Grace?"

Dario winced, closing his eyes. "Stop. Please."

I remembered the community college shirt he sported on the first day I met him. "Yes, I know." He raised a quizzical brow at that, and I reached under the table to give his hand a brief squeeze, understanding this probably made him uncomfortable.

"He doesn't like to talk about it." Aunt Florence gave him a soft smile.

"It's nothing to be ashamed of," I said.

The people around the table gave me an odd look. Alvida's brother, Great Uncle Marino laughed. "She's a card, this one. I like her. Have you seen him play hockey yet? He's amazing."

Dario looked like he wanted to crawl into a hole. I kind of enjoyed this. "No, I haven't."

"He coaches little kids now and plays on a rec team," said Uncle Marino. "But after college, he—"

"Stop," said Dario, putting his face in his hands. "Can we talk about something else, please?"

"Fine. We won't embarrass you any further," said Alvida. "But how are you going to help Lucinda?"

"I'll write about the people of the South Side, starting

with her, for the community pages. They're always asking me to submit material, and it might be the only way to stop this nonsense in its tracks and keep it from spreading. QIVC."

"QIV...what?" asked Uncle Marino.

"Quarantine, Investigate, Vaccinate, Cure," I said, shocked he knew the terminology and used it correctly. "The protocol for dealing with a contagion. I'm surprised you're familiar with it."

Several people around the table chuckled, and one of Dario's uncles, his name also Anthony, shouted out, "He's not as dumb as he looks."

Alvida swatted the uncle on the back of his head, giving everyone even more of a reason to laugh. She called him something sounding like *chadrool*.

Dario leaned close. "It means idiot, but from Nunny it's sort of an endearment."

We walked home after drinking hot, rich espresso and eating large slabs of chocolate cake. Alvida kissed my cheek and gave me plastic containers loaded with leftover lasagna and other goodies. Full to the gills, content, and happy, I got even happier when Dario took my hand, lacing his fingers with mine. He carried the leftovers from Alvida in the other hand, insisting his grandmother's lasagna weighed a ton.

"Thanks for coming. They didn't scare you away?"

I shook my head. "Nope."

"When they brought up college, I thought you were going to bolt."

"They're proud of you, and you shouldn't be ashamed about attending community college."

He came to a halt. "Community college?"

I stopped next to him on the sidewalk. "I've known since the first day we met. You had on a community college T-shirt. But don't worry, Dario, I'd never hold something like that against you."

"How kind of you," he said, letting go of my hand.

Suddenly, the air around me seemed to turn cold. "I told you it doesn't matter to me. Why are you getting angry?"

"Why are you being so patronizing?"

"I meant to be kind. Most of my peers would never even consider..."

"Consider what, Grace?"

I swallowed hard, trying to figure out the right words to say to make this all better. "You have to understand. I'm a PhD candidate at one of the top schools in the country. It's...elite."

"Elitist is the word you're looking for."

The more I tried to dig my way out of this, the worse it got. His face hardened and his beautiful mouth formed a tight, straight line.

"I didn't intend to hurt you, but I see I've touched a nerve. Thank you for a wonderful evening. I can walk the rest of the way by myself." I shoved my hands into the pockets of my coat, turned on my heel, and marched in the direction of the shop. He fell into step next to me, but I refused to look at him. "You don't have to walk me home. I'm perfectly capable of making it there on my own."

"Because you didn't go to community college? It must be great to be so smart. I get lost crossing streets."

I stopped in the middle of the sidewalk and stamped my foot. "Why are you doing this? I told you I didn't judge you. I'm being magnanimous. A lot of people in my position are ruthless, trust me."

"In your position? What is that, exactly?"

He gave me a look so mocking and cruel it felt like a knife being plunged right into my belly. And he spoke the truth. I occupied no position at the moment. I was no one. I shook my head sadly. "You're right. I'm in no position to say anything at all. I've lost everything I ever wanted and have only a slim chance of getting it back. Thank you, Dario. I appreciate the reminder. Goodnight."

I took the bag of leftovers from his hand and stormed off. Just because he'd made me mad didn't mean I wanted to skip out on having Alvida's lasagna tomorrow, but one more word from Dario would put me over the edge. I needed to get back to the shop as quickly as possible and lick my wounds. Alone. With my leftovers.

I walked in front of him, moving as fast as I could in pumps. I wore a beautiful dress and I'd gone on a date with a gorgeous man, but I'd managed to screw it up before I could even get a goodnight kiss.

"Grace...please stop..."

I kept moving, putting distance between us, furious at myself and at him. I kept my gaze trained on the sidewalk. Falling flat on my face would be the perfect ending to what had turned into a terrible evening.

"There's something I have to tell you..."

I ignored him. Since I no longer heard his footfalls behind me, I assumed he'd given up. The shop was now only half a block away. Hopefully, I could make it there without humiliating myself further.

I jumped when I heard the sound of shattering glass and raced around the corner. A man dressed entirely in black stood on the sidewalk in front of the Hocus Pocus Magic Shop. He had on a ski mask.

"Hey," I yelled. "Get away from my shop."

He turned to face me, his eyes meeting mine. For a split second, I experienced a stab of recognition, but before I could process it, he took off, running in the opposite direction. Dario rounded the corner at a sprint and followed him.

I jogged the last few feet to the shop. The man had thrown a rock into the front window, destroying it. Shards of glass twinkled up at me in the orange glow of the lights we'd put up. Once so pretty and festive, now they looked sad.

My heart thumped in my chest. Only seconds had passed since Dario took off after the man, but each one dragged on and on. I took out my cell phone, preparing to call 911, just as Dario reappeared at last. Although he'd run at full speed, he didn't even have to catch his breath, his continued athleticism probably a remnant from his hockey playing days. His temper may have been a remnant, too. He clenched and unclenched his fists, looking a lot like he might want to punch someone. Or check someone. Or whatever they did in hockey.

"Who did this?" he asked, a muscle working in his jaw. "Did you get a good look at him?"

"I couldn't see his face. He wore a ski mask."

He ran a hand through his hair. "Damn it. I lost him when he disappeared down the alley. If only I'd kept up with you, if I hadn't let you walk so far ahead of me..." He took a steadying breath, his eyes on my face. "Are you okay?"

I nodded. I'd begun reciting the periodic table in my head as soon as I heard the glass breaking. "Yes, but I got all the way to tin."

His lips quirked. "Number fifty. Sn."

The fact that he knew that, and understood immediately, made me smile in spite of what just happened. Pathetic, and yet true.

Dario got on his cell phone and called Anthony. He spoke with him in urgent tones, but I barely paid attention. I stared through the broken window, my gaze drawn to a large, black rock sitting in the middle of the shattered glass, right next to a decapitated statue of a witch. It had been a cute little witch with a sparkly cape and hat. How sad. And a once cheery ceramic jack-o-lantern now lay in pieces by her side.

I put my leftovers on the sidewalk, reached through the

opening in the window, and picked up the rock, turning it over in my hands. A small shard of glass imbedded itself into my finger. I winced, pulling it out, but my focus centered on the rock, and the piece of paper attached to it with a rubber band. Removing it, I unfolded the note and read the message written in letters cut from the pages of a magazine.

"WHITCHES WILL BURN IN HELL."

The words caused a tremor to go over my body and all the blood to drain from my face. Not only terrifying, but also confusing. This vandal seriously needed to consider proof-reading their threatening messages.

Dario took the note out of my trembling hands, being careful to touch as little of the paper as possible. "Finger-prints," I said, understanding why he held the paper so oddly. "I didn't think of that. I shouldn't have touched it. I'm sorry."

Suddenly, I couldn't breathe properly. He put an arm around my shoulders. "Don't worry, Gracie. It's going to be okay."

He murmured the words against my hair, as I leaned on him. I was still furious with him, but his warm, solid presence comforted and soothed me.

The low whine of fire sirens started as a faint sound in the distance, but quickly came closer. In the light of the street-lamps, I made out hazy wisps of smoke snaking up into the air. When the smell of burning wood hit my nose, I looked at Dario in horror as we both realized the smoke and the sirens came from the direction of Sally's shop.

CHAPTER 13

LUST STARTS WITH CHEMISTRY, BUT LOVE REQUIRES TRUST AND RESPECT.

Dario took my hand and we ran down the street, his worried face illuminated by the flashing lights of the fire trucks. Sally stood outside, wearing a robe and with her head covered in a turban. She held her dog Bubu in her arms. When she saw me, she pulled me into a fierce hug with her free hand.

"Sally, are you okay?"

"I'm fine. Shaken up, but fine. We both are." Bubu, positively vibrated with fear, and Sally didn't seem much better.

"What happened?" asked Dario. In front of Sally's shop sat a pile of smoldering rubble that the firemen doused with their hoses, but it looked like they'd contained the fire pretty quickly.

"They pulled a trashcan up to the door of my shop and set it on fire, the cowards. I'd just given myself a facial and put my feet up to watch a movie. Ralphie's working late, and Aggie went to meet up with friends from her social club tonight. Thank goodness for that. This would have scared her to death."

Ralphie showed up on the scene a few minutes later,

sagging with relief when he saw Sally. As soon as he reached her side, he gathered her into his arms.

"Sally, darling. I can't believe this is happening." He removed his tortoise shell glasses to wipe the tears from his eyes.

Sally leaned against him and kissed the top of his balding head. "Ralphie Rabinowitz, this is my friend, Grace. Lucinda's niece."

"Nice to meet you," he said. "But not under these circumstances, of course."

"I have to tell you, Ralphie, Bubu is my hero. She barked like a maniac until I looked out the window and saw someone dragging that trashcan closer to the shop." Sally pressed her cheek against the little dog, and Bubu licked her face furiously, making Sally smile. "Brave Bubu."

Ralphie put his glasses back on, straightening them as the worry on his countenance morphed into anger. "Enough is enough. It's time to move away from here."

"No." Sally shook her head, still petting Bubu. "This is my home. I'm not leaving."

"It's too dangerous." Ralphie's cheeks reddened, but Sally refused to budge.

"I don't care. I love this place and I can't let them win."

"I won't stay here if I know you're in danger."

"I won't leave."

They stared at each other a long moment. "Perhaps this is a conversation we should have at a later time," said Ralphie softly.

"Perhaps it is." Sally blinked away tears. She turned to one of the firemen, a tall, handsome man with dark hair and green eyes. "May I go back up to my apartment, Tommy? I'd like to get dressed."

The fireman nodded. "Certainly, ma'am."

She fluttered her eyelashes at him and squeezed his brawny arm, always such a flirt. "Thank you."

Ralphie watched her go with a resigned sigh. "It's too much," he said softly. "The threats were one thing, and that awful online forum, but this is very different, and much more dangerous. She's not seeing sense."

"Someone shattered the front window of our shop tonight, too," I said.

Ralphie took off his glasses again and wiped them with a handkerchief he kept tucked in his pocket. "Then they're upping their game. They're targeting all of us." He let out a sigh. "Excuse me for a moment. I need to check on Sally."

Dario took out his notebook and approached the fireman. "Hi, Tommy. How are you doing?"

"Fine. Were you at Nunny's tonight? Sorry I couldn't make it. I had to work."

"She told me. She saved some lasagna for you."

Tommy grinned. "She always does. She makes enough to feed an army, thank goodness."

I stared at both of them, noticing the resemblance. "He's your cousin, too?"

Dario nodded. "Tommy Belfiore. Anthony's little brother."

Anthony came up the sidewalk from the Hocus Pocus Magic Shop and joined us, nudging Tommy. "Not so little anymore, huh, Tommy?"

Tommy grinned. He stood at least a head taller than Anthony, and only a few inches shorter than Dario. "Is there anyone in this town who *isn't* your cousin?" I asked.

"Yes," answered Dario in total seriousness. "You."

"Thank goodness," said Tommy. "It would be kind of creepy. Like when Anthony crushed on Dario's sister."

Anthony scowled at him. "At least I didn't have a thing for our second-grade teacher."

"Shut up, Anthony. She was hot."

"She was a nun. Her name was Sister Bernice. That's just so wrong, Tommy." He laughed at Tommy's shocked reaction to his words before turning to me. "Can I talk to you for a minute, Grace?"

"Sure."

I tried to hold back a giggle at the outraged expression on Tommy's face. He must have had very fond memories, and perhaps even a case of unrequited love, for Sister Bernice.

Anthony led me away from the noise of the fire trucks. "I called a friend and they're going to board up your window for tonight. They'll come back tomorrow and fix it."

"Thank you, Anthony. That's so kind." I reached out to pat his arm and noticed blood running down my hand. I'd forgotten about the cut I'd sustained from the shard of glass.

"What happened?" He took a tissue from his pocket and wrapped my finger in it.

"I cut myself on the glass from the window. It's nothing. I didn't even realize it was bleeding."

Anthony continued applying pressure to the cut, but his gaze shot to Dario. "Are you okay there, buddy?"

Dario's face had turned deathly pale. "She's bleeding," he said.

Anthony kept his eyes on his cousin. "It's just a tiny cut. She's a redhead. They're bleeders."

At the word "bleeders," Dario swayed on his feet like a giant oak in a strong wind. "Tommy," shouted Anthony. "We may need some help here."

Tommy was talking with some of the other firemen. When he saw Dario's face, he jogged over to him. "Not again."

"He saw blood. She has a cut on her finger."

"I feel funky." Dario swayed again and Tommy grabbed his arm.

"You need to sit for a few minutes, cuz."

He made Dario sit on the curb and ordered him to put his head between his knees. He called to one of the other firemen to bring him a damp cloth, and he put it on the back of Dario's neck. Another fireman grabbed a first aid kit from the truck, so Anthony could take care of my finger.

"It's nothing. The bleeding has already stopped," I said. Dario moaned softly from the sidewalk. "What's up with him?"

Anthony snorted. "He's fine. He just can't stand the sight of blood."

I blinked. "But he's a hockey player."

"Not anymore," said Anthony.

Dario kept his head between his knees. "Is she all cleaned up? Can I look now?"

Tommy glanced back at me and winked. "Yep. You'd never know she was just dripping blood all over the sidewalk."

Dario moaned again and Anthony gave Tommy a stern look. "Stop it, Tommy."

"You're right. My bad," said Tommy. "She's fine, Dario."

Dario got up slowly, the color gradually returning to his face. "Are you okay, Grace?"

I showed him the small bandage on my finger, glad Anthony had wiped the blood off my hand. "It's barely a paper cut. Are you okay?"

"Yes. Sorry about that."

"No apology necessary."

Sally came back, dressed to the nines and fully made up. She gave a statement to the firemen and the police about what she'd seen, and I did the same. By the time Dario walked me home, someone had already boarded up the window with a large piece of plywood.

I picked up my bag of leftovers from the sidewalk, playing with the key ring in my hand, as we stood outside the door.

Unable to figure out what to say, or how to make things better, I stared at a spot in the middle of Dario's broad chest in an effort to avoid meeting his eyes.

"Thank you for tonight," I said, breaking the silence.

"For which part?" he asked. "The part when I dragged you out in front of my whole crazy, nosy family, or the part when I treated you rudely afterward?"

I gave him a small half smile. "The part where you almost fainted at the sight of a tiny cut."

He raised a finger. "First of all, not a tiny cut. You were... gushing..." He shuddered at the memory.

"I'm sorry. I shouldn't tease you. I'm grateful you were here tonight."

He tilted his head to indicate the door of the shop. "Do you mind if I walk you inside? I want to make sure it's safe."

"There's no need."

He stared at me, his dark eyes intense in the dim light of the street lamp. "It would make me feel better."

I fumbled with my keys. "Okay. Fine," I said as I opened the door of the shop and flicked on the lights. Other than the broken window, everything seemed to be in place.

He glanced up the staircase. "Let's check your apartment, too."

As we trudged up the stairs, I analyzed the current situation between us. We didn't seem to be fighting anymore, but I remained clueless about what Dario might be thinking. I'd misread social cues before and had never been good at this whole dating ritual thing. Maybe I needed to do more research on the subject

Dario looked out of place among the doilies and lace in Aunt Lucy's apartment, and filled the tiny space with his presence. He glanced around in amusement.

"Not what I expected."

I slipped out of my coat, happy to see I hadn't gotten any

blood on my pretty new dress, and hung it on a hook. I took Dario's coat, too, and put it on a hanger. Jinx woke up with a yawn and rubbed against Dario's shoes, which were huge. I forced myself to stop staring at his feet and looked up at his face.

"What did you expect exactly?"

He shrugged. "Something darker and more witchy."

"Aunt Lucy is not a witch."

"I know, Grace. I'm teasing."

I clasped my hands in front of me. "Can I get you something? Coffee? Tea?"

Me?

I almost said it out loud. Yikes. I needed to hold myself back. I bit my lip, trying to come up with something normal to say. Sticking to beverages seemed like a good idea.

"Or maybe you'd like something else. It's kind of late for coffee. Aunt Lucy always has a bottle of bourbon around. Would you like a glass?"

"Yes, please," he said, his eyes smoldering. "May I light a fire?"

Oh, Dario. You already did.

"Yes, thank you."

My hands shook as I poured the bourbon into crystal glasses. We were being so polite, but the air teemed with sexual tension. At least I thought it did. I hoped it did. But I didn't know if we were still mad at each other or not.

I did a brief analysis. First of all, he insisted on coming up to the apartment. I hadn't forced him or coerced him in any way. It was his idea entirely. Secondly, he'd agreed to let me ply him with alcoholic beverages, and offered to light a fire, both good signs. If my calculations were correct, things once again moved in the right direction...straight toward my bed.

I wanted to sleep with Dario Fontana. Badly. Other than the weekly, monotonous encounters with Jonathan, my sex life had been nonexistent. I'd deprived myself for too long, and if I didn't do something about it soon, I may self-destruct. Combust. Explode. And not in a good way.

Jonathan accused me of having an over active sex drive. He limited our love making to a strictly regulated schedule and kept track on a calendar. He also instigated rules. Not more than once a week. Always on the weekends. Never in the morning. Or in the shower. Or in a car. I tried, but he shot me down every time.

"You act like a nymphomaniac," he said. Upon researching the matter, I informed him most males enjoyed spontaneous carnal episodes, but he insisted I skewed the numbers and accused me of being insatiable.

To make matters even worse, although adept at many subjects, Jonathan lacked any skills at all in bed. Every time we slept together, I felt vaguely disappointed afterward, but I sensed Dario Fontana would not disappoint. Since I'd decided to follow his advice and pay attention to my gut, I trusted my instinct on this.

I handed Dario his glass and sat next to him on the couch. "Does the problem you have with blood interfere with your job at all?"

"Yes and no," he said, swirling the bourbon in his glass. "Being a war correspondent, for example, would be out of the question, but sports reporting is what I'm best at anyway."

"Has it affected anything else?"

He shrugged. "Well, it ended my hockey career."

"What do you mean?"

"After college, I went pro for a few years. They paid me to play the sport I loved, and I even got to do it for the home team."

"The Penguins?"

"Yes. When the Penguins offered me a spot, it felt like all

I'd ever wanted appeared on a silver platter, especially when we won the Stanley Cup."

Even though I understood nothing about sports, I knew that had to be a big deal. "What happened?"

"My fourth year of playing for the Pens, I went after the puck. A guy from the other team went after it, too, and he didn't stop. I didn't stop either. I could be a pretty aggressive player." He paused, swallowing hard. "My skate sliced his neck. A freak accident, but the guy nearly died. He never played hockey again."

"I'm so sorry," I said. "Well, that explains your phobia."

"There was a lot of blood. Like more than you can even imagine—"

I reached for his hand, twining my fingers with his. "You didn't do it on purpose."

"I know that on a logical level, but it still haunts me. I got cut from the team the next season. I didn't have it in me anymore." He turned to me, his expression haunted. "But it wasn't just about that one incident on the ice."

"What do you mean?"

He stroked my hand with his thumb absentmindedly as he spoke. "I told you my parents died in a car accident," he said, and I nodded. "Well, I was in the car with them. I saw the whole thing from the back seat. Everyone assumed I'd blacked out or something. They'd hoped I hadn't seen..." He seemed to struggle with his words. "What I saw. But I did. And what happened during that hockey game brought it all back, stirring up a pot of repressed memories. The snow-covered road. The ice. The truck hitting us head on. The blood."

"That must have been awful."

"It changed me. I spent my whole life thinking I knew what I wanted to do and who I wanted to be, and I had to start the process all over again. From square one. But sometimes the worst things that happen to you can actually result in something good."

He stared into my eyes and the heat built between us like it always did. I wasn't sure what to say or how to act, but I wanted this man. Badly. As I debated the merits of standing up and leading him straight to the bedroom, he let go of my hand.

"We need to talk."

I didn't need a PhD to figure out what those words meant. He planned to tell me, "Thanks, but no thanks. Hasta la vista. Ciao. Adios. No sex for Gracie."

I moved away from him on the couch, distancing myself from the pain to come. "I'm awfully sorry about what I said earlier, Dario. I didn't mean to embarrass you about where you went to college. It came out all wrong. Interpersonal communication has always been one of my weaker areas. And I have no room to talk since I'm not even in college at the moment, and I've done zero work on my thesis recently. Heck, every time I get close to my laptop, I nearly break out in hives. It's bad. It's like I hit a point so beyond stressed out that I'm now in a different zone altogether."

"Gracie..."

"I get it if you don't want to see me again. It didn't make sense in the first place that you'd want to go out with me. Men like you date women like Tiffany."

I waved my hand to indicate her apartment right across the street. I tried to keep the bitter note out of my voice but found it difficult to even say her name. Perfect blond fluffy woman.

"Gracie..."

"And you shouldn't feel bad about it. If your nunny asks, you can say it didn't work out. We don't have to go into detail. You asked me out in the first place because of her. I get it. I do. You were trying to make her happy, and grandmothers always like me. Grandmothers, babies, and cats for some reason." Jinx rubbed against my legs. "Case in point. He likes me. He showed up in the shop one day. Insta-pet. Yay. It's not like I need another thing to worry about—"

I couldn't seem to stop the ridiculous stream of dialogue pouring from my mouth, but Dario found a way to effectively put an end to it. He leaned forward and brushed my lips with his, giving me the softest, sweetest kiss I'd ever experienced. I blinked at him in surprise.

"You kissed me."

"I did," he said, his voice husky.

He leaned close, tucked a lock of hair behind my ear, and pressed his lips against mine once again. Everything about him felt so muscular and hard, except for his deliciously irresistible mouth.

He leaned back a tiny bit to study my face. "What are you thinking about?"

"I was thinking about Einstein."

He let out a laugh. "No way."

"It's true. He once explained relativity in an interesting and very applicable way. He said if you're talking to a beautiful woman, two hours can seem like two minutes, but if you have your hand on a hot stove, two minutes can be like two hours."

"And how exactly does this relate to what we're doing right now?"

I reached up and put my hand against his cheek. "It's relativity. When we kiss, for that moment, I lose track of time and space. Einstein nailed it."

He kissed me again, pulling me closer, his tongue caressing mine and filling me with hot, aching need. My fingers twisted in his thick hair and his hands gripped my waist, but I still needed to get closer.

I climbed onto his lap, straddling his muscular thighs. His

hands found my hips and I unbuttoned his shirt, pulling on his necktie to remove it. I couldn't do it, and groaned in frustration, but he seemed too focused on the kissing to be of any help.

Giving up on the tie, I slid my hands inside his shirt and stroked his beautifully muscular chest. He had exactly the right amount of hair. When my fingers headed further south, Dario sighed, gathered my hands in his, and brought them to his mouth to kiss my fingertips.

"We need to stop."

I kissed him again. "No, we don't."

"Yes, we do," he murmured against my skin. He lifted me and set me next to him on the couch. I straightened my skirt, embarrassed.

"Is it because of before? Are you still mad at me? I told you I don't care about college."

He buttoned his shirt, covering all that glorious skin, and kissed the tip of my nose. "You aren't an academic, elitist snob anymore?"

I heard the hint of laughter in his voice but answered his question seriously. "Considering my current situation, I have no right to be a snob about anything."

He cupped my face with his big hand and stroked my cheek with his thumb. I leaned against him, like a kitten starved for affection.

"Are you sure? You'll soon be exonerated, and you'll go back. You hold a prestigious position there, one a lot of people envy. One you worked hard to obtain." He watched my face closely. "What would your friends and your peers and your colleagues think about me...about us?"

I stared into his dark eyes, understanding the importance of this moment. It had nothing to do with sex. It was about trust and telling the truth.

"I got thrown under the bus by people I thought were my

friends. It made me understand what's most important. My true friends, the ones who matter, will see what I see." I found no benefit in playing games at this point, so I opened up to him completely. "It doesn't bother me where you went to school, and I don't care what anyone else thinks. Not one bit."

He kissed me so thoroughly my head spun. "Good," he said. "Because I didn't go to community college. I tried to tell you that before you distracted me with your kisses."

"Hey. You distracted me." I frowned. "Wait a second. What do you mean?"

A smile played on his beautiful lips. "I teach a class at the community college. Intro to Journalism. It's through an outreach program I launched at the paper, but I didn't go to school there. I went to Princeton."

CHAPTER 14

FRICTION IS A DRAG.

"Princeton? As in *the* Princeton?" He nodded, trying to kiss me again, but I leaned away from him.

"Yes."

I stood up and started pacing. "You lied to me."

"I did not lie. I never once told you I went to community college. You assumed—"

"But tonight you allowed me to keep believing it. You painted me as so judgmental and wrong, and meanwhile you went to an Ivy League school."

"On a hockey scholarship."

I glared at him. "Who cares? I know the deal, Dario. They won't touch you, no matter how talented you are as an athlete, unless you have the test scores and grades to back it up."

"I achieved the grades, but I didn't have the money. Hockey provided me with a way in. It paid my tuition, and I got a good education because of it."

"You couldn't be honest with me about it? I felt like such a jerk."

"And that's my fault?" He frowned in confusion. "I don't

know why you're so pissed. You looked down on me when you saw me as a community college graduate. This should make you happy."

"Happy? Do I look happy?" I asked, and then a thought occurred to me. A strange, uncomfortable, and extremely superficial thought. "Wait...are you smarter than me?"

I stood up and paced, an angry kind of movement that seemed closer to stomping, but it helped me get my irrational fury more under control. Jinx watched me for a few minutes and didn't seem to find my fit of irritation very interesting. He hopped onto the couch, curled up in a ball, and went back to sleep.

Dario stood up and tucked in his shirt. "And this is why I left academia. To pursue something less egotistical and competitive."

"Journalism is nothing but sunshine and good times?"

He laughed, but it held no humor. "Compared to what I've seen from people like you? Yes."

I held a pillow from the couch in my hands. I'd been plumping it, but now I wanted to throw it at Dario's big, fat head. He must have read something of my intentions in my expression and he raised a dark eyebrow at me.

"What? Now you're going to hit me with a pillow?"

I frowned. "Maybe." The idea that Aunt Lucy's embroidered pillow with lace fringe could do any harm to Dario Fontana struck me as comical, but I refused to laugh.

He came closer, a muscle working in his jaw. "After what your ex did to you, I thought you'd see the truth in what I'm saying."

I straightened my spine. He was probably right, but pride refused to let me admit it. "You don't know what you're talking about."

"Unfortunately, I do." He ran a hand through his hair in frustration. "I'd hoped you were different, that there might be a real heart beating under the whole uptight, neurotic, scholarly persona you have going on, but I guess I got it all wrong."

He'd hit a nerve, and it took all my control not to react emotionally. In truth, I wasn't all that different from Jonathan and Roger and the others back at school, but I certainly didn't need to hear it from him. Not right now, at least. It hurt too much. "Thank you for making yourself so clear. I'll show you to the door now."

He cursed under his breath, but I ignored him. Back ramrod straight and head held high, I walked down the steps and into the shop. I came to a sudden stop when I saw the boarded-up window. I'd forgotten about the window and the fire and the threat and the whole horrible mess.

Judging by the pained expression on Dario's face, he must have forgotten as well. "I'm sorry, Grace."

I stared at the broken pieces of the window display. "It's okay. I'll clean it up tomorrow."

He turned me so I faced him directly. "I'm not talking about the window. I don't know what's wrong with me. I never act like this."

I gave him a sad smile. "It's as if we bring out the worst in each other. Maybe we should quit while we're ahead."

He grew still. "That isn't what I want."

Not able to meet his eyes, I stared once again at a point directly in the middle of his chest. A nice chest, all muscled and firm, and not a bad view at all, but I didn't want to think about that right now. "Let's face it. You aren't my type. I'm not your type. In some ways, we seem compatible, but we argued twice in one night."

He shrugged. "People argue. It's normal. You were at dinner at Nunny's house. Half the conversations I have with my family are borderline arguments."

"People don't argue on a first date."

He inched closer. "Some people do. We're getting to know each other. It's an adjustment period."

"We shouldn't have to adjust. It shouldn't be this hard."

I rested my hand on the crystal ball finial, suddenly wishing it worked, that it possessed magical powers and could tell me the future. But it didn't. Like everything else in this shop, it was fake, a worthless piece of glass.

"Do you know why I stopped you upstairs? When we were kissing?"

I shook my head, not sure if I wanted to hear the answer. "No."

"You're like a bright flash of light that appeared suddenly and unexpectedly in my life," he said, his voice soft, and his dark eyes hypnotic. "And I'm afraid you'll be gone just as quickly if I'm not careful."

"Like a supernova?" I asked, my voice also hushed.

He smiled, tracing the line of my jaw as his eyes caressed my face. "Exactly. I knew you'd get it. You always do. And not everything about tonight could be classified as horrible. Parts of it were rather spectacular."

He probably referred to the moment I'd practically climbed on top of him and ripped off his clothing. Thinking about it made my blood fire up again. Before I could respond, he kissed me softly on the cheek.

"You're a brilliant, beautiful, exceptional person, and I really like you. I want to get to know you better, but it's up to you now. Are you going to take a chance and believe in something you can't quantify or qualify, or will you keep playing it safe? I suspect you hate sports analogies, but the ball, so to speak, is in your court." He gave me a wry smile. "You have to decide if I'm a risk you're willing to take."

He walked out of the shop and I watched him go, stunned. I didn't know much about men, but I recognized sincerity when I saw it, and Dario positively glowed with it.

I locked the door and walked up the stairs to the apartment in a daze. Not a perfect first date by any means. We'd fought. Twice. My shop got vandalized. Sally's shop nearly burned to the ground. But for some reason, one I could not explain, a smile tugged at the corners of my lips, and it stayed there most of the night.

The next morning, Aunt Lucy came into the shop during the installation of the new window. She gasped when she saw it and covered her mouth with her hand. "Oh, Gracie."

I'd called her and told her what happened, mostly because I didn't want her to hear it from someone else. When Mags brought her over, Aunt Lucy looked around in shock. "They could have hurt you, Gracie. This has gone too far. I should close the shop and move to Florida."

I knelt next to her wheelchair, so I could look directly into her eyes. "We are not going to let them win."

She patted my hand. "I'm tired of fighting, and I won't allow you to be in any danger. You've been such a dear to help me, but I'm sure you need to get back to school. You've already stayed longer than you should have, dearie. You're supposed to be working on your PhD right now, not helping an old lady sell potions and charms. It's time to give up, pack up, and say goodbye."

A week ago, I probably would have agreed with her but not now. "I won't do it. I won't give up," I said, as I slowly rose to my feet. "And neither will you."

Mags looked back and forth at both of us. "You two need a chance to talk somewhere private. I'll help Matilda until you're done."

I gave her a grateful nod. "You're right. Thanks, Mags. This will only take a minute."

We hadn't opened the shop yet, but customers already lined up outside. I needed to make this quick and come clean to my aunt. I pushed her into the back room and told her about Dr. Lewis, the charges against me, and everything going on back at the university.

"I decided not to tell you before because I didn't want to worry you."

She made the appropriate noises of shock and outrage. "Does your mother know?"

I shook my head. I'd avoided calling the Human Lie Detector ever since I came here, although I texted her daily about Aunt Lucy's progress. I didn't want to talk with her because I knew she'd worry, and I hated it when she worried about me.

"No one knows, except you...and Dario."

Her eyes twinkled at the mention of his name. "I knew you two would hit it off. You're both so tall."

Unsure how to respond, I nodded. "Yes. We do have that in common. But the important thing is I'm free for at least another month. I can work on my PhD thesis here. I can help you with the party and in the shop until you're back on your feet. I want to do this, Aunt Lucy."

Her hands were clenched in her lap. "These people are dangerous. They nearly burned down poor Sally's shop."

"I'll be careful," I said. "I won't take any unnecessary risks."

She considered it, worry etched on her face. "Can you promise me you'll pack up your bags and head right back to school if anything else happens?"

"Yes."

She sighed. "Okay, but I'm not happy about it."

"It'll be over before you know it. Officer Belfiore is investigating, and Dario's writing that article about you."

She primped her hair. "He's coming to interview me today."

"And we have the Dragon Rouge," I said, knowing how to

cheer her up even more. "I left it upstairs, and have not touched it, as instructed."

"Good girl," she said. "That thing is dangerous. I have no idea why Anton brought it with him from Romania, but if he wants it back, we'll give it to him. I miss my Anton, but it's very disturbing to have his ghost wandering around. Hopefully, he won't bother us again."

"I'm sure everything will be fine," I said, giving her a reassuring smile, but far from reassured myself. Aunt Lucy's muddled mind concerned me. Even though all of the testing came back negative, her unwavering certainty about her delusions continued.

"Now let's get to work," she said, her good mood restored. "We have potions to sell."

She stayed and helped out in the shop. She wasn't able to do much yet but spending time with the customers brought a smile to her face. We set her up near the door so she could greet the people coming in and out, and she laughed and chatted with every single person who arrived.

"If I didn't know she suffered from a problem with her memory, I never would have guessed it right now. She seems so normal," said Mrs. Periwinkle.

"Well, as normal as Aunt Lucy gets," I said, giving her an embarrassed smile.

"Maybe she just needed to be back home," she said. "Where she belongs."

"I guess so. I hope that's all it is." Mrs. Periwinkle meant well, but she didn't hear Aunt Lucy talking about ghosts and dragon boxes and souvenirs belonging to dead husbands.

Missy and Sissy came over to express shock and outrage over our broken window. "Why would anyone do something like this? Weren't you terrified? I shared photos of it on Insta," said Sissy, tapping away on her cell phone. "It's horrible."

"Horrible," echoed Missy, glancing at her own cell phone as she spoke. "Do the police know who's behind it? I'm going to Snap about it right now."

I blinked, trying to follow their conversation. I hadn't seen them since hearing Dario's Party Ark conspiracy theory, but these two appeared to be the least likely candidates to participate in corporate intrigue, and far more interested in taking selfies than in sabotaging local businesses.

"No," I said, "but they suspect it's the same person who set the fire at Second-Hand Sally's."

"A fire is really dangerous," said Missy.

"People can get hurt in fires," said Sissy.

"Or even killed," said Missy.

"I don't know how you sleep at night," said Sissy. "I wouldn't be able to stay. I'd be too scared. What if they try again?"

Aggie, who'd just entered, stood in the doorway with a smoothie in her hands. Her face went pale at Missy's words. I put a comforting arm around her narrow shoulders, waving goodbye to Missy and Sissy, the Party Ark harbingers of doom, as they slipped out of the shop.

"Do you think Sally is in danger?" she asked.

"I'm sure it'll be fine," I said. "Things always get crazy here right before Halloween. Aunt Lucy told me stories about it. This is someone taking things too far."

"I wish Sally would close the shop and get out of here. Your aunt, too. Enough is enough."

Before I could respond, Aunt Lucy called out to her. "Hello, Aggie. Nice to see you today. Did you make another one of your yummy smoothies?"

Aggie visibly relaxed. "Yes, I did. You poor dear. This one has lots of pineapple in it to help your broken bone heal. I added some leafy greens, too, so you can get some vitamin K, and apricot juice for potassium."

"Impressive," I said. "Are you sure you aren't a chemist?"

She smiled. "Math has always been my passion, but I do love chemistry. It's so logical, isn't it? And I love physics, too."

"Because physics is math disguised as a science," I said, and Aggie and I shared a giggle.

Aunt Lucy took a long sip. "I don't understand what the two of you are giggling about, but this smoothie tastes delicious. Thank you, sweet Aggie. You're such a thoughtful person."

Aggie beamed. "You're most welcome. I'll bring another one tomorrow."

After Aggie left, I went outside to arrange a signboard advertising a sale on smudging supplies and voodoo candles. The men cleaned up after installing the new window, and it sparkled in the bright autumn sunshine. As I admired it, I sensed Ivan's presence behind me, due to the now familiar prickling that went up my neck. I turned to face him.

"Good morning, Ivan."

"Good morning. What happened here?" he asked, watching the repairmen pack up their things.

I dusted off my hands on my jeans. "Oh. An accident. How are you?"

"I'm well, thank you."

He looked well. The man sparkled as much as the new window. Today he wore dress slacks that perfectly outlined the muscles of his thighs and a blue cashmere sweater the same color as his eyes. He'd pulled his hair into a ponytail, and wore a scarf wrapped around his neck. Only European men could wear that sort of scarf and still look sophisticated and manly. Americans always looked like posers when they did it.

"Where are you from, Ivan? I'm curious."

He grinned, his teeth white and straight. "Where do you think?"

"Well, at first I wondered if you could be Swedish since you look like Thor."

"Thor?" He laughed, a deep and surprisingly merry sound. "No. Not Sweden."

"I kind of figured because the accent is different. I can't place it."

"I grew up in several countries but spent most of my time in boarding schools in Switzerland. I went to university in England. My accent is a bit...convoluted. This is my first time in Pittsburgh."

A brilliant idea occurred to me. "Wait a second."

I ran inside and grabbed an invitation from the back room. "Do you mind if I invite someone to the party?" I asked Aunt Lucy.

"Of course not," she said, but she seemed foggy and disoriented again.

I frowned at her. "Are you okay? I think you're overdoing it."

"It's been a busy morning. I'll take a quick nap in the back room, and I'll be as right as rain. Now, who did you want to invite to the party?"

I pointed outside. Ivan stared intently across the street with his back to us. "Ivan. He's new in town."

"Oh," she said, admiring him from behind. "Let's call him Ivan the Terribly Gorgeous. You should invite him. The more the merrier, you know."

I went outside and handed him the invitation. "It's for our Halloween party," I said.

His eyes lit up as he read it. "A masked ball? I'd love to come. Thank you."

"It'll be a good chance for you to meet your new neighbors."

"How kind. Speaking of local people," he said, tilting his

head toward Librarie Antique next door. "Do you know anything about that place?"

"Not a lot. I hear the owner knows his stuff. I planned to ask him about an odd little thing I found while cleaning the shop. Well, several odd little things, to be exact."

"What did you find?"

I paused, not keen to talk about my grimoire or the dragon box with a stranger. "Nothing terribly interesting."

He studied my face, a twinkle in his eye. "It sounds like you have a secret."

I laughed it off. "Or it sounds like my aunt is a hoarder who needs to do a major purge."

"No hidden treasure? I'm disappointed. But maybe I will stop in his shop sometime and look around. I'm a collector of 'odd things.' One might call me a hoarder, too," he said, with a smile. "Goodbye, Ms. O'Leary. Thank you again for the invitation."

He walked away and every single female on the block sighed and watched him go, including me. One girl nearly ran into a garbage can.

After her nap, Aunt Lucy woke up so refreshed and invigorated she decided to continue with her scheduled tarot card reading for that evening. She made a few phone calls, and in less than an hour, all the slots filled up. She didn't even have to advertise. Her clients missed her and wanted to see her, which brought an unexpected swell of emotion to my chest.

"Can you go to the Enchanted Garden and pick up the cookies for tonight?" she asked. "I ordered them yesterday, just in case."

"Sure."

I pulled on my cardigan and grabbed my purse from the back room. Today I wore a pale grey pencil dress I'd found at a consignment store. I knew it looked good on me. I tried to fool myself into thinking wearing it had nothing at all to do with Dario coming over later to interview Aunt Lucy, but I couldn't seem to get that man out of my head.

Mrs. Periwinkle, once again dressed in bright blue from head to toe, handed me an invitation for Missy and Sissy, and another for Mr. Dalca of Librarie Antique.

"While you're out, could you deliver these, dearie?"

I tapped my finger on Mr. Dalca's invitation. "I want to ask him to take a look at my grimoire. Do you think he'd mind?"

Mrs. Periwinkle shrugged, a gentle lifting of her shoulders. Her reading glasses hung around her neck on a chain glittering with brightly colored stones and her white hair rested on top of her head in its usual complicated updo.

"He's an odd man," she said.

Aunt Lucy overheard our conversation. "He does most of his business online, but he's usually open on Saturdays. And Matilda is right. He's odd."

Will raised one pierced eyebrow as he stocked shelves. "Not odd. That dude is seriously bizarre."

I bit my lip, taking in Will's kohl lined eyes, black clothing, and various tattoos. "Bizarre, huh?"

Will nodded. "I ran into him once outside the store. There is definitely something freaky about him."

Mrs. Periwinkle headed out the door on her way home. "Shall I come with you?"

"I'll be fine. I'm just dropping off the invitation. And he's a bookseller. Book people always love me."

I decided to deliver Missy and Sissy's first. I'd never been inside Party Ark before, and I found it overwhelming. Cheery music played over the loudspeaker, a catchy dance tune that made me want to tap my feet, but also annoyed me at the same time. Missy and Sissy, working behind the counter, waved to me.

"Grace, it's so good to see you. Is there anything we can

help you with?" asked Sissy, as she wrapped a happy scarecrow in colorful birthday paper.

"Not a terribly scary scarecrow," I said.

"Oh, we don't do scary here," said Missy. "We're a family friendly establishment. We only sell happy, wholesome things."

"Look for the good and you'll see it," said Sissy.

Missy agreed. "Goodness and light make your life bright."

Mr. Dalca wasn't the only neighbor who fell into the "odd and bizarre" category. I pulled out the invitation to the party, wanting to leave as soon as I could.

"We're having a party. I hope you can come."

"Oh, thank you," said Sissy. "Do you need any supplies?"

"We're fine." I checked my watch. "I've got some more errands to run. See you later."

"Here, take this for the road," said Missy. She handed me a bag of what looked like candy corn, but the label read "Harvest Seeds of Happiness."

"What's this?" I asked, trying to read the tiny words on the package.

"Ephesians 5:11," said Sissy. "It says, 'Have nothing to do with the fruitless seeds of darkness, but rather expose them.' It's relevant, don't you think?"

I didn't understand what she meant by it being relevant. She gave me a bright, sunny, guileless smile. Missy pulled out her phone and snapped a quick photo of me holding the candy corn as I stared at her, dumbfounded.

"Another good deed for you today, Sissy," said Missy. "You're on a roll."

I said goodbye and got out of their shop as quickly as I could. Something about the Party Ark twins didn't sit right with me, like a sinister shadow lurked beneath that happy, shiny, goodness-and-light surface. It creeped me out more than anything I'd ever seen in Aunt Lucy's shop, and Aunt

Lucy kind of cornered the market on creepy in the South Side.

I shook off my unease, deciding to deliver the second invitation as quickly as possible. The dark interior of the bookshop offered a total contrast to Party Ark. A sign on the door boasted, "Oddities, Antiques, and Other Curiosities," but mostly I noticed piles and piles of books. I picked one up to look it over and jumped when Mr. Dalca greeted me with a sharp bark from the back. "Who are you and what do you want?"

I put the book down, suddenly doubting my earlier assumption about book people always liking me. "I'm Grace. From next door. I have an invitation for you."

A door closed with a loud click, and a slow, shuffling sound followed. Due to the dim lighting of the shop, I didn't see Mr. Dalca until he stood right next to me. When I glimpsed his face, I jerked in surprise.

"Oh. Hello."

A foot shorter than me with a pale face covered in a long, grey beard, he reminded me of one of Snow White's dwarves. He even donned a funny little hat. I let out a nervous giggle but saw nothing humorous in his eyes. Dark and piercing behind thick glasses, they studied me intensely, like they read my very soul and came up unimpressed.

"You are too tall. What do you want?"

I tried to hand the invitation to him, but he refused to take it. Not sure what to do, I placed it on a pile of books next to a cash register that looked like it hadn't been used in years.

He glared at the invitation. "What is that?" Because of his heavy accent, it took me a second to translate what he said.

"An invitation. To our Halloween party."

"I have no time for parties."

I looked around the quiet, dark shop. "Yeah. It seems like you're extremely busy. Well. Come if you can. It'll be fun."

He raised one bushy, skeptical eyebrow at me. "Fun?"

"Yes. Fun."

I turned to leave and saw an old leather book. It reminded me of my grimoire. I reached out to touch the elegantly embossed leather, and Mr. Dalca smacked away my hand.

"No touching."

"Ow. Fine. Can I ask you something?" He nodded, letting out a huff of annoyance, and I continued. "I found a very old book. If I brought it over, would you take a look at it for me? I'd love to know more about it. It's a family heirloom."

"We can't always have what we want. I'd love to get rid of the bunion on my foot. It's the size of a golf ball."

"Wow. Okay."

Not finished yet, he continued. "I'd love to get rid of noisy neighbors. Talking all night. Yappity yap yap."

He must have heard Fiona, Cat, and me the other night, but we weren't that loud. What a crabby, miserable old man. "Sorry..."

"No, you aren't." He made a noise which sounded like a growl. "And I'd love to find a way of getting out of attending your party."

I narrowed my eyes at him. "Does that mean you're coming to the party or not?"

He looked over his thick glasses at me. "Yes."

"Not a yes or no question." I eyed the door, eager to get away from nasty old Mr. Dalca, but he stopped me with a long, tortured sigh.

"You have twisted my arm. I will come to your silly party. I will also look at the grammar for you. I don't want to, but I will do it. Bring it to the shop tomorrow at three. Do not be late. I have many other things to do. Important things. Things that are not favors for troublesome neighbors."

"Gee, thanks," I said, but he'd already turned away and shuffled back into the dark interior of the shop.

I stepped out into the sunshine and the door banged shut behind me. A moment later, I realized something unsettling.

I never told Mr. Dalca the book was a grammar.

CHAPTER 15

I HAD A SUPER BUSY DAY CONVERTING OXYGEN INTO CARBON DIOXIDE.

Bright, airy, and filled with the aroma of baking cookies and coffee, the Enchanted Garden Café brought back happy memories of my childhood every time I visited. Mags greeted me as I entered.

"You've come at just the right time."

She led me past the displays filled with funky jewelry and eclectic pieces of art. Some odd stone sculptures caught my eye. They looked like phalluses.

"Are those what I think they are?"

Mags grinned. "Oh, yes. Fertility charms from a Shinto shrine in the mountains of Japan. One of our top selling items."

"No way."

She let out a deep, throaty laugh. "The world is a crazy place, and you're about to see some of that craziness right now."

She opened the door to the kitchen and interrupted Fiona and Claire in the middle of a heated argument. Fiona stood with her hands on her hips, cheeks flushed, staring at her mother. Claire folded her arms across her chest and looked skyward as she tapped her toe on the ground and seemed to count to ten.

"We cannot have another party with people getting naked in our back garden, Mom. Don't you remember the bonfire the Wiccans organized for summer solstice? For Samhain, it'll have to be even bigger. We cannot do this again."

Claire made a tutting sound. "The police won't bother with us. It's a religious ceremony. And no one gets naked during Samhain. It's too cold."

Fiona glared at her. "It isn't just the police who worry me. Think about what happened to Sally and Grace. Do you want to be the next target?"

Mags cleared her throat, and Claire's face immediately changed from irritated to welcoming. She pulled me into a big hug.

"So good to see you, sweetheart. How about a cup of coffee?"

"Sure. I'm sorry. I didn't mean to interrupt."

Claire waved her hands. "You didn't. Fiona and I were chatting about the Samhain celebration."

Fiona gave me an apologetic look. "I've tried to get her to see we may need to scale it back. We went through a whole big fiasco the last time we hosted a bonfire, and we don't need any more trouble."

"What's life without a little trouble?" asked Claire.

The door to the garden opened and Simon stuck his head in. "Is World War III over yet?" He smiled at me. "Hello, Grace. Lovely to see you again."

We chatted a few moments, then Fiona gave me a steaming hot cup of coffee and pulled me out into the garden. "I needed to get out of there. My mom is driving me crazy."

We sat on a cozy bench under a tree covered in bright orange autumn leaves. I grinned at her. "She's always driving you crazy. Your father is adorable, by the way. I love his French accent, and he seems wonderful."

"He is, and it's amazing having him in my life. He filled a void I never even realized existed, and we get along perfectly, like two peas in a pod. It's my mother who's the problem." Fiona leaned back on the bench. "She never considers the consequences of her actions."

I took a sip of my coffee. "It's lucky she has you."

Fiona laughed. "Yeah. Lucky. Enough about me. How are things with you? I heard the great Madame Lucinda is doing a tarot card reading tonight. I wish I could come."

"Yes, she is." I stared at the contents of my cup, thinking about the argument I'd overheard in the kitchen. "I promised Aunt Lucy I'd host the after party, but I wonder if we're making the right decision."

Fiona wore a white "Be nice to the cook or she'll poison your food" apron. She tucked a wisp of blond hair behind her ear as she considered my comment. "I think it'll be okay but be careful," she said. "Something feels off to me, but I'm not sure what it is. At first, we faced the normal, random problems in the South Side, like graffiti or whatever, but suddenly it's getting much nastier."

"Like what happened to Sally's shop."

"And your window." She took a long sip of coffee. "Sally is often a target, I'm sad to say. There are many ignorant, hateful people in this world, but she is who she is, and she handles it better than I ever could. I don't remember anyone ever having a problem with your aunt, though."

"They say she's a witch." I shook my head. "On that online forum, at least. I took a look at it, and I hate the way people act when they think they're anonymous. It's disgusting."

"Oh, the lovely SSI forum," said Fiona with a snort. "South Side Improvements. I call it 'South Side Idiots.' It popped up about a year ago. They're nothing but trolls and cowards, hiding behind avatars and trying to stir up trouble."

"It's a double-edged sword for Aunt Lucy. She owns a magic shop. Of course, she can't broadcast that there's no actual magic involved. It also wouldn't help if people knew she learned to read tarot cards from an online course."

Fiona almost choked on her coffee. "Are you kidding me?"

"That's what she told me."

She sat back on the bench, laughing. "She's hilarious, but she's good at what she does. She told me about Matthew before he even arrived."

"She did?"

"She saw someone tall, dark, and handsome entering my life. Cliché, right? But then Matthew showed up a few days later. And she also knew someone would lie to me."

"Who lied to you?"

"My ex." She gave me a crooked smile. "I know it sounds crazy, but she somehow knew."

I held the warm cup in my hands and drank the last of my coffee. "You believe in magic now?"

Her gaze went to the fountain in the middle of the garden. A crumbling old thing, covered in moss, it spewed water over odd-looking symbols carved into the sides. "I believe in *some* magic," she said softly.

Looking at the fountain made me remember something else I'd meant to discuss with her. I told her all about the potion mixing, and how it failed without the fountain water.

Her blue eyes widened in surprise. "Mom told me you'd stopped by. She didn't tell me why."

"I came to get sacred water from your magical fountain in order to mix up love potions." I gave myself a face palm. "I can't believe this is my life now. Your mom was cool about it, by the way."

Fiona rolled her eyes. "Not a surprise."

"It's so strange, Fiona. When I used tap water, the potion looked different. Once I added the fountain water, it changed. Cat said she could set me up with the person running the lab at the community college. Could I take a few more samples?"

"Sure. As I told you, we already did testing to make sure it wouldn't give our customers dysentery or something. I can definitely give you the results."

"Great."

She went inside and came back with copies of a report from the local water authority. I put them into my bag. "And I have something for you." I handed her an invitation.

"The Halloween party," she said. "I can't wait. Are you going to ask Dario to be your date?"

I winced. "I'd like to, but we sort of had a fight."

I told her what happened the night before, and she couldn't keep a straight face. "Gosh. You argued twice on your first date? That sounds like my first date with Matthew."

I looked at her, stunned. "Are you serious?"

She giggled. "We argued all the time. We still do, but now making up is so much fun."

We went back inside, and I gave an invitation to Claire and Simon as well. "Have you ever attended a Wiccan celebration?" asked Claire. "They are incredible. I'm never so in touch with nature and the universe as I am during Samhain."

I tried not to laugh at the expression on Fiona's face. "I haven't, but I'm looking forward to it."

"You'll love it," she said. "But some people get very carried away during Wiccan events."

She gave Fiona a pointed look and Fiona blushed from her neck all the way up to her hairline. "Mom," she hissed, but Claire giggled and went back to work in the kitchen.

"I'll tell you later," Fiona whispered to me under her breath. "It involves Matthew and a rhododendron bush."

I grinned at her. "I'm looking forward to it. I'd better get back to work."

Mags piled my arms high with cookies. "I'll be at the reading tonight," she said. "See you, Grace."

As I walked back, I saw a customer duck out the door of the Hocus Pocus Magic Shop and head quickly down the street in the opposite direction. I only caught a glimpse of her, but she looked an awful lot like Tiffany.

"Did you wait on a girl in a pink raincoat?" I asked Aunt Lucy as I walked in.

Aunt Lucy looked up from the box of charms she'd been organizing next to the cash register. "You mean Tiffany? Yes, I did. A few minutes ago."

"What did she buy?"

She thought about it. "Quite a few things. A ceramic pumpkin. Some candles. She also seemed especially interested in your potions."

Uh, oh. Not good. If my gut instinct proved correct, Tiffany wanted to cause trouble. It made me nervous.

"Great."

"What's great?" Dario stood next to me, surprising me so much I jumped.

"Oh. Hello."

He grinned. "Hello yourself."

Aunt Lucy's face lit up when she saw him. "I'm ready for my interview. I wore lipstick."

She puckered her lips and I suppressed a groan. Dario laughed. "The photographer will be here soon."

I got them set up at a small table by the newly repaired window to the shop, snapped a photo of Aunt Lucy with my phone, and went to the back room to dab some cool water on my face. Between the ever-so-hot Dario and the chance encounter with delectable Ivan Rochat, my hormones shifted into overdrive. There was a shortage of parking spots on the

South Side, but definitely not a shortage of beautiful men. I needed to get Laura here as soon as possible.

I sent her a quick text, telling her I couldn't wait to see her on Halloween. I wanted to text Blythe about the latest threat but decided not to tell her. She couldn't do anything to help, and it would only make her worry. Instead, I sent a group text to my whole family with the photo of Aunt Lucy all dressed up for her interview. They responded immediately with hearts and emojis and messages like, "Tell her we miss her," and, "Make sure she agrees to come here for Christmas this year."

The photographer arrived and Aunt Lucy posed, resplendent in a green velvet jacket with a froth of ivory lace from her blouse poking out near her lapel. She also wore a matching velvet hat. From the waist up, she looked like she could be a typical, sweet little grandmother, but the view from the waist down told a slightly different story. Zodiac symbols covered her long black skirt, and someone inked a pentagram in black marker on her orange cast. She'd been asking the customers all day to sign it for her, and I suspected one of the witches must have drawn the pentagram. I moved closer and adjusted her skirt, covering up as much as I could, but part of the pentagram still peeked out.

"Why can't you have normal friends?"

She laughed. "Variety is the spice of life, my dear. You've dined only on boiled potatoes until now, so you don't know any better."

I took a moment to try to figure out what she meant, and I gave her a squinty-eyed look. "Did you just bash my friends?"

Her blue eyes filled with innocence. "Only some of them. I like Laura. When is she coming to visit?"

"Soon."

Dario watched us with amusement. As the photographer

readied himself, Dario grabbed a throw from the back of one of the threadbare velvet chairs. He gently covered Aunt Lucy's legs with it, and in that one quick motion, he effectively hid the embossed skirt and the pentagram from view.

"There you go, Madame Lucinda."

She beamed. "Thank you, Dario. It is a bit chilly in here."

He smiled and I moved closer to him as the photographer worked. "Great save with the blanket," I said softly.

He crossed his big arms over his chest, making his biceps bulge. I resisted the urge to touch them, but they were so tempting.

"I like her style," he said, watching Aunt Lucy as she preened for the camera. "But I want to make sure we get this right. Other people might not understand the pentagram or the swastika."

I choked on my coffee. Dario patted my back, eyeing me with concern. "Are you okay?"

Once I could speak again, I grabbed his arm and pulled him aside. "She has a swastika on her cast?"

He grinned. "You didn't see it, huh?"

I shook my head. "Why would someone do that?"

"Well, it isn't a Nazi thing, if that's what you're thinking. I'm guessing someone put it there as a healing message. The word 'swastika' comes from the Sanskrit 'swasti,' which means 'good' or 'wellbeing.' No evil intent at all."

Aunt Lucy giggled at something the photographer said and I rolled my eyes. "She makes things so much harder for herself."

"She has a good heart and sees the best in everyone."

I snorted. "She just bashed my ex and most of my friends from college."

He gave me a steady brown-eyed stare. "Maybe that's the best thing she could say about them."

He walked away and I pondered his words. Aunt Lucy

only met Jonathan once, at a family function. He'd barely spoken with her, but her assessment of him seemed spot on. He *was* boiled potatoes. Most of my friends were boiled potatoes, too. No salt, no butter, no flavor at all. Next to them, Dario was decadence personified, a wild explosion of taste and flavors, and a complete sensory experience. He made me think of red wine, dark chocolate, and rich coffee. I wanted to smell and taste and touch him. I wanted to consume him.

Dario caught me looking at him and I blushed so thoroughly heat practically radiated from my face. I turned away and ran smack into the counter, instantly bruising my hip.

"Ow, ow, ow," I said as quietly as I could, hoping Dario missed witnessing my clumsiness. No such luck.

"Are you okay?" he asked, obviously trying not to laugh.

"Oh, yeah." I put my hand on my hip and winced when I touched the spot I'd bruised. "I'm peachy."

The bell above the shop jingled and Missy and Sissy walked in, resplendent in their Party Ark shirts and khaki skirts. Today Missy wore her hair down, and Sissy tied hers up, which made it easier to tell them apart. Missy carried a gift bag from Party Ark.

"We brought you something," she said, pulling out a sparkly pumpkin. Before she handed it to me, she snapped a photo of it. "At Party Ark, they like to see when we perform an ARK, an Act of Random Kindness. We get points for it."

"I'm close to winning a new cell phone," said Sissy with a sunny smile. "I gave a burger to a homeless man yesterday. I got like fifty points."

I frowned, disturbed by the blatant greed in her eyes, but Aunt Lucy didn't seem to notice. She admired the pumpkin, delighted by the gift. "It's beautiful. I love pumpkins. I love this whole season. Speaking of which, will you be able to come to our party?"

Sissy shook her head, ponytail swinging. "We can't. We have a meeting that night."

"On Halloween?" asked Aunt Lucy, confused. "Who schedules a meeting on Halloween? Unless you're witches, of course."

Missy let out a nervous laugh. "Uh, we are definitely not witches. It's an event with our Party Ark friends who choose to celebrate Halloween in an alternative way."

"Oh, I see," said Aunt Lucy, but her forehead wrinkled, telling me she didn't see at all.

"Sorry you can't make it," I said. "Thank you for the jack-o-lantern."

"It isn't a jack-o-lantern," said Missy. "It's a Fall Fantasy Pumpkin. We sell them at Party Ark."

"Well, it's lovely," said Aunt Lucy. "So sparkly and festive. I do love glitter. Some call it the herpes of the crafting world, since once it's on you, you can't get rid of it. I don't agree, of course. I find it cheerful."

Missy and Sissy blinked with identical expressions of confusion and vague horror at Aunt Lucy's words. Sissy came out of her stupor first. "Did she say *herpes...*?"

I jumped in, trying to lead the Party Ark twins to the exit. "If there isn't anything else, ladies, we'd better get back to work."

"Just one more photo," said Missy. "For Insta."

They ended up taking about ten more photos with Aunt Lucy, and of the pumpkin, before they felt satisfied with the results. They brought the art of selfie-taking to a whole new level. After they left, I shook my head. "Perky and pushy. A bad combo."

Dario laughed. "Indeed."

"I don't understand what they have against jack-o-lanterns," said Aunt Lucy. "And did you see the way they looked at my pretty pentagram necklace? It's ridiculous."

"It is," I agreed, and turned to Dario. "Will you be back later? For the tarot card reading?"

He grabbed his jacket from the back of a chair and put it on. "No. I can't make it tonight, but Nunny will be here. She never misses one."

"Oh. Okay." I tried to hide the disappointment in my voice. I wanted to see Alvida again, but I'd hoped Dario would be there, too. "Did Aunt Lucy give you an invitation to the party?"

"She did."

"Will you come?"

"I will," he said with a smile.

A long, uncomfortable silence dragged on and on as I desperately sought a way to fill it. I couldn't come up with anything. Dario stared at me, silent, as I wrung my fingers and wondered what to do next. I'd become a world-class hand wringer recently, and I'd already swooned once as well. I couldn't wait to see what Victorian mannerism I'd adopt next.

"Well. See you soon," I blurted out. "Hopefully. Maybe. If you have time, that is."

He gave me a funny look. I didn't blame him. I turned, about to run away, when he stopped me. "I'd planned to show you the article before it went to print, but my editor says he wants to publish it in the Sunday edition."

I gulped. "Tomorrow?"

"Are you okay with that?"

So many things could go wrong, but I knew Dario wouldn't let us down. "I trust you."

He gave me a crooked grin before he put his bag over his shoulder. "Well, Gracie, that's a start."

CHAPTER 16

YOU CAN'T B. CEREUS.

The tarot card reading commenced at seven o'clock. Aunt Lucy changed into a turban with a huge green jewel and a feather in the front. It fluttered when she moved her head. Beneath her black cape, she wore what looked like one of the tavern wench costumes we sold upstairs, complete with a corset.

"Are you sure you'll be okay wearing a corset all night?" I asked.

"It's one of the most comfortable costumes we have. It's elastic." She gave the bodice a tug, showing me way too much old lady cleavage.

"Whoa, Aunt Lucy. We need to safety pin your shirt shut."

She looked at her chest. "Why?"

I leaned close. "Because you flashed me."

She covered her mouth with her hand, trying to suppress a giggle. "Oops. And I'm not wearing a bra."

I sighed and said, "I noticed," which made her laugh even harder.

I got her pinned up as modestly as possible and hoped she'd remain covered throughout the evening. I'd pondered a long time over what to wear to a tarot card reading, finally choosing a narrow black skirt, black tights, and flats. I'd also thrown on a pale grey cashmere twinset. My only jewelry was a pair of pearl earrings I'd inherited from my father's mother and a matching pearl choker. Aunt Lucy eyed my outfit critically.

"You need some color, girl. Some panache. Some splash."

I smoothed my skirt. "This is the way I like to dress, Aunt Lucy."

She shrugged. "Whatever makes you comfortable, dearie. I wish you didn't always look like you're going to a funeral. You're young and beautiful. If you've got it, flaunt it. That's what I always say."

I looked at her in her turban and silly costume as a rush of something equal parts pity, embarrassment, and love came over me. "Do you know what I always say?" I asked, giving her a stern look. "To each his own."

She giggled. "Touché. Well played, pumpkin."

The guests arrived exactly on time, and the room filled up quickly. Aunt Lucy sat at the large, circular table in the center of the shop, queen of her domain. She dealt the cards and dished out a healthy dose of practical advice with her readings. I'd never seen her do one before, and her skill set impressed me.

"She's good," said Alvida as I put out more cookies. Fiona outdid herself once again. She'd recreated an entire deck of tarot cards in cookie form.

"She is. And these cookies are amazing. Do they taste as good as they look?"

Alvida handed me one on a napkin, a depiction of The Lovers. "Have a cookie," she said. "Live a little. You're too young to act so old all the time."

I took a bite of the cookie. It tasted fabulous. "You're the second person today to insinuate I need to lighten up."

Alvida laughed. "I call a spade a spade. Who else told you that?"

I tilted my head toward Aunt Lucy. Her eyes were huge and her face animated as she clutched the hand of the lady across from her and told her to make sure she gets a yearly physical.

"And you should have a mammogram, too. We all should. I don't care how big or small your boobies are."

Aunt Lucy used her hands to better display her own significant bust, almost popping the safety pin. "Oh, Aunt Lucy," I said, my voice soft.

"She has her own style," said Alvida with a giggle. "But I like what she's doing. It's important. The woman sitting with her right now is Olivia Fabruccio. She'd never listen to me if I told her to go to a doctor, but if Madame Lucinda tells her to go, she does. And it's time for her yearly physical. Your aunt keeps track of those things."

"She does?"

Alvida nodded. "People see the clothes and the turban and think she's some kind of crackpot, but she's got her stuff together. More than most people, at least. Can I give you a piece of advice?"

"Could I stop you if I wanted to?"

She laughed. "Probably not."

I braced myself. "All right. Go ahead."

"It's about my grandson. He hasn't stopped talking about you since the day he met you."

I didn't need a mirror to know my cheeks turned pink. "Really?"

"Yes, and it took a lot for him to ask you out. He's shy."

"Dario is...what?"

"Shy. It may not seem that way, but he is, and from what I understand, the first date didn't go so well."

"We kind of fought. A few times. And there was a fire. And property damage."

"Well, he's a Fontana. It goes with the territory." She gave me a steady look. "You like my grandson."

I met her steely gaze. I had nothing to hide. "I do."

"There is something you need to know about him. He's like your aunt. He isn't what he seems. He won't ask a girl out unless he's truly interested in her, and he might need some prodding to get his feet wet again."

"What do you mean?"

She rolled her eyes. "For someone so smart, you aren't terribly quick, are you? My grandson is more of a nerd than you are, and not the pushy type. If you want to see him again, I suggest you do the asking."

Panic gripped my chest. "Me?"

"Yes, you. Who else do you think I'm talking to here?"

In spite of the hint of harshness to her tone, she gave me a gentle and reassuring pat. I didn't know if I'd ever work up the courage to ask Dario out, but I may have to give it a try if he didn't ask me out again soon.

Aunt Lucy's tarot card reading went remarkably well. I don't know how she did it exactly, but she made the whole group feel happy and comforted. Some people left as soon as their reading ended, but most stayed and mingled. The cookies were a huge hit, our guests also enjoyed the rum punch Aunt Lucy had insisted on serving.

"There's nothing like it to warm up your insides," she said.

When all the readings finished, she called me over to the table. "Okay, now. This is Gracie's first time."

"What are you talking about?"

Alvida grabbed my arm and made me sit in the chair opposite Aunt Lucy. "Sit and be quiet. Your aunt is going to read the cards for you."

"It's okay," I said, trying to rise out of the chair. "I have to clean up."

Alvida kept a firm hand on my shoulder. "Sit here and do as you're told," she said. She leaned forward to whisper in my ear, "This is for your aunt, silly goose. If she wants to do it for you, let her."

I lifted my hands in surrender. "Fine, but I want you to know ahead of time, I don't believe in this kind of thing."

A gust of wind blew into the shop, extinguishing nearly all the candles. Only one remained lit, and it sat right in the middle of our table. Everyone gasped and moved closer, surrounding me.

"Weird," I said. "Did someone open a door?"

Aunt Lucy grabbed my hand, almost crushing my fingers with her rings. "Shhhh," she said. "The spirits want our attention."

I figured the fastest way to get through this was to shut up and cooperate. Aunt Lucy stared at me as she shuffled the cards, her eyes studying my face like she saw it for the first time. She handed me the deck, and told me to shuffle, too. The first card she turned over did not surprise me.

"The Lovers."

"Okay. Thanks. I'll go and clean now."

I glanced at Alvida, but she responded with a stern look in spite of the twinkle in her eye. So did Aunt Lucy. "You have to be quiet or this won't work, pumpkin. I'm not going to tell you again."

"Yes, ma'am." I swallowed hard. She took this seriously.

"Love is like a flame. It can ignite in a blaze of passion, but it can also consume and destroy. What I see is unclear. There is potential for conflict here, and heartache, but there is also something else..." She paused, a happy smile playing on her lips. "I'll let it be a surprise."

I tapped my foot in irritation. "Oh, great."

She ignored me and flipped another card. "The Ace of Wands."

"The Ace of what?"

"Wands." She stroked the card with her finger. "You should be working on a project right now that you've neglected. You're about to get a burst of energy. It will inspire you to take your work in a new and exciting direction. Go for it. You'll be rewarded in ways you never imagined."

My mind went to my untouched thesis and the computer I steadfastly avoided since I arrived in Pittsburgh. I'd been way ahead of schedule on my work, so I maintained some leeway, but if I didn't get my nose back to the grindstone soon, I'd fall behind. But I'd told Aunt Lucy basically the same thing in the shop earlier. Nothing magical about that particular prediction.

She turned over another card. "Oh, this is interesting. The Ace of Pentacles. I see where this is leading. It means your goal is within your reach."

I wanted to believe her. I'd worked for as long as I could remember with one goal in mind; to get my PhD. Right now, it seemed nearly unattainable. I remained frozen in a terrible sort of limbo, my fate to soon be decided by a group of unknown colleagues and faceless professors at the university. I didn't think I'd made any enemies at school, but since Roger and even Jonathan turned on me, I didn't trust my own instincts any more.

When she turned over the next card, her eyes widened. "What is it?" I asked.

"The Ace of Cups." Her sweet face filled with confusion. "Three aces in a row. This is strange."

In spite of myself, I leaned forward in my chair. "What does it mean?"

She nibbled on her lip. "It's often said to represent the

Holy Grail. Joseph of Arimathea sustained himself for an eternity by eating a wafer placed in the grail each day."

And like that, she broke the spell. I sat back in my chair and folded my arms across my chest. "Joseph of Arimathea? Are you talking about the Knights Templar?"

Aunt Lucy didn't seem bothered by my skepticism. "Of course. But I don't think this means you'll embark on a quest. Not any time soon. The cup is the beginning. In your case, it represents the first stirrings of passion and the start of a relationship, one full of potential that may eventually lead to true love and happiness. But it's up to you. The ball, so to speak, is in your court. You have to make the next move."

A shiver went over my skin. Dario had said those exact words to me after our disastrous first date, but Aunt Lucy never heard that conversation.

"Are you sure?" I asked.

I realized what Fiona meant about her tarot cards readings. As much as I doubted the validity of the whole thing, Aunt Lucy's composure and confidence unnerved me, making me wonder if there could be a thread of truth hidden in all this nonsense.

She tilted her head to one side, immediately negating my theory. "Or I could be wrong. It might mean you're thirsty."

"What?" I didn't even try to hide the annoyance in my voice. Alvida giggled.

"She's teasing you, sweetie."

"Is this the time for a joke?"

"I couldn't help myself. You looked so serious." Aunt Lucy cleared her throat, turning over the last card, and her whole face lit up. "The Magician. Oh, this is good. You have magic at your fingertips, girl. You can make something out of nothing. It's a real power. Others know you have it, but you're blind to your own abilities. You need to believe in yourself. Once you do, anything is possible."

Aunt Lucy gave me a smile, but a shadow of worry hovered in her eyes. "Do you mind making one of those fabulous Turkish coffees, Alvida? There's something I'm missing. The cards hint at it, but it's beyond my grasp. I'd like to read her coffee grounds."

"Sure thing," said Alvida and she raced back to the kitchen. No one else moved a muscle. They all wanted to see what happened next. I'd become the freaky sideshow of the tarot card reading.

We waited in awkward silence. Although unsure how I felt about all of this, the reminder to get back to work on my thesis struck a chord. I'd neglected it for months. Not finishing it would be academic suicide.

A few minutes later, Alvida burst through the door with a tiny cup of coffee in her hands. Painted gold and sparkling with jewels, I admired its exotic beauty, certain I'd never seen anything like it before. She put it in front of me, resting it on a dainty, matching saucer.

Aunt Lucy's blue eyes glowed dark and mysterious. "Drink it, Gracie, but make sure you sip. You don't want to drink the grounds. Those are what I'll use to tell your fortune."

"Got it. Thanks for the warning."

I lifted the cup and saucer and tilted the sweet, rich contents into my mouth. When I felt the powdery grounds on my tongue, I stopped drinking.

Aunt Lucy reached for the cup and put the saucer upside down on top of it. She flipped it over, letting the grounds land on the plate. She waited a moment before turning the cup over and staring inside.

"Oh. This is interesting."

Aunt Lucy squinted in the dim light of the shop. She tilted the cup closer to the candle so she could get a better view. "There's a lot going on in here," she said. "Let me try to figure this out. First of all, I see a snake. Actually, two snakes."

"There are snakes in my coffee cup?"

Aunt Lucy unfazed by my sarcasm, continued. "I see something else, too. A mongoose. The mongoose will protect you. They eat snakes, you know. Don't you remember the story?"

"*Rikki Tikki Tavi?* By Rudyard Kipling?"

The fact that I knew exactly how Aunt Lucy's mind worked at this point, and could easily follow her convoluted thoughts, kind of scared me. "Yes. You loved it as a child. A mongoose seems so insignificant and weak, but they are actually quite amazing. I mean, seriously, taking on a cobra is no small task."

"Is that all, Aunt Lucy? Snakes and a mongoose? It doesn't sound too bad."

She let out a sigh. "But it is. I'm worried about you. You're in danger. Watch out for those snakes. Let the mongoose help you. Trust the mongoose, Gracie."

It took a great deal of physical restraint not to roll my eyes. "Okay. Keep an eye out for wildlife. I get it."

"I'm serious. It'll be a tough road ahead. You'll have to be braver than you've ever been, and strong." She put down the cup and stared at me, her face pale in the light of the single candle. "When you think it's over and all hope is lost, you're going to have to turn to the one person you can truly count on and believe in with all your heart."

The silence in the room grew thick and heavy, like a wool blanket covered us. I was scared to hear the answer, but I needed to ask one very important question.

"Who?"

Aunt Lucy gave me a sad smile. "Yourself."

CHAPTER 17
YOU MAKE MY DOPAMINE LEVELS GO ALL SILLY.

I went to sleep with Jinx snoring on my chest and dreamed of shadowy creatures chasing me through a dark forest. Snakes slithered against my feet and sharp fangs gnashed, biting at me. I cried out in my sleep, waking myself in the process and startling Jinx out of a deep sleep as well. He hissed, looking around in such irate confusion I laughed.

"Sorry, Jinx. My bad."

He settled back into the blankets, giving me one last dirty look, as I got up. The sun hadn't risen yet, but I knew I'd never get back to sleep. I couldn't shake the sensation of being chased by something I couldn't see.

"Thank you, Turkish coffee," I muttered as I hopped into the steaming shower. I dressed in comfy yoga pants and a red, long-sleeved "Math Ninja" T-shirt, a leftover from my under-grad days when I could wear whatever I wanted. One benefit to my hiatus? Wearing my favorite clothes again.

"Math Ninja. Hi-ya." I adopted a martial-arts pose as I looked at myself in the mirror. Without glasses, makeup, and my teacher wardrobe, I appeared younger than my actual age, like a high school kid. Not a professional. Not a PhD candidate. Not a TA. Just fresh faced and kind of vulnerable.

I chewed on my lip as I stared at my laptop on the kitchen table. It grew harder and harder to face my thesis with each passing day. Had my hypothesis been as good as I'd initially thought? So much remained undone. Would I ever finish it? *Could* I ever finish it? And should I even bother trying?

"The Ace of Wands," I said softly to myself. "This is the project I need to be working on. This is what I've neglected."

Aunt Lucy said I'd get an inspirational burst of energy. Inspiration was a tricky thing, but due to the amount of caffeine I'd consumed, I practically exploded with energy, so I decided to go for it.

I picked up my laptop and opened it to my work. I read over what I'd done before the big kerfuffle with Dr. Lewis and liked what I saw. I was on the right track but missed something significant. I needed a key component to fill it out and tie everything together, but I couldn't figure out what.

I pondered it as I ate breakfast and watched the sun come up, slowly rising in the east and bathing Aunt Lucy's apartment in its warm glow. The horizon burst to life in a gorgeous show of magenta, purple, pink, and red, and suddenly I knew what to do. I pulled on a long, snuggly cardigan and raced down the steps, my laptop tucked under my arm.

I mixed up two batches of love potion, one using tap water and one using the water from Fiona's fountain. I carefully documented each step of the process, measuring the ingredients precisely and writing down everything. Then I checked and double-checked my own notes. I found some jars I could sterilize, labeled them, numbered them, and filled them with the two different batches of love potion. One turned grey and goopy. The other became a rich purple, swirling and dancing in the jar. I didn't even need labels to show which one contained the fountain water, but I wanted to be able to trust the results when I got to a lab.

As soon as it could be considered a decent hour, I texted Cat, asking her if she could contact her friend at the community college for me. To my surprise, she responded within minutes, saying she'd ask her right away. She called me as I cleaned the back room.

"As it turns out, Delilah is there right now. She went in to catch up on some paperwork since it's quiet at the school on Sundays. She said she'll be there for a few hours if you want to stop by."

"Thanks, Cat. I'm surprised you're up so early." I knew she worked late, especially on Saturday nights.

She paused a second before she spoke. "I couldn't sleep."

Something in her voice caused a tug of worry in my heart. "Are you okay?"

She sighed. "I got a note last night, kind of like the one they left for you. It freaked me out. They said they'd go after my dad." Her voice caught on the last word.

"Do you want me to come over?" I asked.

"No. I'm fine. I called Officer Belfiore last night, and I'm on my way to my dad's right now. Normally, I'd ignore this kind of thing, but it's bad timing. Today would have been my mom's birthday. I'd already planned to close the shop and take a few days off. Now I'm glad I did."

"Oh, Cat. Is there anything I can do?"

She sighed. "Be careful. I've tried to convince myself they're bullies, all bark and no bite, but something in the last letter...it frightened me."

"Oh, I get it. As soon as I saw the note about hurting Aunt Lucy, I fainted."

She laughed, a soft, husky sound. "Into Dario's waiting arms, I believe. At least that's how I heard it."

"Yeah. Kind of. But the point is you're handling this much better than me."

"Thanks. I'll call you as soon as I get back."

I hung up my phone, filled with fury over what had happened to Cat and wanting to hit something, or someone. This needed to stop, but it was essential to think things through calmly and rationally. Anger always caused me to act impulsively. I decided to go to the lab, focus on my samples, do the work, and think it through again once I'd cooled off. Otherwise, I'd do something stupid and make matters even worse.

As I rounded the corner of the block, I ran smack into Tiffany. Wearing black spandex leggings and a pale pink hoody, she must have been heading home from her morning jog. Even all sweaty with her hair pulled up into a ponytail, she still managed to look gorgeous.

"Sorry," I said. I'd nearly knocked her over in my haste to get to the lab.

"Whoa," she said by way of greeting. "You're up early this morning."

"Uh, yeah. I am." I glanced at my watch, wanting to end this awkward encounter as quickly as possible. "I'd better get going."

I turned to leave, but she stopped me. "I saw what happened to the window of your aunt's shop. It's awful. I hope they catch whoever did it."

"Thanks."

"Your aunt has always treated me kindly," she said. "We go way back. Just like me and Dario."

Message received loud and clear. "Good to know. Good-bye, Tiffany."

She gave me a wave over her shoulder and jogged away, annoyingly perfect, right down to her perky behind.

"No one should look so good in spandex," I muttered as I

trudged down the street, hauling my unperky bum to the lab. Her comment about Dario annoyed me, but I had more pressing things to worry about at the moment.

Delilah met me at the door of the chemistry lab, a tiny woman with spiky, platinum hair, grey eyes, and a silver ring in her right nostril. She wore a baggy pair of khakis and a long-sleeved grey T-shirt.

"Thanks for doing this," I said. "I appreciate your help."

"It's nothing. The labs aren't used on Sundays, and it's my favorite time to get caught up on work. Cat told me you're a PhD student?"

"Yes. My aunt broke her leg and I'm here helping her until she's better."

Delilah smiled. "Madame Lucinda is a friend of mine. She introduced me to my girlfriend, Jane. She's quite the matchmaker."

I laughed. "Tell me about it."

Delilah left me alone and I looked around, surprised by the quality of equipment and the lab itself. Although lacking some of the more sophisticated microscopes and computers we utilized at the university, it appeared well organized, clean, and perfect for my needs.

Dario nailed it when he said I'd acted like an elitist snob, but that was not my only mistake. I'd based my conclusions not on facts, but on assumptions. As a scientist, I knew better.

My younger sister Ava once told me, "You're smart, but it doesn't mean you know everything." She'd announced it right after she told me she wanted to study elementary education in school and become a kindergarten teacher. I was opposed to the idea.

"Study chemistry, like me, or computer engineering, like Aishling. You have a great mind for math and science. Don't waste it on runny noses and picture books."

She reacted with a flick of her red ponytail, and a hard look in her normally soft brown eyes. "Maybe I don't consider it a waste of time. Maybe you have no idea what you're talking about."

I'd used my own parameters to judge what she should be doing with her life, and I'd been wrong. She ended up loving her major and planned to pursue her master's degree in education. She'd be a great teacher someday, but I'd wanted her to study something I could relate to, unlike Mary, an accountant, and Blythe, who'd majored in criminal justice. Only Aishling studied something STEM related.

My father took me aside for a chat after I'd argued with Ava, something he often did when any of us fought. He sat next to me on the front porch swing and pulled a box of sweets out of the pocket of his jacket. Lemon drops. My favorite.

I plopped one into my mouth, leaning against his broad shoulder. "Thanks, Pops, but our fight is over. I'm not mad at Ava anymore."

"I know," he said, "but there is something I wanted to show you."

He pulled out a photo of the five of us. The twins were babies, and Mary and Blythe held them on their laps. Mary beamed. Blythe seemed annoyed. The babies sobbed. I stood in between them, looking tall, gangly, and awkward as I tried my best to ignore everything around me and pose for the camera.

"Wow. Nothing's changed."

He laughed. "You're right. And I always knew you were something special. Something precious. From the moment of your birth."

"You did?"

"Of course. And the same happened with each of your

sisters, too. Each of you has a special gift, but you're so smart, Gracie. Maybe too smart."

"What do you mean?"

He put an arm around me. "You see things as black and white, but the world is made up of a million shades of grey. You may need to step back, let go of what you think you know, and realize you're not seeing the whole picture."

Looking around the lab, I knew my father was right, but I had no time to ponder my errors in judgment right now. I needed to save the self-flagellation for later

I set to work, finding my groove immediately. For the first time in weeks, I felt centered and like myself again. Being in a lab did that to me. The closest I could get to describing it was to say I experienced a giddy sense of calm when I worked. It began when I got a chemistry set as a child with a plastic microscope and prepared slides. I looked into that lens and saw a secret world invisible to the naked eye. My first tiny microscope opened a door for me into a wondrous and fascinating place.

I didn't believe in tarot cards and love potions, but something truly magical existed inside a microscope. I witnessed such beauty in balancing a chemical equation, or working in a lab to prove a theory, or studying slide after slide to see something different, special, and rare. Something no one else came across before.

I'd prepared some slides back at Aunt Lucy's and brought them in the wooden box I carried in my briefcase. Now came the moment of truth. Did the water from the Enchanted Garden Café contain something special or not?

First, I put the tap water under the microscope and studied it. I turned on my phone voice recorder so I could describe exactly what I saw without pausing to write. I'd take notes later, after studying each sample and listening to my recordings.

"Slide number one. Sample taken from the back kitchen at the Hocus Pocus Magic Shop. Normal tap water. Nothing unusual detected. Will run a detailed chemical analysis to be certain."

I put the slide away and took out the sample from the Enchanted Garden. When I looked at it through the microscope, I blinked in surprise. I sat back, rubbing my eyes, and leaned in again for closer examination.

"Slide number two. Sample taken from the fountain on the premises of the Enchanted Garden Café. This water appears to contain some sort of bioluminescence, making flashes of light and color appear within the sample. This could explain the purple color and pearlescent quality of mixture number two. I've never seen anything like this before, but I've read about it in regard to deep-sea creatures. I'll check the analysis done by the private lab provided by Fiona Campbell and do a more detailed analysis myself. For lack of a better word, this water...shimmers."

The water came from an underground spring. Something metallic in the water could account for part of the anomaly, but not all of it.

"This is strange." I picked up my phone and spoke into it. "I need to review the report Fiona gave me. I'll do as much as I can at this lab. I may have to send out samples to get a more thorough evaluation. I'll text Megan back at school and ask her if she'd be willing to do this for me. Lastly, I need to have someone else mix the potion and observe to make sure the reactions are identical. If what I'm seeing in this water sample is what I think it is, this could be the breakthrough I need to complete my thesis."

I turned off my phone. I might no longer be a PhD candidate at the moment, but my thesis remained a puzzle I needed to solve. Not because I wanted to impress Dr. Lewis or my colleagues. I did this only for myself.

I lifted a vial of the love potion and turned it around in my hand. It swirled and danced in the sunlight streaming through the windows of the chemistry lab. I picked up my phone and turned it on again to record.

"Is this movement something beginning at an atomic level? Is this an actual visual demonstration of my theory, or am I watching a chemical reaction and mistaking its origins? Either this is the proof I'm looking for or I'm making a huge mistake. Either way, what do I have to lose?"

I turned off my phone and stuck it into my pocket. I could answer my own question. I had nothing to lose. Already persona non grata and an outcast, this could be the last nail in my coffin, or it might be exactly what I needed to redeem myself.

Delilah popped her head in as I cleaned up. "How did it go?"

"I'm not sure. Can you look at a sample and tell me what you see?"

I put the water sample from the Enchanted Garden back on the microscope and Delilah hopped onto a stool and peered into the lens. Seconds later, she glanced up at me in surprise.

"What is this?"

"You tell me." I tried to keep my expression neutral. "Any guesses?"

She moved closer to the microscope and looked again. "It almost looks like bioluminescence, but the markers are off."

"Do you know a lot about bioluminescence?"

She made a "hang loose" symbol with her hand, her eye still pressed against the microscope. "I got my PhD at the University of Hawaii. Aloha, baby."

"Hawaii?"

"Yep. I spent four years underwater, and guess what my thesis focused on?"

"What?"

"Bioluminescent dinoflagellate ecosystems. They are mostly found in tropical lagoons. The Discovery Channel picked up some of my research, and they did a documentary on it. Not on me, of course, just using my research as a springboard to talk about the phenomena."

I thought about the swirling dance of the love potions and chills went up and down my arms. "A springboard."

I quickly jotted some notes in my book. Maybe the atomic motion provided the springboard, propelling the chemical reaction to occur. A catalyst on the most basic level.

Delilah waited patiently for me to finish writing. "Sorry," I said.

"Don't worry. I get it," she said. "What I don't get is this sample. Where is it from? It has to be deep sea, but it's like nothing I ever saw in Hawaii. Is it from Iceland? I'm presuming volcanic activity could cause the metallic glow. I saw it in Hawaii, too. But the difference is the way this...moves."

"Like it's dancing?"

She nodded. "Exactly."

"The sample isn't from Iceland."

She frowned, her pale eyebrows drawing together. "Where did it come from?"

I leaned close, whispering, even though no one was around to hear me. "From the fountain behind the Enchanted Garden Café."

"You're kidding me." Delilah almost fell off her stool. She took another look into the microscope. "*This* came from the South Side?"

I nodded, barely able to control my excitement. I told her about my thesis, and she listened carefully. "Do you want to know what I think?"

Part of me feared hearing her opinion. If I was headed in

the wrong direction, it could mean the end of whatever hope I had left of getting my PhD and becoming a professor, but I wanted to know.

"Yes."

"Bioluminescence like this is only found in salt water, and usually in tropical waters. There is some in colder oceans, but only at deep levels and with different markers." Delilah's steady grey eyes met mine. "I'll tell you what, and I'm being honest about this. I think you're onto something big."

"You do?"

She took my slide out of the microscope and handed it to me. "Yes. If you need my help, I'd love to be a part of this. And you're welcome to use this lab any time you want. My lab is your lab, okay?"

I stared at her, getting choked up. I didn't realize how much I missed working in a lab, and how much the respect of my peers meant to me. I saw respect in Delilah's face, and heard sincerity in her words. After what happened with Dr. Lewis, and after the way other professors treated me at school, Delilah's affirmation soothed my wounded confidence like a balm

"That's so kind of you."

She laughed. "Not really. I'm a sucker for puzzles and what you have on your slide is a mystery if I've ever seen one. I want to be around when you figure it out."

She seemed exactly like me, this woman who taught at the South Side Community College. She saw chemistry as a beautiful puzzle, and she felt the same passion for learning and for teaching as I did. Seeing her lab turned into a lesson for me and getting to know Delilah was a much-needed wakeup call.

Delilah gave me a key and an entry code and promised to let the school security staff know I'd be using the building. As I left, with the key in my pocket and my briefcase full of samples, I practically walked on air. The warm autumn sun shone on my head and I needed nothing more than a cardigan to keep me toasty. I'd pulled my hair up into a messy updo, and as the tendrils caressed my face, I noticed how it came to life in the sunshine, like a flame lit from within. When I caught a glimpse of my reflection in the window of a clothing shop, I liked what I saw.

I tucked a lock behind my ear and grabbed a Sunday paper from a box on the street. Dario said the newspaper would publish the article about Aunt Lucy today. I skimmed through the paper until I hit the "Community" section and came to a dead stop in the center of the sidewalk. Aunt Lucy's photo took up half the page. In the colored picture, her blue eyes twinkled, and a sweet smile hovered on her lips. I read through the article as pedestrians swirled around me, and I probably blocked some people, but I didn't care.

After I finished, I folded the paper, put it under my arm and flew back to the shop. Dario waited outside, peeking in through the window. For a second, he didn't see me, but as soon as he turned, I ran into his arms and kissed his sweet, sexy, adorable face.

"Thank you, thank you, thank you," I said between kisses. We stood in the middle of the sidewalk, in full view of the entire South Side, but I couldn't have cared less. Dario didn't seem to care either. He pulled me closer, kissing me over and over again.

When a delivery truck backed up next to us, beeping loudly, we laughed and stepped away from each other. I dug through my bag to find my key and unlocked the door to the shop. As soon as we stepped inside the dark shop, I kissed him again. Eventually, I curled up on his lap on one of Aunt Lucy's soft, velvet chairs. Dario wrapped his arms around me as I held his face in my hands. I couldn't stop touching him. I felt like I was a person dying of thirst and Dario a spring of fresh, cool water.

ABIGAIL DRAKE

"I take it you read the article."

I sighed. "Yes. Amazing. Perfect. Wonderful."

His face glowed at my praise. "You aren't mad at me anymore?"

I shook my head and pulled him closer, raining butterfly kisses on his forehead. "Nope. It has nothing to do with the article, though. I stopped being mad at you long before I saw it."

"Is it safe to ask you out again?"

I leaned back, still in the circle of his arms, so I could look directly into his eyes. "I think I should be the one to ask you out this time."

He gave me a slow, sexy smile that made my insides get all wobbly. "When are you going to do it?"

I sat up straighter, and he groaned as my bottom pressed against his manly parts. "Sorry," I said, folding my hands primly on my lap. "Dario Fontana, will you please go out with me?"

He pretended to think about it. "Fine. If you insist."

"I insist." I threw my arms around him, burying my face in his neck. "You smell so good."

He wrapped a lock of my hair around his finger. "So do you. Like vanilla and something spicy. Cinnamon. Cloves." He stuck his nose in my hair. "And maybe some ginger."

"I smell like a pumpkin pie?"

He laughed. "Kind of. It figures, though. Pumpkin pie is my favorite." He kissed me again, his lips clinging to mine. "When is our date? Can it be now?"

"Yes." I unbuttoned his shirt, enjoying the warmth of his skin. "Or we could skip the whole dating thing and head up to the apartment."

He made a muffled noise against my mouth. "Grace. You're killing me."

I stood, about to lead the sweetly aroused and delectable

192

Mr. Fontana up the stairs, when I turned and noticed something near the bookshelf behind us. The sky darkened with an impending storm, and a flicker of light caught my eye. It came through a hole in the wall. Someone must have turned on the lights in Librarie Antique next door, but how could I possibly see it from here?

A clap of thunder sounded outside, making me jump. Motioning for Dario to be quiet, I removed a few books from the shelf, giving me a clear view through a large gap in the wall into the main room of Librarie Antique. Dario crouched next to me as I looked through the hole. Someone walked past slowly, pausing right in front of us, but far too tall and buff to be Mr. Dalca. And he wore a suit cut from expensive looking fabric, not Mr. Dalca's style at all. Even his shoes seemed way too fancy and large for our octogenarian next-door neighbor. They had tassels. I didn't know Mr. Dalca well, but he wasn't a tassel wearing sort of guy.

I tilted my head and looked up, my cheek pressing against the wood of the bookshelf. The person inside the shop wore a black ski mask, his face and hair entirely hidden from view. He sifted through piles of books, tossing some on the floor and pushing others aside. One book flew toward me and I gasped but kept my eyes locked on the stranger in Mr. Dalca's shop.

He turned at the sound of my voice but couldn't see me. The dark shop proved to be my friend. When he got close to where I crouched, so close I saw the blue of his eyes inside his ski mask, the facts clicked together slowly in my mind. A ski mask. A stranger. Books being tossed around all willy nilly.

I let out a scream and fell back, bumping into Dario. "Call the police. Someone is robbing the bookstore."

He peeked through the hole, too. "Holy cow. You're serious."

"Would I joke about something like this?" I asked, giving

him a flabbergasted shake of my head before looking through the hole again. The man dropped what he'd been holding and ran toward the back of the shop. "Hurry, Dario. He's getting away."

A loud crash, followed immediately by the sound of breaking glass and the shrill whine of a burglar alarm, blared through the shop. The police arrived only moments later, but the intruder, with his ski mask and his expensive suit and his tasseled loafers, had already vanished.

CHAPTER 18

YOU CAN FAKE MANY THINGS, BUT YOU CAN'T FAKE CHEMISTRY.

Officer Anthony Belfiore arrived first on the scene. He rolled his eyes when he saw us. "You two. It figures."

He called Mr. Dalca as soon as he got there, and the elderly man stood staring around his shop in shock. The intruder had strewn Mr. Dalca's books everywhere, and he'd callously torn pages and damaged many covers. As he bent to pick them up, I hurried over to help him.

"Who would do something like this?" I asked.

He shrugged, looking even older than usual. "I'm glad you heard him. It may have been much worse otherwise."

Anthony took out his notepad. "Here we go again," he said. "Tell me what happened."

"We were in the shop...talking," I said, my cheeks getting hot.

Anthony stared at me. "Remind me never to play poker with this one, Dario. She doesn't give a thing away, does she? Okay, so you were making out with my cousin, and...?"

He'd lowered his voice so Mr. Dalca couldn't hear, but now Dario was the one who turned red. "Stop it, Anthony."

ABIGAIL DRAKE

He winked. "I'm teasing. Did you see anything?"

I showed him the hole in the wall, once hidden from view by a set of books on Wiccan ceremonies. Anthony looked at it in confusion. "Did you know about this, Mr. Dalca?"

"No, but it explains why all their noisy noise comes into my shop. Laughing. Talking. Party, party, party. I get no rest."

"Sorry, Mr. Dalca." A thought occurred to me. "You aren't missing a black kitten, are you?"

He almost growled at me. "Do I look like the sort of person who has a *kitten*?"

I wrinkled my nose at him. "I guess not."

"Do you remember anything about the intruder?" asked Anthony.

"He had blue eyes and wore a ski mask. Most of what I saw of him was from the knees down. Oh, and his shoes had tassels and looked expensive."

Dario agreed. "Also, he wore a suit."

"A burglar in a suit?"

"Yes," I said. "And with very muscular thighs."

Anthony snorted. He wrote down everything and turned to Mr. Dalca. "I know it's hard to tell at the moment, but is anything missing?"

Mr. Dalca responded in a tired and monotone voice. "No. Nothing is missing."

My gaze wandered around the shop and I frowned. How did he know the thief didn't steal anything? The place was a mess. Anthony must have thought the same thing.

"Well, let me know once you have more time to go through your things."

Anthony got a call and closed his notebook. "We caught another group of girls dancing naked in the park. Hopefully, they'll be more sober this morning than they were last night." He put his phone into his pocket and smoothed back his hair. He had dark circles under his eyes, and a weary slouch to his well-muscled shoulders. "This is ridiculous. It happens every single weekend now. I spend the whole night rounding them up, and I spend the whole morning doing the paperwork. I don't have time for this right now."

He promised to call Mr. Dalca if he heard anything. Dario pulled me aside. "Do you mind if I go with Anthony? I want to find out more about the naked girls."

I frowned, hoping this had no connection to my shop or my potions. I also didn't like the idea of Dario being interested in chatting with a herd of naked women. "Sure," I said.

"Is something wrong?" He tilted my chin up, and grinned. "Wait...are you *jealous*? I'm asking about the girls for the newspaper."

"I know," I said and kissed him on the lips. Immediately, his arms wrapped around me. I went on my tiptoes to whisper in his ear, "Can you come over later?"

He nuzzled my cheek. "Of course. And I know you wanted to plan our date, but I have tickets tonight for something you might enjoy. What do you think?"

"Sounds good," I said. "Where are we going?"

"You'll see. I want it to be a surprise."

He kissed me once again, so thoroughly my knees wobbled, and left with his cousin. It took me a second to get my bearings. Mr. Dalca muttered to himself as he picked up books from the floor and put them back on the shelves.

"Kissy, kissy nonsense," he said. "Get a room. Please."

I cleared my throat. "Sorry, Mr. Dalca."

I worked by his side in silence, helping him clean up the shop. Before long, we'd put all the undamaged books back in place. A few seemed beyond repair. We left them in a sad little pile next to the cash register.

"You should photograph those for the insurance company."

Mr. Dalca pulled a brand new smart phone out of his pocket. "I am not stupid. That is what I am doing."

"Good." I glanced at the hole in the wall. "Should I fix this?"

He shrugged. "Leave it."

"But our noise bothers you..."

"Maybe not so much anymore."

I held back a smile at Mr. Dalca's softer and less hostile tone. "We should do an inventory."

He shook his head, still going through the books in the pile next to him. "No. The book he wanted was not here."

"What do you mean?" I crossed my arms over my chest and stared at him. "You know who did this."

He gave me a sharply assessing look, his dark, beady eyes alight with intelligence. "I have my suspicions."

"You should tell Officer Belfiore."

He sighed. "This isn't an issue for the police. It's a personal matter."

"Are you sure?" He made a noncommittal noise and went back to the damaged books. He didn't seem to need any more help. "Well, I guess I should get going."

"Yes. You have a hot date tonight."

I thought I heard laughter in his voice, but I could have been mistaken. "You don't miss much, do you, Mr. Dalca?"

He didn't even raise his head. "I miss nothing."

"Okay. Bye."

"Thank you. He may have done more damage if he'd had more time."

"It was nothing."

"It was something."

I turned to leave, but he stopped me. "I will look at the grammar on Monday for you."

"Are you sure? You have a lot on your plate at the moment."

He scowled at me, his bushy brows drawing together above his eyes. "I would not offer if I did not mean it."

"Got it. Thank you, Mr. Dalca."

He made a grumbling noise and went back to his work but didn't seem as annoyed with me as before. Maybe Mr. Dalca was not grumpy at all. Maybe he was a big softy.

I locked up the shop, bought a stack of newspapers from the market, and went straight to Mag's house. Aunt Lucy waved at me from the porch with a copy of the newspaper in her hands.

"Look at me, Gracie. I'm a star."

I grinned at her. "Yes, you are."

Mags sat next to her on a wicker chair. They both wore sweaters. I reached the porch as the first raindrops fell.

"You made it just in time," said Aunt Lucy as Mags went into the kitchen to make tea. "And you brought me more newspapers. Fabulous."

I wheeled her into the house. "I knew you'd want to share with your friends."

"I do. I hope this helps fix things between you and Dario."

I plopped on Mag's soft, floral sofa. "Well, I'm going out with him tonight."

She clapped her hands together. "I'm so happy. This is what you need. Sex makes everything better."

I blinked. "Said no one. Ever."

She looked confused. "I did. Just now."

"Can we *not* talk about this? Please."

Aunt Lucy sighed. "That's one thing I miss. Sex. I was so good at it."

I put my fingers in my ears. "You need to stop. Now."

She giggled. "You act like such a prude, Gracie, but I know the truth."

I took my fingers out of my ears. "What do you mean?"

199

She leaned closer to whisper. "You take after Maeve McAlroy. I do, too. I didn't get her magic, mind you, but I got her other talent."

"And what was that?" I almost didn't want to know.

Aunt Lucy winked at me. "She was a sexual dynamo. A real firecracker, if you know what I mean. A femme fatale."

"Oh, God."

Mags came in with mugs and a steaming pot of tea. "What are you two talking about?"

"Sex," said Aunt Lucy. I whimpered, covering my face with my hands, but she ignored me. "I miss it."

Mags placed a hand on her shoulder. "It's not over 'til it's over. You may find another one like your Anton. You never know."

"What about you, Mags?" I knew her husband died a few years ago, but Mags was still a relatively young woman.

"Oh, hell no," she said it so vehemently both Aunt Lucy and I laughed. Mags laughed, too, the sound warm and rich. "The last thing I need is some crotchety old man telling me what to do and where to go. No thank you."

"That isn't what I saw when I read your cards, Mags," said Aunt Lucy.

Mags gave her a dirty look. "This is one instance when the cards were wrong, Lucinda. It is not going to happen. No way. No how."

Aunt Lucy shrugged. "Well, at least Gracie has a date tonight."

"With Dario?" asked Mags, and I nodded. "Perfect. The phone has been ringing off the hook. We're all so thrilled about what he wrote for the paper. Have you seen him yet today?"

I told them about what happened at Mr. Dalca's shop and they both reacted with appropriate shock and outrage. "Who robs a store in the middle of a Sunday afternoon?"

asked Mags. "Which makes them either extremely stupid or..."

"Or what?" I asked.

When she looked at me, her dark eyes filled with concern. "Or extremely dangerous. I don't like the sound of this. How did he break in without anyone knowing?"

"I'm not sure, but he left through the back. I startled him."

"Thank the goddess you did," said Aunt Lucy. "I still can't believe there's a hole in my wall. He's probably been watching me this whole time. He may have seen me naked."

I sipped my tea, not wanting to know what she meant by the naked comment. "Who?"

"Mr. Dalca. I suspect he has a bit of a crush on me. He is kind of intriguing. I have a thing for beards. And foreigners."

The idea of Aunt Lucy prancing around naked downstairs in the shop didn't even make me blink at this point but the thought of her hooking up with Mr. Dalca? Yikes. A visual I didn't need in my head right now.

"I'd better get going," I said.

"I forgot to tell you my good news," said Aunt Lucy. "They're putting me in a boot. I'll be able to get around on my own in a few days, and then you can go back home."

"Great." The idea of returning to Philly didn't make me very happy. Here I had the shop, my friends, Aunt Lucy, and Dario. Back at school, I had nothing. No students to teach. Nowhere to go. No one to kiss me until my toes curled. I let out a sigh.

Aunt Lucy eyed me curiously. "Unless you don't want to go back yet."

I shifted in my chair. "There's no need to rush."

I told her about Delilah and how she let me use her lab. "Delilah is such a gem," said Aunt Lucy. "I've always had a real soft spot for lesbians, even though I could never be one myself. I'm too fond of men. I love the way they feel, the way they smell, the way they—"

I winced, knowing exactly where this headed, and suspecting Aunt Lucy possessed nymphomaniac tendencies. "Okay. I get it."

"But lesbians are nice. And Jane is a sweetheart, too. I'm so glad they found each other."

"Delilah said you fixed them up."

"Fate brought them together. I provided fate with an instrument on that particular day."

When I got back to the apartment, I sent a text to my fellow TA, Megan, asking if she'd run some samples for me. I jumped into the shower, and when I got out, she'd already replied. I sank onto the couch to read it, wearing a white robe and with a towel wrapped around my damp hair.

Megan said she'd be happy to help and asked if I felt ready for the review board. I didn't, and I had only three weeks left to prepare.

I jumped up and began pacing back and forth, wringing my hands. If I didn't get reinstated, no other respectable academic institution would touch me.

A glance at the clock told me I only had an hour before Dario arrived for our date, and I stopped pacing. I stopped wringing. I stopped worrying. Suddenly, my path seemed perfectly clear.

I whipped the towel off my head and tossed it into the hamper. Instead of fretting about what would happen in November, I decided to make the most of right now. It meant helping my aunt, working on my thesis, and spending time with Dario. Those were my priorities. I lacked control over the people on the review board, but I could control myself and the way I reacted to whatever came my way. That power remained in my hands.

When I looked at myself in the vintage Yves Saint

Laurent dress with its classic lines and various cut outs, I saw a sexy, sophisticated, powerhouse with the guts to go after what she wanted. And I wanted a lot of things, including Dario.

When he came to pick me up, I met him downstairs. He put a hand over his heart when he saw me. "Gracie. Wow."

He helped me into my coat, his fingers brushing against my skin. I leaned back, enjoying the contact with his body. Maybe I *had* inherited something from my long lost great, great grandmother after all.

"Femme fatale." Dario kissed the side of my neck and I froze. How odd to hear Aunt Lucy's words echoing from Dario's lips.

"What did you say?" I asked.

"You look like one of those old Hollywood starlets. Nunny nailed it when she compared you to Sophia Loren. You have the same air about you. Elegant, beautiful, and sexy as hell."

I lifted myself onto my tiptoes to plant a soft kiss on his lips. He made a sound deep in his throat and pulled me close. By the time we broke apart, Dario's eyes gleamed dark with passion.

"We'd better go," he said, and I heard the edge of frustration in his voice. "We have reservations and--"

I put a finger to his lips. "And then we'll finish what we started."

"I'd like that," he said, and promptly bumped into a table near the door. I bit my lip, trying not to laugh, and kind of enjoyed flustering him. Somehow this big, tall man made me the powerful one.

"I'm in so much trouble," he murmured, as he took my hand and led me outside.

Giving him a grin, I squeezed his fingers. He might be right.

CHAPTER 19

IF I COULD BE AN ENZYME, I'D BE DNA HELICASE, SO I COULD UNZIP YOUR GENES.

Dario took me to a Spanish restaurant called Mallorca with delectable food and an impressive wine list. Afterward, we walked to a club, strolling hand and hand along the river. Music pounded from inside and a long line formed on the sidewalk out front.

"Can we get in?" I asked.

"Of course." He winked at me. "We have tickets, and we also know someone in the band."

Dario held my hand and led me through the crowd, which parted for him instantly. He possessed an air of importance, his presence instantly effecting both sexes. Men automatically liked and admired him. They wanted to *be* him. Women, on the other hand, wanted to be *with* him. Dario didn't seem aware of any of it, which made him all the more appealing.

He helped me out of my coat as we walked through the door. His gaze lingered on my dress, making me silently thank Sally for the vintage Yves Saint Laurent.

He leaned close, his voice a husky whisper in my ear. "What are you thinking about?"

"Apodyopsis. The act of mentally undressing someone or

imagining someone naked."

He blinked. "Come again."

"It's what every single woman outside did to you just now."

He looked over his shoulder, his expression comical. "They were not, but the men ogled you."

I shook my head. "I disagree because the men all looked at you, too. They have man crushes on you because you are extremely ogle-able."

"Ogle-able? You throw a word like 'apodyopsis' at me, and follow it up with that?"

He put his hand on the small of my back, his fingers gently caressing my bare skin. I nearly purred and rubbed against him like a cat.

"Where are we going?"

"You'll see." He led me up to the second floor to a reserved table with a good view of the stage and the people dancing below.

I laughed when I saw the man on drums. "Is that Will Wax?"

Will wore a sweat soaked "South Side Slackers" T-shirt. The band sounded good, and Will's drumming was fantastic. The crowd went crazy for him.

"They're one of the hottest bands in the city. They have an album coming out soon. It won't be long before they're touring."

Will grinned the entire time he played. I'd never seen him smile before. He always seemed to be in a perpetual state of gloom in the shop. Now he acted almost giddy. He saw us and waved a drumstick. When the band took a short break, he came up to chat. Several girls stopped to whisper in his ear. Some asked for autographs.

"You're a celebrity," I said, giving him a fist bump.

He smiled, wiping his face with the bottom of his T-shirt.

Will Wax was small, but he had as much of a six-pack as Dario. "Yeah, well, we're local right now. We play at a few clubs in other cities, and we're doing the college circuit, but we're still waiting to hit the big time."

"It won't be long, dude," said Dario, shaking his hand.

"Let's hope," said Will, with a tug of his braided beard. "And thanks for coming tonight. I appreciate it."

Someone bumped into Will, and I looked up to see Ivan Rochat standing directly behind him, with a very irritated Tiffany by his side. "Apologies," he said to Will, giving him a pat on the shoulder. He turned and blinked in surprise when he saw me. "Miss O'Leary?"

Ivan's gaze slid over me, from the top of my head to my toes. He seemed to pause an abnormally long time on the middle part, which brought a frown to Dario's face.

Apodyopsis. Ivan undressed me in his head.

I folded my arms across my chest uncomfortably. "Dario Fontana, this is Ivan Rochat."

Dario eyed him warily before shaking his hand, and he glanced at Tiffany. "Hey, Tiff," he said. "What are you doing here? I didn't think this was your kind of thing."

"Well, I guess you don't know much about me, do you?"

Tension hung thick in the air. Will stood between the two men with a scowl on his face. "Are there any normal sized people in this city?" he asked. "It's like Giant-ville."

Ivan laughed, thinking Will had made a joke. "We're enjoying your performance, Mr. Wax."

"Thank you," said Will, tugging at his sweaty T-shirt. "Uh, I'd better get back to work."

Oddly enough, Will didn't look as strange in a darkened club as he did in the daylight. His kohl lined eyes and braided beard made him sort of hot and mysterious, or at least it seemed that way, judging by the reaction of most of the girls in the club.

"We should take our leave, Tiffany, before the music begins," said Ivan. "Goodbye, Miss O'Leary. Delightful seeing you again."

I moved to shake his hand, and he surprised me by bringing it to his mouth and kissing it. Dario stiffened, but Ivan ignored him, his lips lingering on my skin a few seconds longer than necessary. An electric jolt surged through my body again, exactly like it had when he touched me in front of the shop. Ivan's eyes met mine, and I knew he felt it, too. If I'd been in a lab, I would have wanted to analyze it because the whole thing puzzled me.

Tiffany studied both of us with interest, before turning to Dario. "Will I see you at work tomorrow?"

"No, I'm covering the Steelers game in Philly. I'll see you when I get back."

Will and his band resumed playing, and we sat through their last set in awkward silence. It would have been nearly impossible to chat over the music, but Dario didn't seem inclined to make an effort. He glowered, his gaze roaming the room, deep in thought.

After the band finished playing, he helped me put on my jacket and we left the club. Will, surrounded by groupies, waved goodbye. Once outside, Dario started walking, his shoulders hunched. I nearly ran to keep up with him.

"Um, Dario. I'm wearing heels. If I'd known we were going for a jog, I'd have put on running shoes."

He slowed immediately. "Sorry, Grace. I..." A muscle worked in his jaw. "How do you know Ivan Rochat? Is there something going on between the two of you?"

"No. Why ask such a thing?"

"Well, apodyopsis."

I came to a dead stop in the middle of the sidewalk. "On my part?"

He leaned against a guiderail and looked out at the river,

his hands gripping the metal. "No, but he did it to you. And then the whole hand-kissing thing. So freaking suave and European of him."

Dario Fontana was jealous. Not a hypothesis, but a fact. It made a warm glow shoot out from my heart and spread all over my body.

I grabbed his hand and made him turn around so I could face him. "There's nothing going on. I just met him. I talked with him twice and invited him to our Halloween party because he's new in town."

He rolled his eyes. "You invited him to your party? Oh, great."

"Do you want me to uninvite him?"

"No." He shoved his hands in his pockets and looked at his feet, kicking a stone with his shoe. "He's way too interested in you."

"Well, I'm not interested in him." I moved closer, my body only inches away from his. "But I am interested in you, and I'm not sorry you asked me out again."

He gave me a sheepish grin. "You sort of asked me this time."

"Yeah. You're right. I sort of did." I pressed closer to him. His hands immediately slid inside my coat to caress my bare back and I sighed. "Can we stop talking about Ivan now?"

"Yes, please."

We walked, hand in hand, and ended up in front of an elegant brownstone. The imposing oak door contained a small, circular window made with brightly colored bottle glass.

"I love this door. Whose house is it?"

He pulled a key out of his pocket. "Mine. Would you like to come in?"

Would I ever.

"Sure."

We went inside and I instantly fell in love with the tall ceilings and elegant staircase. A living room on the left, decorated in muted greys and blues, caught my eye, and an equally tasteful formal dining room sat on the right. The house, well preserved from a historical perspective, included modern touches to make it seem fresh and new.

"I used the money I made from hockey to buy it, and the rest I invested. Since the salary of a sports reporter for a small paper is barely above the poverty line, I'm awfully glad I did. It takes away the stress and allows me to do what I enjoy."

"You're lucky. You found a life for yourself after hockey. That's remarkable. When you spend your whole life building a dream, and it comes crashing down around you, it's not easy to pick up the pieces and move on. You did, and I admire you for that."

He watched my face as I took it all in, lacing his fingers with mine and leading me right into a completely renovated kitchen. He pulled me close, his hands on my hips, and gave me one soft kiss.

"Now, for the reason I brought you here," he said.

My eyes widened and my heart pounded. This could be it. *Let it be sex. Let it be sex.*

He gave me a naughty grin, let go of me, and pulled a giant tiramisu out of the fridge. "I made dessert."

He cooked, too? Could he be more perfect?

"Wait...*you* made this? Not Nunny?"

"She taught me the recipe years ago. I make it myself now."

He ran his finger along the side and put it in my mouth. My taste buds exploded with the flavors of coffee, chocolate, mascarpone cheese, and cream. Not as good as sex, but still pretty fantastic.

"Oh, sweet baby Jesus," I said with a moan. I licked the

rest of it off his finger. Seeing his eyes immediately fill with lust made me bold. I put my hands on his wrist and sucked on his finger, teasing it with my tongue.

"Grace," he said, his voice a tortured whisper.

He pressed me against the island, and I let out a happy sigh as I wrapped my arms around him. That sigh turned into a moan when he tilted his head and kissed me.

"You taste even better than the tiramisu," I said.

I tangled my fingers in his hair, wanting him even closer. He accommodated me. When I pushed his jacket from his shoulders, he yanked off his tie, his eyes hot, cheeks flushed, and breathing unsteady. Dario Fontana on a normal day was heart-stoppingly gorgeous. Dario Fontana fully aroused and partially undressed was a wonder to behold. Six and a half feet of pure muscle and smooth, golden skin.

I opened his shirt slowly, letting my fingers skim his naked flesh. He watched my face the whole time, his eyes dark with passion. As soon as I got his shirt off, I worked on his pants and tried to unbuckle his belt. The belt proved to be more complicated than I expected. He let out a shaky laugh as I struggled with it, but stopped laughing when I undid his zipper, and my hand touched his erection.

Early experiments designed to freeze time were a joke, completely unscientific, but as Dario kissed me, I wondered if freezing time might actually be possible. Right now, we seemed suspended in a moment. For the first time in my life I couldn't think. I couldn't worry. I couldn't even analyze.

He put his hands on my thighs and slid them up beneath my dress. The only barrier between us was the smooth cotton of his tight black undershorts and the thin lace of my panties. When he reached to stroke me between my legs, I grew frantic. He shuddered against me and let out a curse.

"Damn it, Grace. This isn't how I planned it...on the kitchen island..."

I continued kissing him and stroking him, unable to stop myself even if I tried. He let out a strangled noise and lifted me so he could remove my panties in one swift motion. I pushed down his shorts, moving closer to give him better access.

He brought me to the edge of the island and paused, looking deep into my eyes. "Are you sure this is what you want?" he asked.

I cupped his face in my hands and stared directly into his eyes, just so he knew we were clear on this. "Hell yes."

He laughed, a deep and sexy sound, and reached to the floor to get a condom out of the pocket of his pants. "Semper paratus," he said as he slipped it on.

Always prepared. The idea he could use Latin at a time like this almost put me over the edge. "Now. Dario. Please."

His gaze locked on mine as he thrust into me, filling me completely. He reached a point inside me I never knew existed as he kissed my neck and murmured sweet words against my skin.

I still wore my dress. Dario's pants remained bunched around his ankles, his shoes still on his feet. We did this in the middle of his kitchen, right next to a tray of tiramisu, but all I could think about was how Dario Fontana made me feel. Wild. Wanton. Crazed with desire.

I came quickly, my release overwhelming me with its power and intensity, and Dario soon followed, shuddering against me with a groan. At that moment, I realized something important. This was what I'd been looking for, what I'd been missing, and if Jonathan hadn't broken up with me, I may have spent my entire life unfulfilled, sexually repressed, and a little cranky.

I realized something else as well. I *was* a femme fatale. What a delightful surprise.

CHAPTER 20

I STUDY CHEMISTRY BECAUSE 'BADASS INTELLECTUAL GODDESS' IS NOT AN OFFICIAL MAJOR.

After we returned to our senses, Dario sat next to me on the island in his tight, black underpants and fed me tiramisu. We ate straight from the tray, our legs brushing against each other. He kissed me between bites and couldn't stop smiling.

"Sex makes you awfully happy, Mr. Fontana."

He grinned and gave me a kiss. "*You* make me awfully happy."

After we ate our fill, he led me upstairs to his bedroom, his hand clasping mine. He had a gigantic bed, abstract art hanging on his walls, and piles of books resting on his nightstand. More books sat in neatly arranged stacks on the floor.

"There is nothing sexier than a man who reads," I said with a happy sigh as I eyed the books, reading quickly over the titles. He possessed eclectic tastes, which made my insides go all warm and fuzzy. "Except for a man who makes a killer tiramisu."

He grinned. "I do dishes, too."

"Be still my heart."

I sat on the edge of his bed. He knelt in front of me, and

the fire in his sexy, dark eyes held promises of things to come. Wild things. Unexpected things. Things I'd wanted to do since the first moment I met him.

"What are you thinking about?" he asked as he slid a hand up my calf.

"Resonance."

He laughed. "Of course." He trailed a finger up over my knee, made a slow circle, and placed both his hands on my bare thighs. "Do you care to explain?"

Why did I always blurt out my unfiltered musings to Dario Fontana? It made me sound like such a weirdo.

"Well, resonance is something in physics," I explained. "A series of waves and vibrations."

"Yes. When one object vibrates at the same natural frequency as a second object, it makes the second object vibrate as well." His lips followed the same path his hands took up my leg, making it difficult for me to concentrate.

"Oh, God, Dario. You are so....smart."

He grinned, his hair falling over his forehead. "Not the compliment I expected at the moment, but I'll take it."

I cupped his cheeks in my hands. "You *are* smart. Really smart. Brilliant, in fact." I kissed him, working my way across his high cheekbones to nibble on his ear lobe. "And I find your intelligence sexy, too. Even more than all your books. Or your tiramisu. Or your..." He shivered as I whispered in his ear, telling him exactly which parts of him were sexiest and all the dirty things I wanted to do to him.

"Time to get you out of this dress, Miss O'Leary." He unzipped it, sliding it off my arms.

"But we haven't finished discussing resonance yet."

"No, we haven't." His eyes widened when he saw my black lace push-up bra. "Oh, Grace."

I looked at the expanse of white bosom and sighed. "I know. My cups overfloweth."

"No complaints here." He kissed the curve of each breast. "Now tell me about resonance."

I held his head close as he continued kissing my breasts through my bra, cupping them with his huge hands. I took an unsteady breath.

"Music is created because of resonance. Sounds vibrating off surfaces. A hollow space, like inside a French horn, increases the vibration and creates the sweetest sound."

He unhooked my bra and held my breasts, staring at them with something akin to awe. I'd always been self-conscious about my large bust, but the look in his eyes made me feel almost proud.

"I love it when you talk physics to me," he growled. "You make it so damned adorable."

He took one nipple in his mouth and I arched my back to give him better access. "But there is resonance in chemistry, too. It involves bonding and the delocalization of electrons within molecules."

"The delocalization of electrons?" He paused and stared at my face. "You thought about electrons as we made love?"

"I couldn't help it. There's an overlap between the two definitions. An interesting phenomenon."

"Please explain."

My cheeks got hot. "I was that hollow space. Empty. You delocalized everything inside me, and I shattered. Waves...vibrations..."

"Resonance." He reached up to cup my cheek in his hand. "I was hollow, too."

"You were?"

He kissed me deeply with something close to reverence. "Yes, and I love the way your mind works," he said. "I want to know what is going on inside your head. I'm obsessed with it. I love the rest of you, too. The satiny touch of your skin. The color of your eyes." He wound a lock of hair around his finger.

"And I love your hair. It's so bright, like holding a flame in my hands." He looked at my breasts and sighed. "I love those, too."

I giggled. "I kind of noticed."

He stared into my eyes, all joking aside. "I love everything about you."

For a second, I couldn't remember how to breathe. Logically, I knew it to be an involuntary bodily function, oxygen in, carbon dioxide out, but suddenly I'd forgotten how to do it. Fortunately, my lungs remembered, and I exhaled with a funny little noise, sounding oddly like a gasp.

"I love everything about you, too."

He stood up to take off his shorts. In the kitchen, our lovemaking had been frantic, hungry, and desperate. Now he meant to take his time. I saw it in his eyes. He pressed close to me, and I gasped at the sensation of his skin against mine. He took charge, exploring my body with his massive hands and his sweet, clever lips. When we came together, in one simultaneous, shuddering, earthshattering climax, he stared at me, his eyes filled with joy and wonder.

"Resonance," he said, his voice husky and unsteady. "I think that may be my new favorite physics term."

I let out a surprised laugh. "Tell me the truth. Did you honestly have a favorite physics term before I brought it up?" I asked. "Or are you saying that to make me go all geeky and mushy inside?"

"Well, until tonight, the one electron universe model was my favorite," he said. "The derivation of the Dirac equation came in as a close second. But you changed all that when you introduced me to resonance."

He curled up on the bed, holding me close to him with my back against his chest and placed a soft kiss on my shoulder. I let out a happy sigh.

"Resonance. Best. Thing. Ever."

I hated leaving a sleepy, sexy, warm, and tousled Dario Fontana in the morning, but he had to go to Philadelphia to cover a football game. I woke as the sun rose in the sky. I kissed his scruffy cheek and searched for my clothing. He rolled out of bed with a groan and slipped into a pair of pajama pants.

"You can stay and sleep longer if you want," he said. "I'll give you a key."

I smiled at him, oddly energetic in spite of my lack of sleep. "I need to put the final touches on my thesis and restock the shelves at the shop. I'd better go."

"Are you going to make more love potions?"

I giggled as he pulled me into his arms. "I might. But I'd better get prepared for my review board hearing. I'm dreading it. Seth Billings, the student who says he found the copy of my test key on the floor of the classroom, is an entitled jerk who has so far managed to get through school based only on his name."

"What do you mean?"

"His father owns Billings Industries."

Dario's eyes widened. "Seth's father is Silas Billings?"

"Yep. He owns one of the largest chemical-producing companies in the eastern United States. And, from what I've heard, he's bound and determined that Seth graduate from his alma mater and follow in his footsteps. The trouble is Seth has zero aptitude for chemistry. In all honesty, he seems to hate the subject. It almost makes me sad for him."

"I'm not sad for him at all," he said, his face darkening.

Dario believed in my innocence so completely it did funny things to my heart. "The thing I can't understand is, how did he get my key? I know for certain I put it in my briefcase the night after the exam."

"Did anyone else have access to your briefcase?"

I bit my lip. "Jonathan, since we shared an apartment.

And I guess anyone who walked into the TA office that morning. I left it briefly on my desk when I used the ladies' room." I shook my head. "Our department has a reputation, a code of honor. *Sapientia et Veritas*."

"Knowledge and Truth."

"Yes, but one of my colleagues or students purposefully set out to ruin my life and my reputation." I still couldn't think about it without getting a sharp pang in my stomach. "It's against what we're supposed to stand for."

He pushed a lock of hair behind my ear. "It's hard for you to imagine because you're a good person. You have to think like a bad guy to understand a bad guy's motives."

I struggled to maintain my composure but found it hard in the face of such support and trust. I cleared my throat and glanced at the clock on the stand next to his bed. "I'd better go. You have to get moving or you won't make it to Philly in time for the game."

"Let me make you a cup of coffee. I insist." He pulled me close, his nose in my hair. "Mmmmm. You always smell so good. Like cinnamon and cloves and fresh air and--"

"I know. Pumpkin pie, right?"

He paused, thinking about it, and his eyes lit up. "You smell like fall."

I wrinkled my nose at him. "Moldy leaves and rotting vegetables?"

"Not even close," he said, kissing my cheek. He took my hand and led me downstairs and into his kitchen. As he ground the beans for the coffee, his broad back turned toward me, I realized exactly how much I cared for him.

"I think you're amazing," I said.

Dario shot me a confused smile. "Because I'm making you coffee?"

"Yes. I mean, no. I mean..." I paused, because I'd never

felt this way before and it made me a little uncomfortable. "I just wanted to tell you."

Dario came close and stared deeply into my eyes. What I saw there was so pure and honest it made my breath hitch in my chest.

"I think you're amazing, too." He gave me a long, sweet kiss that made my knees go weak. "Especially when you look at me like that," he said, with a cheeky grin. He went back to making the coffee and I sat at the island, pressing my thighs together and trying to ignore the aching need between my legs. If I wasn't careful, I'd turn into a nympho like Aunt Lucy. I seemed halfway there already.

I tried very hard to think of something other than sex. "How exactly do I look at you?"

"Usually, you're analyzing. Thinking all the time. Worrying about things I can't even begin to imagine. But when I kiss you, it all goes away, and you look..." He paused in the middle of measuring out the coffee and putting it into the hi-tech stainless-steel machine on his counter. "Befuddled."

"Befuddled? And you find this attractive?"

Leaning across the island, he kissed me. "Yes. Because you look both befuddled and aroused at the same time."

He gave me a hot cup of coffee and made me a breakfast of eggs cooked inside thick slices of Italian bread. We sat side by side at his island and ate.

"Thank you," I said.

"I couldn't send you off hungry." He gave me a wink.

He got dressed and insisted on driving me home. When we arrived at the shop, he walked me to the door. "Thank you for last night."

I went up on my tiptoes and kissed him senseless right in the middle of the sidewalk. Now *he* was the one who looked adorably befuddled. "My pleasure, Dario."

His gaze caressed my face. "Can I see you when I get back?"

"Of course." My heart actually fluttered. Ridiculous.

"I'll stop by after work on Tuesday." He gave me one last, long, lingering glance. "I can't wait to see you again."

I bit my lip. "You, too."

I went up to the apartment, feeling like I walked on air, but as I undressed and got ready to shower, a strange sense of foreboding hit me. I hesitated, naked, as warm steam filled the bathroom. I wanted to keep his scent on my skin as long as possible.

Jinx sat on the toilet seat, watching me, and I rolled my eyes. "You're right. I'm being silly."

I summed it up to my old fears getting the better of me, but as I put soap on a washcloth and scrubbed myself clean, I couldn't shake the uneasiness in the pit of my stomach. I wrapped a fluffy pink towel around my head and another around my body. When I looked in the fogged-up mirror, I almost didn't recognize myself. My eyes were bright, my cheeks rosy, and my whole body hummed with joy. I pulled the towel tighter around my torso. Even if the voice inside me told me something bad hovered on the horizon, I chose to ignore it. I felt happy, and I refused to let anyone steal it from me, even myself.

CHAPTER 21

LAB RULE #1: IF YOU DON'T KNOW WHAT A
BUTTON DOES, DON'T PRESS IT. EVER.

In spite of my best efforts to hide it, Mrs. Periwinkle knew exactly what happened as soon as she walked through the door Monday morning. She glided into the shop, her signature blue heels clicking on the tile floor, humming a tune. She came to a dead stop as soon as she saw my face.

"At last," she said.

I stood next to the cash register, arranging necklaces on a display tree. The pretty crystals sparkled in the soft morning light, making a rainbow on the wall next to me as they dangled on delicate silver chains. I picked out one in my favorite shade of green and put it over my head. It looked nice with my green cashmere twinset and black skirt, and the color matched my eyes. I felt indulgent today, and pretty, too. I hadn't even bothered with the glasses, and I'd pulled back my hair with a green satin ribbon instead of putting it in my usual serious, no-nonsense bun.

I looked up at Mrs. Periwinkle, distracted. "What?"

She gave me a knowing smile. "You finally slept with Dario Fontana."

She breezed past me and went to the back of the shop to get a cup of coffee, leaving me stunned. I nearly knocked over the necklaces and steadied the display so it wouldn't crash to the ground.

"How did you know?" I asked in a hushed voice when she walked back into the room. No one else occupied the shop, but I whispered anyway.

She tweaked my chin with one perfectly manicured, dainty hand. "It's written all over your face, pet."

I felt different on the inside because of what happened with Dario, but I had no idea it was so obvious from the outside as well. I tried to keep my expression neutral when Aunt Lucy arrived at the shop, but she figured it out as quickly as Mrs. Periwinkle. She hobbled in with a walker, her foot in a boot instead of a cast, took one look at me, and grinned.

"Ohhhh, Gracie got laid," she said.

"Aunt Lucy. Hush."

I put a finger to my lips, looking around in a panic. The shop was empty, but people milled about outside, waiting for the doors to open. The closer it got to Halloween, the busier it became. I hoped no one heard her. Aunt Lucy didn't possess an inside voice.

"Is it so obvious?"

Aunt Lucy laughed. "You're glowing, my sweet. Either you got laid or you have a bun in the oven. It's only one or the other. Unless it's both..." She gave me a penetrating look.

"It *isn't* both," I hissed.

"Well, good, because the cards told me you and Dario won't have a baby for at least three years."

I froze. "The cards indicated I'd have a baby with Dario? You said they told you about animals or snakes in my coffee or something."

She tilted her head to one side and narrowed her eyes at

me. "Did you even pay attention? I told you there were people to watch out for, but I also said some people would help you. And I'm pretty certain I mentioned things I couldn't share yet."

"And having a baby with Dario Fontana was one of those things? It seems like an incredibly vague warning for something awfully specific, Aunt Lucy."

She acted like we discussed the weather and not my entire future. She slowly made her way over to the cash register, propped herself up on a stool, and organized the cash drawer as she spoke.

"Well, you're going to marry him first, of course. It'll be in the fall, which is always gorgeous. Pumpkins. Leaves. A slight chill in the air. My favorite time of year for a wedding."

A wave of happiness rolled over me. Logically, I knew it to be complete and utter nonsense, but part of me wanted to believe it. "Really?"

She patted my hand. "And you'll live happily ever after. I saw it in the cards. That much came out very clear, and I'm never wrong. I didn't want to tell you before because I knew you'd get all strange and skittish. I decided things would work out better on their own and look at what happened. I bet he's good in the sack. I can usually spot them a mile away. And he's a very *big* man, too."

Mrs. Periwinkle giggled as she stocked shelves. "You know what they say, the bigger the sock, the bigger the—"

"Stop right there, Mrs. Periwinkle." I narrowed my eyes at both of them. "We're not going to discuss this. Got it?"

Aunt Lucy winked at me. "Whatever you say, dearie. I've always admired people who don't kiss and tell. I never could. And during sex I was quite the screamer. Our neighbors called the police once. Anton found it hilarious. He always did have such a wicked sense of humor."

I put my face in my hands. "Can you please stop?"

Aunt Lucy lifted her hands in surrender. "Sorry. You can be such a little Puritan sometimes. It's good Dario brings out the wanton woman in you. If you suppress it too long, there could be physical repercussions. Sleeping with him was nearly a medical necessity at this point. Oh. I'll bet he's a good kisser, too."

The memory of Dario's kisses brought a warm flush to my skin. A head to toe flush. A dead giveaway flush. Mrs. Periwinkle giggled even harder.

"I think you're right, Lucy."

I managed to survive their teasing and innuendo all morning. When Mr. Dalca came in, not long after Mrs. Periwinkle left for the day, I embraced the distraction. He stood at the entrance to the shop, his hat in his hands, peering around nervously at the crowd of customers.

"Look at him. It's like a wizard and a hobbit had a love child," said Will under his breath. I nudged him with my elbow and gave Mr. Dalca a friendly wave. He greeted me with his usual frown.

"I have come to look at your grammar, as I promised, but it seems you are busy right now. I will come back later."

"It's okay," I said, leading him to one of the velvet chairs near the window. "Will can handle it, and my aunt Lucy is here, too."

His eyes widened when he saw Aunt Lucy sitting on her stool and chatting with customers as she rang them up. She wore a bright purple dress and a matching jaunty hat. Happy to be back in the shop and around people again, her eyes twinkled brightly, the sound of her laughter contagious.

Mr. Dalca swallowed hard. "I did not know she'd come back already. I thought she was staying with a friend."

He seemed strangely interested in Aunt Lucy's whereabouts. "She is, mostly because she still can't manage the steps to the apartment."

Aunt Lucy glanced over at us. When her eyes met Mr. Dalca's, an odd tremor went through the air. For a moment, it felt like they were the only two people in the room. It ended almost as soon as it started, and I kind of wondered if I'd imagined the whole thing.

"Let us get back to business," he said, but his gaze kept straying to Aunt Lucy. She seemed to enjoy the attention. A lot of eyelash batting and hair fluffing ensued. She even undid the top few buttons of her dress, fanning her face like she was hot, the minx. Mr. Dalca patted his cheeks with his handkerchief. Droplets of sweat appeared on his forehead. Witnessing their mating ritual unfold was as engrossing as watching an episode of *National Geographic*.

"Bring me the book, Miss O'Leary," he said, his voice oddly strained.

"Certainly."

I scurried up to the apartment to get the grimoire and experienced the same pleasure I always did when I touched it. I shook my head, laughing at myself. I currently operated on a lot of good sex, very little sleep, and some awfully strong coffee, all courtesy of Mr. Dario Fontana. No wonder I imagined things at this point.

I made up a tray with two cups of tea and brought it out for Mr. Dalca and myself. He refused the sugar. "I like it bitter," he said.

"I bet you do," I said under my breath. He raised a bushy eyebrow at my words. I gave him a sunny smile in return. Nothing could ruin my good mood today. Not even a grumpy old man or my horny aunt.

When he saw the grimoire, his expression grew rapt. "This is the book you mentioned?"

"Yes. What do you think of it?"

He took the grimoire in his hands, studied the back and the front, and looked inside. "This book, she is lovely," he said as he leafed through the pages. "And she is very old, from the late seventeenth century. I'd guess around 1690."

I enjoyed the way he referred to the book as a female, like a ship. I kind of thought of it as a girl book, too.

"Wow. I didn't realize it was so old. It's in such good shape."

"It is indeed remarkable. The penmanship is impeccable, and the illustrations are lovely. This is a special book."

He touched a drawing of a sprig of lavender on one of the pages, his gnarled fingers gentle and his expression oddly sweet and serene. As I watched him, I wondered if he also experienced a strange sort of connection to the grimoire. Mr. Dalca acted almost mesmerized by it. By *her*.

"Do you feel something when you touch it?" I asked, keeping my voice as low as possible.

"Yes," he said, his dark eyes locked on mine. "I feel happy because I know this book is worth a lot of money."

My shoulders slumped. "Is that it?"

"What else do you want me to say, Ms. O'Leary?"

I sighed. "Nothing, I guess."

"Okay. I will say nothing, but I do have a question. Can you read this?" He pointed to the writing inside the book.

"Yes. It's Latin. I learned it in school."

He snorted. "This isn't the Latin you can learn in a classroom. *Veni, vidi, vici,* and all that useless garbage. This is Latin mixed with other languages. Ancient languages. Languages a young girl like you should not know. Languages long forgotten, and only used by a handful of scholars and practitioners."

"Practitioners?"

"Of the magical arts."

A customer opened the door and a gust of wind blew through the shop, making the decorative chimes hanging near the door clatter and causing me to jump a few inches in my chair. Mr. Dalca freaked me out.

"Look, Mr. Dalca. Some of the words were unclear, so I skipped them. I read the Latin words and figured out the rest based on common sense and a great deal of experience with chemical formulas. It's logical. Each of the 'potions' follow standard scientific practices, even if they are nonsense."

"Nonsense?" He made a growling sound deep in his throat. "If this is how you think about it, you do not need this book. I will buy her from you."

I resisted an urge to grab the grimoire right out of Mr. Dalca's hairy hands. I had no interest in selling it. I didn't even like other people touching it. I opened my mouth to speak, but Aunt Lucy answered for me.

"It isn't for sale."

She stood right behind me, balancing in her new boot and giving Mr. Dalca the death stare. I hadn't heard her approach, oddly enough. She made a lot of noise with the walker and the boot and her various charms and jewelry tinkling with each step she took. Aunt Lucy's many necklaces and bracelets delivered the same effect as bells on a cow. She normally couldn't sneak up on anyone.

Mr. Dalca took a long sip of his tea. "Everything is for sale. It is a matter of price. I will pay you well for this ratty old thing."

She shook her head, her blue eyes blazing. "We've kept it in the family for more than three hundred years. It belongs to Grace."

"And I'll never sell it." I snatched the book out of his hands and held it close to my chest. "Sorry, Mr. Dalca."

He stood up with a grunt. "Sorry? You are sorry? I am

sorry I wasted my time like this. Silly women with a silly shop. I am leaving now."

"Goodbye, Mr. Dalca. Thank you," I said.

He narrowed his furry eyebrows. "But I have one final thing to say. It is a warning."

I frowned at him, confused by his tone. "Are you threatening me, Mr. Dalca?"

He made a sound of pure disgust. "I am not threatening you. Why would I threaten you? I am trying to stop you from making a big mistake because you are obviously stupid."

Aunt Lucy's face grew as red as her hair. "Don't insult my niece, you cruel old man."

She stood nose to nose with him, almost exactly the same height. If the situation weren't so tense, I may have found it comical. Sort of like watching hobbits battle.

But nothing funny showed in Mr. Dalca's demeanor at the moment. His gaze bored into Aunt Lucy's, his expression harsh, even though his voice came out soft. "You are the cruel one, Madame Lucinda. You know she has the gift and you are using her. Exploiting her. For profit. You fill your shelves with her magic even though you know there will be consequences and she alone will have to face them."

Our customers started to take an interest in their discussion, gawking at them as Mr. Dalca's once quiet voice rose in volume. "What are you talking about, Mr. Dalca?" I asked while faking a smile for the benefit of our patrons.

His gaze stayed on Aunt Lucy, but suddenly he looked tired and resigned instead of angry. "She knows. She will tell you. Just remember, some things, once damaged, never fully heal. They stay broken. Forever."

He walked toward the door, his steps uneven and his gait slow. He stopped, his hand on the doorknob and turned to face us. I felt as if some kind of war waged inside of him, as if he was deciding how much he wanted to tell us. Finally, he spoke.

"Your grammar holds white magic. Pure. I can even call it innocent. It should not be misused, but there is no malevolence about it. No evil. Not all magical objects are the same. There is one so powerful and dark, in the wrong hands it could be dangerous. If you find it, do not play with it. Don't try to use it. The consequences will be horrific. For everyone."

A chill swept over my body. "I don't believe in magic. I believe in science."

He laughed, shaking his head. "That is why I call you stupid. You *are* magic. You don't even believe in yourself."

"Have a nice day, Mr. Dalca."

He waved a hand at me, making a sound of complete disgust, and walked out the door. Aunt Lucy shook her head. "What an irritating, impossible man."

"At least he told me how old the grimoire is," I said.

She rolled her eyes. "We already knew that much, silly."

"What do you mean?"

She showed me the spine of the book. Delicately embossed in the fragile leather were the numbers 1690. Aunt Lucy ran her finger gently down the front. I almost heard the book purr.

"And she died only a few years later. I suspect she knew what was coming and wrote down all these things so her ancestors could use the information in the future. Poor Maeve McAlroy."

"Why do you say that? How did she die?"

Aunt Lucy gave me an odd look. "She was hung for being a witch, of course. Her own husband accused her of sorcery, and the entire town believed him."

"How awful," I said as I imagined my redheaded ancestor

furiously scribbling in the grimoire, trying to record her knowledge for posterity.

Aunt Lucy let out a sigh. "Mr. Dalca was right. I should have been more honest with you, but I didn't think you were ready. Now, it's finally time to tell you the truth."

"The truth about what?"

Her blue eyes locked on mine, and for a moment I swear the earth shifted on its axis. "Maeve McAlroy was a witch. And so are you."

CHAPTER 22

LOVE IS IN THE AIR? WRONG. NITROGEN, OXYGEN, AND CARBON DIOXIDE ARE IN THE AIR.

I stared at her, my mouth agape. I wanted to respond to her ridiculous comment immediately and nip the whole "Grace is a witch" thing in the bud, but I got distracted when Sally charged into the shop, tears streaming down her face. Aggie trailed behind her.

"Have you seen Bubu?" asked Sally.

I shook my head, taking her by the arm and handing her a tissue. "What happened?"

"Who is Bubu?" asked Will.

Sally dabbed her eyes. "My Yorkie-poo," she said. "She's gone."

Although born male, Sally insisted Bubu also identified as female, in other words, a transgender Yorkie-poo. I agreed with her. Bubu was the girliest dog I'd ever seen.

"I'll go look down the street," said Aggie. "We wouldn't want Bubu to end up in traffic."

As Aggie ran out the door, Sally let out a wail, and leaned against me. Heavily. She was so distraught and emotional, I feared she might pass out. I led her to a chair by the window and brought her a cold compress. It seemed to help. Aunt

Lucy sat next to her, holding her hand. Will poured her a cup of hot tea, and she spoke between small, hitching sobs.

"Bubu always sleeps in her little bed, right in the corner of my room. It's the most adorable bed with four posters and a canopy. I woke up this morning, and she wasn't there. I thought she must have gone to the kitchen, so I got dressed and ready. I took my good old time with it, too, because I had trouble finding the perfect outfit. Nothing seemed right today, and I could just kick myself. When I saw she wasn't in the kitchen, I panicked. I looked through every inch of my apartment, but I couldn't find her. She's gone."

This brought on a fresh flood of tears. I knelt beside her. "We'll go back to your apartment together and have another look. If she isn't there, we'll walk around the neighborhood."

Sally hiccupped. "Would you, Gracie? I tried to call Ralphie, but he must be in a meeting. He isn't answering his phone."

I helped her up and turned to Aunt Lucy and Will. "Can the two of you mind the store for a few minutes?"

Aunt Lucy squeezed my hand. "Of course, dearest. Go help Sally."

We looked through Sally's shop and her apartment but found no sign of Bubu. We'd decided to give up and search outside of the building, when I noticed a pile of papers on the floor in Sally's living room.

"I must have knocked those over this morning," said Sally as I bent to pick them up. "I was in such a state I didn't even notice."

I put them on her coffee table, and my heart thudded to a stop in my chest. On top of the pile sat a note made of letters cut out from magazines.

I HAVE UR DOG. YOU'LL GET HER BACK WHEN U CLOSE UR SHOP AND LEAVE, U QUEER.

Like the other note, it read like text-speak. Sally knew

right away something was wrong from the look on my face. "What is it, Gracie?"

I handed the note to her and watched the color drain from her face. "Ralphie was right. He told me we should move. We've argued about it for weeks. I should have listened to him. If I had, Bubu might still be with me."

She sank onto the couch, the note clutched in her hands. She looked shell shocked, a nearly catatonic glaze in her eyes.

"I'm going to call Officer Belfiore," I said.

I wondered if I should call an ambulance, too, but Sally snapped out of it by the time Anthony Belfiore arrived. He walked through the house, inspecting the doors and windows.

"It's all locked up tight," he said. "And it doesn't look like someone broke in through the front door. Was it locked when you woke up this morning?"

She nodded. "Ralphie always locks it on his way to work. He's ever so careful."

Ralphie raced into the apartment, his eyes frantic. "What happened? Where is Bubu?"

Sally clung to his impeccably ironed shirt. "She's gone, Ralphie. Someone stole our baby." He patted her back, making soothing noises.

I checked my watch and spoke quietly to Ralphie. "I have to get back to work. Is she going to be okay?"

Ralphie thanked me, and said she'd be fine, but I felt bad leaving her. I needed to get back to the shop, but I called several times to check on her. When my phone rang later that evening, I thought it might be Sally, but it wasn't.

"Hey, beautiful," said Dario.

The sound of his voice on the phone made me smile. Not a little smile. A big, goofy, grin. I'd been sitting by the fireplace in the apartment, sipping a glass of wine and holding Jinx on my lap as I worked my way through Aunt Lucy's private bookshelf. Her tastes ran on the eclectic side, and I was immersed in a rather racy little book of Victorian erotica when Dario called.

"What are you doing?" he asked.

I glanced down at the book in my hands. It showed women doing nearly impossible things in corsets. "Um. Reading."

I told him about what happened to Sally today. "Now Bubu is missing?" he asked, fury and sadness in every word. "Poor Sally. Why would someone take her dog?"

"The weird part is she locked all the doors and windows. Anthony has no idea how someone got in. They're analyzing the note right now, but it seems like the others. I doubt they'll find anything." I heard a beeping noise. It sounded like he was in a car. "Where are you?"

"I'm about to meet with someone for an interview. I've tried to track down this guy all day. It turns out he frequents a bar right next to my hotel. I'm heading back there now. I wanted to make sure we were still on for tomorrow night."

"Yes," I said, smiling in that same silly way once again. Thank goodness this wasn't a video chat. "Let's have dinner here."

"Good," he said, and I heard a smile in his voice, too. "I'll be there around seven."

I spent the whole day counting the minutes until Dario's visit. I'd never been a great cook, but I thought about attempting to make a real meal for him. In the interest of public safety and after remembering several near fatal instances from my past, I decided against it and ordered take out instead.

I put on my shortest skirt and a silky blouse. I unbuttoned it far enough to show off the curve of my breasts and the edge of my lacy bra. I set the table with Aunt Lucy's best china and two long white tapers in silver candlesticks. An elegant gold tablecloth, matching cloth napkins, and crystal cut wine glasses completed the look. I wasn't a great cook, but I could set a table.

When the food arrived, Indian curry, it smelled so good my mouth watered. I put it in the kitchen and opened a bottle of wine. I glanced at the clock as the hand moved toward seven and peeked out the window to the sidewalk below. I expected Dario to be standing there with flowers in his hands and a big grin on his face, but the spot remained empty, and the first whisper of worry wound its way through my mind.

Dario always arrived on time. Something felt very wrong.

I willed myself to calm down. He was probably stuck in traffic, or maybe he got delayed at work. I folded my hands and waited. Minutes passed like hours and time dragged on and on. When the clock hit seven thirty, I picked up my phone and gave him a call. No answer.

I got to my feet and started to pace. What if he'd been in an accident? What if he lay in a ditch somewhere, hurt and unconscious? I texted him, asking him to please call me, and decided to wait a few minutes more before I let myself get worked up into a full-blown panic.

The candles burned low with wax dripping on the pretty gold tablecloth. The stupid clock became my enemy, making each moment excruciatingly long. It was pure torture.

I ran downstairs and found Alvida's number in Aunt Lucy's files. Sitting in the back room, I called her, my hands shaking. She answered on the first ring.

"Hello?"

"Hi, Mrs. Fontana. This is Grace. I'm trying to reach Dario. Have you heard from him?"

A long and very telling pause ensued. "Yes. He's here."

"He planned to stop by tonight. Is he okay?"

I heard some whispering, and it sounded like Alvida put

her hand over the mouthpiece of the phone. My heart slowly sank all the way down to my toes.

"He's fine, but he can't come to the phone right now. I'm sorry, Grace."

Suddenly, I felt like liquid metal gallium filled my throat. Liquid metal gallium had a surface area that could expand up to five times its original size under low energy consumption. Right now, the lump in my throat rivaled any glob of liquid metal gallium.

"Oh. Okay. Bye."

I set my phone on the table, sick to my stomach, and tried to pull my skirt down to cover more of my thighs. I hadn't worn tights, thinking I'd look sexier without them, but my legs now appeared pasty white and flabby. I caught a glimpse of myself in the mirror. I'd put on way too much makeup and my hair seemed unkempt and trashy. I'd gone for a tousled look but ended up with a rat's nest instead. I smoothed my hair and slowly buttoned up my blouse.

I was a fool. A complete and total fool.

Upstairs I blew out the candles, corked the bottle of wine, and put the food into the fridge. Maybe Will could eat it tomorrow.

I curled up on Aunt Lucy's bed, fully dressed. I had an ache in my chest so deep and so powerful it could have split my body in two. After a few minutes, I knew sleep would be impossible, and numbness made way to anger.

I ripped off my blouse and skirt and put on a pair of sweats and a long-sleeved T-shirt. Pulling my hair into a ponytail, I set to work. Typing at a near frantic pace, I inputted all the accumulated data from my earlier experiments into my laptop. It took a few hours, and my fingers cramped, but I didn't want to stop. It kept my mind from churning with thoughts of Dario Fontana.

I looked outside my darkened window. Three in the

morning might not be the best time to walk to the community college and use the lab, but my desire to finish my work and occupy my thoughts overrode my desire for sleep or safety. I shoved my things into my backpack, stuck on a hoodie, and set off down the street.

It didn't take long for me to realize someone followed me. I sensed their presence like a physical touch, as if fingers brushed softly against the back of my neck. I turned to look a few times, trying not to be too obvious, but all I saw were shadows.

"Stupid, stupid, stupid," I muttered in cadence with the sound of my footsteps. I should never have come out this late alone, not after what happened to Sally's dog and our shop. I remembered the look in the eyes of the figure in black as he stood in front of the broken window. He recognized me, and he held a distinct advantage since I never caught a glimpse of his face. He could be anyone.

Distracted, I nearly fell over when someone stepped directly into my path. I jumped back with a shriek as a large shape loomed in front of me.

"Hey, girlie. Why are you out so late?"

A drunk, hulking man blocked the sidewalk in front of me. To make matters worse, his herd of drunken friends surrounded him, and they all stood right in front of Casey's Draft House, a notorious biker bar.

"Excuse me," I said, and tried to duck past him. In spite of his inebriated state, he moved pretty quickly and effectively blocked me.

"Where are you going, little red riding hood?"

My hood was dark grey, but I decided now would not be the time to argue the point. I pulled my cell phone out of my pocket, ready to call for help. I had Anthony Belfiore on speed dial, but didn't want to contact Dario's cousin unless absolutely necessary.

"I'm busy and tired and not in the mood to deal with this at the moment," I said. "Let me pass or I'm phoning the police."

The man let out a laugh. "She's a pissy little thing, but she's cute. Come on, Ginger. I'll buy you a drink and you can show me if you are a true redhead or not."

I decided not to wait for Anthony. I'd get a lot more satisfaction punching this guy in the face myself. I pulled back my arm, my hand clenched in a fist, when a voice from behind me stopped me in my tracks.

"Gentlemen. Is there a problem here?"

Ivan Rochat, in all his well-tailored glory, stood in the middle of the sidewalk like a blond avenging angel. The drunken man did not appear happy to see him.

"We're having a conversation here."

Ivan reached out ever so subtly and pulled me behind him. An oddly reassuring gesture, but I still wanted to punch the drunk in the nose. Ivan seemed aware of my dilemma.

"Now is not the time, Gracie," he said softly, and I heard a note of laughter in his voice.

If the man in front of us had not been so drunk, he would have recognized Ivan was a wolf in sheep's clothing. Under the cashmere and wool beat the heart of a warrior. A predator. A plunderer. When I'd first thought of him as a Viking, I wasn't far off. I sensed something wild and untamed about him, something he kept carefully hidden from view. I caught a glimpse of it as he stared down six drunken men with his steely gaze.

When the behemoth in front of us made a move, Ivan was more than ready. With one fist to the face, Ivan knocked him over and the man fell like a giant redwood.

"Either you let us pass," he said, his eyes on the other men. "Or we can continue to play this game. It is up to you."

They parted in front of him like the Red Sea, and we

walked through in silence. Once we were a block away, he stopped and turned toward me, his hands on my shoulders. He had the nerve to give me a shake, an angry glint in his eyes.

"Why did you go out alone at this hour? Have you no common sense? You could have been hurt."

I tilted my chin and stared up at him with a scowl. "Why were you following me, Ivan?"

He scowled right back at me. "As I walked home from an engagement, I saw you prancing down the street alone at three in the morning. So preoccupied you almost walked right into a biker gang. Where were you going at this hour? Are you mad?"

I turned and started walking to the college again. Although only a few blocks away, I didn't protest when Ivan fell into step beside me, his hands shoved deep into his pockets. I suspected his initial reaction came from worry, not actual anger, and part of me appreciated his concern, even if it did irritate me at the moment.

"Thank you for helping me. I'm on my way to the lab. I have work to do."

And I needed to get my mind off Dario. I burned with shame when I thought about him.

"And you couldn't wait a few hours until the sun came up?"

I shook my head. "I'm on the verge of a breakthrough. I have to get the work done now."

As we walked, I told him about my research, just to fill the silence. He probably understood very little about the subject, but he feigned interest, and it kept me occupied until we reached the door. I pulled out my key and showed it to him.

"See. I have a key. They have a security guard. I am safe now. You can go, Sir Galahad."

He snorted. "I'm hardly Sir Galahad, and you are not a damsel in distress."

"I acted like a total damsel a few minutes ago."

He gave me a crooked smile. "Not really. You seemed perfectly prepared to take on those men, but even the strongest people need help sometimes."

I let out a long breath, not wishing to discuss this any further. "Can I go now?"

He laughed. "Yes, but I want to tell you one thing."

"What?"

I tried hard to keep the annoyance out of my voice. I had one hand on the door and the lab was only a few feet away. The lab was my sanctuary, and I needed it now more than ever. I wanted to throw myself into my work until I could think about what happened between Dario and I without doubling over in pain.

Ivan surprised me by tucking a wisp of hair behind my ear. "If this is about a certain big, grumpy Neanderthal of a reporter, you are far too good for him. Don't allow him to make you sad. He is simply not worth it."

And with a swish of his wool coat and a flutter of his scarf, Ivan disappeared into the night, leaving me standing at the door of the lab all alone.

CHAPTER 23

IF IT SQUIRMS, IT'S BIOLOGY. IF IT DOESN'T WORK, IT'S PHYSICS. IF YOU CAN'T UNDERSTAND IT, IT'S MATHEMATICS. IF IT STINKS, IT'S CHEMISTRY.

I finished up in the lab as the first students started pouring in for class. I'd come very close to tying it all together. Once I received the results from Megan, I'd be able to finish my thesis. Even if I never had the chance to defend it, a sense of personal satisfaction enveloped me. I knew I'd done something original and unprecedented, and it made me proud.

From the first time I stepped into a chemistry lab, it all made perfect sense to me. The lessons seemed familiar, like remembering something I already knew rather than learning a new subject. I loved all the sciences, but with chemistry, it was different. It came naturally.

Unfortunately, the same did not apply to relationships. What happened with Dario proved it. I rehashed it over and over again in my mind but couldn't figure it out. It did, however, make me pose the same question Dario suggested regarding the problems I faced at the university.

Why?

Something changed after Dario's single phone call from Philly. He told me he planned to meet a guy in a bar, but maybe he didn't meet a guy. Maybe he met a girl. Or maybe he hooked up with someone randomly, but why lie to me? Our relationship had barely started. Nothing was official yet. It seemed out of character for Dario to behave this way, but perhaps I didn't know him as well as I thought.

In a lab, I'd have trashed the experiment and started again, but in real life I didn't have such an option. Even if I could, I'm not sure I wanted to erase the memory of my one night with Dario. No matter how it pained me to think about it now, at the time it had been pretty close to perfect.

After finishing in the lab, I stumbled home, exhausted. The morning air made me shiver, and I couldn't wait to crawl under my warm blankets and enjoy a few hours of sleep.

As I dug through my backpack, searching for my keys as I neared the shop, I stepped in something sticky and strange. Confused, I stared down at my feet, and for a moment I could not process what I was seeing. The entire sidewalk in front of the Hocus Pocus Magic Shop was bright red. The color of blood.

I forced myself to calm down and analyze the situation logically. Yes, it looked like blood, but it wasn't. The consistency and color were both off. It had to be paint, but why had someone dumped paint all over our sidewalk? I wondered if it could have been an accident, but then I saw a message, written in the same red paint, on our window.

WHICHES, U R SATAN'S HORES.

The vandal had struck again, and the paint wasn't even dry yet, which meant they did it not long ago. I checked my cell phone for the time. Eight o'clock. They must have done this right after I left the apartment to go to the lab, which made a question pop into my head.

Was someone watching me? If so, who...and why?

I'd handled the broken window and the threats and the

missing dog, but the paint proved to be the final straw. This pissed me off, and the time for action had come.

I called Anthony Belfiore, hoping I didn't wake him. He answered on the first ring, the sound of traffic in the background.

"Don't touch anything," he said, after I explained what happened. "I might be able to get prints this time."

He arrived a few minutes later and shook his head when he saw the damage. "This guy is turning into my full-time job." He took a statement and investigated the scene. When he got a closer look at the writing on the window, he let out a frustrated curse. "He wrote this with his finger, but he used gloves."

"It figures. Do you mind if I check on the Black Lotus? Cat is out of town."

"Be careful," he said.

Fortunately, whoever hit my shop left Cat alone. When I told Anthony, he shook his head in confusion. "There is a big 'closed' sign on her door. Isn't that the perfect time to do something to her shop?"

"Yes, unless..."

"Unless what?"

The events of the last few weeks whirled around in my head. "Unless the goal is fear. We assumed this guy wants to scare away customers. Maybe he's actually trying to scare us away."

"Why?"

I remembered Dario's theory about Party Ark, and how similar things occurred in other areas. "It could all be part of a bigger plan, a way to get rid of the shops that don't fit into the new and improved version of the South Side."

"You might be right." Anthony said. "Dario mentioned something like that as well. You think this is calculated?"

"It has to be. The threats, the paint, the vandalism. All are pretty personal."

"True. Stealing Bubu indicates a direct attack on Sally. And Mr. Dalca's robbery felt personal, too."

"These things are related. I'm sure of it," I said.

Anthony shrugged, his lean muscles emphasized by the well-fitted blue uniform. "I agree, but I don't know what we're missing. It all started a few months ago, around the time Mrs. Trabuski said the ghost of her husband appeared."

I winced, closing my eyes. "Oh, no. She told you that, too?"

He let out a chuckle. "Well, she seemed pretty sure someone had pushed her. What if she was right? Not about the ghost, of course, but about the pushing part. By the way, I didn't put the supernatural stuff in my official police report. I left that nugget out."

"Thank you," I said, trying to form a logical answer to this equation. "I had the distinct impression Mr. Dalca knew who robbed his store."

Anthony nodded. "So did I. Maybe I should have a talk with Mr. Dalca today. Did you call Dario?"

I shook my head. "No. We aren't...I mean...well...he's not taking my calls."

Anthony frowned. "What are you talking about? When I spoke with him on Monday, he was over the moon about you."

I looked at my tennis shoes, now splattered with red paint and ruined. "Not anymore."

"It changed in one day? No way. I know Dario better than I know anyone in this world. He's not like that at all, unless you were the one..."

I shook my head, embarrassed, but I refused to let Anthony know how much his cousin had upset me, so I changed the subject. "Well, these shoes are ruined, and I'd better get the sidewalk cleaned up before our customers come. Do you need anything else?"

"No." He tilted his head, forcing me to make eye contact. "Do you want me to talk with him?"

That sounded like a very bad idea. "It's fine. Truly. Thanks for your help today, Anthony. I appreciate it."

He gave me a crooked smile. "Don't mention it. I'm going to request extra patrols for this area, but be careful, Grace."

I bought a newspaper, made a path over the paint, took off my shoes, and walked into the shop. Everything inside looked untouched, so I fed Jinx, made a pot of coffee, grabbed some cleaning supplies, and set to work. The windows and doors were easy to clean. The sidewalk took a hard brush and nearly an hour on my hands and knees to complete. I finished just as Mrs. Periwinkle arrived.

"Oh, dear. What happened?"

I stood up slowly, rubbing my lower back. "Vandalized. Again. You should have seen it a few hours ago."

Mrs. Periwinkle's bright blue eyes blazed with fury. "This needs to stop. Now. And you're the only one who can do it."

My shoulders sagged from exhaustion, my hands red from the paint. I wiped them half-heartedly on my hoodie. "Me? How?"

She pursed her lips. "We can't discuss it now. You're nearly falling over. Go upstairs, take a hot bath, and have a nice long rest. I'll gather supplies and we'll work on it when you wake up."

Too tired to argue, I did as she said and trudged slowly up the stairs. After washing my hair several times and scrubbing my body from head to toe, I felt marginally better. I sent a text to Sally asking for news about Bubu. She hadn't heard anything but promised to call if she did. I lit a fire, curled up on the couch with Jinx, and fell into a deep and dreamless sleep. When I woke, I heard Will's voice in the shop, so I knew I'd slept into the afternoon.

I'd fallen asleep with my hair wet, leaving it a kinky, curly mess. I tried subduing it, but it refused to cooperate, so I gave up. No sense in fighting the inevitable.

I put on black tights, a long black skirt, and a dark grey turtleneck sweater. I needed comfort right now. I stuck my glasses onto my nose and slipped into a pair of black flats. I didn't bother with makeup. I looked like I was going to a funeral, which perfectly mirrored my emotions at the moment.

I walked into a crowded shop. As soon as Aunt Lucy and Mrs. Periwinkle saw me, they exchanged a long look, but fortunately it was too busy for them to question me right away. I hovered on a cliff at the moment, precariously close to the edge. One word and I could tumble over into the abyss. The abyss would involve a great deal of ugly crying, and I didn't want to break down in front of an audience. I didn't want to do it at all.

Aunt Lucy placed a soft hand on my cheek, looking like she might cry herself. "I spoke with Alvida," she said softly. "Poor poppet."

Mrs. Periwinkle saved me. "Grace, have you seen the black flame candles? I can't find them anywhere."

I slipped into my work routine, and it helped almost as much as being in the lab. Mrs. Periwinkle told me she couldn't locate all the ingredients needed for her "project" and we'd have to wait until she found them.

I had no idea what she meant. I felt numb, like I existed in a robotic state. It may have been lack of sleep, but I knew I still reeled from what had happened with Dario.

Sally stopped by with posters of Bubu, and we hung them on the door and near the cash register. "You're offering a reward?" I asked.

She nodded, her face pale and drawn. "Ralphie didn't like the idea, but if there is any chance..." She sniffed and her lips trembled, but she managed to steady herself.

I gave her a big hug. "We'll find her, Sally."

She left, her pile of posters clutched in her gloved hands, and fury combined with a healthy dose of embarrassment overtook me. Sally had faced obstacle after obstacle in her life, and yet she'd remained upbeat and positive. Two men had dumped me, albeit in quick succession, but I acted like the world was ending. I had to stop moping around feeling sorry for myself. I needed to put on my big girl panties and get over it.

Missy and Sissy came over right after Sally left, carrying another gift, assorted Halloween candy. The label read, "Autumn Splendor Assortment."

"What do they have against Halloween?" asked Aunt Lucy softly as the Party Ark twins chatted with Will and fussed over the photo of Bubu. "It's like they're afraid to even say the word."

"Lots of people are scared of the unknown," I said. "And it can be pretty spooky, I guess."

Aunt Lucy waved my words away. "They aren't afraid of the unknown. What they truly fear is the darkness dwelling inside them, because that's the scariest thing of all."

I looked at Missy and Sissy, two perfectly perky blondes radiating wholesomeness and good intentions. They didn't appear dark to me. Shallow, and perhaps not future members of MENSA, but dark? Not likely.

"Poor little guy," said Missy, her lip pouting adorably as she looked at Bubu's photo. "I sure hope someone finds him soon."

"He's such a cute doggie," said Sissy.

"*She*." Aunt Lucy and I spoke at once, automatically correcting Sissy's pronoun.

Sissy looked confused. "But it's a boy dog."

"She identifies as female," said Aunt Lucy. "She always has."

She snorted. "A dog with male parts is a male dog. It's pretty simple."

"The world is not simple," said Aunt Lucy with a tight smile. "It's a beautifully complicated mess, thank goodness."

Missy opened her mouth to respond, but I stopped her. "Thank you, ladies. We appreciate the candy, but we need to get back to work now, and I'm sure you do, too. Bye."

With flicks of their matching blond ponytails, Missy and Sissy left the shop. I exhaled in relief, not sure if I could have handled another moment with them. With my emotions so unsteady at the moment, the comments about poor Bubu infuriated me.

I found a black, sparkly Halloween wreath in one of the boxes of new inventory. As I hung it on the front door, a tingle went up my spine signaling the arrival of a certain blond Viking. I recognized the sensation now. At a saner moment, I may have enjoyed studying the phenomena of how his presence affected me, but this did not qualify as a saner moment. I turned and gave him as much of a smile as I could muster.

"Sir Galahad returns."

Ivan responded with a gallant bow. "As I already told you, I'm no knight in shining armor."

"Maybe not in shining armor, but you are wearing a nice suit. That has to be custom made."

The suit, in dark wool, fit his body perfectly. His tie was silk, his shoes Italian, and the sexy grin on his face adorable. He opened his jacket and modeled for me.

"I got it in on Seville Row. Do you like it?"

I assessed him from head to toe. He looked delicious. He

smelled delicious. He *was* delicious but I didn't want to flirt with Ivan Rochat, or anyone else for that matter.

"What's not to like?" I asked and went back to adjusting the wreath. I'd found some pretty ribbon to make a bow but dropped it on the ground. Ivan and I both reached for it at the same time, bumping heads.

"Ow," I said, rubbing my forehead. "This day just keeps getting better and better."

"Let me see," said Ivan, pushing my curls away from my face. He winced at the damage. "Well, it appears out of the two of us, I have the harder head. Lucky for me, but unfortunate for you."

His proximity, and his hands on my face, made me uncomfortable, but I couldn't explain why. "Wow. I've never met someone with a harder head than me."

"There is a first time for everything," he said and surprised me with a gentle kiss on my forehead.

At that moment, Dario appeared on the sidewalk behind Ivan. He glared at us, storm clouds gathering in his eyes. I glared right back at him. He had no right to be angry. He'd thrown me out like an old newspaper. I got even more irritated when I noticed Tiffany beside him in her pink raincoat. As she gave me a smug smile, Ivan put an arm around my shoulders.

"An unexpected pleasure," said Ivan. "What are the two of you doing here?"

"We're just passing by." Tiffany pulled on Dario's arm, trying to lead him away, but he couldn't seem to take his gaze off me.

"I came to check on Grace," said Dario, a muscle working in his jaw. "I heard about what happened this morning." For a second, I thought he referred to the way Ivan had rescued me from the drunken bikers, but he was talking about the paint on the sidewalk.

"I'm fine." I leaned closer to Ivan, purely to garner a reaction from Dario, and was instantly rewarded by a flash of anger in his dark eyes.

Ivan frowned. "What happened? I knew I shouldn't have left you alone at three in the morning. I was worried about it all day."

Dario's face turned a color I'd never seen in nature, a red so bright it pulsated. He played the jealous act well for someone who'd just dumped me. I ignored him.

"Don't worry about it, Ivan," I said. "Someone spilled paint on the sidewalk in front of the shop this morning. Nothing important."

Dario's hands balled into fists. "Anthony called it another threat. What are you going to do about it, Grace?"

I gave him a dirty look. "That's none of your concern, is it?"

He muttered something sounding like a curse in Italian and stomped away. Tiffany trailed behind him, following as quickly as she could in high heels. As soon as he left, the sky darkened, and the first heavy raindrops fell. The weather suited my mood perfectly. I stepped away from Ivan and went back to fitting the bow on the wreath.

"You should be pleased," he said. "It worked."

I looked at him in confusion. "What?"

He gave me a crooked smile. "We made him jealous."

"Are you referring to Dario? Well, I couldn't care less." A total lie, and judging by the wicked gleam in Ivan's eyes, he didn't buy it.

I fussed with the wreath, pulling off a tiny, glittery pumpkin by accident. I shoved it back on hoping it might stick, but it didn't, and I got even more frustrated. Seeing Dario with Tiffany turned me into a mess. I hated this.

Ivan leaned closer, speaking in a low, conspiratorial voice. "Do you know how to make him even more jealous?"

I scowled. "What are you talking about?"

"If you joined me for dinner one night, it would drive him crazy." He kept his expression neutral, but something in his eyes told me this was a serious offer.

I pretended to be very concerned about the renegade pumpkin that refused, in spite of my best efforts, to stay on the wreath. "Do you really think so?"

Ivan nodded. "He'd be insane with jealously and regret ever letting you go."

I liked the idea because Dario had hurt me. Badly. Even more than Jonathan. Revenge sounded sweet right now. "And you'd be okay if I went to dinner with you in order to annoy another man?"

He shrugged. "If that's what it takes to get you to go out with me, yes. But I hope you'll agree to a second date for different reasons."

I could think of no better tool for revenge than the smooth, sophisticated, and handsome Ivan Rochat. But I came up with one question. "How would Dario even know?"

"He'll know because I already have a plan." Ivan took the pumpkin from my hand and placed it gently on the wreath. To my surprise, it stayed put. "Tomorrow is the press banquet. Dario is getting an award. He has to be there."

"How do you know about that?"

He winked at me. "I have my sources, and I also have two tickets to the event. I'd like for you to be my date."

I knew I'd probably regret it, but I couldn't help myself. "Fine. As long as you know why I'm doing this."

He took my hand and kissed the back of it in his suave, European way. "I am aware of your motives. Mine, however, are simple and selfish."

"What are your motives, Mr. Rochat?"

When he smiled at me, it made me forget, for a moment,

that I was a dowdy, plain bluestocking with frizzy hair and a fractured heart. "I want you to be mine."

He left as a loud clap of thunder sounded in the distance and the storm intensified. Aunt Lucy hobbled over and we both stood in the doorway and watched Ivan glide down the sidewalk under a black umbrella.

"Are you sure you know what you're doing, sweetness?"

I sighed, certain I'd just made a huge mistake. "No, but I'm going to do it anyway."

CHAPTER 24

WHAT IS LOVE? A NEURO-CHEMICAL CON JOB.

I breezed through Sally's door as soon as she opened the next day. "Help. I need a dress."

She hastened over to me, obviously hearing the panic in my voice. Aggie, who'd been hanging dresses on a clearance rack, joined her.

"This sounds like a fashion emergency," said Sally. "What kind of dress?"

"A dress to make someone wish he'd never broken my heart."

"Oh, Gracie." She put a hand over her mouth. "It's not Dario, is it?"

I couldn't speak, and Aggie squeezed my hand, her gaze sorrowful. "Men," she said. "Are aleph zero."

"Alpha what?" asked Sally.

"Not alpha." I shared a tremulous smile with Aggie. "*Aleph*. The smallest possible number. The lowest of the low. Thanks, Aggie. I agree with you. Men are the worst."

"Well, some men at least." Sally pulled me over to a soft, antique couch in a tiny alcove in the back of the shop and held my hand. On the table rested photos of Bubu and a few candles, like a shrine. Heartbreaking, but Sally being Sally put her own sorrow aside so she could help me. "Tell me what happened, darling. A burden shared is a burden halved. Not mathematically accurate, but true."

Surrounded by sea of tulle and satin, I told her everything. She and Aggie shook their heads and made all the appropriate noises. Sally took out an embroidered linen handkerchief, in case I needed to cry, but I didn't. If I could cry, I'd probably feel better.

"You poor sweet baby," said Sally.

"I'm a complete idiot. First Jonathan, then Dario."

"Did you love Jonathan?" she asked.

I thought about it for less than a nanosecond. "No. I did not."

"But you loved Dario."

I shrugged. "I'd started to, and I thought perhaps he might even love me, too..." I paused, shaking my head. "Like that could ever happen."

"What do you mean?" asked Sally.

I waved my hands, indicating my wool skirt, serviceable shoes, and tightly controlled bun. "How could a man like Dario Fontana ever fall for a girl like me? It was an aberration. An anomaly. A glitch in the matrix. As soon as he came to his senses, he must have realized men like him don't date tall, dorky, bookworms. They date blond princesses who wear pink all the time, like tiny mutant dolls."

"Men never want a woman with brains," said Aggie. "It's against their nature. They're all animals. Beasts."

Sally spoke to her sister but kept her eyes on me. "Aggie dear, do you mind running to the post office for me? I have a package I promised to mail, and nearly forgot. Silly me."

"Of course," said Aggie. "And I'll bring Lucinda another smoothie while I'm out."

"Thank you, Aggie," I said. "She'll appreciate it."

Aggie gave me a small, almost hesitant pat on the shoulder. "Remember what I said, Grace. You cannot trust them, and men will never, ever appreciate all you do for them. You're better off on your own."

With those cheery words, she went to the back of the shop. Sally watched her go with sadness in her eyes. "She's suffered, poor Aggie, but she's wrong. Not all men are bad. Dario certainly isn't."

I pursed my lips. "When presented with such absolute evidence to the contrary, I have to go with my initial hypothesis. Dario played me."

But I had so many questions. Why did he call me from Philly sounding sweet and wonderful, and then treat me callously the next day? And why act the part of the injured party now, feigning hurt and jealousy?

It all came back to the same question, over and over again. *Why?*

Sally sighed. "And you think going to this party will make things better?"

"No, but at least it'll help me save face. It's about walking away with what pride and dignity I have left."

"Pride and dignity?" She touched a finger to her chin as she considered it. "Then you need something to knock his socks off, and I have just the dress."

Sally pulled me into the dressing room and ordered me to strip. When she handed me the dress through the door, I gasped. "I can't wear this."

"Why ever not?"

I stuck my head out and wrinkled my nose at her. "It's red."

"Yes."

"I'm a redhead."

"Yes."

"It's against the rules for me to wear red. Or pink. Or orange."

Sally tapped me gently on the nose with one well-manicured finger. "Rules were made to be broken, child. Don't they teach you anything at that fancy university of yours?"

As I closed the door of the dressing room, the wheels turned in my head. Rules were made to be broken in chemistry, too. And so were chemical bonds. Suddenly, it all became perfectly clear. I let out a squeal and hopped up and down in my underwear in the changing room.

"What happened?" asked Sally. "Are you okay?"

"I'm more than okay," I said, still bouncing up and down. I flung the door open, not caring who saw me in my undies and bra. "You solved it, Sally. My thesis. I was headed in the right direction, but I'd tried to follow the rules. Bioluminescence versus biofluorescence. Light produced from an organism versus light reflected by an organism. Except there is no organism. The water is the organism, or at least the vehicle for the biofluorescence. It broke the rules, like you said."

"Yay," she said, bouncing up and down with me as she held my hands in hers. "I have no idea what you're talking about, but I'm so excited. Yay."

"This is big. Bigger than big."

"Good girl," said Sally. "Now put on the red dress and let's celebrate by making you irresistible."

I snorted. "Like that could ever happen."

Sally put her hands on my shoulders and stared straight into my eyes. "Listen to me, young lady, and listen well. You are beautiful and powerful and strong, and no one can make you an aleph zero unless you allow it. Are we clear?"

I got choked up all over again. "Yes. Thank you, Sally."

"Good. Now let's get to work."

After Sally outfitted me with red heels, a glittering choker made of blood red gemstones, matching earrings, and a white faux fur stole to keep me warm. I looked pretty good. I'd been wrong about the redhead rule. Completely and absolutely wrong.

I turned around in front of the mirror. The heavy satin dress, designed to look like it might fall off my shoulders if I moved the wrong way, showed a creamy expanse of white skin. It displayed my ample bosom nicely as well. It clung to my curves, emphasizing my waist and my bottom. A long slit reached nearly to the top of my thigh.

"What if someone sees my undies?"

"You'll wear this, just in case. It's the right color."

Sally gave me a red lace strapless teddy with a built-in push up bra. It snapped at the crotch. I raised an eyebrow at her. "Seriously, Sally?"

She batted my hand with a giggle. "Always wear the prettiest lingerie you can find. It's not about looking sexy, it's about *feeling* sexy. And that starts with the right underclothing."

She gave me a wink, and after we hung the dress in a bag, Sally insisted on doing my hair and makeup. The idea terrified me, but I didn't want to offend her. With the shop quiet today, and Aggie off running errands, I knew it provided a welcome distraction for her.

As soon as Sally finished and handed me a mirror, I gasped, barely recognizing myself. "Sally. You are a genius."

She studied her handiwork with a proud gleam in her eyes. "No one knows better than a drag queen how far a little mascara can go, honey."

More than a little mascara, the amazing Sally had turned me into a completely different person. My appearance startled me, and not just because of the makeup. "I look like sex on a stick," I said, blinking at my reflection. "Exactly what I'd been going for. Thank you, Sally."

She put a hand over her heart. "My pleasure."

Aunt Lucy had already left by the time I returned. She'd put a note for me on the cash register saying she needed to nap, so Mags had taken her home. She still hadn't fully recovered from her fall, and it seemed like even being in the shop a few hours wore her out. I wondered how long it would take for her to get back to normal, and if she'd ever be okay again.

I poured a glass of wine and sat in front of the fire. Opening my laptop, I decided to search for information on Ivan. I knew nothing about him and thought I ought to be prepared. I typed in his name, Ivan Rochat, and, other than a Facebook profile for a man who was definitely not the same Ivan Rochat I knew, I found nothing.

I frowned. Strange. Ivan was wealthy, successful, and worldly. He should have some kind of online presence, but he didn't.

"A ghost," I said softly. Not the spooky kind. The invisible-on-the-internet kind.

Too late to cancel the date in spite of my qualms, I shut my laptop and got dressed. I put on the teddy, slipped into a silk robe, and painted my nails red to match my dress. As I sipped wine, waiting for my nails to dry, I found my gaze wandering over and over again to the spot on the bookshelf hiding the wooden box.

No longer able to stop myself, I moved the books aside so I could see the dragon box again. Picking it up, I traced the elegant lines of the painted dragon and carried it over to the couch with me. My grimoire always felt warm, and holding it calmed me. Not so with the dragon box. Oddly cold to the touch, in spite of the heat from the fire, it made a chill go over my skin. It seemed...reptilian.

"Dragon Rouge."

I said the words aloud and a gust of wind from the chimney made sparks fly in the fireplace. Jinx jumped straight onto my lap, causing me to spill some of my wine on the floor.

"Jinx, Settle down."

I grabbed some paper towels, glad no wine had gotten on Aunt Lucy's pink and white oriental carpet, and picked up the dragon box again. The carvings on the sides and back of the box brought to mind reptilian scales, and the dragon on the front looked so real I almost heard the flapping of the creature's wings as it soared into the dark sky.

I grabbed Aunt Lucy's keys and opened the lid. Tonight, the stone inside seemed to glow even brighter. A trick of the firelight, but it made the hair on my arms stand on end. Although beautiful and mysterious, I didn't like it much at all.

About to close the box, I noticed a folded piece of parchment tucked inside the lid. I took it out and opened it, being careful not to tear the fragile paper. As my eyes scanned the yellowed page, brittle from age, I couldn't believe what I saw. Spells, written in the same convoluted Latin as Maeve McAlroy's book, covered the entire surface.

I skimmed through the words as a terrible realization hit me. Unlike the love potions and constipation remedies in my grimoire, these were *evil* spells, and they simultaneously intrigued and terrified me.

I brought the paper closer to my face to better read the tiny print. The spells promised great and terrible things. Ways to destroy an enemy. Ways to take revenge on an unfaithful lover. Ways to kill another human being.

Dark, sinister, ugly things.

I put the parchment paper back and slammed the box shut. Mr. Dalca said not all magical objects were good, and nothing about this thing seemed good. Even for a person who didn't believe in magic, I understood this box contained something vile.

I didn't want to touch it again. I put it back where I'd

found it. Once I could no longer see the box, I felt better, stronger, and more than ready to face Dario.

A smile curved on my lips at the thought but not a nice smile. Dario didn't deserve a nice smile. He deserved to suffer.

I frowned. Where did that come from? Yes, Dario hurt me, but the plan for tonight focused more on self-preservation than revenge. Or at least that's what I'd told myself when I initially agreed to go with Ivan. Now I couldn't be sure.

After dousing the fire, I slipped out of my silk robe and into the elegant red dress. Putting on the antique choker, I checked myself in the mirror. The stones glowed in the dim light of the apartment, reminding me of the stone inside the dragon box. I pushed the thought of it out of my mind. I needed to focus on tonight.

Sally gave me long, red satin gloves to match the dress. They reached my elbows. My newly polished toes peeked out from under the skirt, and my skin looked as smooth as polished alabaster. My appearance added to my level of confidence. Red, it turns out, was my color. Who knew?

After one last worried glance at the spot on the bookshelf containing the Dragon Rouge, I patted Jinx's head. "Guard the place for me, and don't go near that nasty box."

He winked at me, letting out a yawn and stretching before he curled up on one of the cushions. The grimoire sat on the end table, and I decided to hide it, too. I put it in a pink lingerie bag and stuck it in Aunt Lucy's underwear drawer. She owned a surprising number of thongs for an elderly lady. I cringed at the visual popping into my head.

I heard a knock on the door downstairs and locked up the apartment before heading to the shop. Leaving it open tonight made me uneasy. The discovery of those spells inside the dragon box, and the repeated visits by the dyslexic vandal, made me decide to go with my gut and be cautious.

Ivan stood at the door, in a tux, carrying a bouquet of red roses. When he saw me, a broad smile lit up his face. "Miss O'Leary. You are stunning."

"Thank you."

His gaze roamed over my body, taking it all in. Apodyopsis. Ivan undressed me with his eyes again, and I suspected my cheeks got redder than my dress when his gaze lingered on my bosom. I grabbed my stole from a chair, eager to cover myself. Even though things ended on a bad note with Dario, the odds of having two extremely handsome and desirable men admire me in the span of only a few short weeks were incalculable. It made me very uncomfortable.

Ivan straightened my stole, his fingers caressing my shoulders. Once again, a tingle went over my skin as soon as he touched me. I tried not to react, even when he leaned close, his breath warm on my ear.

"They say revenge is sweet, but you are much sweeter, my dear."

I turned to look at him, trying to judge how much sincerity existed in his words. Either he played his part well, or he actually liked me.

"You don't even know me."

"I know enough."

Ivan's driver waited outside the shop, ready to take us to the fancy hotel downtown hosting the party. I locked things up and slid into the leather interior of the limo. Ivan climbed in after me and poured perfectly chilled champagne into expensive crystal flutes.

"Cheers," he said, and we tapped glasses.

"You think of everything," I said, taking a sip. Being with Ivan was easy. Uncomplicated. And his attentiveness soothed my wounded pride. He didn't make my heart soar like Dario did, but that might be a good thing. Soaring hearts tended to hit hard when they crashed.

I took another sip of champagne and looked out the window at the glittering city. People stared at the limousine as we rolled by as if someone important rode inside, maybe an athlete or a local celebrity. If they'd known the eyes looking back at them belonged to a person who spent most of her time thinking about molecules, chemical equations, and things invisible without the use of a microscope, it would have sorely disappointed them.

"Now what kind of musings brought such a lovely smile to your face?"

"I was thinking that the people watching us have no idea about who's actually inside."

"It's kind of a metaphor for life, isn't it? Do we ever truly know what's inside another person?" he asked.

I studied his face, trying to figure out where he went with this. "We don't, and I've only just met you, but I'm glad we're being honest with each other. We have no expectations or false hopes. It's refreshing."

I saw something odd pass across his blue eyes, but in the intimate lighting of the limousine, I couldn't tell what it indicated. I polished off my glass of champagne, and he did the same, refilling both of them immediately.

I needed to be careful. After not eating all day, my head already buzzed from the champagne. Getting drunk with someone like Ivan would be a huge mistake and could lead to serious consequences. I eased away from him ever so slightly and he gave me a knowing, wolfish grin.

"To new beginnings," he said, raising his glass to me.

"And happy endings."

The words came out of my mouth before I could stop them. Aware of the double entendre almost immediately, I gasped, covering my mouth with one gloved hand. Ivan blinked in surprise and tossed back his head, laughing.

"I didn't mean it..." I said, but he waved aside my words.

"No need to explain," he said. "I happen to be a sucker for happy endings myself."

As we pulled up in front of the hotel, I wondered again if I'd made the right decision by being here tonight, but then I realized something. Dario was receiving a big award tonight, but he never mentioned it to me, which meant either he'd been extremely remiss and unorganized, or he'd already asked someone else. I voted for option number two, figuring his date was none other than Miss Bubblegum Pink.

I squared my shoulders, trying to ignore the way the idea of Dario being with anyone else caused such agony. Almost a physical manifestation of my emotional pain, another topic I'd eagerly study if any possibility existed for me to view it objectively. I knew I couldn't, though. I could be unbiased about many things but not this.

We timed our arrival perfectly. Cameras flashed as Ivan reached for my hand, helping me out of the car. I remembered reading something about how celebrities practiced exiting a limo. Leaning too far forward could cause a cleavage issue and unwanted exposure. Not sliding forward far enough meant flailing legs and the flashing of panties. I did neither. I exited the car like a graceful swan or a queen, placing a gloved hand on Ivan's arm as I smiled for the cameras. The press ate it up, asking for my name. I gave them a coy smile as Ivan looked on proudly. "This is the lovely and brilliant Grace O'Leary."

Beyond the cameras, I saw Dario standing on the steps to the hotel, watching me with an unreadable expression in his eyes. Tiffany stood next to him in a hot pink dress. I lifted my chin a little higher and stared right back at him. His face hardened and he turned away.

"What are you thinking about, my dear?" asked Ivan, his lips nearly touching my ear as he led me into the hotel.

"The old saying, 'Revenge is a dish best served cold.' They had it wrong."

"How so?" he asked, as he took the stole from my shoulders and handed it to the coat check girl.

I grinned at him, knowing Dario still stood behind us, his eyes boring into my back. Dario's anger made me feel almost as tipsy as the champagne.

"It's delicious piping hot as well."

CHAPTER 25

IF AT FIRST YOU DON'T SUCCEED, TRY AT LEAST TWO MORE TIMES SO YOUR FAILURE IS STATISTICALLY SIGNIFICANT.

After a long, monotonous dinner with standard hotel fare and a series of speeches, Dario received a big award, Sports Reporter of the Year. He accepted it graciously, his acceptance speech short and to the point. Distracted, his gaze kept wandering over to where I sat with Ivan. I ignored him, but knowing my presence disturbed him brought me no small satisfaction.

Make him hurt. Make him suffer.

Cold fury lurked inside me like a monster in a child's closet. I normally wouldn't classify myself as the vengeful type, but part of me truly wished to ruin this night for Dario. I rubbed my forehead with my fingertips, frowning as I realized I wanted to ruin more than this night. I wanted to ruin everything.

My blood ran cold. Where had those thoughts come from?

I took a deep, steadying breath, quelling my rising fury, and forcing myself to calm down. No matter how Dario behaved, I refused to retaliate. I was a good person, not spiteful or mean, and knowing that made those whispers go silent.

When the dancing started, Ivan pulled me onto the floor. "I'm not a good dancer," I said.

"Let go, Grace. Follow me. Your body will know what to do, but you need to shut off that magnificent brain of yours for a few minutes."

I'd sipped wine throughout the evening, and it gave me the confidence to go for it. Surprisingly, Ivan was right. I let him lead me around the floor, and before I knew it, I'd learned to waltz.

"This is amazing," I said. "Like muscle memory, but I've never used these muscles and I've never done this dance. I wonder how it happens."

I looked at my feet and stumbled. Ivan lifted my face with a finger under my chin. "Stop thinking. Just enjoy it."

We danced and danced until the band took a break and the music stopped. Breathless, and tipsy, I sought out a bathroom as Ivan spoke with some business associates. Rather than fight my way into the crowded ladies' room near the party, I walked down a quiet hallway until I found a deserted restroom at the opposite end of the hotel. I opened the door and turned on the light, surprised to find a small lounge with soft furnishings and toilets in a separate room in the back. As I dabbed my face with cool water, the door opened, and Dario stepped inside. I jumped away from the sink with a squeak.

"This is the ladies' room."

He prowled toward me, like a panther about to strike. I backed up until my bottom hit the sink, but still he kept coming. He stopped right in front of me, hands balled into fists at his side.

"Why are you doing this to me?"

I glared at him. "Why am I doing this to *you*? Why are you doing this to me?"

I pulled my gloves back on with swift, angry tugs. The right glove got twisted, so I took it off and tried again. Dario watched me, finally pulling off the glove himself and helping me put it on properly. The touch of his hands on my skin made my entire body react immediately.

When Ivan touched me, I experienced a tingle. When Dario touched me, it felt like I'd stuck my finger into an electric socket. Two hundred and twenty volts. *Bam*.

I tried to control my pulse, but my heart raced. Dario watched me closely, before turning on his heel and going straight to the door. I thought he intended to leave, and my body sagged in an odd combination of relief mixed with disappointment. He didn't leave, however. He locked the door and spun around to face me.

"I should get back to the party," I said, but didn't make a single move toward the door. My breath came out as a shallow pant and my breasts nearly popped out of my dress. Dario noticed this, his eyes darkening with what looked a whole lot like hunger.

"I'm doing what I've wanted to do ever since I saw you get out of that limo...what I should have done as soon I saw Ivan with you in front of your shop."

He reached for me, pulling me close and crushing my lips with his. I tasted anger in his kiss, and jealousy, but also desire. I responded in kind, giving him angry, frantic, hungry kisses. Trying to show him with my lips how much he'd hurt me. Our kisses were brutal and demanding. Intense. Nothing sweet or gentle passed between us, but I didn't want sweet. I didn't want gentle. Not right now, at least.

He took my hand in his and pulled off my glove, tugging at each finger before sliding it off. He did the same with the other glove, and I watched, transfixed, as he kissed the pulse point on my wrist. He inhaled my scent as if he'd missed it. As if he couldn't stop himself.

I should have laughed in his face, but instead I pulled his head down, wanting more. Wanting his lips on mine. He made a sound in his throat, part ecstasy and part agony, and I understood it well. I felt exactly the same way myself.

He cupped my cheek with one hand, staring deeply into my eyes like he searched for the answer to some kind of puzzle. I'm not sure what he saw there, but I knew as soon as he came to a decision. He yanked off his bow tie, his mouth a hard line, and tossed it to the floor. I unbuttoned his shirt, needing to have the smooth warmth of his skin against mine, and not caring anymore whether or not I'd regret this later.

He teased and caressed my mouth with his, his desire overwhelming me. When he kissed his way down my neck, and his lips touched the curve of my breasts, I shut off the voice in my head warning me to be careful. I hated that voice, because I wanted Dario right now. Immediately. In the ladies' room. It might prove to be a horrible mistake, but as Ivan said about waltzing, if I shut off my brain and stopped thinking, my body would know what to do. And my body screamed for me to do this. Now.

Dario lowered me onto a large chaise lounge in the center of the room. Made for a time when ladies wore formal dresses with crinolines and puffy skirts, the design permitted several women to sit on it and chat as they powdered their noses and reapplied their lipstick. Perhaps not originally designed for fornication, but Dario and I were about to turn it into an extremely multi-functional piece of furniture.

I grasped the sides of the red velvet cushion. With my voluptuous breasts, and my pose one of complete abandon, I must have looked like the subject of a Rubenesque painting, a curvaceous redhead in the throes of passion waiting to be ravaged by a dark god.

Dario fit the part. He unzipped his pants, as his eyes raked my body with a hunger and possessiveness that sent a thrill through my heart. Stupid, but true.

He leaned over me, his beautiful body only inches from mine, and I gasped as he unsnapped my red lace teddy. I'd never felt so vulnerable in my life, but when he reached out with a trembling hand and touched me, gently caressing me, I arched against him, unable to stop myself.

"Grace," he said, his voice a husky whisper.

I hushed him, placing a finger on his lips, afraid he was going to say he'd changed his mind, and I didn't want him to stop.

"You make me crazy. You know that, don't you?" he asked.

"Then at least we have something in common."

I couldn't stop touching him. My hands ran over his body desperately. Wantonly. I touched his back. His shoulders. His ever-so-delectable bottom.

He let out a groan and plunged into me, his eyes filled with something akin to wonder, but I tried not to read into it. I'd done that last time, in the throes of passion, and he'd played me for a fool. Instead, I pulled his dark head down so I could kiss him over and over again. His tongue met mine in a wild dance as he thrust in and out of me, bringing me to a shattering climax in moments. He came with me, calling out my name, but as soon as the sex was over, reality set back in, and Dario stood, pulling up his pants, unable to meet my eyes.

"We didn't use a condom." He went to the sink, washed his hands, and buttoned his shirt. I managed to get my teddy snapped back together without looking too ridiculous, but my cheeks felt raw from rubbing against the stubble on his jaw.

"I'm on the pill. It should be fine."

I watched him put on his bow tie, knowing he'd checked

out emotionally. The person who'd made passionate love to me on the settee was already gone. In his place was someone cold, someone I didn't even recognize.

He swore under his breath and sat next to me, so close our thighs nearly touched. We shared the most intimate contact, and yet now we could barely handle sitting next to each other.

"Why are you with Ivan?"

I frowned. If he wanted to believe that, my pride told me to let him. "Why are you with Tiffany?"

"I asked her to come to this dinner with me weeks ago, before I even knew you, but only as a friend." He laughed, a sound without humor. "Not that it matters."

I studied his profile, the arrogant nose and stubborn chin I'd grown to love. The tousled head of curls I itched to run my fingers through even now. The most beautiful man I'd ever met, but bad for me. And I was bad for him.

"We need to stop doing this," he said, his voice tight.

"I agree. By the way, you have my lipstick on your collar."

"And you have a hickey on your neck," he said with a smirk.

I shot a quick glance in the mirror. He was right. Tonight, my hair covered it, but I'd have to wear turtlenecks for a week.

"Dario, how could you?"

Sadly, I liked having a giant purple mark on my pale skin because he'd put it there. He'd stamped me as his, even if only for a moment, but now he ran a distracted hand through his hair.

"I'm not like you. I've always been monogamous. This is new for me. I realize we didn't promise each other anything, but I'm not comfortable. It's not fair to Ivan either."

Like a slap to the face, his meaning became painfully clear. I smoothed my hair, straightened my dress, and made sure my makeup looked passable. Dario watched me, unspeaking, from the settee.

Calm now, and back in control, I turned to him, putting my lipstick back in my clutch. "I never slept with Ivan. You're a fool for thinking I did." Ignoring the shocked look on his face, I walked to the door, pausing with my hand on the door-knob. "I've never cheated on anyone or anything in my life, but lately everyone seems to be accusing me of it. First Dr. Lewis, because of the answer key, and now you, because of Ivan. Both of you are completely wrong. Maybe there's something in the water."

I laughed at my own joke, since the water from the Enchanted Garden definitely played a big role in my life at the moment. Dario stared at me with an oddly pained look on his face, like I'd just punched him in the stomach. He had no right to look like the injured party. It was getting old. "Grace—"

I stopped him by holding up one red-gloved hand. "Don't say another word. I may not be able to fix what happened to me back at school, but I can certainly fix this. Leave me alone, Dario. I won't allow you to make me feel like this ever again."

Unlocking the door, I squared my shoulders and walked away. Ivan found me before I made it to the ballroom. When he saw my face, he pulled me aside. "Are you okay?"

I sighed. "Our plan worked, but the outcome wasn't what I expected."

His blue eyes turned gentle and contemplative. "Shall I slay the dragon for you?"

My mouth curved into the barest hint of a smile. "No slaying necessary."

He pulled my hand into the crook of his arm. "Then allow me to get you a glass of wine."

"That would be lovely."

I drank and danced and put on a brave face, which was turning into a full-time occupation for me. I didn't relax and let my guard down until the ride back home. Resting my head on Ivan's broad shoulder, I let out a long, slow breath.

"Thank you for being such a good friend."

He lifted my hand and kissed the back of it. Even through my gloves, I felt the warmth of his mouth. "I wish I could be more, but I sense your heart is already taken."

"The only problem is the person who took it doesn't seem to want it."

It would be so easy if I loved Ivan, but I couldn't. I'd given Dario my heart, the poor, battered and bruised little thing, and I didn't know how to get it back.

Ivan's eyes, bright and piercing in the dim light of the limo, locked on me. "He is a fool."

I couldn't have agreed with him more. "The only problem is I'm a fool, too. A big one."

When we arrived at the shop, Ivan insisted on walking me to the door. He took the key from me to open it, always the gentleman, but before he unlocked it, he put a hand on my cheek.

"Let me know if things ever change."

Suddenly, he didn't look powerful or sophisticated. He looked like a man. An incredibly handsome, extremely kind, and slightly vulnerable man.

I went up on my tiptoes to kiss him softly on the cheek. "I will."

He unlocked the door, and handed me my key, giving me a bow. "Adieu, Miss O'Leary."

"Goodnight, Ivan."

Once back in my apartment, I stepped out of my shoes, slipped out of my dress, and took off the teddy with a dull numbness in my chest. I showered, washing every vestige of makeup from my face, and the scent of Dario off my skin.

After putting on a pair of flannel pajamas, I looked in the mirror. The mark Dario made had darkened on my neck. I touched it, remembering how his mouth felt, how he looked, how he tasted.

Taking my cell phone out of my bag, I saw several missed calls and messages, all from Dario. I slowly deleted them one by one and tossed my phone onto the couch. I was done.

CHAPTER 26

HEY, GIRL. THOSE GOGGLES AND GLOVES LOOK GREAT ON YOU. I LOVE HOW YOU ALWAYS THINK OF SAFETY FIRST.

I picked up Jinx and went to bed, exhausted both emotionally and physically. With the help of all the wine I drank, I hoped to fall into a deep, dreamless sleep and remain that way until morning. Most importantly, I wanted to stop thinking about Dario. It hurt too much.

Things didn't work out exactly as planned. I'd only slept a few hours when Jinx jumped up, hissing and arching his back. He stared at the door of my room, his fur standing on end.

"What is it, boy?" I asked, groggy and confused.

A soft thump echoed from the front room, and I came fully awake in an instant. Whoever, or whatever, lurked out there now moved closer and closer to my room. Reaching for my cell phone, I remembered leaving it on the couch. Trapped in my room, without a weapon and without any other options, I pulled Jinx close and waited.

A figure appeared in my doorway. The darkness swirled around him, like a cape. Was he actually wearing a cape? I couldn't tell. I scooted back to the head of my bed, trying to put as much space between us as possible, the hissing kitten clenched tightly in my arms.

"Who are you and what do you want?"

As the figure drifted further into the room, I saw a pale face and black, menacing eyes. A hood covered most of his head, but what I could make out terrified me. Tall and intimidating, a cape covered him from the top of his head nearly to his toes. He reminded me of an illustration I'd once seen of the grim reaper in one of Aunt Lucy's book. Could this be him? Was I about to die?

"I want the Dragon Rouge."

The voice, deep and heavily accented, sent chills up and down my spine. I stared at the apparition in confusion, my brain numbed from fear and shock.

"Uncle Anton?"

He moved even closer, standing at the foot of my bed. "Where is it?"

My cell phone rang, shattering the silence of the quiet apartment. The ghost turned toward the sound as Jinx flew out of my arms and hissing loudly, scratching him. The man jumped back with a yelp, nearly landing on the floor. Jinx scrambled under the bed, and the man ran out of the room, banging his leg on the coffee table and letting out a curse. As soon as he left, I locked it behind him and turned the dead-bolt as my phone continued to ring. I answered it with shaking hands.

"Grace?"

Tears of relief sprang to my eyes at the sound of Dario's voice. "Someone broke into my apartment. He woke me up."

"Are you okay?"

"I think so," I said, even though I was so far from okay I didn't even know where to start.

"I'm coming over. Lock yourself in."

"I did," I said. "Dario?"

Hearing his footfalls over the phone, I suspected he must

be bolting down the stairs of his house and heading to the front door. "What, Gracie?"

"I'm scared."

He spoke after the briefest pause. "I'll be there soon."

My teeth chattered. "Please don't hang up."

"I need to call Anthony. I'm going to put you on hold. Go over the periodic table. I'll be back before you hit potassium. Cobalt at the latest."

As soon as he put me on hold, it got hard for me to breathe. "Hydrogen, helium, lithium, beryllium, boron..."

He returned just as I got to potassium, and I let out a sigh of relief. He talked to me as he careened through the dark streets in his Jeep, ignoring traffic lights and running straight through stop signs. He told me the details of his ride to keep my focus away from the person who'd invaded the apartment.

"Oops. I went through another red light."

"Stop running those, Dario. Please."

"I'm pulling up in front right now. Can you come and unlock the door for me?"

I turned on the lights, and moved as quickly as I could, but the journey to the front door of the shop felt like one of the longest in my life. I held Jinx tightly and as soon as I opened the door and Dario came inside, I fell into his arms.

"I saw the ghost of Uncle Anton."

He pushed my hair out of my eyes. "What are you talking about?"

"Jinx woke me up, and the ghost came into my room, stood by my bed, and asked for the Dragon Rouge. Jinx attacked him and he ran away." I paused, frowning. "Wait a second. Jinx scratched him. How could he scratch a ghost? Incorporeal beings, by their very nature, are not made of matter."

"True." Dario held me close, as if protecting me. It may not have been reality, but it felt pretty darned good.

"And he tripped, knocking his leg on the coffee table. Ghosts can't trip. They don't curse when they hit their shins, and they don't make sounds when they run away."

He shook his head. "Nope."

"It was a man."

"Yep."

He remained calm, but worry filled his eyes, making it seem like he cared for me. Like he had something invested in this relationship. I frowned, backing away.

"Why did you call me?"

He opened his mouth to speak, and my cell phone went off, buzzing in my hand and startling me. I answered it automatically and heard Ivan's voice.

"I hope I didn't wake you. You seemed sad when I left. I wanted to make sure you were okay."

"I'm not okay, Ivan. Something happened." I told him the bare basics, and he made sympathetic noises.

"I shouldn't have left you," he said.

"There's nothing you could have done. The police are on their way."

"I'll be out of town for a few days, but I'll see you as soon as I get back."

I hung up the phone to find Dario glaring at me. "Why is he calling you in the middle of the night? Doesn't that seem odd?"

It did seem strange, but I refused to admit that to Dario. That phone call may have been Ivan's attempt at a booty call, but I wouldn't admit that either.

"Don't be ridiculous. He just wanted to check on me."

"Great. Peachy."

I wanted to question his sneer and the sudden anger in his voice, but sirens sounded as Anthony pulled up in front of the shop. His partner, Officer Miller, stepped out of the car with him. Officer Miller, older, paunchier, and not as good looking as Anthony, carried a resigned air about him. He took careful notes and listened to my story as Anthony and Dario checked out my apartment.

"No forced entry," said Anthony. "All doors and windows secure."

I frowned, still in my flannel pajamas with Jinx snoozing in my arms. "Then how did he get in?"

Anthony's eyes scanned the shop, as if hoping he'd find the answer to my question somewhere among the spell books and potions. "Does anyone else have a key?"

I shook my head. "Only Aunt Lucy and Mrs. Periwinkle."

Officer Miller scratched his chin. "This is the second time this week it's happened on the same street. First, someone stole a dog from a locked apartment, and now this. Do you think he wanted something in particular?"

"The Dragon Rouge." I shivered, remembering the deep voice and the shadowed face. "It's an old wooden box with a stone inside. I'm pretty sure it's valuable, but I couldn't even begin to estimate the price. It belongs to my aunt. He asked for it."

"Just like the other intruder asked your aunt for the same thing," said Dario, and I nodded, hugging myself close.

"Can you give me a description of the man who was in your room?" asked Officer Miller.

I showed him the photo of Uncle Anton near the cash register. "He looked a lot like this."

"Dario's right. This could explain what happened to your aunt," said Anthony, taking a picture with his phone. "If the intruder looks like your uncle, she must have noticed the resemblance, too, and mistook him for her husband. Or rather, the ghost of her husband."

Officer Miller raised his eyebrows but didn't comment. Working in the South Side meant he'd likely seen lots of interesting things.

I scratched Jinx behind the ears, trying to calm down. He'd become my therapy cat at this point.

Anthony looked over his notes, a frown on his face. "There are too many similarities and too many coincidences here. I don't like coincidences."

A call went off on their radio and Officer Miller let out a sound of pure disgust. "More naked women in the park. I swear this whole town is going crazy. We'd better go. Let us know if you think of anything else."

He went out to the car. Anthony tipped his hat at me. "I'll stop by tomorrow. Dario, do you want to come with us? It's the third time this week we've made an arrest like this. Maybe you can use it for the paper."

"I should stay here with Grace."

"No." I put down Jinx, who'd started to fuss, and folded my arms across my chest. "You should go."

"Come on, Dario," said Anthony, sticking his head back in the door. "We have to move."

He held up an impatient hand to Anthony and spoke to me. "Can we talk later?"

I gave him a wobbly smile. "Why? So we can argue again?" He opened his mouth to respond, but I stopped him. "Let it go, Dario. Please."

He muttered something under his breath and got into the police car. I locked the door to the shop behind him and rested my head against it with my eyes closed as the car sped away. I'd done the right thing, but it didn't make it any easier.

Sleep no longer an option for the rest of the night, I poured a cup of hot tea, and set to work on my thesis. Megan told me the final results would be back in a day or two, but I didn't need them to complete my work. They'd be the icing on the cake.

I finished before the sun came up, showered, dressed, and went downstairs to mix potions. I called Aunt Lucy to let her know what happened, reassuring her I was fine. Not exactly the truth, but she let me get away with it, promising to be in soon. By the time Mrs. Periwinkle arrived, I'd already made coffee and prepared the shop to open for the day.

"Aren't you the busy bee this morning?"

She carried a large box in her blue-gloved hands and set it on the table by the cash register. I followed her into the back room as she took off her coat.

"I couldn't sleep," I said.

I told her about what happened, and she gasped, putting a hand over her heart. "This has gone on far too long." She marched out and opened the box she'd brought into the shop.

"What is all this stuff?" I asked as she took out seven purple candles, a black candle, a white candle, and bags full of different powders, including one that looked like soil. I picked it up and studied it.

"Graveyard dirt."

I dropped it with a *plop* onto the table. "Why did you bring graveyard dirt with you to work today?"

"I ordered it online, from the Hoodoo Supply Store. It's a Wall of Protection Kit."

She pulled out a card with an angel on it, and a piece of wood resembling a decayed tree root. "Is this something we're going to start selling?"

She shook her head. "It's a specialty item. I got it for you."

I poked at the piece of root with one finger. "Wow. Thanks."

She gave me an exasperated sigh. "It will keep invaders out, and it'll keep vandals away from your property."

"Or we could install cameras."

The bell above the shop jangled as Aunt Lucy walked in with a cane. She still wore the boot, but she got around much better at this point. Her eyes lit up when she saw the box of supplies.

"Oh. The Wall of Protection Kit is here. Let's get started."

I rolled my eyes. "Must we?"

She hobbled over to me. "Yes, and we'll do it for Cat and Sally, too."

"You two go ahead. I'll stay behind and mind the shop."

Aunt Lucy's forehead wrinkled into a frown. She wore a velvet hat today in sapphire blue. It looked vintage and had a small bunch of feathers on the side.

"You have to do it, Gracie."

"Why me?"

She took off her gloves. "Well, the ghost visited *you* last night."

"Not a ghost, Aunt Lucy, a man. Jinx scratched him, and he fell over your furniture. He did resemble poor Uncle Anton, but a real live person broke into your apartment last night. Not an apparition."

"Which is why the Wall of Protection will work. It's useless against ghosts. It'll only keep you safe from the living. To keep you safe from spirits, we'd need an exorcist, not a hoodoo kit. Thank goodness we don't need one of those. It was terribly expensive the last time we called one."

"You called an exorcist..."

"Yes, but as you said, this time we need protection from a man. Hence the hoodoo." She gave me a triumphant smile, knowing she'd backed me into a corner.

I lifted my hands in surrender. "Fine, but we should do Mr. Dalca, too."

Aunt Lucy let out a huff. "If we must, even though he doesn't deserve it, miserable old man."

We decided to take care of the shop first, and Aunt Lucy gathered the other items we needed. A white handkerchief. A piece of tin foil. A blank sheet of paper.

"What's this for?" I asked, holding up the blank sheet.

"To write the name of the perpetrator," said Mrs. Periwinkle. "Nine times. It's very clear. Since we don't know his name, we'll write, 'Anyone who means us harm.' I think it'll work, don't you, Lucy?"

"Of course. And the added bonus is that it'll give us a clue as to who's doing this. If they normally come into our shop, but suddenly stop, we can add them to the list of suspects because it will literally keep them from entering our space."

I wanted to slam my face into the table but managed to contain myself as Mrs. Periwinkle looked over the instructions, her glasses perched on her nose. Aunt Lucy peered over her shoulder, the feather waving on her tiny blue hat. They appeared, for all intents and purposes, like two little old ladies reading over a recipe or instructions for bridge club. I felt a migraine coming on.

"What exactly is hoodoo and how do the two of you know so much about it?"

"Wait. I have a description right here," said Mrs. Periwinkle, reading aloud. "'Hoodoo is African American folk magic. It's a mix of African beliefs with Native American botanicals and European folklore.' Lovely, isn't it?"

"See, Gracie. Nothing strange about it at all," said Aunt Lucy.

The migraine curled its way past my eye sockets and into the back of my head. "Can we get this over with?"

It took nearly an hour to burn the incense, sprinkle powders, carve the candles with the names of angels and protectors, and complete the ritual. By the time we finished cleaning up, customers streamed into the shop.

"What now?" I asked, already exhausted.

"Well, we have to take all of this to the graveyard and dispose of it," said Mrs. Periwinkle, matter-of-factly.

"Of course, we do," I said with a yawn.

"Then onto Sally's."

"Hooray."

Aunt Lucy stayed behind to take care of the shop. After we made our trip to the graveyard, we trundled over to Sally's with our giant box of hoodoo supplies.

"Wouldn't this be more effective in the middle of the night?"

Mrs. Periwinkle stopped walking, perplexed. "Magic doesn't have to be scary. Do you need to mix your potions at night?"

A few people passed by as she spoke and glanced at us curiously. I guess we did look kind of strange, a tiny blueberry of a woman in a bright cerulean dress, cardigan, and shoes, and a tall redhead wearing a wool skirt, tights, and a beige turtleneck reaching nearly up to her chin. The turtleneck covered up the hickey Dario had given me the night before. I was a sad mess of a person this morning.

I hushed her, pulling her aside. "No, I don't mix them at night because they aren't magic. They're simple, herbal formulas combined in such a way to induce health and stimulate good emotions."

She gave me a knowing look. "Explain the water."

I pursed my lips. "I haven't figured it out yet."

She winked and continued walking toward Sally's shop. "And explain the customers. They flock to buy your potions. Why do that if the potions didn't work?"

"Because they have impossibly romanticized views of love and relationships, fed to them by the media, and incredible pressure put upon them by our society to find love, get married and make babies, all before they turn thirty, preferably."

She stared at me like she wanted to shake me. "Out of all the things you said, only one is true."

"What?"

She paused on the stoop in front of Sally's shop. "We all

want to find love. We're desperate for it. Not because of what the television tells us to do, but because we crave it in our hearts and with every fiber of our being."

She wasn't wrong there. Every fiber of my being certainly craved Dario last night. "True love is a myth," I said. "A fairy tale."

She gave me a gentle pat on the cheek, her eyes filled with compassion. "No, it isn't. Love is the most powerful force in the universe. And once we find it, once we experience the real thing, it's awfully hard to let it go."

Sally greeted us at the door of her shop in a flourish of black and purple. She even wore a turban. Strains of *That Old Black Magic* echoed from the interior of her store. This had turned into a very interesting morning.

Sally lifted her arms to the sky with a dramatic wave of her black-gloved hands. "Let the hoodoo begin."

CHAPTER 27

RESISTANCE IS NOT FUTILE. IT'S VOLTAGE DIVIDED BY CURRENT.

The process to create a wall of protection around Sally's business took less time than ours did. Possibly because we'd already done it once.

"By the time we finish Mr. Dalca and Cat, we'll have it down to a science," said Mrs. Periwinkle.

"*Not* a science. This is a system of ritualistic and shamanistic beliefs based on primitive customs and fear." I shook my head in disbelief. Once again, I'd willingly participated in the propagation of irrational nonsense. The only benefit was that Sally seemed to enjoy it, and she needed cheering up.

"Any news yet?" I asked as we set up our supplies.

She shook her head. "Nothing. It's as if dear Bubu disappeared off the face of the earth. And Aggie went out of town for a couple of days to take care of some personal business. It's so lonely here without Aggie and my Bubu."

Mrs. Periwinkle gave her hand a squeeze. "You'll find Bubu. I'm sure of it, and you're lucky to have a sister like Aggie."

"I am," said Sally, beaming. "And it's even more precious to me now. We were estranged for years, you see, and a few months ago she came back into my life. Aggie was in a bad state, poor thing. I stepped in and helped. She needed to be with family. She's always been a fragile sort. That's why I'm kind of glad she went out of town for a few days. Bubu's disappearance really upset her. It's like she can't bear to be in the shop anymore. She spends most of her time wandering the streets, looking for my little doggie. She doesn't say so, of course. She makes excuses to leave, but I can tell. She wants to find her so desperately."

"As we all do," I said.

"They need to catch whoever is behind all this as soon as possible," said Sally. "Ralphie is beside himself. He wants me to sell the shop and move to San Francisco with him. And those Party Ark girls, the bookends..."

I smiled in spite of the seriousness of our conversation. "Missy and Sissy."

"Yes, those two. They said the police have no clues at all, and we as a community need to take care of this ourselves. They look like baby dolls, but they sound like vigilantes."

I frowned. "They do?"

"Well, not quite. They're all into the whole ARK community involvement thing. Even Aggie joined it."

I looked at her in surprise. "Wait. Aggie is in ARK? Why?"

"Well, she was lonely when she first came here, and it's been good for her. It's a social group, and it makes her feel more like part of the community." Sally gave us a sad smile. "We could use some Acts of Random Kindness at the moment. Whoever is behind all this crime must be clever if he can elude the police like this."

"But how smart can the bandit be if he can't spell?" I asked.

Sally gave me an odd look. "Whatever do you mean?"

"Well, the culprit misspelled something in every message.

It's almost like he writes in text-speak and doesn't have auto-correct."

"I see," she said, her face pale beneath her expertly applied makeup. "Oh, this hurts my heart."

Sally's reaction confused me, but she was under a great deal of stress. Mrs. Periwinkle gave Sally a thoughtful look. "It'll be all right, dearie, but we need to focus on the task at hand. You need to choose seven guardians and carve their names on these candles." Mrs. Periwinkle pulled the grave-yard dirt and purple candles out of the box. "Grace chose Dario as one of her guardians, of course."

She winked at me over her glasses. I didn't find it amusing. As angry as I was with him, he seemed an obvious choice, mostly because he kept showing up whenever trouble did. Sally, on the other hand, loved the idea.

"I'll take Dario, too. He's so nice to look at, and whether he's a good guardian or not, having someone that handsome hanging around is always enjoyable," she said with a wink.

Imagining Dario's reaction to that assessment, I held back a laugh, keeping my face serious as I tried to explain the process to Sally. "According to the instructions, it's a symbolic thing, and it works better if the guardians have some kind of connection. That's why we chose other people from Dario's family, too. Alvida, Anthony, and Anthony's younger brother, Tommy."

"Alvida is a matriarch, a powerful protector," said Mrs. Periwinkle. "And it's always good to have police and firemen as guardians."

"Firemen. Yummy," said Sally.

"And our last three were Mags, Claire, and Will Wax." Mrs. Periwinkle folded up her list and put it back in the pocket of her wool cardigan.

Sally put a finger to her chin. "I agree with Mags and Claire. And I adore Will, but I could squash him like a bug."

"What about Ralphie?" I asked, preparing to write his name.

Sally shook her head, a hint of sadness in her eyes. "No," she said clearing her throat. "Not Ralphie. How about Ivan."

I blinked. "Ivan Rochat?"

"The one and only. Who would be better to protect my castle than a big, handsome Viking? And he's so kind. He stopped by several times to ask about Bubu."

It didn't exactly surprise me Sally showed a fondness for Ivan. Only Dario seemed to immediately dislike him, and Dario had his reasons.

"We barely know Ivan," said Mrs. Periwinkle. "Where does he come from, and what does he do exactly?"

She made a good point. "I know he went to boarding school in Switzerland, but I have no idea what he does for a living, or why he's here," I said. "Which is disturbing. I even tried to Google him, but nothing showed up. It's weird."

Mrs. Periwinkle agreed with me. "We should stick to Will. He's small, but mighty. And the role of the guardian isn't a physical one. It's about forming a psychic circle of protection. Since Will is always here, he's the most obvious choice."

Sally waved a hand at us. "You're right. Of course. This isn't the first time I've gotten distracted by a pretty face and a muscular set of thighs. Will Wax it is. Good call."

After we finished the Wall of Protection, a thought kept niggling at me as we packed our things and headed off to the cemetery to dispose of the ashes. "Wouldn't Ralphie be the most logical guardian for Sally?"

Mrs. Periwinkle lifted her shoulders in a dainty shrug, a pensive frown on her face. "Not necessarily. Sally may think Ralphie needs protection, too, or…"

"Or what?"

For a second, I didn't think she'd answer. She sighed.

"Sally and Ralphie have been going through a rough patch lately."

"I suspected as much," I said.

"Well, I guess he moved out. He left without saying a word. Sally is trying to put on a brave face, but she's hurting."

"Oh." My heart went out to her. I'd put on such a brave face lately my cheeks ached from the effort. "It makes me sad. They seemed so perfect together."

She gave me a pat on the arm. "Even perfect couples go through hard times. Relationships are like the ocean. It's not all about smooth sailing. It's also about how you maneuver during the storms."

As if on cue, the sky darkened, and thunder sounded in the distance. "We'd better hurry," I said.

We managed to make it to Mr. Dalca's shop before the first fat raindrop hit the pavement. He looked less than pleased to see us. "Mrs. Trabuski told me you were coming. She said I had to be nice to you. She asks too much of me."

He sat on a stool next to his cash register, a pile of dusty old books by his side. Mrs. Periwinkle gave him a sunny smile.

"It's lovely to see you again, too, Mr. Dalca." She handed him the purple candles and he carved names into them right away. I stared at him in surprise.

"You've done this before?"

He scowled at me. "Haven't you?"

Mrs. Periwinkle flitted around the shop, lighting the incense and sprinkling powders. "Mr. Dalca is more magical than he lets on."

He turned away from her with a grunt of pure disgust. "Magic, schmagic. True power is located right here." He tapped his finger on the pile of books and a tiny cloud of dust rose into the air. "Knowledge is power. Books are power. I do this to make you stop bothering me."

For once, I agreed with Mr. Dalca. "We're in the same boat."

He looked at me from under his bushy eyebrows. "I heard the ghost who is not a ghost came to visit."

"Who told you that?"

"Your aunt. She is worried." He leaned close, his voice soft. "And he wanted something? Something *red?*"

I almost dropped my candle. "How did you know?" I asked and rolled my eyes. "Wait. Aunt Lucy again, right?"

"Maybe I can help you."

"How?"

"Your ghosty man is looking for something, and you cannot let him have it. It's important."

I gave him a steady look. "Why do you want to help us?"

Mrs. Periwinkle went to the back room of the shop to sprinkle powder there. I heard her softly humming to herself as she went about setting up the wall. It sounded like she sang, "Bibity, Bobity, Boo," an odd choice for a hoodoo ritual.

"Because it is vitally important that the thing he wants does not fall into the wrong hands."

"You know who he is, don't you?"

He tugged on his beard. "I have my suspicions."

"He's the same man who broke into your shop."

"I believe so."

"Tell me who he is."

"I cannot. It would put you and others in danger. It's a problem only I can deal with."

We engaged in a stare down. "I don't want your help."

Mr. Dalca narrowed his beady eyes at me. "You are making a foolish mistake, but you must promise not to give it to him."

"Give what to him exactly?" I asked, deciding to test him.

Mr. Dalca crooked his finger at me, telling me to come closer. I leaned forward, catching a whiff of exotic spices and pipe smoke on his clothes. "The Dragon Rouge," he said, his voice soft and his tone intense. "Don't play with it, Miss O'Leary. Don't touch it. And, most importantly, don't let him have it. The consequences could be dire."

We heard the sound of Mrs. Periwinkle's heels as she came back to the main room, and we finished the ritual, but Mr. Dalca's words echoed in my ears. They stayed with me as we went to Cat's and made a Wall of Protection around her shop. She wasn't back yet, so we did the ritual on the sidewalk, much to the entertainment of people passing by. It stopped raining, but the sky remained dark and ominous. When Mrs. Periwinkle finished and we made our last trip to the cemetery, I couldn't wait to go back to the shop.

Mrs. Periwinkle left with Will, promising to see us bright and early the next morning. I asked Aunt Lucy to stay. As soon as we closed up for the night, I lowered the blinds on the window and covered the hole to Mr. Dalca's shop with a book called *Smudging Made Simple*. I ran up the stairs to the apartment, taking them two at a time, as Aunt Lucy sat in the back room, waiting for me. When she saw what I held in my hands, she gasped.

"The Dragon Rouge. It's been a long time since I've seen it."

"You said it originally belonged to Uncle Anton?"

"Yes," she said, trembling. "And the man, the one who pushed me, looked so much like him. It frightened me."

I sat and took both her hands in mine. "He looked like Uncle Anton, but it wasn't him, Aunt Lucy. We were both scared when we saw him, so our memories could be skewed. Also, his dark cape and hood obscured most of his face. In actuality, he may not have looked that much like Uncle Anton at all, but when we saw him, our minds automatically filled in the blanks. It's a normal reaction."

She frowned. "You're right. He *did* have on a hood. Anton

never wore hoods. He hated them. Oh, Gracie. It's so obvious now. It couldn't have been him. What was I thinking?"

Always amazed at how Aunt Lucy could take such an illogical path to a logical conclusion, I held back from commenting further on Uncle Anton's fashion choices. "So, this flesh and blood man, who is not Uncle Anton, broke in at least twice looking for this." I tapped my hand on the box. "But why? And how did he know we have it?"

I turned the box over in my hands and Aunt Lucy wagged her finger at me. "Be careful. It can affect you. It changes people."

I put it down. I found her irrational belief in magic and fear of inanimate objects ridiculous, but I had to admit something about the dragon box felt off. It wasn't just its scaly exterior or the blood red stone or the dark spells tucked inside, but the dragon itself; like it studied us with its beady eye as we studied him.

"What do we do about it?"

Aunt Lucy stared at me with blue-eyed determination. "We figure it out."

The lights in the shop flickered as a clap of thunder sounded outside, and someone knocked on the front door. I let out a scream so loud I startled myself and slapped a hand over my mouth. "I'm sorry," I said, trying to control the racing of my heart.

"You are a nervous Nelly this evening." Aunt Lucy hobbled over to the door. I followed behind, grabbing a broomstick on the way in case I needed a defensive weapon. She glanced through the blinds. "Oh. It's Mags. And Claire is with her."

I heaved a sigh of relief. I didn't think the vandal would act while there were still people around, but he'd gotten awfully bold.

"I stopped by to see if Lucy was ready to go home," said Mags.

"And I brought soup." Claire gave me a kiss on the cheek and handed me a heavy pot.

"I brought wine," said a voice from behind Claire. Sally stood there, resplendent in a shiny red raincoat, hat, and matching boots, holding a bottle of merlot. Cat huddled next to her, shivering in a thin sweater.

"When did you get back?" I asked, pulling Cat into a hug as I ushered all of them into the store.

"Not long ago," she said. "I had this weird urge to come see you, and here I am. Is that okay? It looks like you're having a party."

"Not a party. A...spontaneous gathering." I smiled at her but found it odd so many of our friends showed up at once.

"I love spontaneous gatherings," said Aunt Lucy, clapping her hands together. "Although you're wrong about this, dearie. There is nothing spontaneous about it."

Before I could ask her what she meant, she'd already shuffled off to chat with our guests. The rain fell in earnest now, and they put their umbrellas into a stand near the door and peeled off their wet raincoats. Sally slipped out of her boots and set them on a mat. Even in her stocking feet, she towered above us. Her red dress perfectly matched her rain gear, as did her ruby red lipstick. She kissed me loudly on the cheek.

"How is Aggie?" I asked.

"Fine, I think," she said, patting her hair to make sure it was in place. "She should be back in town tomorrow, and I'm so glad. It's been lonely."

Sally smiled, but her normally bright eyes appeared haunted. I suspected I knew the cause. Ralphie moving out, combined with her missing dog, must have put a strain on poor Sally. I patted her shoulder, not sure what to say, and headed to the back room to put on the kettle for tea. As I went, I grabbed the Dragon Rouge from the table and carried it with me. It didn't seem prudent to leave it in the main room of the shop. As I tucked it into one of the kitchen cupboards in the far corner of the back room, a clap of thunder sounded so loudly it rattled the walls. I put a hand over my heart, willing myself to calm down, but I felt strangely tense and wound tighter than a top at the moment. I wrapped my cardigan around my body, put cups and saucers onto a pretty tray, and carried them out as another knock came at the door. I jumped into the air with a squeak, making the teacups clatter.

Aunt Lucy rolled her eyes. "Stop it, Gracie. Goodness me. It's enough to give an old lady a heart attack."

She opened the door to Alvida, who stood there flanked by three of her grandsons, Anthony, Tommy, and an irritated looking Dario. Each of them carried a tray of food.

"We wanted to stop by and check on you," said Alvida. "We brought dinner."

"Oh," I said, my cheeks getting pink. Dario watched me closely and I didn't know how to act around him now. "You didn't have to do that."

Alvida handed me her raincoat and brushed my protests aside. "Yes, we did. We're Italian. We cook when we're stressed. Tommy made the cannoli. They are to die for."

Tommy gave me a sheepish grin. "If Nunny approves, they must be good."

"Please come in," I said.

I ushered them into the room, and we chatted as Aunt Lucy set the table. Only Dario hung back, looking decidedly uncomfortable. I almost pitied him. Almost, but not quite.

His eyes met mine, and something pulsed within me, like my body recognized his on some basic cellular level and craved his nearness. I couldn't help but think about what happened between us, the arguing and the anger, but also the hunger and the passion. I needed to be careful. Dario Fontana was not good for me. Our relationship had been rocky and painful and doomed to failure, but I still felt this tremendously confusing connection to him. It gave me a new appreciation for what life must be like for drug addicts.

Aunt Lucy came up to me with a twinkle in her eye after we'd pulled together a mishmash of tables and chairs. "You know what's happening, don't you?"

I shook my head, thinking she'd tapped into all the weird sexual tension between me and Mr. Tall, Dark, and Gloomy. Aunt Lucy was not particularly observant, so I decided to feign ignorance.

"What do you mean? Nothing is happening."

She clasped her hands together, a giant, happy smile spreading across her face. "How can you be so clueless?"

"What are you talking about?"

"Our guardians have assembled. The hoodoo magic...it worked."

CHAPTER 28

THERE IS THE GOOD KIND OF CHEMISTRY
THAT MAKES THINGS LIKE GUMMY BEARS,
AND THE BAD KIND THAT CAUSES
EXPLOSIONS AND CAN WIPE CITIES OFF A MAP.
WE HAVE THE BAD KIND.

My jaw dropped as I looked around the room. "No...because Will isn't here."

The back door of the shop opened, and Will strolled in, shaking raindrops off his jacket. He looked up in surprise at the crowd gathered around the table.

"Sorry. I didn't mean to interrupt. I forgot my umbrella."

Aunt Lucy pointed to the last empty seat at the table as the rain picked up and the wind howled. "We were expecting you, Will. Now the circle is complete. Sit, and we'll begin."

The entire dinner tasted fantastic. Soup from Claire, a huge salad and eggplant parmesan from Alvida, and Tommy's cannoli for dessert. He unwrapped the platter after we cleared the dinner dishes and set it in the middle of the table.

"For some reason, I decided to make cannoli today. Then Nunny called and said we were going to stop by and visit Grace, so I brought it with me. How lucky is that? The only thing better would have been Dario's tiramisu. Have you tried his tiramisu, Grace?"

My cheeks got so hot I thought I might melt the cream inside the cannoli. "Uh, yes. I have."

I remembered his tiramisu quite fondly, but sitting across the table from him and talking about it tortured me. Being near him tortured me, too. My eyes were drawn to him constantly, and I felt his gaze on me as well. Why was he here? Alvida must have bullied him into it.

The night he made tiramisu for me, the night he made passionate love to me, remained something special and beautiful in my memory. Last night, in the ladies' room, we'd had sex. Nothing more, nothing less. I'd enjoyed it at the time, but it now seemed dirty and wrong.

I stood up, needing to get away. "Spoons," I said. "We need spoons."

"But we have forks," said Mags, holding one up. "They'll do."

I waved a hand. "I'll grab a few, just in case."

In the back room, I put both hands on the counter and took long, deep breaths. I needed to center myself, and I'd gotten close to doing so when Dario walked in.

"Can I help with the spoons?" he asked.

At first, I couldn't answer. I found myself staring at the way his dark hair curled rebelliously around his forehead, the way his eyes seem to soften when he looked at me, and the way he bit his lower lip self-consciously. I wanted to bite his lip, too, but I gave myself a mental slap, and shot him an incredulous look.

"Uh, no thank you," I said, opening a drawer and pulling out a handful of random teaspoons. "I can manage on my own. I don't need *anything* from you."

I slammed the drawer and made a pretense of wiping the spoons with a dishcloth. The spoons weren't dirty, but I couldn't go back to the main room with Dario, the great wall of muscle, blocking the doorway. If I tried to walk past him, I'd have to touch him, and I knew exactly where that would lead—to me, flat on my back, and devoid of both my panties and my self-respect.

"Grace..."

"Don't. Go back with the others. Please."

He moved closer and gently pulled at the neck of my sweater, wincing when he saw the giant purple bruise. "Sorry about that," he said, touching it with a soft caress and making my heart beat erratically in my chest. "I hurt you. And I'm not talking about your neck."

I stepped away, pulling my turtleneck up protectively. "Water under the bridge."

He shook his head. "No, it isn't. I have feelings for you. That should be pretty obvious, especially after last night."

"Last night we both made a huge mistake. Dating you in the first place was a huge mistake. And when Tommy brought up your tiramisu..." I let out a laugh, but it held no humor at all. "I wanted to crawl under the table and die."

"We need to talk."

"About what? About how you broke up with me by hiding at your grandmother's house? About how you weren't man enough to tell me the truth? About how you dumped me and started hanging out with Tiffany the next day? I don't want to talk, Dario." I tossed the teaspoons onto a tray. One clattered to the floor, and Dario leaned over to pick it up for me. I took it from his hand. "When we try to talk, we either fight or have sex."

He tucked his hands into the pockets of his jeans. "Is that necessarily a bad thing? I mean, I don't like the fighting, but the other part—"

I threw the towel onto the counter. "This isn't funny. You said it yourself. It's hurtful. You *hurt* me."

"I know," he said, reaching for me again. "And I want to explain."

I backed away from him. "You dropped me like...like...

liquid metal heated in an insufficiently insulated crucible and you didn't have a pair of tongs."

Not my best analogy, but, judging by the sudden flash of pain in his eyes, I assumed he got my point. "It wasn't like that," he said, coming closer.

"Stop it." I held up the spoons for protection, a ridiculous gesture. He pushed them aside as he put his hands on my cheeks and stared deeply into my eyes.

"Stop what?" he asked, his voice husky. I recognized that voice. It was his sexy pre-kiss voice. It had gotten me into a lot of trouble on previous occasions.

"You're doing this because you're jealous," I said. "You do realize that, right?"

His thumbs caressed my cheeks as he touched his forehead to mine. "I *am* jealous," he said. "But I miss you. So much. Your smile, your laugh, your incredible brain...all of it. All of you."

"You're the one who broke it off. And now what? You've changed your mind?"

"I wish I could explain why I did it, why I reacted that way, but I can't," he said, and he no longer carried the sexy, husky note in his voice. Now he sounded almost...tortured.

I gave him a tight smile, trying to hide my pain. "You belong with Tiffany. You deserve each other. Consider last night our final f..." My voice increased in volume, as the front room grew quiet as they all sat out there listening to us argue. I lowered it to a whisper. "Our final farewell."

I pushed past him and went back into the main room, struggling to put on a good face. Our friends resumed their conversations as soon as I walked in, all the while giving me awkward, pitying glances.

I didn't fool anyone. Alvida watched me like a hawk, making it even worse. She missed nothing. She pulled me aside as I cleared up the dishes. "You argued. It sounded awful. What's going on with the two of you?" She folded her arms across her chest and tilted her head to one side. "You care about him, and I know he cares about you."

I struggled to stay calm. "Judging by the way he dumped me, I think you're wrong about that one, Mrs. Fontana," I said, walking away.

Unfortunately, Alvida followed me, like a little Calabrian bulldog. "For being two of the smartest people I know, you're both pretty stupid."

I struggled to control my temper, knowing she wanted to help. "I think I made it clear. *He* broke up with *me*. If you want answers to your questions, ask him. He can't seem to tell me what happened, so how am I supposed to tell you?"

Her shoulders slumped, and she looked weary as she shook her head in disbelief. "It makes no sense. Dario was over the moon, and a day later he acted like he'd lost his best friend in the world. Then he started going out with that blond thing. The one named after the jewelry company."

"Tiffany," I said with a sniff.

"Yes, her," said Alvida. "And he doesn't even *like* her. He's so unhappy. Miserable, if you want to know the truth of it. And so are you. I see it all over your pretty face."

"And what am I supposed to do about it?"

She grabbed me by the shoulders and gave me shake. "Fight for him. There is something wrong here, honey. The night he came to my house, he acted like a zombie. Even now, he's not himself. Something isn't adding up, and I intend to figure out exactly what it is."

"How reassuring."

"Trust me. No one is as relentless, or as nosy, as an Italian grandma." Her gaze went to Dario, who currently looked at her with an expression of absolute horror mixed with panic. He shook his head, mouthing the word, "Stop," to her, but Alvida ignored him. "I have some theories, but we need to talk about it later. Alone. I'm getting the death stare from my grandson right now, and the cannoli can't wait forever. I need to serve the coffee so we can eat them."

Alvida made espresso, and we sat around the table. Although hard to focus with the rather gloomy Dario sitting across from me, I did my best to ignore him. Especially when the subject of last night's break-in came up.

"We haven't found a single lead," said Anthony. "Not about the vandalism or the break-ins or about Bubu. Do you ladies have any idea who might be trying to scare you?"

Sally blushed adorably. "I love it when you call me a 'lady,' Anthony. It makes me go all warm and fuzzy inside."

He seemed confused. "But you are a lady. What else would I call you?"

Alvida kissed the top of his head as she handed him a tiny cup filled with steaming hot espresso. "And that is one of the reasons why we love you so much, sweet Anthony."

Tommy snorted. "*Sweet* Anthony," he said, giving Dario a nudge. Alvida rewarded him with a none-too-gentle smack on the back of the head. He ducked. "Ow. Nunny, stop it. I'm laughing because he wasn't so sweet last night while rounding up all those naked women. He turned into Mr. Tough Guy Cop then."

Anthony rolled his eyes. "They're driving me nuts. It's the same thing over and over again. Naked women running around in a city park at midnight. It's not normal. And the only answer I get from them to explain their behavior? They said they had to do it for the love potion to work. They said it's 'in the instructions.' Can you believe it?"

Dario's eyes widened. Cat choked on a bite of her cannoli. Will immediately patted her on the back. "Are you okay?" he asked. She nodded, but shot me a long look, and I knew we both thought the exact same thing.

My silly love potions had caused all the naked dancing in

the South Side. Fiona came up with those instructions as a joke, but they were on *my* love potions. And since I was the one selling them that made me the responsible party.

I'd turned into a public menace. I tried to keep my expression as neutral as possible but wondered if I'd face legal repercussions down the line for more than false advertising and selling something not verified by the FDA. If the instructions on my potions actively encouraged naked frolicking in the moonlight, could I be held legally responsible?

"I cannot even tell you how many hours I have wasted in the last few weeks on paperwork," said Anthony, rubbing his face. "Let alone how difficult it is to try to corral naked women without being too rough or accidentally inappropriate. They're usually inebriated as well. One lady told me she'd never be able to dance naked in the moonlight without a few glasses of chardonnay. It was Candace, the nice teller who always waits on me at the bank. Candace. I couldn't believe it."

Now I choked on a cannoli. Tommy gave me a funny look. "What's up with all of you choking on my cannoli tonight?"

Sally covered her mouth to suppress a giggle. "Choking on a cannoli is the worst, isn't it?"

Tommy seemed perplexed, and the older ladies at the table struggled not to laugh. Aunt Lucy put a hand on her chest. "I once choked on a cannoli so huge—"

I interrupted her, not wanting to hear the end of her story. "Sorry, Tommy," I said, taking a sip of water. "Ignore them, please. The cannoli are delicious, but I got greedy and ate it too fast."

"Me, too," said Cat.

Aunt Lucy looked from me to Cat and back again. "Or did you choke because the naked ladies dancing outside might have something to do with—" I shushed her effectively by kicking her in the good leg under the table. "Oh. Never mind."

Now Anthony eyed us, full on suspicious. "Is there anything you want to tell me?" We shook our heads, mirroring expressions of wide-eyed innocence. Anthony tilted his head to one side. "You know more than you're letting on, but I'm mainly concerned about the threats at the moment."

Something tugged at the corners of my mind, elusive, like a wisp of smoke. "Sometimes when I have an especially perplexing problem in the lab, I get lost in the details and I need to simplify. I find the answer by going back to the basics and using the scientific method of problem solving."

Dario nodded. "Start with defining the problem."

As always, he immediately understood where I went with this. I hated that about him now, mostly because I'd loved it about him when we were together.

He was so smart, it pissed me off. I narrowed my eyes at him. I wanted to say something snarky, about how he should define his own problems first, and he could benefit from employing the scientific method to keep his you-know-what in his pants, but I held myself back.

"But how do we know what the problem is?" asked Mags, bringing me out my reverie. "We can't define it until we iden- tify it. How does this help us figure out who is trying to frighten all of you?"

"We have to turn it around, and view it from a different angle," I said. "We may be misinterpreting the data or over- looking something significant."

Dario agreed. "We need to think like the bad guy."

Sally closed her eyes and rubbed her temples. "Be the bad guy. Be the bad guy," she said. She opened her eyes, shaking her head. "Nope. I can't do it. I can't figure out who'd vandalize Lucy's shop, nearly set fire to mine, steal Bubu, sneak into Grace's bedroom, ransack Mr. Dalca's shop, and write all those nasty notes. How could one person do all of those things? They'd almost have to make it their full-time job."

"Or be in two places at once," said Aunt Lucy.

"Unless it isn't one person," I said.

The whine of sirens filled the air as Tommy and Anthony's phones rang in unison. They jumped to their feet, faces serious, and whispered something to Dario.

"What is it?" I asked, following them to the door. "What's going on?"

Dario put his big hands on my shoulders, his eyes worried. "Stay here," he said. "Don't leave the shop."

"Where are you going?"

Anthony answered, his face grim. "Someone found a package. The bomb squad is on their way, but we have to go help." His dark eyes went to Cat, and she paled instantly. "It was in front of the Black Lotus."

She leapt to her feet, and started for the door, but Tommy grabbed her and held her back. "No, Cat. It's too dangerous. You need to stay here. We'll call you as soon as it's safe."

"But you don't understand," she said, pushing against him. Although tiny compared to Tommy, he struggled to hold her back. "My dad is in the shop. He's working tonight."

At her words, both Anthony and Dario shot out the door. Tommy kept a grip on Cat, his face kind. "We'll take care of him, I promise, but you need to stay here. Are we in agreement?"

"Yes," she said, her voice small and scared. "Help him, Tommy. Please."

Tommy motioned to Sally, the tallest and strongest person in the room, to help with Cat. She pulled Cat into her arms and spoke to her in soothing tones as Tommy raced out the door after his cousins. "It's okay, sweetness," said Sally. "Your father is going to be fine."

"We should go to the back room," said Alvida, her lips tight and her face drawn.

She didn't say she was concerned about us being near the glass windows in the front of the shop if the bomb exploded, but we all understood. As we sat in the back room, huddling together, we tried to find a way to comfort Cat. No murmured words of reassurance calmed her, however.

"What if I never see him again?" she asked, her delicate face pinched and worried.

I stared at her, realizing I might never see Dario again. Dario with his broad shoulders and brilliant mind and sweet kisses that stole my breath away. Yes, I was mad at him, and I hated him at the moment, but it didn't change how much he meant to me, or how much I cared about him.

Acknowledging it felt like a blow to the gut. Unable to stop myself, I did the only thing I could think of. I jumped to my feet, grabbed my jacket, and headed straight to the door.

"Grace, where are you going?" asked Aunt Lucy.

I didn't answer. I couldn't. Instead, I raced out of the shop and headed straight to the Black Lotus.

CHAPTER 29

ACCORDING TO CHEMISTRY, ALCOHOL IS A SOLUTION.

I ran, expecting to hear an explosion at any moment. I waited for the sound of breaking glass and the smell of burning plastic and sulphur, but does a bomb even smell like sulphur? I had no idea. I wanted to Google it but lacked time at the moment due to having more important things to worry about. Mostly Dario.

He'd never have the good sense to hang back. He'd jump in and put himself in danger if it meant helping others. He wouldn't think twice about it.

I ran past the gawkers and the fire trucks and the police cars, my eyes searching for him. I worried someone might try to stop me, but no one did. I expected to see barricades and bomb sniffing dogs and lots of tense professionals trying not to get blown up. Something quite different greeted me.

A small crowd formed in front of the Black Lotus, but they didn't act like people in the middle of a crisis. I even heard the sound of someone laughing.

"What happened?" I asked a police officer carrying equipment back to his car. My breath came out in puffs as I tried to regain my composure.

"A new clock for the tattoo parlor," he said. "The delivery guy didn't have the sense to leave it in the doorway. He put it in the middle of the sidewalk. Some idiot heard it ticking as they walked past and called it in. Like bombs even tick these days. Got a whole bunch of people upset over nothing."

"Everyone is okay?"

"Of course," he said, getting impatient. "Scared the crap out of the shop owner though."

He pointed to a big man with brawny arms covered in tats. Cat's father. He looked nothing like his petit, dark-haired daughter, but he wore a Black Lotus T-shirt. Standing right next to him was Dario.

I let out a sigh of relief. He was safe. Perfectly and absolutely safe. And I realized something both important and terrifying.

I loved Dario Fontana.

Not a neat, tidy, happy kind of love. Oh, no. The way I felt made me desperate and sad as a painful wave of emotions engulfed me, nearly knocking me to my knees. Being named persona non grata at the university wounded me to the core, destroying my reputation and shredding my professional aspirations to pieces, but I'd learned from it. And this experience had taught me a valuable lesson as well. Loving someone who didn't love me back hurt on a far deeper level. A cellular level. Being named persona non grata may have broken my spirit but being rejected by Dario broke my heart. I didn't know how to move on.

As I gathered the courage to go and speak with him, I noticed someone in pink standing beside him. Tiffany tossed back her blond head and laughed at something Dario said. As soon as her eyes met mine, she wrapped her arms around Dario's waist, resting her head against his side, and shot me a nasty, victorious smirk.

I didn't stay to see anymore. I turned and trudged back to

the Hocus Pocus Magic Shop, weary and despondent. At the
end of the block, Cat hurried toward me, a huge smile on her
pretty face.

"Did you hear? He's okay. It was a stupid ticking clock. He
must have ordered it online and forgotten about it." She practically danced as she walked.

"That's great news," I said, giving her a hug.

She kissed my cheek. "I'll be back in a few minutes. I
want to see my dad."

At least something turned out well tonight. Not for me, of
course. Seeing Tiffany with Dario was the perfect ending to a
perfect week.

When I got back to the shop, Alvida and Aunt Lucy sat at
the table, waiting for me, a bottle of whisky between them.
They were drinking it straight.

"Where is everyone?" I asked.

"They went home," said Aunt Lucy, pouring me a glass. "I
told Mags I'd sleep here tonight. There's a couch in the back
room. I'll be quite cozy."

They raised their glasses, and I joined them. "Cheers," I
said. "What's going on?"

"We need to talk," said Alvida. "But we want your friends
to be here for this, too. I called Fiona. She's on her way. And
Cat should be back any minute now."

"Oh, great. An intervention."

Alvida finished her whisky, slamming her glass on the
table. "Most definitely."

Fiona arrived a few minutes later. Even in a hoodie and
jeans she somehow looked glamorous. "Did you hear about
the bomb scare?" she asked, her blue eyes huge in her face. "It
was just a clock, right?"

"Yes," I said. "Someone heard the ticking and freaked out.
Strange, huh?"

"It gets stranger," said Alvida. "Anthony rang us before

you got back. The caller was an anonymous tipster using an untraceable phone. They're looking into it right now."

The door swung open and Cat came back into the shop, the sleeves of her sweater pulled over her hands to ward off the cold. A brisk wind rustled the dry, fallen leaves on the sidewalk and made the sign hanging above the front door sway and creak. We poured her some whisky, but Aunt Lucy kept her eyes on the storm brewing outside.

"Something wicked this way comes," she said softly as she watched the leaves swirl and scatter. Her words sent a tremor up my spine. I got up to lock the door of the shop and jumped when I saw Aggie standing on the sidewalk.

"Aggie?" I asked, stepping outside. "Come in. You must be freezing."

She wore only a dark grey sweater and a matching skirt, but no jacket. Her face pale, she looked so thin and tired I worried the wind could blow her away like it did the dried-up autumn leaves.

"I can't come in," she said. "Is Sally here?"

I shook my head. "She went home. Are you all right?"

"I heard about the bomb and wanted to check on you."

"Not a bomb, thankfully. Just a misunderstanding and possibly a prank call. We're all fine."

"A misunderstanding?" She wrinkled her forehead, as if trying to figure something out.

"Are you okay, Aggie?"

She looked at me in surprise. "Yes, I'm just tired. I needed to go back to my house in Grovetown for a few days, to check on things. It's stressful going back there. Lots of bad memories. I'm sure you know what I mean."

"I do," I said, remembering exactly how it felt to be the academic equivalent of a leper on campus. But something about Aggie's vacant, confused expression worried me. "Why don't you come in and chat? Aunt Lucy and Alvida are forcing us to drink whiskey. It should be an interesting evening."

"No, thanks. I need to get back to my...to Sally." She fixed her eyes on mine. "Be careful. Things are not what they seem."

A chill went over my body at the fear lurking in her eyes. I wanted to ask what frightened her so badly, but she'd already turned and walked away...heading in exactly the opposite direction of Sally's shop.

A sign in front of the store advertising Samhain supplies, clattered to the sidewalk, making me jump. I bent to pick it up, but someone else beat me to it.

"Ivan?" He'd come out of nowhere.

"Hello, Grace," he said, handing me the sign. "You'll want to bring this inside. The wind is picking up."

"Thank you." I set the sign next to the entrance of the shop and rubbed my arms to keep warm. "Did you hear about the bomb scare?"

He nodded. "A false alarm, from what I understand. Are you okay? No more threats or other issues?"

"Nope," I said with a snort. "My aunt and her friend put a protective hoodoo charm on the shop. It's supposedly keeping the bad guys out, so we're good...at least for the moment. It expires on the night of the full moon." I shook my head. "This is what I'm dealing with. Hoodoo and love potions and spell books and a dragon. My life is like one of those silly old horror movies. I keep waiting for Bella Lugosi or Lon Chaney to pop out and scare me. Well, I guess we do have Mr. Dalca. He's close enough."

"A dragon?" he asked, leaning close. "How interesting. Was it fire breathing? Can you show it to me? I've always wanted to meet a dragon."

I knew he teased me, but he made me uncomfortable, mostly because Ivan radiated sexuality the way a lighthouse emitted a beacon of light. He practically pulsated with it. And he smelled as good as he looked, like expensive cologne and fine wool and luscious man. I backed away so he wouldn't realize I was sniffing him.

"No, not fire breathing, just a carving on an old wooden box..." I stopped myself from saying anymore. I kind of wished I hadn't said anything at all, especially when I saw something strange spark in Ivan's blue eyes. Something intense and kind of scary.

"What sort of box?"

I shrugged, backing away even more. "Just a silly old box. It's nothing. There's been some weird stuff going on here lately, and it's starting to affect my brain."

He scanned my face, his expression so neutral it seemed forced. "This time of year affects us all, don't you think? As the days get shorter and the nights grow long and cold, it puts everyone on edge."

"I guess you're right."

He placed a finger under my chin and tilted my face up to his. "Grace, would you like to go out to dinner sometime? Not to make Mr. Fontana jealous, but to spend time with me."

"I wish I could, but I can't. I'm sorry."

He put his hand back by his side. "You still have feelings for Dario."

"Sadly, I do."

He shook his head, biting his lip in the sexiest way possible. "Such a pity. Well, enjoy the rest of your evening, Grace O'Leary. I'll see you soon."

I waved goodbye, and watched him walk away, his blond hair shining under the light of the street lamps. He possessed the most beautiful backside I'd ever seen, and his front side didn't disappoint either.

"I'm an idiot," I said under my breath. "Definitely an idiot."

I brought the sign inside, glad to be out of the wind. With unexpected visits from both Aggie and Ivan, I was gone long enough for everyone else to pour a second round of drinks. Alvida, Aunt Lucy, Cat, and Fiona sat around the table, sipping whiskey and chatting. Aunt Lucy already looked toasted.

"Finally," she said. "You're back. Now we can start."

I sank into a chair. Cat handed me my whiskey. "You're going to need this," she said.

"Oh, no. What are we doing, Aunt Lucy?"

"We're creating the antidote."

"The...what?"

Alvida took my hand in hers. "We figured it all out. Dario is messed up in the head because that blonde girl gave him one of your love potions. He isn't in love with her. He's under a spell. We have to figure out how to make the antidote and save my grandson."

"I sold the love potion to her," said Aunt Lucy. "It's true."

Almost too puzzled to respond at first, I stared at them. "Wait. You think Dario is no longer interested in me because Tiffany gave him one of my love potions?"

"Absolutely," said Alvida. "Why else would he be with her?"

I fought to remain calm. "So it doesn't make sense that he's with her because she's beautiful and well-dressed and perfect, but being under the power of a love potion *does* make sense?"

They nodded in unison. Fiona bit her lip. "It is kind of weird how he was crazy about you one day and hanging around with Tiffany the next."

"Oh, please. Not you, too. He's a man. Are we forgetting

this? Men do these things, especially men who look like Dario. They're kind of known for it. He cheated on me."

"He didn't cheat on you," said Alvida.

Unbelievable. Would this nightmare of an evening ever end? I struggled to answer her in a patient, rational manner. "I saw him outside with Tiffany only moments ago. They looked like a couple, Alvida. I'm sorry to disappoint you."

"They looked like a couple, but they aren't a couple," said Alvida. "They haven't slept together. He hasn't even kissed her."

"And how do you know?"

"I have my sources," she said.

"Tommy," said Aunt Lucy with a bright smile. "I'm sure it's Tommy."

"You're right," said Alvida. "It's Tommy. It's always Tommy. He's the best source of information in the South Side, and he knows Dario better than anyone. Do you know what he told me? He said even when Dario is with Tiffany, the only person he can think about, or talk about, is you. Does he sound like a cheater?"

"Well, he's still with Tiffany. That says it all."

Alvida leaned closer. "Tommy thinks something fishy is going on, and I trust Tommy's judgment. He told me it's like Dario is under some kind of spell. Tommy's words, not mine. I got to thinking about your love potions, and it clicked." She snapped her fingers. "Dario is under the influence of one of your potions. I'm sure of it."

"You can't be serious." I looked at the others for support, but they seemed to be on board with Alvida's crazy theory.

"Sorry, Grace. I have to agree with them," said Cat. "I know it sounds far-fetched, but what if it's true?"

"You're kidding me." I stared into each of their faces. Aunt Lucy and Alvida had managed to get even Cat and Fiona on their side. "Fine. This flies in the face of everything I believe in, but I give up. Let's make an antidote. I'll find a way to give it to Dario. And, when it doesn't work, you'll all promise to leave me alone, right?"

"Well, you'll have to dance naked under the light of the moon first," said Aunt Lucy. "It's part of the spell, so it has to be part of the counter-spell."

I lifted my hands in surrender. "Why not? I'll dance naked, act like a crazy person, and most likely get arrested. Tomorrow, when you see it's all nonsense, you can break me out of jail, and we'll move on. Sound like a plan?"

I downed my whisky in one gulp and coughed as it burned my throat. Aunt Lucy wagged a finger at me. "Slow down, girlie. Jameson should be sipped, not chugged. Show some respect. Also, how are you going to mix a decent antidote for poor Dario if you're three sheets to the wind?"

"Poor Dario?" I asked, scowling at her, but she was right about one thing. Getting wasted tonight would make all of this so much worse. "What about 'poor Gracie'?"

"You're both poor," said Alvida. "And you're both stupid."

I laughed. "Thank you, Mrs. Fontana. I can always count on you for honesty."

"You can, and it's a valuable thing," she said.

"And you can count on me, too, sweetheart," said Aunt Lucy. "Because I love you. We all do."

I put down my glass and got to my feet, trying to quash a swell of emotion at her words. "Fine. Let's make the antidote and get it over with. I assume the instructions are in my grimoire somewhere?"

"Maeve McAlroy wouldn't have left out something so important," said Aunt Lucy. "I'm sure of it."

I rubbed my forehead with my fingers. Aunt Lucy's words made sense to me, which meant I'd seriously gone off the deep end. "I can't believe I'm participating in this nonsense."

Aunt Lucy took my fingers in her hand, her normally

sweet expression serious and intense. "It's not nonsense. This is what I've tried to tell you. It's magic, *your* magic, but in order for it to work, you have to believe in it. And you have to believe in yourself. If you can't, all hope is lost, and I'm afraid Dario will be lost, too."

She got up and hobbled to the back room, leaning heavily on her cane. Alvida, Cat, and Fiona followed. Jinx jumped on the table, his green eyes fixed on mine in what seemed like a challenge. He let out a sharp, "Meow," and I got to my feet.

"Fine," I said, picking him up. "Even the cat is yelling at me. I guess I have no choice."

As I went to the back of the shop to join the others, my palms began to sweat. Every part of my scientific brain knew this was a load of rubbish, and no antidote could make Dario mine, but a tiny part of my heart still wanted to believe it. And as my brain shouted, "They are wrong. They are most definitely wrong," my heart whispered ever so softly, "But what if they are right?"

CHAPTER 30

WHEN LIFE GIVES YOU MOLD, MAKE PENICILLIN.

As soon as I touched the grimoire, I immediately experienced the now familiar surge of connectedness. I couldn't explain it, and didn't want to try, but it seemed like the grimoire was as much a part of me as my red hair, my tendency to freckle, and my inability to form cohesive sentences when Dario Fontana entered a room. It made no sense, but I felt a strange spiritual bond to the little leather-bound volume, perhaps because my ancestor penned it. Or maybe because the spells written inside seemed more like chemistry than magic to me. I couldn't say, but the way I felt about the grimoire made all this nonsense about creating an antidote for Dario more palpable. Not logical exactly, but acceptable.

"I cannot believe I'm doing this," I muttered as I opened the book. As we'd predicted, Maeve McAlroy left instructions for antidotes. I translated for the others. "It looks like we should put the ingredients together in reverse order. By the way, there is nothing about dancing naked at midnight. It's not part of the formula."

"Oh, remember I added that part," said Fiona with a

giggle. "As a joke. I never imagined anyone would actually do it."

"Maybe we can leave it out," I said.

Aunt Lucy shook her head. "Oh, my. No. You can't leave anything out. You have to replicate exactly what put Dario under this spell. Otherwise, it won't work."

I counted slowly to five before responding. "First of all, it's pretty cold outside, and not naked dancing weather. Secondly, where do you suggest I perform this task? If I go to the park, Anthony will have to arrest me."

"True," said Alvida. "He's been arresting a lot of naked women lately, poor kid."

"What about the Enchanted Garden Café?" asked Aunt Lucy. "It's private there, and I'm sure Claire won't mind lighting a bonfire to keep you warm."

Fiona pulled out her phone, unfazed by Aunt Lucy's convoluted logic. She sent a text to her mother and got a response almost immediately.

"As luck might have it, my parents already lit a bonfire tonight. I told them to keep it burning and leave the premises as soon as we arrive. They were fine with it. They didn't even ask any questions."

"They should join us," said Aunt Lucy. "It'll be fun."

"Um, no one is watching me dance. I want to be clear here."

"I agree," said Alvida. "It's private, and I'm far too old to be dancing around in my birthday suit. Also, you just broke your leg, Lucinda. Do you think you should be hopping around on it in the dark?"

Aunt Lucy frowned. "You're never too old, Alvida. Don't be such a stick in the mud. But you're right about my leg. It could be dangerous. Fine. No dancing for us."

"I'm glad that's settled," I said. "We still have some water from the fountain, and all the other ingredients, but there is one additional thing we need, and I'm not sure how we can get it."

"Oh, no," said Aunt Lucy. "What is it?"

I pointed to the last line in the section about antidotes. "It says we need 'The broken-hearted tears of the one most grievously injured.' I guess that's me, but if I have to cry, it's not going to happen."

"What do you mean?" asked Cat.

"I don't cry, especially not in front of other people."

"True," said Aunt Lucy. "You've never been a crier, even when you were a little girl. It's your practical nature. You see things in such a scientific way, like normal human emotions are a mystery to you."

I stared at her. "I experience emotions. I feel things deeply, in fact. I'm not a robot."

She patted my hand. "I know, dearie, and I'm not criticizing. I wish I could be more like you. I cry at the drop of a hat. You're able to separate yourself from the emotion of a situation and look at it objectively. It's a talent. The problem is now you need to jump inside and experience it, and it'll be hard for you."

"Or she could cut an onion. Onions make everyone cry," said Alvida.

Aunt Lucy shook her head. "The tears have to be from the heart. Grace has to cry because she's sad, and she has to let it all out, or it won't work."

I wrapped my arms tightly around myself. "I'm not sure I can."

Aunt Lucy removed the sleeping Jinx from her lap and hobbled over to me, placing both hands on my cheeks. Much smaller than me, she had to stretch. "Gracie-bug. What are you afraid of?"

"If I start to cry," I said, my voice a whisper. "I might not be able to stop."

She gave my cheek a gentle pinch. "You will, darling. But, like the storm brewing outside, it will bring quite the downpour."

Alvida raised a finger. "Speaking of which, we'd better get started. If you plan to mix a magic antidote for my grandson and dance naked at midnight, you're running out of time. It's almost eleven. Let's get the show on the road."

I opened the cupboard and took out the marble bowl, as per the instructions. "Since we added water from a sacred pool last for the love potion, we'll do it first this time."

I poured in the water, cherry juice, brandy wine, honey, rose water, and all the other items listed. After I stirred it up, I stared at it in shock.

"It isn't purple and swirly," said Aunt Lucy. "It's as black as night."

I frowned. "Which makes no sense. We added all the same ingredients, just in reverse order. Why would it end up like this?"

"I can't wait to see what happens when you put the tears in," said Alvida, munching on one of Fiona's cookies. "This will be quite the show."

The tears. I'd forgotten about the tears. "How am I going to do this? I can't make myself cry."

"Are you sure you don't want to try the onion?" asked Alvida.

"No." Aunt Lucy shook her head so vehemently her long dangly earrings jingled. "It has to be an emotional cry. Not onions. You need to forget about the onions, Alvida."

She shrugged. "I'm Italian. Almost everything we cook starts with onions. I have onions on the brain."

"And Grace, you have Dario on the brain," said Fiona softly. "What you need to do is let him into your heart."

"I have. I did. And where did it get me?" I stared at the black, goopy potion. "We're wasting time. It'll never work."

"It won't until you believe," said Aunt Lucy. She grabbed one of my hands. Alvida grabbed the other. Fiona and Cat joined in until we formed a small circle. "Close your eyes and think of Dario. The good and the bad. The beautiful and the hurtful."

I did as she said and felt nothing at first. But the energy created by all of us standing together and touching changed my thoughts. Instead of remembering Dario's face, I saw the details, too. The stubble on his jaw, the dark silk of his hair, the deep brown of his eyes. I heard the timbre of his voice in my ear, felt his touch on my skin, and even smelled the unique spicy, clean scent that was all his own, and the tears finally came. They rolled down my cheeks one after another, wetting my face and neck. Aunt Lucy let go of my hand and gathered them into a small glass tube with a stopper she kept next to the sink.

"How many do you think we need?" asked Alvida, looking for another vessel to store my tears in.

"This will be enough," said Aunt Lucy, watching my face. "Are you okay, Gracie?"

I wiped my cheeks. "Yes," I said, my voice catching. "I think so."

Even though my eyes were now open, images of Dario seemed burned into my brain. I couldn't stop thinking about him, and I couldn't stop crying, but my tears weren't only about Dario. I also cried about Dr. Lewis's accusations, and the way Roger took over my classes, and because Jonathan was a weak, disloyal prick.

"I knew it," I said, weeping uncontrollably. "I can't stop. I c-c-c-can't stop crying."

Alvida, of course, managed to snap me right out of it. "Enough already. You have a job to do, and it's time to do it. Put those tears to use, young lady. Mix them into this antidote, and let's get moving. You have to be naked and dancing in forty minutes or this was all for nothing."

Like a slap in the face, it jarred me from my self-pity and brought me back to the task at hand. "You're right," I said. Alvida handed me a damp cloth and I used it to pat my face. "Let's do this."

I emptied the vial of my tears into the bowl, and we all gasped as the mixture changed from black to a yellow as bright as sunlight. "What happened?" asked Fiona.

"I have no idea," I said. "It's...well, it's not possible. It makes no sense at all."

"Magic doesn't make sense, silly," said Aunt Lucy. "Magic is in your bones. It's in your heart. You can't explain it, or see it, but, if you're lucky enough, you get a chance to come across it and to know it."

"Like love?" asked Fiona.

"More like an orgasm," said Aunt Lucy. "Some people never experience it, and they have no idea what they're missing out on. But, once you do, you recognize when it's about to happen again. And some serious magic is about to happen tonight, ladies. I know it."

CHAPTER 31

A CHEM LAB IS LIKE A WILD PARTY. SOME DROP ACID, OTHERS DROP THE BASE.

The orange glow of the bonfire greeted us as we entered the walled garden behind the café. With trees blocking the autumn wind, the bonfire provided a surprising degree of warmth. As the fountain gurgled next to us, and wood crackled in the fire, my body relaxed. It felt so peaceful and calm here, like we weren't in the middle of the city, but in a quiet, hidden garden far off in the country.

Claire and Simon left out a bottle of wine for us and three glasses. Smart move. Fiona uncorked the bottle and poured each of us a glass. I took a long sip. "I've never undressed in a public place before."

Cat laughed. "None of us have. Right, Fiona?"

Fiona paused, and even in the dim light I saw her cheeks redden. "Well, the summer solstice party did get pretty crazy last year."

I studied her face. "Didn't you mention something about you and Matthew behind a rhododendron bush?"

She pointed to a large bush in the corner of the garden. "The pagans weren't the only ones frolicking that night."

Cat snorted. "Frolicking? You meant to use a different 'f' word, Fiona."

The whisky I'd consumed, plus the wine, gave me a bad case of the giggles, but nerves contributed to it as well. I'd never done anything like this before, which brought on a worrisome thought.

"Can I get arrested for this?"

"I don't think so," said Fiona. "Or the police would have put the pagans in the slammer years ago."

Her use of the term "slammer," and the way she slurred her words when she said it, made all three of us dissolve into another fit of giggles. Fiona took a deep breath. "Sorry. I'm not much of a drinker. What time is it, Grace?"

I glanced at my watch. "It's nearly twelve." I emptied the contents of my glass, needing liquid courage at the moment. "I'd better do this. Wish me luck."

They went into the café, leaving me alone next to the bonfire. Stars twinkled in the sky, and trees swayed in the breeze, causing leaves to flutter to the ground around me like a gentle rain. Someone turned on music, probably Claire. Dark, mysterious, and sensual, it created the perfect setting for casting a counter-spell at midnight.

"It's now or never," I said to myself as I removed my clothing. I piled it carefully on a bench near the fountain as the clock at the church down the street chimed midnight.

For a moment, I stood by the fire, unsure what to do. But as I listened to the sounds of the music and the night, an odd peace enveloped me. The warmth of the fire contributed to it, as did the alcohol I'd consumed, but it was more than that. I became a part of the trees and the flowers and the burning flames. I'd never experienced this sort of connection to the world around me, and it brought me such joy and happiness I did the only thing I could.

I danced.

I forgot about being naked. I forgot about being worried. I even forgot about being sad. I may not have believed in love potions and counter-spells, but I did believe in what I felt right now, and I knew exactly what it was.

Magic. Pure, sweet, delicious magic. It flowed through me, ancient and mysterious, yet familiar, too, and even more intoxicating than the wine I'd drunk.

As the music throbbed, I twirled and danced, raising my arms into the air. I became part of the night and the fire and the sky. I'd never felt so free or powerful in my life, and I knew I possessed a strength greater than the potions I'd mixed, greater than the accusations made against me back at school, and greater than the people trying to threaten and frighten us into closing up shop. I could handle anything life threw at me...because I was magic, too.

As the clock stopped chiming, the music changed, increasing in tempo. My dance grew wild and I spun around the bonfire, laughing, my face raised to the night sky. The moon was nearly full, and Halloween only a few days away. Soon I'd have to return to school, and face the review board, but I chose not to worry about what might happen next. Instead, I planned to deal with one thing at a time.

The rhythm of the music slowed, and the melody became something soft and sweet, like a lover's kiss. I stopped dancing and stared into the light of the fire. One thing remained. The final instructions of Maeve McAlroy.

Fiona had placed a bucket of water near the bonfire for this task. I lifted it and carried it over to the fire.

"As water meets fire, this spell comes undone," I said, pouring some of the water onto the fire. It landed with a hiss.

"As water meets fire, this spell is now broken." I doused the fire with more water. Now only a few bright embers remained.

"As water meets fire, I am free." Lifting the bucket one

final time, I dumped the rest of the water onto the fire, extinguishing it completely. I had one line left to recite, the last and most important part of the ritual.

"Blessings be, so mote it be."

I stared at the ashes from the bonfire, thinking about what I'd just said. A mote was something small, like a speck or an atom. Invisible to the human eye, and yet so powerful.

"So mote it be," I repeated softly.

The words slipped off my tongue so easily, even though it was a phrase I'd never uttered before. Another weird thing, but weird was becoming my new normal.

I needed to acknowledge the truth in front of my eyes. I'd seen the potion go from black to bright yellow with the simple addition of my tears. I could assume it had to do with the salt found naturally in tears, but salt, formed by an acid and a base, was a neutralized reaction. Perhaps something in the water or the cherry juice or the brandy caused my tears to go from neutral to reactive, but I couldn't explain it using chemistry. I couldn't explain it at all.

"Isn't it kind of cold for nude moon bathing?"

I jumped at the sound of Dario's voice behind me, and grabbed my clothes, holding the bundle against my chest. Could the antidote have worked this quickly? If so, Maeve McAlroy really knew her stuff.

"What are you doing here?" I asked.

He stood in the shadows, but I could make out the gleam of his eyes and the white flash of his smile. He laughed at me, the jerk, not that I blamed him. The situation was fairly ridiculous.

"I came to speak with you. I wanted to apologize, but when I got back to the shop, my nunny and your aunt told me you'd come here. They were drunk, by the way. I had quite the adventure getting Nunny back home." He moved closer, his hands in the pockets of his jeans.

"Stop," I said. "I'm naked."

"I noticed." The predatory look returned to his eyes, the one that got me into trouble before. "I saw you dancing."

"Oh, so you're a peeping Tom now?"

He shrugged. "I didn't mean to, but I couldn't help myself. It was the sexiest thing I've ever seen."

My hands shook, partly from his words and partly because it had gotten colder with the fire out. "I'm not doing this. You're going to have to behave. Turn around and be a gentleman so I can get dressed."

"I'm not a gentleman," he growled. "Not by a long shot. And the way I've behaved with you up to now is the opposite of gentlemanly, as you well know."

But he did as I asked and turned around. I put on my skirt and pulled the turtleneck over my head. I didn't bother with my panties, bra, or tights. I wanted to cover as much as possible as quickly as possible and get out of there.

"Okay. I'm decent," I said. "Now why are you skulking around in the dark exactly?"

He turned slowly, and his eyes trailed from the top of my head to my shoes. When he gazed at me like that, I felt naked once again. I tucked my bra discreetly into my purse and folded my arms across my chest.

"I told you," he said, kicking a stone with his shoe. "I wanted to speak with you."

"Why?"

He let out a frustrated grumble. "I can't explain it. It goes beyond 'wanting.' I yearned to see you, and I needed to do it tonight. It was almost like..."

"Like what?"

"Like I couldn't stop myself from coming here."

"Grace, are you done? We want to drink." Fiona stuck her head out the door, and her eyes widened when she saw Dario. "Oh. Sorry. Hi, Dario."

"Dario's here?" asked Cat, looking over Fiona's shoulder. She bit her lip, obviously trying to hold back a giggle. "Well, that was quick."

Dario waved. "I came to walk Grace home."

I wanted to say I was perfectly capable of walking myself home, but Fiona intervened. "Good idea. See you later."

"Wait. What about Cat?" I asked, uncomfortable with the idea of being alone with Dario right after I'd messed around with spells and potions all involving him. Of course, if he did come home with me, it would be the perfect opportunity to offer him a drink. One laced with a potion containing my tears, sacred water, and a drop of cherry juice.

"My dad's coming to get me," said Cat, a bit too brightly. "You kids have fun. See you tomorrow."

I scowled at them, but they ignored me, smiles plastered on their faces. "I guess I'm going with you."

He nudged me. "Don't act so happy about it."

"Sorry," I said, knowing I was being ungracious. "I'm tired."

"I'm sure you are," he said. "Dancing naked in the moonlight can take a lot out of you."

I covered my face with my hands. "What did you witness exactly?" I asked, worried he may have heard me say the counter spell.

He moved so close I thought for a minute he was going to kiss me, but he didn't. Instead, he stared deeply into my eyes. "I saw you dancing naked in the garden like a goddess come to earth, your skin glowing from the warmth of the fire and the light of the moon. And I imagined you had to be a dream because nothing so beautiful could exist in real life."

A goddess come to earth? Holy guacamole.

"But I have one question for you." He grinned at me, a twinkle in his dark eyes. "What happened to your bra, Miss O'Leary?"

CHAPTER 32

IF AT FIRST YOU DON'T SUCCEED, TRY BLACK MAGIC AND MAD SCIENCE.

Aunt Lucy waited for us when we got back to the shop. Still tipsy, she fawned over Dario, thanking him for walking me home. "I put the kettle on. Sit and have a cup of tea. Or maybe something stronger?" She tilted her head toward the half-finished bottle of whisky.

"I don't want to intrude," he said.

"Oh, hogwash. Stay." She pushed him into a chair, an achievement since he stood nearly two feet taller than her.

He gave me a crooked smile. "Tea sounds nice."

I followed Aunt Lucy to the back room just as the old-fashioned kettle on her stove let out a whistle. Two tea cups sat already prepared on a fancy tray, with silver spoons, a jar of honey, and a bowl of sugar next to them. Aunt Lucy removed the kettle from the stove and made the tea.

"How did you know to make tea?" I asked.

"The cards told me." I blinked at her in surprise, and she giggled. "And Fiona called to let me know you were on your way home."

"You're ridiculous," I said, trying not to laugh. It would only encourage her.

"I know I am."

The antidote to the love potion still glowed an eerie yellow. I picked it up. "How much should I put in?"

Aunt Lucy placed a hand on mine. "Magic is not an exact science. You have to listen to your instincts. Add whatever amount seems right to you."

"Magic isn't a science at all," I muttered, but I did as she said. I put a few drops of the antidote into Dario's tea, and gave it a gentle stir. At first the tea sparkled the tiniest bit, and when the sparkle disappeared, it looked exactly like my tea. I kept the spoon in his, to be sure I didn't mix them up.

I looked around for another cup. "Aren't you having some tea, too?"

"Oh, no. It's past my bedtime." She gave me a wave as she toddled over to the couch. "Goodnight, dearie. And good luck."

I carried the tray with the teacups out to the main room of the shop. Dario scrolled through his phone but put it away when I came through the door. "Where's Aunt Lucy?" he asked.

"She went to bed. She's worn out."

"Whisky can do that."

Uncomfortable with the whole idea of the spiked drink, I gave him his teacup with a trembling hand. I'd never roofied anyone before. Did an antidote for a love potion technically count as drugging someone? I frowned as I considered it.

"Are you okay?" he asked as he took a sip of his tea.

I picked up my cup, nearly knocking over the sugar bowl in the process. "Yes. Fine. I forgot to ask if you wanted sugar or not."

He shook his head, taking another sip. "This tea is delicious. What's in it?"

Oh, Dario. If only you knew. "Um, I'm not sure. It's one of Claire's."

I stared at him, watching him swallow the tea, and wondering when it would work exactly. Maeve hadn't been specific. She'd left out several key details. But I guess knowing people wanted to hang you for witchcraft could be distracting.

"How are the preparations going for the party?" he asked.

"Pretty well. The entire neighborhood is helping, of course. The Samhain celebration itself will be at the Enchanted Garden. People are just coming here afterward."

"It's a masked ball again, right?"

"Yes, and a formal one, which seems out of place for the South Side. I see more tie-dye than tuxes here."

He laughed. "They used to do a different theme each year, but one time the toga party got out of hand. Some people equated togas with a Roman orgy." He flashed me a grin. "Which is more in line with what I'd expect from a party in the South Side."

I smiled back at him. Could this new peace between us be the result of the antidote to the love potion? Or was I reading into it?

I put my elbows on the table, leaning closer to him. I opened my mouth, about to speak, but before I got my chance, he glanced at his watch. "I'd better leave. It's getting late, and I'm going out of town tomorrow." He drank the remainder of his tea. "Can I see you when I get back?"

I tried not to show my disappointment as I walked him to the door. The antidote obviously hadn't worked. I'd failed. Big time. Again. "Yes. Sure. Whatever."

"What's wrong?"

I shrugged. "You said pretty much the same thing to me the last time you went out of town, and we both know what happened."

He put his hands on my shoulders and locked his dark

gaze on mine. "It won't be the same. I give you my word. Be safe and try to stay out of trouble until I return."

"Trouble?" I fluttered my eyelashes at him. "I don't know what you're talking about."

He looked skyward, probably praying for patience. "I'm serious. The bomb scare just adds to the list of weird things happening here lately."

"What do you mean? It was a false alarm."

"Or so we thought, but no one from the tattoo parlor ordered a clock. The box had no postage on it, and no return address. Someone stuck a message inside, but we didn't find it until one of the policemen took the clock out and saw it taped to the bottom."

"A message?"

He nodded. "It read 'Times up.' No apostrophe."

"No apostrophe? Oh, they truly are evil." I tried to make light of it, but my stomach clenched at the significance of this disclosure. With each note the vandal got braver, and progressively more dangerous.

Dario tucked a strand of hair behind my ear. "If this is some kind of prank, it's a bad one. Promise me you'll keep an eye out for anything strange."

I glanced around at the charms and witches' hats and pentagram jewelry in the shop and bit my lip. "Define 'strange,' please."

"I mean it. Be careful." He leaned forward, kissing me softly on the cheek. His lips felt warm and he smelled delicious, but before I could respond, he opened the door and stepped out into the dark, cold night. Moments later, thunder sounded as the skies opened and rain fell. I stood by the window a long time, watching the storm and knowing Aunt Lucy's words from earlier were true.

Something wicked was coming.

Almost on their own volition, my feet took me to the

back room where Aunt Lucy snored softly, curled up on a sofa. I tiptoed across the floor and opened the cupboard door, carefully taking out the Dragon Rouge from where I'd stashed it. Aunt Lucy and Mr. Dalca both told me not to touch it, but I couldn't stop myself. I loved mysteries and this was a mystery plain and simple.

The pot still held some tea, so I poured myself another cup, and sat at the wide table. I opened the box, looking again at the list of spells on the old parchment paper.

Unlike the glowing, peaceful goodness of my grimoire, a dark and sinister power emanated from the words inked on the crumbling page. Spells to curse people and make them suffer. Spells to bind people by fear, and hexes to cause disorder and chaos. Bad, evil, terrible things, and one in particular caught my eye.

A spell for revenge.

"Tiffany," I said softly. I could create a revenge spell against Tiffany. I hated her. She caused all my problems.

Make her hurt. Make her suffer.

As the words twisted around in my brain, like a coiled serpent about to strike, I went to the pantry and pulled out ingredients one by one. Focused on my task, I didn't notice when Aunt Lucy's snoring stopped.

"Don't do it, Gracie," she said softly, sitting up on the couch. "Close the box and give it to me."

"No." I shook my head. "I need to do this. She's a bad person, and I want revenge. I deserve it."

Make her hurt. Make her suffer. Make her pay.

I had experienced the same powerful urge the night of Dario's awards ceremony, but this time it seemed even stronger. A wave of red anger washed over me, as the stone inside the box pulsated with an odd glow.

Aunt Lucy limped over to me, putting a soft, pale hand on mine. "No, you don't. It's making you say those things, honey.

I worried this might happen, which is why I stayed here tonight."

"You worried what might happen?" I spoke to my aunt but couldn't pull my gaze away from the Dragon Rouge and the red stone inside. I wanted to create a revenge spell so badly my fingertips tingled. The voice got louder.

Make her suffer. Make her pay. Do it now.

Aunt Lucy reached up and placed her hands on my cheeks, turning my face so I had no choice but to look into her bright blue eyes. "You are magic, child, and tonight you created more magic. You're positively brimming with it at this point. Magic calls to magic, which is why what is in this box calls to you. The lure of the darkness is strong. You need to be aware of it, and you need to stay vigilant, so you don't get sucked in."

"The darkness?" I snorted. "That's nonsense, Aunt Lucy."

"No, it's reality," she said, her sweet face pinched with worry. "There has to be a balance between darkness and light. The lighter you are, the more the darkness calls to you. The more it tries to dim your light."

"I don't care. I hate Tiffany. I want to make her suffer."

Aunt Lucy smiled, shaking her head sadly. "Do you even know her? Yes, she gave Dario the love potion, I'm certain of it, but have you asked yourself why?"

"Because she's evil," I said, frowning. I didn't want to think about Tiffany's motivation. I wanted to wreak havoc and destroy her, like a tall, redheaded Godzilla.

Aunt Lucy pulled me over to the couch and made me sit next to her. "Tiffany is a sad, pathetic person who deserves your pity, not your anger."

"My *pity*?" I nearly spat out the words.

"Yes," she said. "I've known her since she was a girl. She moved away for college but came back a few years ago. Her parents never planned to have children, and they treated her like an accident, an inconvenience. She spent most of her days with nannies and babysitters, not truly loved. When her parents passed away last year, her loneliness only increased. Dario showed her kindness, so of course she fell for him. How could she not? But he never reciprocated. Then you came into the picture and swept poor Dario off his feet."

"Again, with the 'poor Dario'?"

"I do feel for him," said Aunt Lucy. "And I'm sorry for Tiffany, too. She became jealous of you, and jealous of your relationship with Dario. She did what she could to get what she wanted. Is she a nice girl? Not terribly. Not at the moment at least. Are you a nice girl? Yes, which is why you have no business messing with that awful box."

I shot a glance at the table where the Dragon Rouge sat tempting me. I still heard its call, but the sound grew fainter. I got up, closed the lid, and brought it over to Aunt Lucy. She tucked it into the pocket of her skirt, and I curled up next to her on the couch.

She stroked my hair, like she had when I was small. "We need to sell this to Mr. Dalca. He wants it, the greedy old man, and I plan to let him have it. For a price, of course."

"But aren't you worried about it falling into the wrong hands?"

"I believe Mr. Dalca, for all his faults, will keep it safe. Mostly because he, better than anyone else, acknowledges how dangerous it truly is."

"This is all so strange to me. Magic and potions and evil spells and witches. It's beyond my comfort zone."

Aunt Lucy laughed. "Trust me. I spent time in your shoes once, when I first got married. Your uncle Anton opened my eyes, and my mind, to a world I never knew existed. He opened me up to things of a sexual nature, too, but that's another story." I stifled a groan, and she continued, unfazed. "The point is the dragon box embodies something truly evil.

You, my love, are the opposite of evil, which means we need to get it as far away from you as possible, and we need to do it quickly."

"But I still want revenge—"

Aunt Lucy interrupted me. "The best revenge is happiness. Fix things with Dario, as I know you will. I saw it in the cards, remember?"

I rolled my eyes. "You saw a marriage and babies and a happily ever after. But I don't believe in the cards, Aunt Lucy."

"You don't have to," she said with a laugh, as she kissed the top of my head. "The cards tell the truth whether you believe in them or not."

CHAPTER 33

BILLY WAS A CHEMIST'S SON, BUT BILLY IS NO MORE. WHAT BILLY THOUGHT WAS H_2O, WAS H_2SO_4.

The next morning, I woke long before the sun came up. My thoughts churned, and my emotional state remained unsettled. Had I seriously wanted to harm Tiffany? It seemed so unlikely, and yet I knew the truth.

Last night, anger and hatred had curled like a dark vine around my heart, squeezing it until all I thought about was my own pain and the desire to inflict pain on someone else. Giving in to such fury created a heady sensation. Luscious and dark. I felt powerful and in control, something I hadn't experienced since the day Dr. Lewis accused me of cheating. I wanted to feel the same way again, but not by casting evil spells. I shuddered. If Aunt Lucy hadn't stopped me when she did, I may have done something terrible.

I checked my phone. Dario neither called nor texted, so I surmised the antidote must have failed. Oddly enough, it came as a surprise. I'm not sure what I expected exactly, but the way I'd felt, especially while dancing around the fire, had been magical. No other word could describe it.

I may not believe in everything Aunt Lucy said, but I did believe in what I experienced personally. The evil lure of the

Dragon Rouge had been real, and the sweet call of the grimoire, with its lovely, logical, white magic, was real, too. Sadly, it seemed even a magical antidote couldn't fix things between Dario and me.

I made some coffee and sat to read over the final draft of my thesis. It had all come together beautifully, thanks to the water from the fountain at Fiona's café and the strange biolu-minescence I'd accidentally discovered there. The tests Megan ran supported my conclusions. As I read the last para-graph, I knew I'd finally finished it. The research was flawless, the results amazing, and the science spot-on, but would I ever actually get a chance to defend it?

My shoulders slumped. This hurt even more than the failure of the antidote. What if my work remained on my laptop forever, unread and unappreciated by anyone except me? As much as I got satisfaction from knowing I'd done my job well, at this point, my chances of being reinstated looked slim. I'd become the pariah of the chemistry department. An outcast. A leper in a lab coat. And it hurt to imagine never teaching or working in my field again.

"How depressing," I said to Jinx. He responded with a yawn and a stretch, before rearranging himself more comfort-ably on the desk and falling asleep. I petted his soft, black fur, enjoying the throaty purr my touch elicited.

I closed my laptop, and got ready for work, dressing in a black and white polka dot sheath dress with a black cardigan, black tights, and black suede heels. I added a string of pearls, real ones, a high school graduation gift from my nan, and stuck in some pearl earrings as well. I brushed my hair and decided to pull it into a low side ponytail. I might be a mess on the inside, but at least I could look polished and profes-sional on the outside.

I went downstairs to wake Aunt Lucy for her physical therapy appointment but found her already dressed and standing by the door. She wore a purple jacket, a matching beret, and a bright orange dress. The effect was jarring and yet adorable.

"Good morning," she said. "Mrs. Periwinkle is already here. She's sorting out some inventory in the back. Mags offered to take me to PT today. It'll give you time to work on the ball preparations. I called Mr. Dalca and told him to come and pick up this dreadful box. He said he'd be over around ten."

She handed me the Dragon Rouge. It whispered to me softly now, telling me about all the awful, terrible, wonderful things it could teach me, but I blocked it out without much effort. It didn't pull me the same way it did last night. I was much more in control today.

"Are you all right, dearie?" asked Aunt Lucy.

"It's quieter now. And I'm stronger." I blushed, realizing what I'd said. "I mean it's only a box with a rock inside it, but—"

She held up a hand to silence me. "Not a rock, a ruby, and it's cursed, but you don't have to explain it. I understand. The more you learn about magic, and the more comfortable you get with it, the less a problem something like this will be."

"Holy cow. Wait, it's a *ruby*?" I snuck a look inside the box. The red stone was larger than my fist.

"Of course, it's a ruby. What else would it be?"

"Um, I don't know. Colored glass. Fake...like everything else in this shop." She scowled at me, but I ignored her. "Where did Uncle Anton get it?"

"He described it as a family heirloom. I don't know anything else."

"Well, if that's the case, you should keep it. Don't get rid of it because of me."

"There are lots of evil things in this world. I don't need one living in my own house," she said. "Besides, Anton hated this thing. He only held onto it because he swore to keep it out of the wrong hands. He made plans to give it to someone else, someone he trusted, but he died before he could take care of it, and it ended up with me."

"And you kept a priceless ruby tucked away on your bookshelf behind a copy of *Dracula*?"

"Anton was Romanian. Where else should I put it?"

I decided not to mention Aunt Lucy forgot its location, probably for decades. "None of this explains the hooded man. How did he know the Dragon Rouge was in your apartment?"

She pondered this. "I have no idea. Unless..."

"Unless what?"

"Well, Anton's friend may have known. Of course, he's probably long dead by now. Or, if he's alive, he'd be far too old to sneak into bedrooms or push people down stairs."

Her logic, although once again convoluted, made sense. It didn't explain anything at all about the man in the hood, but it made sense. Scary, but true.

A small cooler sat on the ground in front of the shop. "What's this?" I asked, bringing it inside.

"Oh, dear. Aggie must have left me another one of her smoothies. She's such a peach, but I can't drink it this morning. I promised Mags I'd take her to Pamela's Diner for breakfast. Why don't you have it? I'd hate to see it go to waste."

I opened the cooler and took out the smoothie. Pink and cold, I saw bits of strawberry in it, my favorite fruit.

"Sounds good," I said, taking a sip. "I'll get to work on decorating. Is the box still up in the attic?"

"Yes, but don't go up there by yourself. It's haunted. Oh, look. Mags is here. See you later."

She left with a wave of her purple-gloved hand. Mrs. Periwinkle came up next to me and smiled as she watched her go. "The attic is *not* haunted," she said.

"I didn't think so."

"We took care of all of that last year during the exorcism."

I almost choked on the smoothie. "Wait a second. What exorcism?"

Mrs. Periwinkle smoothed her blue skirt and straightened her matching sweater. "Nothing serious, just a minor demon infestation. Father Reilly from St. Francis took care of it. He did a fine job indeed. So what's on the schedule for today?"

I still hadn't absorbed the whole demon infestation idea but decided to simply accept it and move on. "Getting ready for the ball, I guess."

"Do you want me to come up to the attic with you, or do you think you can find the decorations on your own?"

I sucked down more of the smoothie and set it next to my cell phone by the cash register. I'd need both my hands free to carry the boxes out of the attic. "I'm sure I'll be fine."

As I climbed the stairs, I tried to forget the words, "minor demon infestation." I'd never liked going into Aunt Lucy's attic, but I was no longer a child, and I could handle the dark, dusty, creepiness of it.

"Watch out for bats, though," said Mrs. Periwinkle, and I froze in mid-step.

"Bats?"

"Aunt Lucy sometimes gets them in her belfry," she said, and chuckled at her own joke.

Bats. Great.

I grabbed a flashlight from above the refrigerator in Aunt Lucy's apartment, and headed to the back hallway. A rope dangled down from the ceiling there, and I pulled it to lower the ladder. Clambering up the steep, rickety ladder would be tricky in heels, so I tossed my shoes aside. The ladder squeaked and swayed as I climbed, but I made it easily to the top. Once there, I popped my head up through the hole, and shone the flashlight around the dim room. I heaved a sigh of relief as I looked around, my feet still on the ladder. No bats in sight, and no demons either. All in all, a good start.

I climbed the final steps and found a string to turn on the light. Nothing but a bare bulb hung from the ceiling, but it provided enough light for me to turn off the flashlight and set it down.

I found the decorations quickly. Aunt Lucy packed them in small, light boxes, which made going up and down the ladder much easier. As I dropped the last one to the ground, and placed my hands on the ladder to push it up and close the attic door, a strange sense of exhaustion came over me. I swayed on my feet. My brain seemed fuzzy and strange, reminding me of a time I stayed up all night cramming for a test as an undergrad.

"What's going on?" I asked myself out loud. My words sounded slurred, and my face felt oddly numb.

I left the packages by the ladder and walked to the door of the apartment, leaning against the wall for support. Something was terribly wrong. I could barely keep my eyes open and putting one foot in front of another became a challenge. Also, the white polka dots on my dress swirled around in dizzying circles, not a normal occurrence.

I wondered if I was having a stroke. It would be just my luck to die on the day I finally finished my thesis. At least that had turned out perfectly. A small consolation.

I wished I could tell Dario about my thesis. I knew he'd appreciate the beauty and brilliance of it because he understood me like no one else ever had. That was probably what made losing him hurt so much.

The thought of Dario kept me occupied as I struggled down the steps toward the loft above the shop. I wanted to curl up on the floor and take a nap, but part of me was seriously terrified I might not wake up again. I wished I'd carried my cell phone, but I'd left it next to the cash register. I sensed

THE HOCUS POCUS MAGIC SHOP

I was running out of time. If I didn't get help soon, I could have a serious problem.

I made it to the loft and paused at the top of the main staircase, the same one Aunt Lucy fell down when the ghost who wasn't a ghost pushed her. If I did the same in my current state, I'd break more than a leg. The staircase swayed and moved in front of me, and I could barely even see the first step.

"Mrs. Periwinkle?" My voice sounded weak, my words barely discernible. I tried to make it louder. "Mrs. Periwinkle?"

She didn't respond, so I did the only thing possible. I held onto the bannister and inched my way down one step at a time on my bottom. It took forever. When I finally reached the last step, I collapsed in a heap on the floor, unable to move another inch. I couldn't keep my eyes open, no matter how hard I fought against it. As I faded into unconsciousness, I heard frantic banging on the front door of the shop and someone shouting. Could it be Ivan, or was I dreaming? I had no idea. Mrs. Periwinkle's worried cries sounded real, though. They echoed in my ears, before everything went silent and still.

I didn't remember the ambulance ride to the hospital. I also didn't remember being given activated charcoal to drink or vomiting up the contents of my stomach. Thank goodness for that much at least. I woke to a massively raw and aching throat and a circle of worried faces surrounding my bed. Mrs. Periwinkle, Ivan, and Dr. Mallinger.

"She's back," said Dr. Mallinger with a smile.

I squinted, trying to focus on his kind face and hazel eyes. "What happened?" My voice sounded raspy and rough.

"You passed out. Thank goodness you didn't fall," said Mrs. Periwinkle. "Ivan saw you and got my attention. He's the one who called the ambulance. Our knight in shining armor." She gave his arm a pat, and to my great surprise, he blushed.

"Not even close, but I'm glad I stopped by the shop when I did. I saw you collapse, and I nearly broke the door down trying to get someone's attention."

"And I apologize," said Mrs. Periwinkle. "I was in such a state I couldn't even get the door of the shop unlocked until the ambulance arrived. I left poor Ivan outside."

"Please don't worry yourself about that, madam," he said.

Mrs. Periwinkle dabbed her eyes with an embroidered handkerchief. "And thank you for riding to the hospital with her."

"You rode to the hospital with me?" I asked, giving him a wobbly smile. "Sir Galahad."

He took my hand, the one without the IV needle in it, and kissed it gallantly. All the ladies in the room, including the nurse who'd come in to check on my IV, let out a collective sigh. Ivan was rather swoon-worthy.

"I'll leave you to get some rest," he said with a bow. "Take care, Grace. I'll see you soon."

He left and we all watched him go. Even Dr. Mallinger.

"He reminds me of someone," said Mrs. Periwinkle.

"A Viking," I said.

"Oh, yes," said Mrs. Periwinkle, fanning herself. "Ready to plunder, but in a good way. I wonder if he has a broadsword."

Dr. Mallinger eyes widened at her naughty double entendre, just as Aunt Lucy and Mags came into the room.

"Gracie. I just heard. Are you okay?" asked Aunt Lucy, her face pale and tearstained. Mags and Mrs. Periwinkle stepped outside so we could have some privacy.

"I'm fine. Don't worry," I said, reaching for her hand.

"How can I not worry? This is awful. I knew I should have sent you home." She turned to Dr. Mallinger. "What happened?"

"We aren't sure yet." He studied my face, his expression serious and probing. "We suspect you may have overdosed on something, and we emptied your stomach using charcoal as a precaution. Which is why your teeth and mouth are black."

"My teeth are...what?" I wiped at some drool at the corner of my lips and looked at the back of my hand. Yep. Definitely black. "Do you have a mirror?" I asked Aunt Lucy.

"I do," she said, pulling a big silver one out of her giant handbag. "But don't be alarmed, sweetheart. Appearances aren't everything."

I gasped when I saw myself. My teeth and tongue were indeed black, and streaks of black ran down the sides of my mouth and onto my neck. "I look awful," I said, cringing at the way I'd smiled when Ivan kissed my hand. He probably felt like he'd been kissing a corpse.

Aunt Lucy took her mirror back. "If I didn't know we'd already taken care of the demon infestation, I'd have worried we still had a problem when I first saw you. You looked positively terrifying. Thankfully, they say the black color will fade away in no time. If not, you can be a ghoul for Halloween. Wouldn't that be fun?"

"Delightful," I said, and turned to Dr. Mallinger. "What exactly happened to me?"

"We're not sure," he paused, as if trying to figure out what to say. "Are you taking any medications, Grace, or is there something we should know?"

I shook my head, my brain sloshing back and forth inside my skull. "No. Nothing."

His face became grave. "You came to the ER with all the signs and symptoms of a drug overdose. Drowsiness, a rapid heart rate, low blood pressure. As soon as we emptied your stomach, you improved. I need to know something, and please be honest. Did you purposefully try to harm yourself?"

"No. Absolutely not."

He seemed relieved. "Well, we should know exactly what caused this in a few days, after we get the test results back. Did you have anything at all to eat or drink this morning? Perhaps something you didn't prepare yourself?"

I frowned, remembering the smoothie. "Well, Aggie brought over a fruit smoothie. I drank half of it right before I went up to the attic."

His face tightened. "We'll need a sample of that smoothie."

I swallowed hard, wincing over the pain in my throat. "It's back at the shop, right next to the cash register." My mind still seemed muddled and strange, and a massive headache curled its way through my skull. "When can I go home?"

He glanced at his watch. "Tomorrow, I think. We'll discharge you as soon as we can rehydrate you, and you're able to have something to eat and drink. Are you hungry?"

"Starving."

He smiled, giving my arm a reassuring pat. "A good sign. We'll order lunch for you right away." He checked a few items off on my chart and put it into the slot at the bottom of my bed. "Be careful, Grace. I'm not sure if the smoothie made you sick or not, but you said you saw it outside in a cooler?"

"Yes," I said.

"Which means anyone walking by could have tampered with it. We need to talk with the police about this, but I have an important question. Is there anyone who wanted to harm you?"

I shook my head, realizing a horrible truth. "The smoothie wasn't intended for me."

Aunt Lucy's face got pale. "Oh, my. You're right. It was for me."

Dr. Mallinger considered this new information with a worried frown. "That adds a whole new set of questions. If someone purposely tainted the smoothie, they did it with something dangerously strong. Drinking only half of it made you sick, and if you'd fallen asleep alone, you may have slipped into a coma."

"Heavens," said Aunt Lucy, her face getting paler still.

"I'm not trying to be an alarmist. You're young and healthy and most likely would have survived. Possibly even without significant brain damage. I can't say the same about your aunt."

"What do you mean?" I asked, suspecting I knew what he was about to say, but hoping I could be wrong.

He explained, his expression somber. "If someone gave the smoothie to your Aunt Lucy, knowing what it contained, we're not talking about an accidental drugging here. We're talking about attempted murder."

CHAPTER 34

I'D NEVER TRY TO POISON YOU," SAID THE
EVIL CHEMIST. "NOW SHUT UP AND EAT YOUR
PB AND JELLY SANDWICH."

Mrs. Periwinkle went back to the shop, but Aunt
Lucy and Mags stayed with me a few hours,
trying to keep me entertained and as comfort-
able as possible. It had been a close call...too close. If Aunt
Lucy had drunk her smoothie this morning instead of me, she
could have died, and I would be planning her funeral right
now instead of chatting with her.

She reassured me, saying she'd stay with Mags tonight,
and promised she'd be extremely careful about everything
she ate or drank. "That nice Dr. Mallinger will have the
results back soon. I'm sure it's all some kind of terrible
mistake."

Although not quite as certain about her conclusions, I
couldn't exactly accuse sweet, fragile Aggie of trying to kill
Aunt Lucy. It seemed impossible.

"Either way," continued Aunt Lucy. "The hoodoo ritual
worked. Whoever mixed that smoothie left it outside. They
didn't bring it into the shop."

I remembered Aggie on the night of the bomb scare. Pale
and strange, she'd flatly refused to come inside, but it must be

a coincidence. The only problem was a scientist never believed in coincidences.

Giving myself a mental shake for even considering such nonsense, I changed the subject. "I'm so sorry I can't help you with the ball preparations today. How are you going to do this on your own?"

"Mrs. Periwinkle and I have it under control. Don't worry yourself for a moment. We put on this party every year. It's old hat for us."

After they left, I ate some lunch, and since I could manage to eat and drink without any problem, a kind nurse came in and took out my IV. It allowed me to hobble to the bathroom to take a much-needed shower. Feeling like I'd been hit by a truck, I checked out my appearance in the small mirror above the bathroom sink. Pale face, lank hair, and lips still black from the charcoal. I *did* look like a ghoul. I almost scared myself.

I took off the hospital gown and stepped into the shower, enjoying the hot water on my skin. After a thorough scrubbing, I got out, wrapped my body in a towel, and heard a faint knock on the bathroom door.

"Grace? Are you in there?"

"Laura?" I asked, flinging open the door.

She pulled me into a fierce hug. "You poor thing. Are you okay?" Her short blond hair shone under the fluorescent lights of the hospital, and she wore a pair of faded, ripped jeans and a concert T-shirt for an indie band from Pittsburgh called Surf Bored. Laura did love her indie rock bands.

"Much better now, and I'm so glad to see you. What happened? You weren't supposed to come until tomorrow."

"I wanted to surprise you," she said. "But I got the surprise when I showed up at the shop and heard they'd taken you to the hospital. What the heck? Your aunt said someone tried to drug you."

"We won't know for sure until we get the results of the lab work," I said, and explained how the smoothie was intended for my aunt.

I shivered, and not only because I wore nothing but a damp towel. Nurse Laura leapt into action. "You need to get warmed up. Your aunt packed a bag for you. She knew you'd prefer your own things to a hospital gown, and she sent your cell phone, too. Sadly, she didn't include a charger, so it's already dead. I'll have to bring you one tomorrow, but let's get you dressed and back in your bed. First things first. Then we'll talk."

It felt so good to be in my own comfy yoga pants and a long sleeved black "25.8069: The Root of All Evil" T-shirt. Laura snorted when she saw it. "You and your nerd shirts."

A nurse with dark hair came in with a giant bouquet of flowers in a crystal cut glass vase. "I'm Brenda," she said, with a smile. "I'll be taking care of you this afternoon. How are you doing?"

"Much better, thanks. Wait. Are you Anthony Belfiore's friend? I've heard about you."

"Yes, I know Anthony," she said, but something in the coolness of her tone told me maybe they might not be such good friends at all. "He stopped by earlier to ask some questions, but you were groggy at the time. He said he'd come back later."

"They still think someone drugged me?"

"The lab work isn't back yet, so I can't say." She put the flowers next to my bed. "Well, if you weren't better already, these flowers would do the trick. They're gorgeous."

I suspected I knew the identity of the sender, and reading the card confirmed it. *Get well soon, Grace, and save a dance for me at the Halloween Ball. Yours truly, Ivan.*

I handed the card to Laura and she read it, raising her

eyebrows. "Hmmm. 'Yours truly'? Sounds like someone's crushing on the chemist."

I shook my head. "We're friends. He's actually one of two options I planned out for you this weekend."

She put her face in her hands. "Oh, no. Are you trying to fix me up again? It never works. You've tried before." Laura narrowed her eyes at me. "Wait...who is the other option?"

Dr. Mallinger walked into the room, a big smile on his face. "You look a lot better than you did this morning, Miss O'Leary." He extended his hand to Laura. "Ryan Mallinger. Nice to meet you."

Laura introduced herself, and they chatted about her work at Children's Hospital in Philadelphia. Dr. Mallinger took a look at my chart and promised to discharge me first thing in the morning.

"Will you be able to make it to our Halloween Ball?" I asked, giving Laura a pointed look. She fiddled with the flowers, blooms in the warm, lush hues of a fall sunset, and didn't notice.

"Definitely," he said. "It's the first Halloween in a long time I won't be working in the ER. I'm looking forward to that almost as much as I'm looking forward to your ball."

Laura laughed. "I know, right? Halloween is the worst."

They shared war stories about horrible Halloween nights in various ERs, and after he left, I tugged on the sleeve of her T-shirt. "Well?"

She looked confused. "Well what?"

"Do you like him?"

She shrugged. "What's not to like?"

I rolled my eyes in mock frustration. "No, I mean are you attracted to him? Gosh, Laura."

"Please don't try to set me up again," she said. "Seriously."

"But I'm so good at it."

She laughed. "No, you aren't. And we have more important things to deal with, like getting the black gunk off your teeth. I know a rinse that could help. I'll pick it up from the drug store later."

She brushed out my hair for me and dried it gently with a towel. Then she tucked me into bed, pulling the blanket nearly up to my chin. I blinked away tears. Ever since I created the antidote for Dario, I cried at the drop of a hat. It unleashed something inside me. Apparently, I possessed an inner well of unshed tears just waiting to be tapped.

"I'm so glad you came."

"Me, too," she said. "And we want to make sure you're all better and ready to party on Halloween, so you need to rest up."

"I will," I said.

She smiled at me as she left my room, but the smile didn't quite reach her eyes. She was scared for me.

I leaned back on my pillow, worry tightening my stomach into a knot, because I was scared for me, too.

CHAPTER 35

IF YOU HAVE CHEMISTRY, THE ONLY OTHER THING YOU NEED IS TIMING, BUT TIMING IS A BITCH.

I woke the next morning to sun streaming through my window and Dario fast asleep in the chair next to my bed. I reached out to touch his face, stroking the stubble on his chin, and his eyes flew open. He looked adorably rumpled and sleepy. He took my hand in both of his and kissed my palm, breathing deeply as if savoring the contact.

"I finished my thesis," I said, my voice a whisper.

"Tell me about it." He climbed into the narrow hospital bed, pulling me gently into his arms. The bed was way too small for two people, but we managed to fit, and I told him all about the water from the fountain and how it provided the missing link I needed to support my whole hypothesis.

"What do you think?" I asked, when I finally finished.

"I think you're amazing," he said. "But I've told you that before."

"It's nice hearing it again." I traced a lazy finger along his jaw, noticing the dark circles under his eyes. "You look exhausted."

"Well, you look great," he said. "Especially for someone who got poisoned yesterday."

"Poisoned, drugged." I pretended to weigh the options. "Not sure which one yet. What are you doing here?"

He kissed my palm again before lacing my fingers through his. "I left Philly just after midnight. Nunny called and told me what happened, and I jumped in my car and started heading back to Pittsburgh the minute I heard. I tried to reach you on your cell phone but couldn't get through."

"My cell phone died. Hold on, you left Philly after midnight?" I glanced at the clock. "But it's not even six in the morning. You must have driven all night to get here."

"I did."

"Why?"

He stared deeply into my eyes. "I can't stay away from you. I don't *want* to stay away."

I frowned. "But you dumped me...for Tiffany."

Letting out a sigh, he snuggled closer. "Since you can't get up and walk away at the moment, this might be my chance to finally explain what happened."

"I'm a captive audience," I deadpanned. "Go for it."

He rested his head on my pillow, his face only inches from mine. "The day after the first time we slept together, I went to Philly."

"Yes, and everything seemed fine when we spoke. You said you planned to meet someone Monday night for an interview." My eyes searched his face. "What happened after that phone call?

"My meeting took place in my hotel bar. As soon as it finished, Tiffany showed up."

This could explain everything. "And you hooked up with her?"

"No," he said, shaking his head vehemently. "Absolutely not."

I studied his face, not sure if I could believe him. "Then what happened?"

"We had a few drinks. That's it." His expression grew tense, haunted. "And then she told me something about you, something terrible."

"What could she possibly know about me?" I frowned, perplexed.

He held my gaze. "She said you'd slept with Ivan."

"And you believed her?"

"She showed me time and date stamped photos of him leaving your place in the middle of the night. The most recent one was taken the night after we first slept together." A flash of pain crossed his eyes. "She said she asked Ivan if the two of you were involved, and he confirmed her suspicions. He said you 'bewitched' him."

Bewitched. An odd choice of words from Mr. Rochat.

"She showed you pictures of him leaving my apartment?" I shook my head in disbelief. "How could she have photos of something that never happened? Ivan has never been in my apartment. I mean, I've spoken with him on the sidewalk in front of the shop once or twice…" My voice trailed off as I put several parts of the equation together. "She lives across the street."

"She does."

"If they weren't faked or photo-shopped, it means one of two things. Either Tiffany and Ivan worked together to stage them, or…"

"Or what?"

"Or Ivan entered my shop in the middle of the night without my knowledge or consent."

Hard to fathom, since I liked Ivan, and he didn't seem the type to break into people's houses. The first option seemed the most likely, but why?

"What are we going to do about it?" he asked, his voice hard.

"Nothing," I said, unable to even look at him. "Even if Tiffany and Ivan set us up, you allowed it to happen."

"What do you mean?" he asked.

I tried to imagine how I'd react under a spell. I definitely hadn't been myself when I touched the Dragon Rouge the other night. It nearly controlled me. But when Aunt Lucy spoke to me, I pulled myself back and listened to reason. Dario never gave me that chance.

"You didn't ask for my side of the story." I moved away from him, hard to do when his big body took up most of the bed. "Which is all I really need to know."

"You're angry, but please believe me. I didn't want to hurt you. I can't explain why I acted the way I did. I behaved like a different person or something. And the night we were together at the awards ceremony—"

"In the ladies' room," I said, glaring at him.

He had the decency to look chagrined. "Yes. After that happened, I realized I'd treated you horribly. I started, I don't know, waking up, I guess. Then the night I saw you dancing naked, I understood what I should have done, how I should have handled this. It felt like coming out of a fog, or a dream, or some kind of crazy nightmare. I was in a muddle. I can't offer an explanation except to say I messed up big time."

The night he saw me dancing naked. The night I'd given him the antidote. Could he be telling the truth?

He waited for a response, but my ego, still too hurt and bruised, refused to let me give him one. No matter how much of a spell he'd been under, he should have confronted me. He should have come to see me as planned and yelled at me. I'd have found a way to make him listen to reason. We would have made up the same night and eaten yummy Indian food and gone straight to my bed. Instead, we'd both suffered for weeks.

I turned my head on the pillow to look into his eyes. "When Dr. Lewis accused me of cheating, no one asked to hear my side of the story. They all assumed the worst, and I didn't have a chance to defend myself," I said, my voice cold. "The same thing happened with you. It wasn't about Tiffany or the photos or Ivan. You chose to let your anger and pride overpower your feelings for me. You never asked. You never gave me a chance, so I'm not giving you one now."

Dario got up and gathered his things, his expression one of such deep disappointment and despair, I nearly changed my mind and told him to forget everything I'd just said and come back to my bed. But I didn't. I kept my mouth firmly shut, and my emotions completely under control.

He took an envelope out of his bag and put it on my bed. It had my name on it, written in his strong, bold handwriting. When he finally spoke, his voice sounded hollow and sad.

"I'm better at writing than I am at talking. I always have been. But I have to say one final thing to you." He looked deeply into my eyes. "Who is letting anger and pride get in the way now? Not me, Gracie. Not this time."

He grabbed his jacket off the back of the chair, and he left. I considered throwing the envelope into the garbage but couldn't do it. The scientist in me burned with curiosity about the contents, but the woman scorned in me simply needed to know. To understand. To overcome this. I opened his note and read it, several times, the pain almost too much to bear. Laura came in, and as soon as she saw my face, she knew something was wrong.

"What happened?" she asked.

I couldn't speak. I handed her the letter Dario wrote to me and closed my eyes, picturing the words on the page, and the expression on his face as he left my room.

"I love you, Grace. Truly. You touched my mind, captured my heart, and set my body on fire. From the first moment we met, you've held me spellbound...with your brilliance, your beauty, and your sweet, generous heart. I love every single thing about you. Do you know how rare that is? You are all I've ever wanted, but never even knew existed. If you give me another chance, I promise I'll make sure you never regret it. You are so passionate about chemistry, but do you know what chemistry is to me? Do you know what makes me passionate? It's all the magic and mystery and beauty I see in you."

I pressed my hands against my eyes as a fresh flood of tears came. Why did this have to be so hard?

"Wow. He loves you," she said. "I mean, like a lot."

I teared up again. "It seems so."

Laura sank into the chair Dario recently vacated. "What are you going to do?"

I folded my hands over the sheet. "Nothing. I want my life back. I want to return to school, get back in my lab, and pretend none of this ever happened."

"Even this part?" she asked, indicating the note. "The Dario part?"

I pulled the covers up to my chin with a frown. "Especially that part," I said, but we both knew I lied through my teeth because Dario had been right. Maybe I was the one letting my anger and pride get in the way now. But, if so, how could I stop it?

Wisely, Laura didn't say anything more on the subject. She hung out, distracting me with mindless chatter as I ate breakfast and waited for Dr. Mallinger to complete the discharge paperwork.

"We'll have the lab results back by tomorrow," he said. "And your aunt brought us a sample of the smoothie you ingested as well. In no time, we'll know exactly what made you sick, and hopefully, the police will be able to figure out where it came from."

"Thank you, Dr. Mallinger," I said.

He handed me the papers. "You're a lucky girl. Take it easy today. Get some rest. I'll see both of you at the party."

Nurse Brenda wheeled me to the front of the hospital where Laura waited in her Subaru. "Curbside service," said Brenda with a smile. "Tell your aunt I'm sorry I won't be able to make it to the party this year."

"You can't come?" asked Anthony, who appeared without a sound, making all three of us jump. I introduced him to Laura, and he helped me get into her car, holding the door open as he spoke. "You didn't come last year either, Brenda. Maybe you could stop by after you're done."

"I can't," she said, and Anthony's handsome face fell. "I got stuck with the night shift, unfortunately. There is nothing worse on Halloween. And with a full moon that night it'll be a madhouse."

A full moon. It meant our protective hoodoo spell would vanish when we needed it most.

I covered my face with my hands, glad I hadn't said those words out loud. This whole South Side craziness affected me as well.

"Are you okay?" asked Brenda, her face concerned.

"I'm fine," I said. "Just realizing how much I need to get done before the party and wondering how I'll do it."

She put a reassuring hand on my shoulder. "It'll be fine, and you need to focus on resting at the moment. If you push it, you'll regret it. Trust me."

"Brenda's right," said Laura. "And don't worry about the party. It's in good hands."

Anthony gave me a wink. "I stopped by the shop a few minutes ago, and the party committee is already hard at work."

"The party committee?" My heart sank, wondering what Aunt Lucy could be up to now.

"Yes. The entire South Side is pitching in to help. I stopped by there to check on you, and make sure you had a ride home."

"Thank you, Anthony. You're so kind."

"I have some questions for you, too, but most of them can wait until after we get the results from Dr. Mallinger's lab tests." His phone buzzed. He looked at it with a worried frown. "See you later, ladies. Take care."

He gave us a wave, answering his phone as he walked to his police car. All of us, including Brenda, took a moment to appreciate the perfection of Anthony Belfiore's retreating form. No one compared to Dario in my book, but Anthony may have been a close second. He was even hotter than Ivan.

"Do all policemen look like him on the South Side?" asked Laura. "If so, I'm moving here. Tomorrow."

Brenda snorted. "Nope. Not even close. Anthony is one of a kind."

We said goodbye to Brenda and headed back to the shop. I almost dreaded going inside. I fretted about what the "party committee" may have done in my absence, and knew I'd have no time to fix it.

Laura opened the door for me, and I stepped inside. Instead of an eclectic, slightly run-down little shop, they'd transformed the space into a magical Halloween fantasy. The bookshelves, draped with dark curtains and decorated with sparkly bats, moons, pumpkins, and ghosts, provided the perfect backdrop. The display tables, now cleared of their wares and covered with black cloths and candles, added an elegant touch. Even the centerpieces, made of black silk roses arranged inside skull vases, appeared charming rather than macabre. Aunt Lucy hobbled up to me, leaning on her cane, and gave me a kiss.

"I'm glad you're back, sweetie. How are you?"

"Fine," I said. "Better. You've gotten so much done. How did you do all of this?"

"With lots of help. What do you think? The candles are awesome, aren't they? I forgot we kept them in stock. When you light them, the wax drips red, like it's blood. Fantastic, aren't they?"

"They are." I stared around the shop, perfectly decorated to be dark and yet whimsical.

Will, Fiona, and Cat came out of the back room and fussed over me. Fiona grinned when she saw my reaction to the decorations. "Surprise," she said. "Isn't this awesome?"

"It's perfect."

I turned to Laura, whose gaze locked on Will. Will stared back at her, his expression confused.

"Have you two met?" I asked.

Will studied Laura with his pale, blue-eyed gaze. "I don't think so—"

Laura cut in, interrupting him. "Will Wax," she said, her voice oddly high pitched. "The drummer from the South Side Slackers. I've seen you play. You're amazing. I'm kind of a groupie."

Will's pale eyes lit up and he shot her a grin. "Cool."

Suddenly, Laura, the little blond nurse, and Will, the Goth rocker, were the only two people in the room. Laura's cheeks turned a brilliant pink. Will's gaze grew even more intense. I shot Fiona and Cat a shocked look, making both of them giggle.

Laura only had eyes for Will, and it seemed like I'd failed as a matchmaker once again. I knew Laura so well, but I never saw this one coming.

"Love is a strange and beautiful thing," said Aunt Lucy, giving me a nudge.

"This doesn't surprise you at all, does it?"

She shook her head. "Nope."

"You saw it in the cards?" I raised an eyebrow, waiting for her response. She smiled at me.

"Nothing so mysterious. I paid attention." She pointed to the "South Side Slackers" button prominently displayed on Laura's backpack. "I figured she'd recognize our Will when she saw him, and it would be a surprise."

As I watched Laura and Will engrossed in a discussion a few feet away, I knew she was right. "I bow to your skills, Aunt Lucy."

"Surprises are always the best," she said. "Unless, of course, you're talking about a missed period or a venereal disease." She pushed me toward the velvet couch in the corner. "Now you sit and rest. Doctor's orders. And watch us work our magic."

CHAPTER 36

WHAT DID THE MASS SPECTROMETER SAY TO THE GAS CHROMATOGRAPH? BREAKING UP IS HARD TO DO.

I spent the rest of the morning on the couch with my feet up, feeling like a total slug as people scurried around me, working like crazy to get ready for the party. When Alvida came, she set down a giant tray of spinach and ricotta stuffed shells and pulled me into a fierce hug. She examined my face, her sharp eyes missing nothing.

"You look pale, but all right," she said, and lowered her voice. "I'm not sure I can say the same about my grandson, though. You took about ten years off his life with this."

A tear rolled down my cheek. I sniffed and brushed it away with an irritated swipe of my hand. "I can't stop bawling. It's like I've sprung a leak."

She pinched my cheek. "Or maybe you're emotional because you found something special and you don't want to lose it." She took both my hands in hers. "He's sorry, kid. I've never seen anyone sorrier in my whole life. Also, I know you don't want to hear this, he *was* under the power of your love potion when he started hanging out with Tiffany, so it's kind of your fault."

My jaw dropped. "*My* fault—?"

Alvida swept my words aside with a wave of her hand. She wore several gold rings. They sparkled in the sunlight coming through the window. "I won't say another word. I never interfere. But I will say this—give him another chance. He was so happy with you, and I think you'd say the same."

Tommy, standing behind Alvida, and holding what looked like a giant pot of spaghetti, cleared his throat. "Excuse me, Nunny. Did you tell Grace you never interfere? Because we both know it isn't true. You have to go to confession. Pronto. Or you are going straight to hell for lying."

"Shut up, Tommy," she said, her lips quirking as if trying not to laugh. "Put the spaghetti in the kitchen and make yourself a plate of food. You have to go to work soon. You can't fight fires on an empty stomach, *mio caro*."

He walked away shaking his head. "I mean it, Nunny. Straight. To. Hell."

She smiled as she watched him go. "I need to find a nice girl for him, and for Anthony, but I'm taking care of Dario first. He's worth the trouble, and you should give him another chance. There. I've said my piece. I'm done now. Let's eat."

Rather than eating in the kitchen, everyone insisted on pulling up chairs so I could remain on the couch. "I'm not an invalid," I said with a groan, but they ignored me. Alvida handed me a giant plate of food and a napkin.

"*Mangia*," she said. "You're too skinny. We need to put some meat on your bones."

"Skinny?" I asked, but Aunt Lucy jumped in before I could finish.

"You have lost weight, Gracie, and you're as white as a sheet. Of course, it fits in well with Halloween if you planned to be a ghost. Or maybe even a vampire. Not one of those pretty, sparkly ones. I mean the scary ones that look like walking corpses."

"Thanks, Aunt Lucy. Exactly the look I've been going for," I said, making Cat and Fiona laugh.

Tommy went to work after shoveling down a plate of food in record time. "Firefighters," said Alvida with a shake of her head. "Fastest eaters on the planet."

Laura sat next to Will, so close their knees touched. His dark head bent close to her fair one as he listened to her intently. I had no idea what a pediatric nurse and a funky emo rocker might have in common, but they clicked. Why didn't I see that coming?

Alvida took a seat on the couch next to me, and so did Aunt Lucy, like two geriatric bookends. Fiona and Cat rested cross-legged on the floor, and Mrs. Periwinkle settled comfortably in a high-backed chair. The bell above the door tinkled as Sally dashed in.

"Grace," she said, pulling up a chair right next to me. She had no makeup on, and she'd obviously been crying. Her eyes looked red and swollen, and her face blotchy. "I heard all about what happened. Oh, my word. Did Aggie put something in the smoothie that hurt you?"

I reached out to hold her hand. "I don't know, Sally. We'll get the results back from the lab work soon."

She gave my hand a squeeze. "If it is her, I don't know how I'll ever forgive myself. I knew Aggie had issues but never suspected anything like this. When I got the call from Grovetown College..." Her voice trailed off.

"What call?" I asked.

She pulled out a tissue and dabbed her eyes. "From campus security. They called a few days ago. I told you she experienced a problem with one of the other professors, right?"

I frowned, confused about where this might be leading. "He was inappropriate with her, and the human resources office refused to help."

Sally sniffed. "Yes, that's the story she told me, but it seems the truth is different." She opened her tissue and blew her nose loudly. "Aggie wasn't the victim. They asked her to leave, quietly, because she stalked a fellow professor. A married man. She became obsessive, imagining a non-existent relationship, and it scared him. He didn't want to press charges, and she agreed to stay away from him and the college, but someone spotted her there a few weeks ago. Which is the reason campus security called me. I'm her next of kin, and they wanted to verify her whereabouts. I told them the truth, I haven't seen her in weeks."

"She came here," I said, sitting up straighter. "The night of the bomb scare. I saw her right outside, and she said she was looking for you."

"I haven't seen her. Not once." She let out a sob. "First Bubu disappeared, and Ralphie left me without a single word. Now Aggie's in trouble. But there is one thing I can't understand. Why would she want to hurt you, Grace? She adores you."

I couldn't meet her eyes. "She didn't prepare the smoothie for me."

Sally's tearful gaze flew to my aunt. "Lucy. Oh, dear. That's...horrid. I should have known."

"How is any of this your fault?" asked Aunt Lucy.

Sally's hands shook. "Aggie has problems. She's on anti-psychotics, you see. When she takes them as directed, she's the sweetest, kindest woman you've ever met. But when she goes off them...well..." She paused, her expression sad. "Let me just say she's not herself."

"That has nothing at all to do with you, Sally," said Alvida.

"It does because I know how she is," said Sally. "When Aggie stops taking her medication, her mind gets cloudy. She has trouble with certain things, and one of them is spelling. Without her medicine, Aggie becomes almost dyslexic."

Cat covered her mouth with her hand. "You think she wrote those threatening notes?"

Sally nodded. "It's possible. I thought of it the day Grace mentioned the spelling errors in the notes but dismissed it as foolishness. Aggie seemed to be doing so well. She'd adjusted. She'd made friends. She'd gotten involved in ARK and a few other community groups. Then when I heard about the smoothie..." She shook her head. "It's hard to imagine someone you love doing such terrible things."

I considered it. "Aggie might have issues, but she isn't the one behind the vandalism."

"How can you be so sure?" asked Sally.

"The person who shattered our front window that night wasn't a woman. I'm certain."

Sally exhaled, leaning back in her chair. "Oh, thank goodness."

"Then who did it?" asked Cat. "Who's behind all of this?"

I chewed on my lower lip as I thought about it. "I don't know, but they're escalating their behavior, and getting more dangerous."

"And tomorrow is the party," said Aunt Lucy, wringing her hands together. "Should we cancel it, Grace?"

I shook my head. "No. Tomorrow we'll find out what made me sick. It'll give us something to go on, right? The police already know we're having the party tomorrow, and Anthony will be here. We'll talk with him ahead of time and let him know our concerns."

"He'll want to question Aggie," said Aunt Lucy. "If he can find her. Oh, dear. I hope she's okay. Poor thing."

Acting so kindly about someone who may have tried to murder her said a lot about Aunt Lucy's character. It also said a lot about her refusal to see the bad in anyone, one of her most endearing and yet frustrating qualities.

I closed my eyes, sleepy after the big lunch. Aunt Lucy

and Alvida fussed over me, making me lie on the couch and covering me with a soft quilt. As I rested, watching the others work on the party preparations, I thought about Dario. I couldn't seem to stop thinking about him, and I felt guilty after speaking with Alvida. Yes, he'd wronged me terribly, but was I any better when he tried to apologize? I hated to admit it, but probably not.

I only had a week left before the review board. The possibility of returning to my old life, hovered on the horizon like a beautiful mirage, but I hated to leave like this, with so many things unfinished and unresolved. I worried about Aunt Lucy, Cat, and Sally. They all faced threats. Even without any proof, I knew someone attempted to kill Aunt Lucy with the smoothie. I hoped it wasn't Aggie, but who else could it be? If Aunt Lucy ingested it instead of me, if she finished the whole thing, if she'd been alone when it happened...

I sighed, snuggling deeper into the couch and allowing my heavy eyelids to close. I'd worry about one thing at a time, and first I needed to regain my strength. Trouble loomed ahead, I sensed it in my bones. Tomorrow, on the night of the full moon, the Wiccans would dance, and the person behind all this might make his final stand. He'd grown braver and bolder with each attempt to frighten us, but instead of being afraid, he'd pissed me off.

"Bring it on," I muttered under my breath.

CHAPTER 37

"TAKE CHANCES, MAKE MISTAKES, GET MESSY." MISS FRIZZLE

I rested most of the day. As evening fell, Aunt Lucy insisted Laura and I use her apartment. She preferred to stay downstairs and sleep on the couch in the back room. It made me nervous to leave her alone, but she waved away my worries. "I'll be fine. Spend time alone with your friend. No one is going to bother us tonight. I'm sure of it."

Oddly enough, I agreed with her. We were safe, for now. Or until tomorrow at least.

Laura and I made a fire and curled up to have a chat. She relaxed in a comfortable old tapestry covered chair. I parked myself on the couch with my grimoire on my lap and my legs propped up on an ottoman.

"What are you holding?" she asked, indicating the grimoire.

My face grew hot, and not from the fire. "Um, a magic spell book written by one of my ancestors who died by hanging during the Salem witch trials."

"Oh. Is that all?" She laughed. "First, I need a glass of wine. Then I want to hear the whole story."

She poured a glass of red, as I sipped herbal tea, not quite

ABIGAIL DRAKE

ready for alcohol yet. I told her all about finding the grimoire, making the love potions, and falling for Dario. I talked a *lot* about Dario, in fact. By the time I finished, she'd drunk several glasses of wine. Sloshed, she pointed a finger at me.

"That explains it," she said. "Tiffany gave Dario the potion, which made him believe all her lies about you. He never would have believed them otherwise. You gave him the antidote, and he woke up. It all makes perfect sense."

I blinked in surprise. "You don't think I'm crazy?"

She put a hand over mine. "I've seen things in the hospital impossible to explain. Miracles of the highest order. Children who should have died walking out of the hospital like nothing ever happened. If miracles exist, why can't magic?"

"But it's cherry juice and water," I said. "It shouldn't work. There is nothing magical about it."

Laura waved away my explanation. "The potion isn't magic, silly. You are. Remember how many times I said you have some kind of unnatural gift when it comes to chemistry?"

I frowned. "I work very hard and I study. A lot."

"No," she said. "It's like you know things no one has ever taught you. Tell the truth. Most of the time, when you were in class and the teacher covered something new, did it seem new to you, or was it more like you were remembering something you already understood?"

I bit my lip. She'd summed it up perfectly. "Maybe it's because I've always been so interested in chemistry—"

Laura cut me off. "Nope. That's not it. I sort of assumed you were the reincarnation of some famous dead chemist or something."

"A very likely explanation," I said with a roll of my eyes. I assumed Laura would laugh it off, but she surprised me.

"Exactly," she said, ignoring my sarcasm. "But now I know the truth. You're like Maeve McAlroy."

368

"I'm a witch?" I let out a laugh. It sounded more like a cackle, so I immediately cleared my throat and gave Laura a serious look. "Okay, I have accepted there is something about the potion that is...different. I'm not sure if it's truly magic, or the power of suggestion, or what, but I do concede the potions seemed to work. Sort of. And I experienced something strange and compelling and mysterious the night I mixed the antidote. But I cannot support the whole witchcraft thing. It's complete nonsense, so please don't tell me you believe in all this stuff. I get enough of it from Aunt Lucy and her buddies."

Laura shook her head. "Not a witch in the sense of devil worship and pointy hats and what not. I don't think Maeve McAlroy was a witch in that way either. I'm guessing she was probably more of a Wiccan, or maybe even a healer, poor thing. You have the same skills, and those skills are something good. Something pure."

"What do you mean?" I'd stopped laughing. I wanted to know her theories on this.

"Some people are naturally talented. Born with special gifts. Singers. Dancers. Mathematicians." She swirled her wine in her glass. "You're like that, too. This ability you have with chemistry is magical, and it's powerful. Which is why you have to forgive Dario and move on. It's your fault this happened in the first place."

I scowled at her. "You're the second person to blame this on me today."

"Who was the first?"

"Dario's grandmother, Alvida."

Laura laughed. "Well, she's right. We're both right. The question is what are you going to do about it?"

"I don't know," I said softly.

I put my empty cup of tea on the table and played with the edges of the blanket. Laura, my most grounded and rational friend, believed in all this. It made me rethink my whole stance on the magic issue. I'd been afraid Aunt Lucy and her whack-a-doodle friends had rubbed off on me, but now I thought Laura might be right. Perhaps I did take after my ancestor Maeve.

"I want to be with him," I said. "But how can I ever trust him again?"

"You'll find a way. After all, from what you've told me, he never technically cheated on you. It sounds like he went out with her once or twice to make you jealous. Kind of what you did with Ivan, right?"

"I guess so. Speaking of Ivan, he may have been involved in the plot to make me look bad in front of Dario, so I can't fix you up with him now. Not that it matters. I've noticed the way you took a shine to a certain drummer we all know and love."

She sighed. "Will Wax."

"You like him, huh?"

"Definitely." She hugged her legs to her chest, her stocking feet on the edge of the chair. "You of all people should understand."

"Why?"

"It's *chemistry*," she said, her lips quirking into a smile. "On a fundamental level, my atoms dig his atoms, and I'm pretty sure his atoms dig mine right back. It's not something you can explain. It can only be experienced. Think about the first time you saw Dario. Didn't every part of you scream out, 'It's him,' and recognize it immediately?"

"I guess," I said, remembering the pull I'd perceived when I met him, and how hard I fought it.

Laura got out of her chair to join me on the couch. The firelight played on her short blond hair and her delicate, almost angelic features. "There is no guessing," she said, her voice firm. I imagined this was the tone she used with her young patients before giving them a shot.

"What do you mean?"

"Dario is the man for you. We both know it. The only thing holding you back is your own insecurity and your stubborn Irish temper."

I narrowed my eyes at her. "Is that what you think?"

"Yes, it is." She stood up and grabbed my hand, pulling me off the couch. "And it's time for you to go to bed, young lady. Tomorrow is going to be a busy day, and you need your sleep."

"You're the best, Laura."

"Nope. *You're* the best, which is why I want you to be happy." She kissed my cheek. "Goodnight, my friend. Dream sweet dreams of mascarpone cheese and handsome Italian men ravishing you on their kitchen island."

"Ugh. I should never have told you," I said, heading to my room.

She laughed. "But you did, and that's what I'll picture when I finally meet Mr. Fontana." I gave her a dirty look, but it made her laugh harder. "See you in the morning."

After I climbed into bed, I heard Laura tidying up in the kitchen before she went back to the living room. When it grew quiet, I guessed she'd fallen asleep on the couch, but sleep eluded me. I kept thinking about Dario, and what Laura had said.

I had feelings for Dario, but I needed to make a decision. Should I act on those feelings, or should I ignore them and go back to Philadelphia where I belonged?

I tossed and turned, but even after thinking about it late into the night, I woke up the next morning still unsure about what to do. My review board hearing was in a week. I needed to focus on arguing my case and getting reinstated. If all went well, I'd finish my work, defend my thesis, and hopefully get offered a job. Or I might be blackballed forever.

I pushed aside the covers and stood up, letting out an angry huff. No wonder Dario hated the world of academia. It was a festering boil, a cesspit of ego, arrogance, and snobbery.

I smiled, wanting to share the analogy with him. I knew how he'd react. He'd laugh and say I'd summed it up nicely.

What are you thinking about, Grace?

I missed the way he always asked me that question, wanting to understand the inner workings of my mind, and genuinely interested in my answers.

He'd been right about how elitist and competitive things were at school. I needed to get away from it for a few months in order to truly see it. But it didn't mean I wanted to give it up. I loved the students and the energy there, as well as the excitement of learning and exchanging ideas. Not everything about academia was bad, but, sadly, a lot of snobs like Jonathan and ruthless, selfish people like Roger, found a place in those hallowed halls. Yes, I also liked winning, and craved recognition for my work, but it wasn't my main focus. I loved learning for the sake of learning, and it separated me from the Jonathans and Rogers of my world.

I got dressed and went downstairs, feeling more like myself. We'd closed the shop for the day, but people hurried about, setting up tables and bringing in food. I found Aunt Lucy and Laura in the event room in the back. Most of the year, Aunt Lucy used it for storage. Once the rear garden of the shop, someone had covered it with a glass ceiling many years ago, turning it into a large sunroom. It lacked temperature control, however, which meant in the summer, the heat coming through the glass made it too hot, and during the winter, it got too cold. In October and in the early spring, the temperature was exactly right.

Aunt Lucy smiled when she saw me. "You look much better this morning."

Laura, who stood on a ladder hanging fairy lights, agreed. "Have you heard from the hospital yet?"

I checked my phone and shook my head. "Nope."

Rows of tables filled the space, also covered with black tablecloths and candlesticks. Instead of skull vases and black roses, however, hollowed out pumpkins full of fall floral bouquets were the centerpieces. They added a bright pop of color. Carved jack-o-lanterns dotted the room as well. The result, tasteful and yet spooky, surprised me.

Aunt Lucy seemed to read my mind. "Samhain is a religious holiday for our Wiccan friends," she said. "The candles light the way for the dead who walk the earth on this holy night. Jack-o-lanterns scare away evil spirits. But we keep the rest to a minimum."

"It looks beautiful."

"Thank you," she said. "I'm proud of my handiwork."

I pushed up the sleeves of my favorite fall T-shirt, one with a picture of a pumpkin on it and the mathematical symbol for pi inside. "What can I do to help?" I asked.

She pointed to a pile of black robes sitting on one of the tables. "Those are for tonight. We have to wear black for the Samhain celebration, but we can take off the robes once we get back here and show off our fancy dresses. Could you air them out for me? Bring them to the costume loft and hang them up. Then, if you're up to it, maybe we could do a walk through together. I'd like to make sure I didn't miss anything for tonight."

I hung the robes up as she suggested. They consisted of a variety of different lengths and materials. The longest one, made of black velvet, had my name pinned to it, so I tried it on. Warm and soft, it reached to my toes and a wide hood with a thick, black satin ribbon tied at the neck. The perfect fit. I took it off and hung it next to the others, checking to make sure they didn't need any ironing or repairs. They seemed fine, so I trotted down the steps to find Aunt Lucy. Alvida intercepted me with a plate full of food.

"Oh, no you don't," she said. "Breakfast first. You have a big day ahead of you."

I cleaned my plate, much to Alvida's great satisfaction, and did the walk through with Aunt Lucy. She didn't need my help. She'd arranged it all perfectly and planned out even the smallest details.

"You're amazing. How did you do all of this?"

She smiled, clearly pleased with my words. "Years of practice, dearie. It's not difficult."

"A few weeks ago, you could barely manage to deal with the shop," I said. "And now you're the Martha Stewart of Samhain celebrations."

"I'm back to being my normal self. I'm not all sleepy and groggy anymore, which makes this so much easier."

I paused, as realization dawned on me. "The smoothies made you feel that way, Aunt Lucy. Your exhaustion and forgetfulness got worse every time you drank one, but to everyone else, it looked like dementia or old age."

"I'm not old," she huffed, but she agreed with my conclusions. "You're right. My tiredness started when Aggie began making me those drinks. It's hard to believe, isn't it? Why did Sally's sister want to drug me?"

"I don't know," I said. "But we need to take this one step at a time. Once we get the results back from the hospital, it'll give us a clearer picture, but we have to leave everything else in the hands of the police, okay?"

Her lips quivered. "It breaks my heart. For Sally and for Aggie."

It broke my heart, too, but soon I got too busy to think about it. People came in and out, bringing food and drink and offering to help wherever needed. Once we finished setting up, Laura and I went upstairs to change. Aunt Lucy went home with Mags, promising to meet us at the Enchanted Garden Café at sunset.

We did our hair and makeup and chatted as we got ready. It felt like the old days, when Laura and I went out together for a night on the town. Laura dried her short blond hair quickly and worked on her makeup. Smoky eyes, soft blush on her cheeks, and pale pink lipstick. It suited her perfectly, as did the strapless asymmetrical black mini-dress with a long sheer organza overskirt.

"Laura. You look so hot you could melt tungsten."

She put a hand over her heart. "You flatter me."

I took the hot rollers out of my hair. It fell in soft waves around my shoulders. I had on more makeup than I usually wore but decided it was a good night for something dramatic and wild. My lips were red, my lashes long and thick, and my eyes lined in black to make them look more cat-like and tilt up at the corners. The green dress matched my eye color and showed off my creamy curves.

"Yowza," said Laura, making me turn around and show it off. "Dario is not going to know what hit him."

I sighed and put on the sparkly green earrings from Sally. "We'll see, I guess."

Laura rested a gentle hand on my arm. "Have you decided what you're going to do about him yet?"

I shook my head. "No, but I have to be realistic. I live in Philly. He lives in Pittsburgh. We're on opposite sides of the state. Why start something I can't finish? If all goes well, I'll be back at the university, working toward my PhD and making up for two lost months. I won't have time for a relationship, let alone a long distance one. And, worst case scenario, if the review board expels me, I'll have to find a job. Who knows where it will be or who will even hire me? With a mountain of student loans to pay off, I'll have to take what I can. Either way, I can't get involved with Dario. It...well, it doesn't add up."

"Very logical, but you're leaving one important factor out of your equation."

"What?" I asked, perplexed.

"How you feel about him," she said.

I pursed my lips, unable to lie to my friend. "It doesn't change anything."

"It changes *everything*. When something as special as this comes along, you have to grab it with both hands and hold tight. "

I stared at her, knowing she spoke the truth. "But I don't know what to do," I said softly. "I don't have a plan."

"You don't need a plan." She grinned at me, her blue eyes shining. "And you don't have to worry. As soon as you see him, you'll know. It'll be as clear as crystal."

I frowned. "Most crystals are opaque, not transparent, so your analogy is off—"

She interrupted me. "You'll know, Grace. Stop fussing."

We put on our black cloaks to cover our fancy dresses and pulled the hoods up over our heads. With the ribbon tied at my neck, and the soft velvet of the cloak covering me nearly to my toes, I felt even more like my ancestor Maeve McAlroy. She probably dressed in a similar fashion a long time ago.

As we walked to the Enchanted Garden Café, arm in arm, the dry leaves swished around our feet and a sense of excitement filled the air. Children pranced around in costumes, shouting "Trick or Treat" as the shopkeepers handed out sweets. The scent of candles inside jack-o-lanterns wafted toward us with the aroma of pumpkin, smoke, and burning wax.

The sun had just set as we turned the corner and saw people walking into the garden of the café. In my cloak, anonymous and hidden, I scanned the crowd, searching for Dario, but I didn't see him.

We moved to the center of the garden and found a place to stand near the gurgling fountain. Aunt Lucy joined us, easily recognizable due to her short stature and her limp. Also, her cloak was purple and covered in orange glittery pumpkins, a sure giveaway.

"Oh, there's Eliza Dragonsong," said Aunt Lucy, pointing to a tall, elegant woman with blond hair standing in the center of the circle we'd formed. The light of the bonfire behind her illuminated her figure. "She's a Wiccan priestess, and also a divorce attorney. Kind of a good combination, don't you think? She can put a hex on all those cheating spouses." I stared at Aunt Lucy, trying to figure out if she was serious or not. I couldn't tell.

"What happens now?" asked Laura.

"The normal things," said Aunt Lucy. "We'll drink a little, dance a lot, and celebrate as much as possible."

"So this isn't about Halloween?" Laura's face was barely visible inside the darkness of her hood.

"Yes, and no," said Aunt Lucy. "Listen, girls. Eliza is about to speak."

Eliza lifted her arms to the sky, and the crowd went quiet. "Tonight, we celebrate Samhain," she said. "The end of summer. The cold nights of winter wait on the other side for us. The bounty of our summer labors, the abundance of the harvest, the success of the hunt, all lie before us. We must thank the earth for all it has given us this season, and look forward to winter, a time of sacred darkness. Blessed be."

"Blessed be," the crowd repeated.

After casting a circle and calling the quarters, the Wiccan way to commence a ceremony, Eliza stood in front of a large altar covered with an orange cloth. Two candles sat in the center of the altar, one silver and one gold. As she lit the silver one, she said, "Dark mother, ruler of the night, goddess of death and of rebirth, I honor thee. I stand humbly before thee, asking for thy blessing. Lift the veil between the worlds as this time-out-of-time begins."

A tremor went over my body as the wind rustled the dry leaves in the trees above us. Laura gripped my arm even harder, her blue eyes huge in her face. "What the heck?" she asked. "Did you feel something?"

"Yes, but I'm not sure what it was."

Eliza spoke again, lighting the gold candle. "Dark father, consort of the crone, lord of the underworld, I honor thee, and ask for thy blessings and favor. As this time-out-of-time approaches, we ask you to stand guard as the veil lifts. Keep safe our ancestors, and all of our loved ones here on Earth."

She stepped back from the altar as the flames from the candles flickered and grew larger. Several people in the crowd gasped. One woman from the opposite side of the garden shouted. "They're here. The goddess and god have arrived."

"Don't be scared," whispered Aunt Lucy. "It's no different from shouting out a hallelujah or two in a church. This is exactly the same"

"Uh, okay," I said, not convinced. The ceremony didn't scare me, though, or make me uncomfortable. It seemed natural and somehow right. Strange, but true. Even though I'd been raised in a strict Catholic home, maybe I was more of a pagan than I'd realized.

The Wiccans chanted together. "Tonight, as the barrier between the two realms grows thin, spirits walk amongst us once again. Be they family, friends, or foes? Under cover of darkness no one knows. Trust the goddess to lift the veil. Trust her lord to guard it well. Trust in the magic of this holy night. Trust tomorrow all will be right."

Eliza lifted her arms to the sky. She said, "Embrace your ancestors, your departed love ones, and all who dwell here on earth. Embrace yourself with love and pride and embrace the magic within you. Blessed be. Blessed be. Blessed be."

I found myself lifting my arms to the sky and chanting with them. It may have been my imagination, but I sensed the spirit of Maeve McAlroy standing next to me, chanting along with me. Aunt Lucy seemed to have felt it, too.

"It's always so nice when relatives come for a visit," she said, with a little smile. "Even long dead ones."

Before I could question her further, Eliza rang a bell and said, "Let the feasting begin."

We dined on succulent roasted meats, vegetables, and dark bread. Platters were piled high with fruits and pastries and sweets. Claire and Fiona had outdone themselves. Fiona gave me a quick peck on the cheek as she rushed back and forth from the kitchen. "Are you having fun?" she asked.

"Yes, it's wonderful."

"I see Will," said Laura, waving to him. Will wore his normal clothing to the Samhain party. He always dressed in black. "Do you mind?"

"Go," I said, giving her a nudge. "Have fun."

Although happy to see Laura and Will together, I searched for Dario, and tried to stifle my disappointment when I didn't see him. Even though I still didn't know what I'd say when I saw him, or how I'd act, the idea he might not even show up made me sad.

And then it happened. Suddenly, through the crowd of people, I felt his eyes on me. Dressed in black, with his dark hair curling against the collar of his midnight hued shirt, he looked delectable and kind of dangerous.

I doubted he'd recognize me with the cloak covering my clothing and hair, but his eyes bored into mine as he made his way through the throng of people. I experienced a moment of panic because the time had come to make a decision.

In the lab, I added certain materials together to get

certain results, but real life wasn't so simple. I didn't know right from wrong anymore. With no clear guidelines to follow, what if I made a poor decision? Like a rock thrown in a pond, it could be a catalyst for other bad things to happen, and I might get hurt again.

I lifted my skirts with my hand, about to turn away, but Dario reached me at that very moment. It seemed like the noise and people surrounding us got sucked into a vacuum. All that existed were Dario's warm brown eyes, and what I saw inside them.

Doubt. Fear. Sorrow. And something else, too.

Could it be love?

At last, I found my answer. As soon as I saw him, as soon as I looked into his eyes, the realization made my heart stutter to a stop and start right back up again. Laura nailed it, even though she used a flawed analogy to describe it. Unlike an opaque crystal, my decision was truly and perfectly clear.

I just knew.

CHAPTER 38

ROSES ARE RED, BROMOTHYMOL IS BLUE
(ABOVE PH 7.6 AT LEAST), THERE IS NO
ENDPOINT TO MY LOVE FOR YOU.

"**Y**ou have that look again," he said. "The one telling me you figured out the answer to a puzzle."

"I have a look?"

"You do." He reached out like he wanted to touch my cheek but shoved his hand into his pocket instead. "Tell me, Grace. What are you thinking about right now?"

"Carl Jung's theory on synchronicity," I said. "The simultaneous occurrence of psychic and physical events which don't seem to be linked."

His forehead wrinkled adorably. "What I know about Jung has more to do with libido. So, is this theory about coincidences?"

I shook my head. "The opposite. There no coincidences...according to Jung's theory at least. Each thing occurring is significant and purposeful, and we're all interconnected in a giant web of action, reaction, and causation. It's also what Jung used to justify his beliefs in the paranormal, but I won't get into it right now because it's a whole different branch of the synchronicity theory and unrelated to what I'm trying to say."

I'd started babbling. Even worse, I babbled about Carl-freaking-Jung. Who does that?

Dario came a step closer. The smell of the bonfire and the sounds of the Wiccan celebration faded away. A bare-chested man walked past us wearing a mask and giant antlers, but I barely noticed him. All I cared about was Dario, and what was happening between us right now.

"What are you trying to say exactly?"

I bit my lower lip. "Meeting you cannot be an accident, or a coincidence, or a blip on the radar of my life. It was meant to happen."

"Fate?"

"Yes." I took a deep breath and dove in. "But there's something else I want to say, and I need to get it out right now."

"Okay. I'm ready for it," he said, appearing to brace for bad news.

I moved a step nearer to him, closing the distance between us as I stared into his face. "I don't always believe words. I don't even believe actions. What I do believe in are patterns, and what I see with you is the same pattern repeating itself over and over again."

"What pattern?" he asked, his eyes still worried. He probably thought I referred to the way we bickered, or even his relationship with Tiffany, but that wasn't it at all.

"It's simple." I put my hand on his cheek. "I can't seem to stop loving you. It's a pattern now, and I don't want it to end. I think you're stuck with me."

He closed his eyes and covered my hand with his own, turning his face so he could kiss the center of my palm. "I'm stuck with you, huh?" he asked, opening his eyes. The catch in his voice surprised me. "Then I guess I'd better make the most of it."

He pulled me into his arms and kissed me until the world

spun around us. His lips were gentle, but possessive, strong and sure. I laced my fingers through his thick hair as he groaned against my mouth.

"I missed you," he said, resting his forehead against mine. The hood of my cloak fell back, exposing my face and hair. He pushed a few tendrils away from my cheek, his eyes filled with emotion. "And I'm so sorry."

"Shhh," I said, covering his lips with my fingertips. "We won't talk about it again. I missed you, too."

Dario gave me another sweet, passionate kiss as the sound of drums filled the night and the pagans danced. Aunt Lucy appeared at our side.

"Come on, lovebirds. It's time to celebrate," she said, nudging us into the circle of dancers who spun around the bonfire with hands clasped. She stayed back, smiling at us as she leaned on her cane, the scamp, and we got pulled into the dance.

The bonfire crackled and warmed us on the cool fall night, and we laughed as the rhythm of the drums grew faster and faster. It built to a crescendo pitch, and then everything stopped. A moment of total stillness occurred as we all panted, trying to catch our breaths. When a new song began, and the dancing resumed, Dario and I didn't join in. Instead, he led me to a dark, secluded corner of the garden, and I went. Most willingly.

He pulled me into his arms, holding me close. His lips caressed my heated skin as his hands explored the curves of my body. The dancing and the bonfire had stirred my blood, but nothing affected me as much as Dario's touch.

I unbuttoned his shirt, wanting to touch his skin, and he groaned. His hands slid up my waist to cover my breasts, lifting them until they nearly popped out of the already low bodice. He teased my nipples gently with his thumbs, making it hard to concentrate on anything else.

"Do you know Samhain is a time to start anew?" he asked.

"It is?" I honestly couldn't care less about Samhain at this point. All I cared about was getting Dario naked. Pronto.

"Yes." He cupped my face in his hands, forcing me to focus on his words. "It's like the Wiccan New Year's Day. And I want a fresh start. A new beginning. What do you say?"

"Yes. I'm in. Totally." I nodded, maybe a little too vigorously, and went back to unbuttoning the rest of his shirt.

He let out a deep, throaty laugh, lifting his face to the starry sky. "You aren't going to think about it or analyze it or worry about it first?"

I shook my head. "Nope."

"Why?"

I went up on my tiptoes to kiss his delightfully perfect lips. "Because life is an experiment. I've already made my hypothesis; that you're the one for me. Now I simply have to test it to see if my theory is correct. I don't need to analyze it or think about it. I need to live it."

He pulled me into his arms for a fierce hug, and this time, when he kissed me, it felt like a vow. "We'll get it right this time," he said softly against my lips. "I swear. But we'd better go. It's almost time for your party."

"The party," I said with a gasp. "Am I late?"

He shook his head. "The pagans aren't done dancing yet." He glanced in the direction of the fire, where the dancing continued. Giving me a soft kiss on the cheek, he buttoned up his shirt and pulled my hood back over my head, tying the ribbon at my chin. Lacing his fingers with mine, he steered me out of the garden.

"I thought they'd dance naked tonight," I said. "Fiona said they did that during summer solstice."

He gave me a crooked smile. "Maybe it's too cold tonight for naked dancing."

"It wasn't so bad the other night when I did it."

"True. You're turning into quite the pagan, aren't you?"

"Funny you should say that, Dario. There's something I have to tell you."

Time to face up to what I'd done, both with the love potions and the antidote, so I told him the whole story. He listened without saying a single word, nodding occasionally as we walked. When I finished, he finally spoke. "So you and your aunt and my nunny and everyone else in the South Side thinks I was under the influence of a magical love potion?"

I winced. "I know it sounds stupid—"

He shook his head. "No, it doesn't. It makes total sense. I remember the night Tiffany showed up in Philly clearly, and I remember how things got weird after we shared a drink together in the bar. She roofied me, but with your love potion. She made a big miscalculation, however."

"What?" I asked, surprised he accepted this whole story so easily.

He stopped walking and gathered me close, staring deeply into my eyes. "The potion may have played a part in making me act like a total and absolute fool, but my love for you is stronger than any magic, even *your* magic, my sweet little witch of a chemist."

My heart slammed to a stop in my chest, and then beat so rapidly I worried I may be tachycardic. "You never loved Tiffany? Not even a tiny bit?"

He didn't hesitate a second. "Nope. But it is possible your potion made me more prone to the power of suggestion."

"What do you mean?"

He blew out a long breath. "After that drink with Tiffany, I went out of my mind with jealousy. That's not like me. I'm usually level headed. Under normal circumstances, I would have wanted to listen to your side of the story before jumping to conclusions." He shook his head sadly. "I'm a reporter, and yet I believed her without checking my source. That's rule number one, and I broke it. I messed things up between us, too."

"Tiffany isn't in the picture anymore?"

"She never was. And she never will be."

Light poured through the windows of the shop as Aunt Lucy, Laura, Will, and the others put the last touches on the party preparations. I had to go in and help, but I needed to clarify one more very important fact for Dario.

"Ivan was a friend. Nothing more. I swear it to you."

"I know," he said, cupping my face with his hands and stroking my cheeks with his thumbs. "I believe you. I won't doubt you again."

As he leaned forward to kiss me, Mrs. Periwinkle stuck her head out the door. "You're back, and you're together. Thank goodness. I feared we'd have to take drastic measures if the two of you couldn't work things out on your own."

"Drastic measures?" I asked, and immediately regretted it, scared of what she might say. "Never mind. Sorry I'm late."

She waved aside my words. "Pish, posh. We're nearly done. The moon is full, the stars are shining, we have lots to drink, and our friends will soon arrive. It's going to be a glorious night," she said. "As long as the spirits behave themselves. They are exceptionally restless at the moment. I only hope they'll keep mischief to a minimum. I can't promise the same for the humans." She let out a laugh and ushered us into the shop.

As we walked in, I noticed a single light on at Party Ark, and saw someone watching through the window. Before I could identify the person, however, the light switched off, and the shop went dark. It struck me as odd. Missy and Sissy said they planned to attend an ARK meeting tonight. If so, who hid behind the fall pumpkin display in Party Ark?

Aunt Lucy took my arm in hers. "There is evil afoot tonight," she said softly. Dario, commandeered by Mrs. Periwinkle to hang up a sign, didn't hear her words. "Stay on alert, Gracie my dear."

"What do you mean?" I asked.

She rubbed her arms. "Can't you sense it, too?"

I did, from the odd prickle going over my skin to the way the hairs on the back of my neck stood up. "I do," I said, and noticed the Dragon Rouge sitting next to the cash register, in plain view of our guests. "Aunt Lucy, why is that thing out?"

She pursed her lips. "I'm selling it to Mr. Dalca. It's a monstrosity, and I want it out of my house and away from you. I planned to let him have it earlier, but you got poisoned. I'll give it to him when he comes over for the party."

I frowned. "But why tonight, when so many people will be here?"

"It can't affect non-magic folk. Stop worrying about that hideous thing and help me set out the food. We have creepy canapés and a frightening assortment of sweets. It's going to be a Samhain to remember. I just know it." She looked at her watch. "Oh, my. It's nearly time. Turn on the music, Will," she called out. He gave her a thumbs up, and "The Monster Mash" blared over the sound system. She grinned at me, raising her arms into the air. "Let the wild rumpus begin," she said, and flung open the doors to the shop.

CHAPTER 39

WHAT WAS THE CHARGE WHEN NACL WAS ARRESTED? A SALT.

The Wiccans arrived promptly at nine. We planned to eat, drink and be merrily masked until the stroke of midnight. Then we'd reveal our true identities, say goodbye to the spirits wandering the earth, and continue partying until the wee hours of the morning.

My mask, made of black lace and tied with a ribbon, did nothing to hide my face or my identity. Dario, in a plain back mask, looked very dashing.

"Hello, Zorro," I said with a giggle, grabbing his hand as we went back to the kitchen to check on the food. "You're extremely handsome this evening."

"And you look amazing, as always," he said, pulling me close. "I cannot keep my hands off you. It's embarrassing."

"You're right. It *is* embarrassing," said Alvida from behind us. She wore a simply cut dress in a rich burgundy and a sparkly mask in the same color. "No noogie in the kitchen. It's a rule." She smacked Dario's arm, but I heard the laughter in her voice.

We'd hired a bartender for the event, someone from Paddy's Pub across the street, and a caterer helped prepare and serve the food. Everyone seemed to be having a good time. The front area of the shop bustled with people chatting and drinking. They filled their plates in the kitchen area and moved to the event space in the back to sit at the long banquet tables under the glass ceiling glowing with fairy lights. With room provided for dancing, and Halloween music playing in the background, many of our masked guests made their way to the dance floor.

"Aunt Lucy, it's going perfectly," I said, wrapping an arm around her shoulders.

"They're having a lovely time, which is what this party is all about, isn't it?"

She smiled up at me, adorable in her orange dress embossed with pumpkins and a headband made with silly bats bouncing on springs. She didn't wear a mask, worried it might impair her vision. We agreed the last thing she needed was to trip and fall, so instead she put on wacky glasses in a neon green color with black stripes.

"Hello, Grace," said a voice behind me and I jumped.

"Oh. Ivan. You startled me." Uncomfortable now in his presence, I stumbled on my words. "This is my aunt, Lucy."

Ivan turned and bowed to her, in an elegant and European way, of course, and kissed the back of her hand. "Charmed."

He wore an impeccably tailored tux, and his mask hid all his features except his perfect lips. His blond hair glinted in the light cast from the candles on the tables, and his mouth curved into a smile at the befuddled expression on Aunt Lucy's face.

"Do I know you?" she asked.

"I haven't had the pleasure," he said. "But thank you so much for including me. This is a delightful affair."

"You're most welcome," she said, and nudged me. "What a gentleman."

I wasn't sure about the last part. My eyes shot to Dario,

who stood across the room, chatting with his grandmother. He watched us warily.

Ivan noticed where my attention went and gave me a resigned smile. "I've truly lost my chance I see," he said softly. "How sad."

I wanted to tell him he never stood a chance, but Aunt Lucy interrupted me by hopping up and down and waving to Mr. Dalca. "Constantine. We're over here."

Ivan's body stiffened as Mr. Dalca approached, his gait unsteady and awkward. He held the Dragon Rouge in his gnarled hands.

He didn't wear a mask or a costume. He came as himself, which was scary enough. He moved slowly through the crowd, giving people dirty looks, and swearing at them under his breath.

Ivan cleared his throat. "Pardon me. I must bid you adieu and leave you to your other guests. Goodbye, ladies," he said with another bow. "Thank you again."

"Wait, Ivan..." I wanted to ask him a few questions about Tiffany, but he slipped through the crowd of people so quickly I couldn't even see where he headed.

"Are you sure I haven't met Ivan before?" asked Aunt Lucy, her brow wrinkled in a frown. "He seems so familiar."

"You saw him outside the shop the other day," I said, trying to reassure her. After her memory issues lately, she doubted herself.

She seemed placated, and as soon as Mr. Dalca reached us, the Dragon Rouge in his hand, she turned positively coquettish. "Hi, Connie," she said. "I see you found the box. Maybe later I'll show you how to unlock it." She stroked a finger over his hand, her voice positively dripping with some kind of odd sexual innuendo. I stared at her, mortified, but she didn't seem to notice. She only had eyes for Mr. Dalca. Connie. Yuck.

"Lucinda, why on earth would you leave this out front?" he asked, yelling and waving the box around. He drew the attention of several of our guests. "It is not a toy."

She rolled her eyes. "Don't be such a drama queen, Connie. Dance with me."

He shook his head. "No. You're a naughty girl."

"Will you punish me later?" she asked, batting her eyelashes at him.

His cheeks reddened, and not from embarrassment. He leaned close to Aunt Lucy. "Definitely," he said, his voice a growl.

"Go eat first." She squeezed his arm. "You'll need your strength."

He raised a bushy eyebrow at her and tucked the box into a large pocket inside his jacket. Without another word, he marched straight into the kitchen.

"Ew," I said. "You're sleeping with Mr. Dalca?"

Before she could answer, a man approached in a black suit, white shirt, and narrow black tie. He wore a top hat and a full-face mask. He lifted the mask when he saw us and gave us a wink.

"Dr. Mallinger," said Aunt Lucy, placing a hand over her heart. "You scared the beejeezus out of me."

"I'm sorry. Is there a place we can talk quietly for a moment?" he asked. "There is something I need to show both of you, and it's urgent."

"Sure," I said. "It's so noisy in here. Shall we step outside?"

"We can go to Mr. Dalca's shop," said Aunt Lucy. "He won't mind, and I have a key."

I groaned. She had a key? I needed to drop some major hints about the increase of STDs in the elderly, yet another item on the list of things I didn't want to do tonight. The list was growing rapidly, but other things required my more immediate attention.

We stepped into Librarie Antique and Aunt Lucy fumbled for the light. Dark and quiet in the old bookstore, the noises of the party sounded muffled, even though we could still hear the steady beat of the music and an occasional burst of laughter.

We settled into chairs, our masks off. Dr. Mallinger leaned against a table next to us and removed his top hat, too. He took a folded piece of paper from inside his jacket and handed it to me.

"The lab report," I said.

"Our initial diagnosis was correct. Someone put a very strong dose of medication in that smoothie. It's fortunate you got to the ER when you did. Without immediate intervention, the results could have been much more serious."

"Clozapine," I said, my eyes skimming the report as my heart filled with dread. "An anti-psychotic?"

"It is," he said. "But not a typical one. It's normally prescribed if all else fails. My guess is this person must have tried several other meds before ending up on this one."

"They were probably sick a long time," said Aunt Lucy. "Like for years."

"Probably."

"What do we do now?" I asked.

He cleared his throat. "I passed this onto the police. They're looking for Agatha Stein."

"It was Aggie all along?" I asked.

"It seems so. She made the smoothies, and, according to her records, she has a prescription for clozapine. But I have more bad news."

"What is it?" I asked.

He sighed. "The police are looking for her sister, too."

Aunt Lucy clasped a hand over her mouth. "Sally? But why?"

"She never showed up for a meeting this morning with her

sister's doctor to discuss options for Aggie's care, and no one has been able to reach her. It might be nothing, but the police stopped by her apartment to check on her. The place looked deserted."

"I didn't see her at the bonfire," I said, sick with worry. "But then I got busy and it slipped my mind."

"We can't jump to conclusions," said Aunt Lucy. "Sally could be fine. Aggie may be unpredictable, but she'd never hurt her big sister...would she?"

"It's hard to say." Dr. Mallinger folded his arms. "I spoke with the doctor who prescribed clozapine to Aggie years ago. She's never acted in a violent way, but if she used her medicine to drug you, it means she hasn't been taking it herself. That could be dangerous—for her and those around her."

"Poor dear Sally," said Aunt Lucy. "And poor Aggie."

"Could the clozapine be responsible for Aunt Lucy's symptoms, too?" I asked. "The fogginess, and memory loss?"

"Definitely," he said. "If someone without psychotic problems takes these meds, the results would be what you experienced—extreme tiredness and confusion."

"Is weight gain a symptom, too?" asked Aunt Lucy, squeezing the roll of fat around her belly. "Because I've packed on the pounds lately. It's worrisome since I have a gentleman friend now, and he likes to get intimate during the daylight hours since he falls asleep so early at night."

Dr. Mallinger blinked in surprise but managed to maintain his composure. "Well, yes. Weight gain is also a side effect."

I covered my face with my hands. "What do we do now?" I asked, hoping I could erase the mental image of my aunt and Mr. Dalca having sex in the bright light of day. So many wrinkles. So many saggy parts. So much I did not need to know.

"Nothing, for the moment. I wanted you to keep your eye out for Sally and to be aware in case Aggie should approach you at some point. She's not in her right mind. What she did is criminal. If your aunt ingested the smoothie instead of you, the results could have been fatal."

I put my hand over Aunt Lucy's and squeezed it. She still wore her bobbing bat headband and neon glasses, but the look in her eyes belied the comical nature of her costume. "You honestly think that poor, sweet, fragile woman wanted to kill me?"

Dr. Mallinger rubbed a hand along his square jaw. "We can't be sure murder was her intent at all. When a person has delusions and is not properly medicated, it's difficult to tell how much they comprehend. I'm not a mental health special-ist, but I can tell you the priority is to help her as much as it is to protect you...and Sally."

"I should have known something was wrong," said Aunt Lucy. "Sally never misses a Samhain celebration."

"You can't blame yourself," said Dr. Mallinger. "And the best thing you can do to help Sally now is go back to the party and pretend everything is normal. Which is what the police advised. Officer Belfiore is already at the party, and there are policemen watching the shop from different vantage points outside. If Aggie shows up, they'll be ready for her."

"But how will they know her? We're all wearing masks," said Aunt Lucy.

"They're aware it's a masked ball, and they know the masks come off at midnight," he said, glancing at his watch. "Which is less than an hour away. Can you two manage to hold on that long?"

We nodded. I stood up and put my mask back on. "Let's do this for Sally," I said with as much bravado as I could muster, but my hands shook as we went back to the shop.

Dario approached me right away. "Anthony's here," he said, tilting his head to indicate his cousin standing by the entrance of the shop. He dressed in black as well. "He told me what's going on. The entire police force is out looking for Aggie and Sally." His eyes said what his words did not. He worried about Sally, too. "Stick close to me, okay?"

"Who will keep an eye on Aunt Lucy?"

Dario's lips quirked. "Tommy," he said, and I followed his gaze to a tall man dressed as a mummy standing next to Aunt Lucy. "He says he went to a party for children at the fire station before he came here, but I secretly think he just likes wearing costumes."

For the next hour, we danced and socialized. Laura and Will already looked like a couple as they danced to the strains of "Witchy Woman." I found it oddly romantic, probably due to my new witch-like status. Fiona and Matthew were there, too, and Claire and Simon. Cat hung out with Mags and Alvida. Mrs. Periwinkle, resplendent tonight in a pale blue ball gown, had stars in her hair, stars on her mask, and a color-changing wand in her hand with a star on the tip. I loved seeing everyone together, but with Sally missing, it left a huge void.

Where was she? Did something happen to her?

Surrounded by friends, I found it hard to imagine danger could be close by, but like Aunt Lucy, I knew it was coming. I also knew there was nothing I could do to stop it. I just needed to be prepared.

"It's nearly midnight," said Aunt Lucy. "We have to announce the unmasking."

We climbed the staircase to the balcony, walking on the same steps Aunt Lucy fell down not so long ago. Had Aggie pushed her? If so, why didn't Aunt Lucy realize it was her?

It didn't make sense. Even in Aunt Lucy's forgetful, drug-addled state, she never once swayed from her story. A man in black demanded she give him the Dragon Rouge. A man in black broke into the apartment and asked the same of me. The most logical conclusion? It had to be the same man.

My thoughts whirled around in my head as we climbed the steps. Even if Aggie drugged us, she couldn't be the vandal. I saw a man in front of our shattered window the night I arrived home with Dario after dinner at Alvida's. A man. Not Aggie.

Aunt Lucy looked out at our assembled guests from the balcony and raised her arms into the air. "Rattle my bones and twist my thumbs, the bewitching hour has begun. The veil between the worlds is thin. Remove your masks and let the spirits in."

The church clock, a block away, pounded out a slow, deep chime.

One, two, three.

My eyes scanned the room as people prepared to remove their masks as soon as the countdown ended.

Four, five, six.

I frowned, knowing I'd missed something critical. I needed to figure it out right now.

Seven, eight, nine.

No, not something critical. *Someone* critical. I'd missed a person, and I realized it with sickening clarity. The person I saw in my room was the same person I saw near the broken window of our shop. The same one in Tiffany's photos.

Ten, eleven, twelve.

I took a deep breath, remembering blue eyes and a muscular physique. I knew his identity. I'd recognized him without even comprehending it.

Dario put a hand on my arm. "Grace, what's wrong?" he asked. He'd taken off his mask, and I removed mine, crumpling it in my hands.

"I know who did it. I know who pushed Aunt Lucy down the steps," I said, but the words no sooner left my mouth when the entire shop went dark, and I heard someone scream.

Aunt Lucy.

I reached for where she'd just been standing, right next to me, but grabbed only air. She no longer stood by my side on the balcony. She'd disappeared.

CHAPTER 40

"EVERYONE YOU MEET WILL KNOW SOMETHING YOU DON'T." BILL NYE

The darkness closed around me, oppressive and terrifying. My hands reached out frantically as I tried to locate my aunt. I stumbled, and nearly fell, but Dario's strong arms wrapped around me holding me close.

"Anthony," he shouted over the panicked cries from our guests. "Can you find the light switch? It's by the door to the kitchen."

"I'm on it," came a voice from below. I saw the glow of Anthony's flashlight as he searched the walls. Several people pulled out their cell phones and used them for light. Their worried cries turned into tense whispers as they waited for the lights to come back on.

"Where's Aunt Lucy?" I'd left my cell phone downstairs, but Dario used his to cast light around the balcony. What I saw made my blood run cold.

Mr. Dalca sat slumped against the wall, right beside the door leading to Aunt Lucy's apartment. He looked pale, and he had a hand over his chest. Aunt Lucy hovered over him.

"Connie. Wake up. What happened?"

We reached Mr. Dalca as the lights came back on. I put a comforting arm around Aunt Lucy as Dario knelt next to him on the floor and searched for a pulse. Anthony ran up the steps, holding his cell phone.

"Should I call an ambulance?" asked Anthony, kneeling next to his cousin.

Mr. Dalca, eyes still closed, growled at Anthony and pushed Dario's hand away. "I'm not dead, you idiots. I'm resting."

We all exhaled in relief. Dario sat back on his heels and raised a dark eyebrow at the older man. "And this seemed like a convenient place to take a break?"

Mr. Dalca shrugged. "I got knocked over when one of your guests stole my box."

"Someone stole the Dragon Rouge?" I asked. "What happened? I knew we should have put it somewhere for safe-keeping."

"You did," said Mr. Dalca. "You gave it to me."

"Yes, and I blame both of you," I said, pointing at my aunt and Mr. Dalca. "First, Aunt Lucy left it in the front room, and then you waved it around for all to see. It's no wonder this happened. What are we going to do?"

"Is the Dragon Rouge that old box you told me about?" asked Dario. "The one Aunt Lucy's ghost wanted?"

I cringed at his words, but he'd summed it up accurately. "Yes."

"Why would someone steal it? What's so important about it?"

"I'm curious, too," said Anthony, scratching his chin.

"It's not the box itself. It's what it contains. Inside is a valuable red stone, and some very evil spells."

Anthony's eyes widened. "Evil what—"

"Don't ask, Anthony. You don't want to know," I said.

"There's something weird about it. Something malevolent. Something that should not be in the wrong hands."

Dario helped Mr. Dalca up, dusting off the back of the old man's jacket. "Grace, right before the lights went out, you told me you knew who was behind this. Could it be the same person who stole the box from Mr. Dalca?"

"It has to be Ivan. I'm sure of it. He was the person who broke into my room somehow, and the one who shattered the front window of the shop. I knew the vandal looked familiar, but I couldn't put my finger on it. It wasn't until I saw him masked tonight, that I recognized him, and everything clicked into place."

"You are so slow," said Mr. Dalca. "Of course, it's Ivan. I knew that a long time ago."

"How could you have possibly known?" I asked.

"It is a long story. Maybe you take care of the party people first, and I will tell you."

I'd forgotten about our guests, who stood in the front room of the shop waiting for us to do or say something. I walked to the edge of the balcony.

"Everything is fine, folks. Sorry for the interruption. Resume your revelry please."

Our guests laughed it off, thinking we'd planned this, with the lights going out exactly at midnight. Ivan possessed a flair for the dramatic. Thankfully, no one had gotten hurt.

"I need more information about Ivan," said Anthony, taking out a notepad. "And a description of the box as well. I'm going to call it in, and maybe someone will spot him."

I told him what I knew, which wasn't much. He jotted it on his notepad and then went outside to make a phone call.

After we got the party rolling again, Aunt Lucy put Mrs. Periwinkle and Cat in charge, and we went upstairs to her apartment with Dario and Mr. Dalca. Climbing the steps behind Mr. Dalca and Aunt Lucy proved to be a lesson in patience. They went slowly, due to Mr. Dalca's age and Aunt Lucy's recent injury, and they kept stopping every few steps to chat.

"They can't talk and move at the same time, can they?" asked Dario, biting his lip to keep from smiling.

"That would be impossible."

We finally reached the apartment and got Mr. Dalca settled on the couch. Aunt Lucy sat there, too, insisting he rest his head on her lap, and she stroked his wispy white hair. As much as I hated imagining the two of them having sex, seeing moments of true tenderness between them did my heart good. Aunt Lucy had been alone for a long time. She deserved to have someone in her life, but Mr. Dalca cut the beautiful moment short.

"Let me up, woman. I'm not an invalid," he said, rising to a seated position on the couch.

I looked at Dario and rolled my eyes. He glanced away, trying not to laugh.

"Grace, do you mind putting the kettle on?" asked Aunt Lucy. "We need a cup of tea. Or would you rather have something stronger?"

"Stronger," we all said in unison.

I took out Aunt Lucy's decanter of bourbon and poured each of us a glass. "So, Mr. Dalca, how did you know it was Ivan?" I asked as I took a sip, enjoying the way the alcohol instantly warmed me.

He swished the amber liquid around in his glass. "We've tracked him for some time. I worked for the Ministry of Romanian Antiquities but in a secret division. We locate things others cannot. Dangerous objects."

"Like the Dragon Rouge," I said.

"Obviously," said Mr. Dalca, his eyes stern under his bushy eyebrows. "I heard you were smart. You said she was smart." His accusing gaze landed on Aunt Lucy.

"I *am* smart," I said. "But I'm missing half the equation."

He let out a sigh of long suffering. "I will explain, and I'll speak slowly so you understand. The Dragon Rouge was placed in the hands of the Trabuski family for safe keeping hundreds of years ago. Queen Maria of Romania, the grand-daughter of England's Queen Victoria, engaged in an illicit affair with Prince Barbu Alexandru Stirbey. She gave the Dragon Rouge to him. She trusted him and deemed it far too dangerous to give to anyone else."

"Why is it dangerous?" I asked. "And what does it do exactly?"

"It's not what it does, it's what it is. The stone is cursed. Evil. And especially perilous for someone like you."

"Someone like me?"

"Magic people," he said. "Aren't you even paying attention?" He let out a huff. "Legend has it the stone is as old as the world itself, and the devil created it when God gave us free will. Satan liked the whole free will thing. He saw it as a loophole, a way of encouraging people to do terrible things. Which is what the Dragon Rouge does. It's the whisper of the devil in your ear."

I shivered. His words summed up how I'd felt when I touched the stone. "Why does it only affect people who are... you know...magic, or whatever?" I'd accepted the truth about my condition, but I still wasn't comfortable saying that sort of thing out loud. Thankfully only Dario, Aunt Lucy, and Mr. Dalca heard it.

"Who knows?" he said. "The important thing is it does, and whenever a bad person has it, bad things happen. Queen Maria knew this. She witnessed her own country ripped apart by war when her weakling husband acquired the stone. She knew her first-born son was even worse than his father, and if the stone fell into his hands, it could be catastrophic. Which is why she gave it to her lover, Prince Barbu. Your husband

Anton's great-great-great-grandpoppy. After Queen Maria got exiled, by her own son no less, Prince Barbu honored his promise to her and he kept the stone safe. Eventually, he married and had four daughters, all of them idiots. Not because of the stone. They were just stupid and made poor choices. One of them married a Trabuski, and so on and so forth. It passed down your line from Trabuski to Trabuski."

"Oh, I get it. That explains the Mama Regina part," said Aunt Lucy with a triumphant smile. "The nickname of Queen Maria. I knew it sounded familiar when Anton...I mean the ghost...I mean Ivan said it."

"Yes, you are clever," said Mr. Dalca, wiggling his bushy eyebrows at her. "Wickedly clever."

I cringed, not comfortable with the blatant sexuality between them. "I understand how Uncle Anton obtained the box, but who is Ivan and how did he find us?"

Mr. Dalca chuffed impatiently. "I am getting to that part. Ivan is Anton's great nephew. His parents got divorced many years ago, and he grew up with his mother and stepfather in Switzerland. When his father died, he went back to Romania to claim his property and his title."

"Title?" I asked.

"Your uncle Anton was a count, dearest," said Aunt Lucy. "Like on the cereal."

I felt a headache coming on. "I know what a count is Aunt Lucy. I didn't realize Uncle Anton had a title."

"Oh, yes, but he gave it to his younger brother. He didn't want to stay in Romania. He was a nomad, my Anton. Never satisfied staying in one place. He kept a few things, including the Dragon Rouge...mostly to keep it from falling into the wrong hands."

"And Ivan is the wrong hands," said Mr. Dalca.

"He's bad?" I asked.

"Not bad." Mr. Dalca shook his head. "Just dangerous. He

doesn't understand the power of the Dragon Rouge, and he doesn't appreciate why it needs to be kept safe. He has a bit of magic, all Trabuskis do, but not enough to control the stone." He lifted a finger. "Oh. And he's an art thief. Interpol has kept an eye on him for many years, but he is slippery. Like an eel. No one can prove anything, but things go missing when Ivan Trabuski is around. Very valuable things."

I slapped myself on the forehead. "His last name is Trabuski? Like Aunt Lucy?"

"Of course," said Mr. Dalca.

"He told me it was Rochat."

Mr. Dalca shook his head. "That's his stepfather's name. Ivan is a Trabuski."

No wonder nothing popped up about him online. "And he's an art thief? Seriously? Well, I guess that explains how he got in and out of my shop. If he's a thief, I'm sure he's good at breaking and entering."

"Didn't your woo-woo bad guy radar go off at all?" Mr. Dalca made a tsking sound. "So easily distracted by a handsome face. What kind of witch are you?"

My head ached from all this talk of magic and other nonsense. Especially worrying, since I'd actually started to believe it. "What are we going to do?" I asked.

"Nothing," said Mr. Dalca.

I frowned. "What do you mean? We need to get the box away from Ivan."

"No, we don't," he said, giving me a sly grin. "Because Ivan doesn't have it."

I slammed my glass onto the coffee table. "Oops. Sorry. I didn't mean to do that so violently, but you're not making sense, Mr. Dalca."

"Yes, I am. I may not be magic, but I know some tricks. One of them is sleight of hand." He stood up and wiggled his fingers. "Trick number one: Clever Lucinda leaves the Dragon

Rouge out front where all the party people can see it. Trick number two: I act angry. I hold it up. Ivan sees it. He watches me put it in my pocket. But he does not see what he thinks he sees. Best trick of all: I put a box in my pocket, but it is not the Dragon Rouge. It is another box. It looks like the Dragon Rouge, but it is not the same. When the lights went out, Ivan took the wrong box."

"So where is the Dragon Rouge?" I asked, confused.

"In my special secret hiding place," he said, patting his crotch.

"I know that place," said Aunt Lucy, giving him a saucy wink.

I cringed again. "Please don't tell me you put it in your pants."

He unbuckled his belt. "I'll show it to you."

I stood up and turned around to face the wall. "Oh, no. Don't. I beg you."

"I'll show you the box, not my winkie. Ah, here she is. The Dragon Rouge. Safe and sound."

"You can turn around now, Gracie," said Dario. "His winkie is back in custody."

"Thank goodness."

Mr. Dalca tried to give me the box. "Do you want to see it?"

I lifted up my hands. "No thank you. You can hold onto it from now on."

He slipped it into his jacket pocket. "Much better. But there is one thing I do not understand. Maybe Miss Smarty Pants can tell me. After Ivan took the box, he ran up the stairs to this apartment. It's on the second floor, right? Well, third if you include the loft in the shop. How did he escape?"

I frowned. "I have no idea."

We looked around the apartment until we found an unlocked window in Aunt Lucy's bedroom. "Now I get it.

From here, he jumped onto the roof," said Mr. Dalca. "Then he hopped over to my shop, like a Romanian kangaroo."

Dario's lips twitched. "As much as I enjoy the visual, Mr. Dalca, it doesn't explain how Ivan got into your shop."

Mr. Dalca pointed to a tiny window at the highest point of his attic. "It would be easy to open a window that old. I think he went from here to there. Hop, hop, hop. In through the window, down the steps, out the door, and on his way. I told you he is slippery." He let out a laugh. "I'm sure he knows by now he has the wrong box. Oh. I wish I could see his face. It would be so funny."

"Which box did you give him?" asked Aunt Lucy.

Mr. Dalca could barely talk, he laughed so hard. "Count Dracula. I took one of the silly boxes you sell downstairs, the ones with the vampire teeth inside. It seemed appropriate. Another Romanian. Another count."

It was kind of funny, but one thing still bothered me. "But how did you end up owning the shop right next door? How did you know Ivan would come and look for the dragon box?"

He shook his head, giving me a crooked smile. "I am not so clever, but I am lucky. Also, Anton was my friend a long, long time ago in Romania. Before I went to jail. But that is another story."

"You were in jail?" asked Dario.

He dismissed Dario's question with a wave of his hand. "Romanian stuff. Not important. What is important is this: Before I went to jail, I worked for the ministry, and the Dragon Rouge was one of my first artifacts. I knew Anton had it in his possession, and while he remained alive, it stayed safe. I took care of the other things on my list, lots of nasty business. I didn't hear about Anton's death until long after it happened." He turned to Aunt Lucy. "I'm sorry, Lucinda. I would have come to pay my respects. I wanted to tell you sooner how well I knew him and how much I loved him, but

I couldn't, so I will tell you now. Anton was a good man. A good friend." Mr. Dalca got choked up. He pulled out a tissue to wipe his eyes.

Aunt Lucy patted his hand. "It's okay. You couldn't come. You were in a Romanian prison. I understand. It's the thought that counts."

"Thank you," he said. "But I got out of prison and heard about Anton's death. I sold my property in Romania a few years ago and bought the bookstore so I could be close to you."

Aunt Lucy clasped her hands together. "My hero."

He gave her a dry look. "Not even close. I've always wanted to own a bookstore. Also, I obtained a green card. My son is American. He lives in Milwaukee. But I owed a great debt to Anton. He saved me during the war from a sniper's bullet."

"A sniper's bullet?" asked Dario, his reporter's curiosity once again piqued. "What war? What happened?"

"No, no, no. Different story," Mr. Dalca grumbled. "For another time. I can't tell you all my stories at once. I'm eighty years old. It would take forever." He shook his head in annoyance. "Young people. So impatient."

"Okay," I said, trying to piece the story together. "You bought the shop to protect Aunt Lucy."

"No. To protect the box. Aunt Lucy is a strong woman. She protects herself."

"Fine. To protect the box. How did you know Ivan was coming?"

"I didn't," he said. "I got lucky. Ivan is a powerful, wealthy man, and he is also determined. When he wants something, he won't let anything, or anyone, get in his way. He thinks he has a right to the Dragon Rouge, he considers it his inheritance, but he has no right. That's like saying the descendants of whoever created the nuclear bomb have the right to keep one for themselves in their kitchen. No, they do not. Property rights do not apply to weapons of mass destruction."

"And you consider it to be a weapon?" I asked.

He tilted his head to one side. "It could be, which is why I plan to give it to someone I trust. Someone powerful enough to both keep the dragon box safe and keep Ivan away. "

"Who?" asked Dario.

"The white magic witch, Eliza Dragonsong."

Aunt Lucy agreed. "Yes. She's the one. Can you go fetch her, Gracie? And her sister, Amanda, too. They should both be aware of what's going on."

Dario and I went downstairs and found Eliza chatting with a group of Wiccans. A tiny young woman wearing glasses stood next to her, smiling shyly. She had masses of curly brown hair pulled into an updo, big blue eyes, and freckles dusting her nose. Eliza introduced her as her younger sister Amanda.

"Would the two of you mind coming up to Aunt Lucy's apartment for a moment? Mr. Dalca wants to speak with you. Privately," I said.

A few minutes later, I poured bourbon for Eliza and Amanda. With her perfectly styled blonde hair and elegant hot pink evening dress, Eliza didn't look like the same person in a black hooded cape who'd led the Samhain rituals in the garden. She became every inch Eliza Dragonsong, high-powered attorney, and it grew even more evident when Mr. Dalca spoke.

"We need to enlist your help," he said, and told her the whole story about the Dragon Rouge and Ivan. She listened carefully. Amanda, her assistant, pulled a small pad out of her purse and discretely took notes.

"When you say he has 'some magic,' what do you mean exactly?" asked Eliza.

"He fancies himself a witch, like you," said Mr. Dalca.

"Wouldn't he be a warlock?" I asked.

Eliza shook her head. "Both males and females are witches. It's gender neutral. There is no such thing as a warlock." She turned back to Mr. Dalca. "Why aren't you taking it back to Romania?"

"Let me say I am not certain how safe it is in Romania at the moment. I kept Lucinda's address secret and told no one I was coming here. They think I'm with my son in Wisconsin, eating cheese and having a wonderful time. But someone must have peeked into my files and given Ivan the information he needed to find us."

"Or maybe he found her online?" I asked.

He dismissed my question with a disgusted wave of his hand. "There are too many Trabuskis, and he had no idea about where Anton lived or whom he married. Anton purposely kept it a secret from all of them."

"It's sad he couldn't trust his own family," said Aunt Lucy.

Mr. Dalca snorted. "We're Romanians. We trust no one. The idea of me trusting all of you means I'm getting soft in my old age." He gave Eliza a piercing look. "And I especially trust you. You are both magical and good, a rare combination. I've only seen a few people like that. Grace is one, but she's new at this, and too silly to appreciate the significance of her own power at this point."

"Hey—" I began, but he ignored me.

"What do you think, Ms. Dragonsong? Can you keep the box safe? At least for a little while?"

She pondered it, looking like an old photo I'd once seen of Marilyn Monroe, with the same coloring, creamy skin, and satin gloves extending to her elbows. She lacked the breathy voice and fragility, however. Other lawyers called Eliza "The Dragon Lady" for a reason. She exhibited a spine of steel. And it seemed appropriate someone with her name should be the one to guard the dragon box.

"Yes. I'll do it. I'll keep it safe until you figure out what's going on back in Romania." She extended a satin-gloved hand, and he gave it to her with a sigh of relief.

"Thank you, Ms. Dragonsong. But be careful. If Ivan finds out you have it, he'll do anything to get it back. He's ruthless, and he's charming. A dangerous mix."

Eliza's lips curved into the tiniest hint of a smile. "I'm a divorce attorney. I deal with men like him on a daily basis. I can handle Ivan. Don't worry."

She stood, putting the Dragon Rouge into the purse dangling from her wrist. It looked barely large enough to accommodate it, but it fit. Amanda stood, too, adjusting her glasses and straightening her skirt. She wore a flowing blue dress. It shimmered in the light of the fire and brought out the color in her eyes, but she seemed uncomfortable with getting dressed up and wearing heels. She proved my theory correct when she stumbled and tripped on the hem of her gown.

"Sorry," she said, cheeks reddening as Dario reached out a hand to steady her. He stared at her face.

"Do I know you?" he asked.

She gave him a dimpled smile. "We met a long time ago. I went to St. Alphonse. I was in the same grade as your cousin Tommy."

Dario's face lit up. "I remember you now. Didn't you move away for a while?"

"Yes," she said, a shadow crossing over her clear blue eyes. "But I'm back now."

"Great," he said. "Tommy's downstairs. You should find him."

Her blush deepened with her cheeks looking almost painfully hot at this point. "He won't remember me."

"How could anyone forget the girl whose rendition of 'Ave Maria' made Sister Bernice and all the other nuns weep and cancel classwork for the rest of the day?" asked Dario. "You're legendary. Do you still sing?"

She shook her head so vehemently she nearly dislodged her glasses. "Oh, no. Not at all. Not anymore. I work for Eliza now."

"Speaking of which, we'd better get back downstairs, Amanda. The Wiccans are waiting," said Eliza. She looked at Mr. Dalca and patted her purse. "I'll keep it safe."

"And keep yourself safe as well," said Mr. Dalca. "In spite of his good looks and engaging personality, you must take Ivan seriously. I fear we have not seen the last of him. Not yet. Be careful, Ms. Dragonsong. It's not the Dragon Rouge you're protecting from Ivan, you're protecting him from it as well."

"What do you mean?" she asked.

"He thinks of it as his birthright, but it's an evil thing. It could cost him his soul."

As soon as he spoke, a gust of wind rattled the panes of the windows on either side of the fireplace.

Something wicked this way comes.

Aunt Lucy said those words before, but now I felt them more than ever. Just as I'd known something bad was going to happen tonight, I also knew we weren't done yet.

CHAPTER 41

YOU ARE THE MOST PERFECT LITTLE ARRANGEMENT OF ATOMS.

Eliza and Amanda went back to the party. "Maybe we should go, too," I said. "Are you ready, Aunt Lucy?"

Aunt Lucy smoothed her skirt and gave her cleavage a discreet adjustment. "We'll stay up here," she said, not meeting my eyes. "Connie looks tired."

Mr. Dalca frowned at her. "I am not tired. What are you talking about?" She gave him a pointed look, and his eyebrows went up to his nearly non-existent hairline. "Oh. Maybe I am tired. Maybe I need to rest. You two go. We'll stay here."

As Dario and I walked down the stairs, I made a noise of pure disgust. "Yuck," I said softly. "Yuckity, yuck, yuck."

"Are you okay?" he asked with a laugh. "You look like you bit a lemon."

"They're going to have sex, aren't they?" I asked, keeping my voice a whisper.

"Oh, most definitely," said Dario.

"Ugh. I'll never be able to sleep in that bed again. I'll have to crash on the couch downstairs."

He stopped and turned around, facing me. Because I stood a step higher than him, it made me nearly equal to him in height. He put his hands on my hips and stared at my face, his eyes lingering on my lips.

"Well, I may have a solution to your problem." He kissed the tip of my nose, each of my cheeks, and, finally, my lips. "You could sleep in *my* bed."

"Sounds like a good plan," I said, leaning close to whisper in his ear. When I nibbled on his earlobe and gave it a tug, he shuddered against me and closed his eyes.

"Can we skip the rest of the party and go home now? Please?"

I shook my head. "Tempting, but I can't."

He rested his forehead against mine. "You're right. You're always right. Let's go. Let's do this." He took my hand and led me down the steps.

"I'm not always right," I said, when we reached the loft area of the shop. "I certainly got you wrong."

"What do you mean?" He put an arm over my shoulder, and I wrapped mine around his waist as we surveyed the people partying below. They seemed to be having fun, but not out of control or wasted. A good sign.

I looked up at him, amazed we were together. Amazed he was mine. "I assumed you were a typical jock, good looking and not exactly..."

"Cerebral?" he asked.

"Oh, no," I said, shocked by his question. "I knew you were brilliant. But big, athletic, handsome men are usually the ones most intimidated by someone like me, so I avoided them."

His hand still rested on my shoulder, and he began stroking the smooth column of my neck with his thumb. "What kind of men did you date? Men like Jonathan?"

"Yep, but you have to understand. In high school, I was kind of a geek."

"No way," he said, teasing me with an expression of mock surprise.

I elbowed him. "Yes, and some insecure guys did everything possible to bother me. To make matters worse, I was also the tallest girl in my class, and even more awkward than I am now."

He leaned close and gave me a kiss that made my toes curl. "Maybe I was as much of a geek in high school as you."

I rolled my eyes. "The big hockey star? No way. I'm sure you were popular."

He tilted his head back and forth as he considered it. "You're right, but only because I kept my geek flag hidden."

"A closet nerd. I get it. Do you fly it now?"

He grinned. "I wave it for all the world to see."

Mrs. Periwinkle called up to us. "Grace, Dario. There you are. Anthony wants to speak with you." Eliza and Amanda stood next to her.

Anthony waited for us at the bottom of the steps, his face tense. "No sign of Aggie," he said. "She didn't come. No sign of Sally either."

"Where could she be?" I asked.

"We have no idea," said Anthony, his jaw tight. "But we'll find her. I promise."

Anthony walked away, his shoulders tense. He looked like he carried the weight of the world on them.

"Sally and Anthony are old friends," said Dario. "She helped him when he was a skinny kid who sat the bench every single football game. Thanks to her, he ended up being the star quarterback, and played in college. He owes her a lot, and he's protective of her. We all are."

"I understand," I said. "I feel the same way."

"They'll find her soon," said Eliza. "I'm sure of it."

"Amanda?" Tommy, still dressed as a mummy, waved to Amanda from across the room. She waved back hesitantly, her blue eyes appearing even bigger in her face when Tommy walked over to her. "What are you doing here?" he asked, grinning from ear to ear.

"I work for my sister now," she said, tugging nervously on her skirt. "I hear you're a fireman."

"I am," he said, puffing out his chest. "You know, saving people from a fiery death and all that stuff. I thought you went to California. Didn't you have a big singing contract?"

She ducked her head. "That didn't work out. I have to go help out in the back now. Nice seeing you, Tommy."

She turned, about to dart away, when he stopped her. "Wait. Do you want to go out to dinner sometime?"

She froze. "Why?"

"Why what?"

"Why would you want to go out with me?"

Now Tommy blushed. "We could catch up on old times. Chat. You know. And eat food."

Dario rolled his eyes. "Oh, this is so painful," he said under his breath.

I agreed. Amanda's blush became a full body experience at this point. Each bit of exposed skin from her head to her toes pulsated red.

"Um, I'm really busy right now. Learning the ropes at my new job and getting used to being back home. But thank you, Tommy. See you later."

She dashed off into the crowd, and Tommy stared after her, his green eyes perplexed. "Well, that's a first. I think she turned me down," he said, pushing back pieces of the white cloth he'd wound around his head and exposing more of his dark curls. "What the heck just happened?"

"She definitely turned you down," said Dario. They both

watched Amanda scurry away. "The question is what are you going to do about it?"

Tommy straightened his costume. "Tonight? Nothing. But I'm not giving up. I'll launch another attempt to woo Miss Amanda Dragonsong at a date to be determined. For now, I'll drink beer."

"Sounds like a plan," said Dario.

Dario and I didn't drink. We stayed stone cold sober. When the last guest finally left, Dario grabbed my cloak, bundled me up in it, and waited as I locked up the shop.

We drove back to his house in silence. He held my hand in his, his thumb stroking me absentmindedly. He seemed deep in thought. When we reached his place, he ushered me inside, and ran a nervous hand through his hair.

"Look, I don't want to pressure you. If you'd rather stay in the guestroom, I understand. There's no rush. I'll give you all the time you need."

Time. The one thing I didn't have. One week until my review board hearing. Seven days, 168 hours, 10,080 minutes. I'd do anything for more time with Dario and regretted wasting so much of what we'd had.

"What are you thinking about?" he asked, his brown eyes caressing my face.

"Theoretical physics," I said.

"Of course, you are," he said, biting his lip and giving me a sexy grin.

"Have you ever heard of the B-theory?" I asked as I removed my cloak. My emerald colored satin dress glowed in the soft light from the lamp in his foyer.

He shook his head. "No, I haven't."

"B-theorists argue the flow of time is nothing but an illusion. They think the past, present, and future are equally real, and that time is, well, timeless."

"I understand the theory, but not how it relates to our current situation."

I blew out a breath. "I only have seven days left here in the South Side, and I want to make every minute count. I don't believe in the B-theory. It's a load of crap. I believe in now, and I believe in you."

"Are you saying you *don't* want to sleep in the guest room?"

"Bingo."

He responded with a kiss and kept kissing me as he led me up the stairs and into his bedroom. Undressing me slowly, he explored every inch of skin with the gentle touch of his hands and the warmth of his lips. When I stood naked in front of him, he gazed at me, his eyes filled with passion and desire. "If you've put a spell on me, I honestly don't mind."

"No spells," I said as I pulled off his tie and unbuttoned his shirt, kissing the warm curve of his neck, then his muscular chest and perfectly sculpted abdomen. "And definitely no love potions."

I reached for his zipper, feeling both naughty and brave, and he stared at me transfixed. When I lowered his pants and knelt in front of him, taking him into my mouth, he groaned.

"Grace," he said, gasping out the word. "That is definitely magical."

I rose to my feet, trying not to giggle. "I'm magical now?"

"You were always magical, my sweet, I just didn't know you were a—"

I raised a hand to stop him. "If you say, 'wicked witch,' I'll definitely put a hex on you."

"Never," he said. "Because you aren't a wicked witch. You're a wondrous witch. A winsome witch. A well-endowed witch."

"Alliterations are annoying." I ran a finger slowly down his arm. "But your vocabulary gets me hot."

"Pneumonoultramicroscopicsilicovolcanoconiosis,"   he said, wiggling his eyebrows at me suggestively.

"What is that?" I asked in surprise.

"The longest word in the English language. It's a lung disease."

I put a hand over my chest. "Be still my heart," I said. Then, feeling both naughty and brave again, I pushed him onto his bed, and we didn't talk about B-theory, or anything else, for a very long time.

CHAPTER 42

THE UNIVERSE IS MADE UP OF PROTONS, NEUTRONS, ELECTRONS, AND MORONS.

The next morning, we woke to the sound of Dario's cell phone ringing. Cozy and warm in his arms, I groaned, not wanting to get up. He answered, and I listened to the soft murmurs of his conversation.

"I'll be there in a few minutes," he said, and turned off his phone.

"What happened?" I asked.

"I have to cover a story about vandalism at the Prince of Peace church. Apparently, someone snuck in and stole some holy water. The reporter who normally handles this is still hung over after your aunt's party. He asked if I could go, since I know the area and the priest."

"Halloween pranks, probably," I said. He kissed my shoulder and I snuggled closer to him. "I don't want to get up."

"Stay here," he murmured, putting his scratchy cheek against my bare breast. I stroked his face. "I'll be back soon."

"I have to get back to the shop. There's a lot of cleaning up to do, and I don't want to leave it all for Aunt Lucy and Mrs. Periwinkle."

"I've been meaning to ask you. What's the deal with Mrs. Periwinkle? According to Nunny, she comes and goes, but always seems to show up when your aunt Lucy needs her. Also, you might think I'm nuts, but I swear I saw her hovering a few inches in the air one time." He winced. "That *did* sound nuts, erase the last part."

I sat up in bed. "No. I saw it, too. I'm so glad you said something."

"The mysterious Matilda," he said with a wink, and I groaned.

"No more alliterations. Please. You're making my head hurt."

He held up his hands. "Fine. I'll stop." He gave me a kiss. I'm not sure what happened, but within seconds I climbed on top of him, my hands in his hair and my body once again eager for his. His body seemed awfully eager for mine, too. Bonus.

"Oh, Grace." He positioned my body over him, and lowered me slowly, sweetly onto him. He prolonged the sensation, filling me completely, inch by delectable inch.

"You said you needed to go to work." My words came out in short, breathless pants.

"The holy water can wait," he said.

Even though we'd made love only a few hours before, I wanted to have him over and over again. Needed him, actually. His hands found my bottom, and his lips were on my breasts as I rose up and down, riding him. I'd grown addicted to this man, and each time we came together our bond grew.

"What are you thinking about?" he asked afterward, as our breathing returned to normal.

"Bonds," I said, my words unsteady.

"As in bondage?" He sounded extremely hopeful.

I laughed. "No, as in the energetic interaction occurring between two atoms." I smacked myself on the head. "Ignore me. Please. I'm such a total geek sometimes I even surprise myself."

He lifted my chin and kissed me firmly on the lips. "I get it, Grace. I get *you*. Don't ever act shy about being so freaking smart. I love the way your brain works. I love everything about you. I love you...on an atomic level. Hell, on a subatomic level."

And with that, he completely took my breath away, but somehow I managed to respond. "Good. Because my atoms happen to like your atoms very much."

He bit his lip. "Are your atoms dirty right now? Because mine kind of need a shower."

We showered together, and I discovered nothing quite matched the feeling of Dario's warm, wet, soapy body next to mine. He washed my body thoroughly, being adorably careful not to get soap in my eyes when he shampooed my hair. Afterward, he dried me with a fluffy white towel.

I put my dress back on, knowing the emerald green evening gown seemed excessive for a bright Sunday morning. Luckily, I had my long velvet cloak and could cover myself. The cloak looked strange, too, like a modern-day Hester Prynne, but better than just a ball gown.

Walk of shame, here I come.

I laughed at the idea because I felt no shame at all. I was happy I'd slept with Dario and didn't care who knew it.

He dropped me off in front of the shop, kissing me thoroughly and promising to stop by to help clean up the party remnants as soon as he finished interviewing people at the church. I waved as he drove away. When I saw my reflection in the glass, I noticed my cheeks were flushed, my lips pink from his kisses, and my hair still damp. I looked like a woman who'd spent the night in her lover's arms, which was completely accurate.

As I pulled out my keys, I sensed someone approaching from behind and froze. "Aggie?"

Her pale face seemed even thinner, her clothing wrinkled, and she had dark circles under her eyes. She carried a large duffle bag on her shoulder.

"Grace, I need to speak with you. It's urgent."

I backed away, fumbling for my cell phone. My danged cloak got in the way, and I nearly spilled the contents of my purse onto the sidewalk. "I know what you did with the smoothies. You made me sick. I ended up in the hospital, and you could have killed Aunt Lucy."

She shook her head. "I didn't do it. I swear. I mean, that was my medication, and I made the smoothies, but..."

I finally located my phone and held it up. "That's it. I'm calling 911."

She clasped her hands in front of her. "Please don't," she said softly. "If you do, they'll hurt my sister."

I lowered my phone. I'd never heard Aggie call Sally her sister before. In fact, it seemed like she'd purposely avoided using that word. Something very significant must have changed.

"What are you talking about?"

"Sally, Ralphie, and Bubu are locked up in one of the Stash and Store units on twenty-sixth."

"Did you put them in there?" I tried to imagine tiny Aggie overpowering either Sally or Ralphie and couldn't do it. Bubu maybe, but not the other two.

"Of course not," she said, mortified. She pushed a strand of hair off her face. "They took my medicine and replaced it with a placebo. It made everything so confusing."

"Who took your medicine?"

"The same people who locked up Sally and Ralphie." Aggie spoke slowly, like she was annoyed at me for not keeping up. "I've been taking sugar pills for weeks without my knowledge. I went to Grovetown to see my doctor because I thought I was having some kind of breakdown. He gave me a new prescription, and I'm better already. It's been so hard, not knowing the truth. But then I understood. Tautology."

I frowned. "Tautology? Propositional logic?"

"Yes. The truth of the overall formula can be deduced by looking at the truth or falsity of each variable. It applies to you. You haven't seen what's truly going on. You've used false variables in your equation, which is why you came up with the wrong solution."

I gave her a dirty look. "Dang you for pulling the math card on me. You knew I'd be unable to argue with it."

"Because it makes sense." She ticked off her fingers. "You think I hurt my sister. False. You think I put drugs in your aunt's smoothie. False. You think I'm crazy." She tilted her head from side to side as she considered it. "That's an ill-defined statement. True and false at the same time."

I blew out a breath. "Even if I believed you, why come to me? Why not go to the police?"

She looked right into my eyes and seemed as lucid and as sane as anyone I'd ever met. "Do you think they'd believe me?"

I weighed my options. I might be making a huge mistake here, but Aggie hooked me with the tautology argument. Some of the variables did seem false in my equation.

"I don't like this."

"Because I made you question your own theories. You hate being wrong." She grabbed my hand, her cold fingers gripping me tight. "We have to go. We're running out of time."

I pulled my hand out of hers. "I'll come with you under three conditions," I said. "One: We call the police as soon as we locate your family. Two: I call Dario right now. Three: I'd like to change my clothes."

"I agree with conditions one and two, but three will take too long." She glanced at her watch, as she looked nervously up and down the street.

"Fine," I said. "I'll wear the ball gown. Why not? This is the South Side. No one will even give me a second glance."

I called Dario, but it went straight to voice mail. I left him a message, telling him exactly where we were going and why, and held onto my phone, waiting for him to call back. He didn't, and the more I walked, the more I worried about my current course of action.

Aggie had issues. Big issues. Even if my intuition told me she spoke the truth, should I trust it? Was it the real truth, or only the truth as she saw it?

My anxiety increased when we changed direction and headed to the smaller and less populated side streets. I tried to call Dario again, and left him another message, hanging up my phone in frustration. Where was he, and why didn't he answer?

"Here we are," said Aggie, stopping in front of the Stash and Store. She opened her duffle bag and took out two wrenches.

"What are you doing?" I asked.

"Opening the lock."

"Shouldn't you ask someone to let you in?"

She shook her head. "It's Sunday. They're closed. This is the only way."

She put a wrench on either side of the padlock and popped it open by pressing the wrenches together like scissors. Not easy with her tiny, delicate hands, but Aggie's skills included more than a knack for logic problems and a brain for discrete mathematics.

"How do you know how to do something like this?"

"I learned online."

"You're scaring me."

She laughed, putting the wrenches back into her duffle bag and opening the gate to the storage units. "I scare myself sometimes."

She walked in, and I looked around, unsure what I should do. We were breaking and entering and doing it in broad daylight while I wore an evening dress. If our goal was to attract as much attention as possible, this was the way to do it.

"I'm not sure about this."

Aggie gave me a stern look, and I saw a glimmer of disappointment in her eyes. "I need you. I wouldn't have asked for your help if I didn't."

"But you never said why."

She gave me another stern look. "Why tell you when I can show you? It's so much simpler."

"Fine," I said, lifting my hands in surrender as I followed her down the row of storage units with bright blue doors. "If we get arrested, I'm requesting to be your cell mate so I can torture you forever with unsolvable math problems."

Aggie smiled at me but seemed preoccupied. She studied each door before stopping in front of one that looked exactly like all the others. She paused, resting her ear against it. "This is it," she said softly. "We found them."

I stared at her in disbelief. "You think they're locked in here?"

"I'm sure of it." She opened her duffle bag again, this time taking out a drill and something else that looked like a clamp. "And this is where you come in. This tool is called a disk buster. I need you to hold it as I drill through the lock, or I won't be able to get the pins out."

"How do you..." I paused and answered my own question. "You learned this online as well, didn't you?"

She grinned at me, giving me a pair of safety goggles and putting on a pair herself. "Research is a beautiful thing."

"And a little knowledge can be dangerous."

The more time I spent with Aggie, the more I believed her version of the story. Now, as she clamped on the disk buster and carefully aligned the drill, I was sure of it. Either Aggie could play normal really well, or she boasted a much better hold on her sanity than any of us suspected.

After drilling through the lock, she pulled a large mallet out of her bag. "Geesh, Aggie. What else do you have in there?"

"This is it," she said, resting the mallet on her shoulder. "The final step. I couldn't get the drill and disk buster to work on my own, no matter how hard I tried. The angle was wrong. Thanks to you, I could finally do it. Now we have to get the pins out of the lock. Easy peasy."

"With a hammer?" I asked. "Won't it make a lot of noise?"

"Yes, so we have to be quick about it. Get ready. I need five pins. Can you hold your hand under the lock and count as the pins drop out?"

"Fine," I grumbled.

The pins were tiny, but it took a couple swings of the mallet to dislodge them. The noise deafened me, and the slam of the mallet on the lock accompanied by the clatter of the metal door echoed throughout the compound.

I wanted to cover my ears, but I counted the pins as Aggie requested. When the fifth one dropped out, I exhaled in relief. "Last one. We're good."

The soft wail of a police siren sounded in the distance. "Hurry," said Aggie. "Let's get them out."

She opened the door, and we both gasped at what we saw. Someone had tied Sally and Ralphie up and left them on two bare mattresses on the concrete floor of the unit. Bubu, locked in a kennel, barked his head off. Duct tape covered

Sally and Ralphie's mouths, silencing them. I hurried over to Sally, pulling the tape carefully off her face as Aggie removed Ralphie's. Sally looked so different without a speck of makeup on her skin and no perfectly coiffed wig on her head. She seemed bare, and exposed, and she wore men's clothing, which, on Sally, was bizarre.

"Grace," she said. "You shouldn't have come. It's too dangerous."

I saw real fear in her eyes. "We're here to rescue you."

"And who is going to rescue you?" asked a voice behind me.

I turned as the door to the storage slammed shut behind us. The only light came from a wonky looking lamp sitting on the floor next to Sally's bed.

"Tiffany?" I asked.

She wore pink, of course, and Missy and Sissy flanked her on either side. They didn't have on their Party Ark uniforms. Instead, they wore dresses and flats. Sissy had a ribbon in her hair.

"It's lucky we left church early," said Missy, looking at Aggie, who cowered in the shadows. "Someone's been a bad, bad girl."

"And bad girls need to be punished," said Sissy.

"They do indeed." Tiffany reached into her pink cross body purse and pulled out a gun. The gun was pink, too, of course, and Tiffany coordinating her weaponry with her clothing was terrifying indeed.

Sissy clapped her hands. "Let's play 'Naughty or Nice.' We'll each tell the worst thing we've ever done, and the best. The winner gets to walk out of here unharmed, and the loser...well...let's just say the loser doesn't deserve to leave. It's a fun game. You'll love it. We play it at Camp Ark Angel. Now, who should go first?"

"Grace," said Missy, with a nasty gleam in her eyes. "She's

wearing the same dress she wore to the party yesterday. I saw her through the window of the shop. Grace didn't go home last night, did she?"

"Naughty, naughty," they said in unison, chortling with glee. Tiffany's mouth narrowed into a hard line. I did not like where this was going.

"Yes," said Sissy. "Let's begin with Grace. You have two minutes to tell all or face the consequences." She glanced at the sparkly purple watch on her wrist. "And the time starts *now.*"

CHAPTER 43

ARE YOU COMPOSED OF BARIUM, SILICON, CARBON, BISMUTH, TECHNETIUM, AND HYDROGEN? BECAUSE YOU ARE A BASIC BITCH.

I stared at them in surprise, trying to mentally process all the pink combined with the weapon and the pure evil in their eyes. They looked like homicidal baby dolls.

"Wait," I said, knowing I had to stall them as long as possible. "I'm confused. What is the point of this game exactly?"

"It's girl time," said Sissy. "We're bonding. Hurry up."

This was the reason I hated board games as a child. "But I don't get it," I said. "I need examples."

Sissy grew more exasperated. "It's not rocket science. Just confess. Get it off your chest."

Missy nodded. "Confessing the bad will make you glad."

"I have an idea," said Tiffany. "Ask Grace to tell us about her love potions."

"Why?" asked Sissy.

"Because I bought one and it didn't work."

Missy frowned. "That's witchcraft, Tiff. We're against witchcraft. Goodness and light make your life bright. It's in our mission manual."

"You have a manual?" I asked. "What are you talking about?"

"We're Ark Angels." Missy rolled her eyes in annoyance. "We follow the manual and do good deeds. Things like cleaning up the neighborhood. Helping people. Getting rid of all the garbage." She waved a hand to indicate Sally, Ralphie, and possibly even Bubu.

"A clean place has no space for perverts," said Sissy. Her voice exhibited a singsong quality to it, like some kind of messed up nursery rhyme. "It's in the manual."

Aggie rose to her feet. "My sister is not a pervert," she said, her voice echoing off the walls of the metal structure. "She's a good person. And so is Ralphie. You're monsters."

"And you're pathetic," Missy snorted. "But convenient. Everyone trusted you, and your clozapine was the perfect way to get rid of that old witch."

"My clozapine? How did you get it? I keep it in my room."

"We took your keys and made copies," said Missy, staring at her nails in boredom. "That's also how we got the freaky dog and those two abominations over there."

"It's amazing what flunitrazepam can do," said Sissy. "Sally and Ralphie were ever so cooperative."

"The date rape drug?" I asked. "Is there anyone in the South Side the two of you haven't drugged? You do realize that's a felony, right?

"Unimportant," said Sissy, her expression smug. "We answer to a higher power."

"But how would you even get your hands on something like flunitrazepam?" I asked.

"Sissy's dad is a pharmacist," said Missy. "She knows all about drugs. And it's lucky for us your doctor prescribed those meds for you, Aggie. They were the perfect thing to drug the old witch. A little clozapine added to the protein powder we gave you and people thought she'd gotten dotty. You handed us the ideal tool for our mission. And you believed in our mission, too. Don't forget that part, Aggie."

"You took advantage of me, acting like you were my friends and convincing me you needed my help. I wasn't in my right mind," she said, chewing on her lip.

Missy laughed. "And what excuse can you give for how you treated your 'sister' before?"

Aggie's gaze went to Sally, who still lay on the mattress, and her face softened. "I was stupid and judgmental and cruel. As a child, I thought you could do no wrong, Sally. You were my hero, the big strapping football player and the shining star of our family. When you changed, I couldn't adjust. My problem, not yours, and I'm so sorry for hurting you. But you showed me how to be better. When I needed you most, you were there for me. You taught me what acceptance, and forgiveness, is all about."

"Wah, wah, wah. I love my shemale tranny brother. Good for you. But you have to admit he looks so much better now. Dressed as a man like nature intended. And the dog is dressed like a boy dog at last." Sissy pointed at Bubu, who glared at her from the kennel. "Oh, and FYI, Aggie. We're taking all the ARK points you earned and sharing them between us. You don't deserve them anymore." Sissy lifted her phone and took a selfie. "Winning."

"Such a disappointment." Missy shook her head sadly. "It's time to get this over with, but I'm not sure about sharing those ARK points. I'm the one who copied the keys."

"But I stole the medicine," said Sissy, outraged.

Bubu barked again, and they yelled to be heard over the noise. As they argued back and forth, Aggie slowly unzipped her duffle bag. She pulled out the mallet and held it behind her back. If Aggie planned to take on the Party Ark twins and the evil Pink Princess, she couldn't do it on her own. I needed to help her.

I scrutinized the room, hoping to find a weapon, and I noticed Tiffany trying to catch my eye. As the Party Ark twins argued, she tilted her head and motioned for me to untie Ralphie and Sally. I took a step toward them, not realizing the room had grown silent. Bubu stopped barking, and the Party Ark twins stared at Tiffany with identically irritated expressions on their pretty faces.

"What are you doing?" asked Missy, stamping her foot. "Are you trying to *help* them?"

"Of course not," said Tiffany. "Why ask such a thing?"

"Because you just instructed the big red-headed witch to untie them. Why would you do that?" Sissy inched closer to Tiffany. "Unless you weren't truly an Ark Angel. Unless you pretended to be one of us."

"Stop right there," said Tiffany, pointing her bubble gum pink gun at Sissy. Her hands shook, but her voice sounded steady. "I already called the police. They're on their way."

"And how did you call them exactly?" asked Missy, holding up a pink cellphone. "We snatched this from your purse hours ago, while we were still in church."

"You stole from me in church?" asked Tiffany.

"Again with the same question. In church, out of church, it doesn't matter. We doubted your sincerity, especially when we found out you worked for the newspaper," said Sissy. "By the way, you can stop pointing your pink plastic gun at us. I grew up shooting guns, and I knew the moment I saw it that it wasn't real."

Missy pulled a small black handgun out of the pretty floral quilted purse hanging off her shoulder. "But this one is."

"*Now*, Grace," shouted Aggie as she swung her mallet, hitting Missy on the arm and dislodging her gun. It fell to the floor and went off, the noise amplified by the metal walls of the storage unit. As Sissy went for the gun, I knew it was up to me.

I threw my black cloak over her head and tackled her from behind, landing on top of her with a thump. Her head hit the concrete floor of the storage unit with a sickening crunch. Tiffany grabbed the real gun off the floor, pointing it at Missy.

"You can get up, Grace," she said. "Sissy is down for the count."

She was right. I'd knocked Sissy out cold. When I removed my cloak and stood up, I saw a tiny trail of blood coming from a large lump on her forehead.

"Grace." I knew as soon as I heard Sally's voice that something was terribly wrong. Tiffany must have heard it, too.

"Call the police," she said. "And an ambulance. Tell them to come quickly."

I thought, at first, she requested the ambulance for Sissy, but she meant it for someone else altogether. Aggie lay sprawled on the cement floor of the storage unit, blood seeping from her chest. I dialed 911 as I freed Sally, and she ran to her sister's side.

"Aggie, no. Please, no," she said as she hovered above her sister. "Help me. I don't know what to do."

"Untie me, Grace," said Ralphie. "I can help."

As soon as I untied his bound hands and feet, he hobbled stiffly over to Aggie. He applied pressure to her wound. My call didn't go through, so I dialed 911 again.

"I'm so sorry," said Aggie, her voice faint. "For all my mistakes, but especially for hurting you, Sally."

"Shhh. You're going to be fine. Help is on the way," Ralphie said as Sally cried softly next to him. He glanced up at me as I waited for my phone to connect, and the look in Ralphie's eye told me Aggie was not fine at all. "Will that ambulance be here soon, Grace?"

"I can't get a signal," I said, my hands shaking. "I'm going to try outside."

I gasped when the door of the unit flew open, blinding us with bright morning sunlight. Dario stood on the threshold, flanked by Anthony and his partner, Officer Miller.

"Call an ambulance," I said, running toward them. "Missy shot Aggie."

Dario saw the blood and swayed on his feet. I worried he might faint, but he managed to pull it together. It seemed to take superhuman effort. "Are you hurt?"

"I'm fine. Call for the ambulance, Dario. And hurry."

The next few minutes were the longest of my life. Officer Miller checked on Sissy, who remained unconscious. As he handcuffed Missy, and got a statement from Tiffany, we knelt in a circle around Aggie. Anthony took over for Ralphie, applying pressure to her wound, but the blood kept flowing out of her in an endless river of red. How could one small body contain so much blood?

Sally held tightly to her sister's hand. "Stay with us, Aggie. Help is almost here. Come on, Aggie-boo. You can do this."

Aggie's pale lips curved into a smile. "You haven't called me Aggie-boo in ages. I missed it."

"I'll call you that every day from now on," said Sally. "I promise. And as soon as you're better, we're going to take that cruise we've talked about. We'll need some sun and fun after this, won't we, dearest?"

"I wish I could," said Aggie, closing her eyes. "But it's too late, Sally. I love you. You're the best sister a girl could ever have."

Aggie let out a long, ragged breath. It seemed to come from somewhere deep inside her, and then she grew silent and terrifyingly still.

Sally wailed, a sound that tore at my soul. Anthony started CPR as the ambulance pulled up outside. He continued it as

they put Aggie on a stretcher and carried her into the ambulance. He climbed in with her, refusing to give up. We all
watched him pressing desperately on her chest, begging her
not to die. The door to the ambulance closed, leaving us
staring after it in stunned silence as it sped away.

CHAPTER 44

SUMMARY OF ORGANIC CHEMISTRY: CARBON IS A WHORE.

Aggie's survival ended up being more of a miracle than anything even the zealot Ark Angels could have imagined. She needed several blood transfusions, however, and faced a long road to recovery.

"A Class IV hemorrhage," explained Dr. Mallinger, his face pale and drawn from exhaustion. "She lost nearly forty percent of her body's blood volume. If Anthony hadn't started CPR when he did, Aggie wouldn't have made it."

After being checked over by Dr. Mallinger, Sally joined her sister. Ralphie needed some treatment for minor cuts and bruises, but he was otherwise okay.

"I have to take our doggie home." He looked at his blood-covered hands. "And I need to get some fresh clothes for Sally. It'll do her good to get back to being herself."

Anthony leaned against a wall in the ER waiting room, his shoulders drooping with fatigue. I still wore my evening gown, splattered with Aggie's blood and torn on one side. Dario sat next to me.

"I'm sorry I didn't answer when you called," he said. "I turned off my phone when I went into the church. Father

Bob was celebrating mass, and I had to wait until it ended before I could speak with him."

"You made it just in time," I said, leaning against him. "And you handled the blood so well. A total rock star."

"I didn't 'swoon' at least, which is what you called it the last time it happened." He kissed the top of my forehead and rose to his feet. "I have to call Nunny and the others. News spreads fast in the South Side, and they'll want to know what's going on. I'll be right back."

As soon as he left, Tiffany walked up to me, her pink heels making a clicking sound on the faded linoleum floor. She sat in the chair Dario just vacated, crossing one long leg over the other.

"Do you ever wear anything but pink?" I asked.

She shook her head. "It's my signature color."

"Kind of weird for a woman who writes obituaries."

"Yeah, I'm hoping to get out of that soon. I'm going to take a stab at investigative reporting, which is why I joined the Party Ark gang in the first place."

"You were working undercover?"

"Yep. The paper didn't know about it, but I saw it as an opportunity to break out of the obituary racket. It all came about thanks to you. And Dario."

"What do you mean?"

"As you already know, I live right across the street from you. It gave me a unique vantage point, and it's how I caught Ivan sneaking in and out of your establishment on numerous occasions."

"I never slept with Ivan—" I said, but she interrupted me.

"So I hear. Whatever. The point is what started as a chance to spy on you, turned into something else entirely." She pulled a pile of photos out of her handbag. "I took these the night someone broke the front window of your shop."

I leafed through the pictures. The first one clearly showed

a woman in a hoodie throwing a rock at our window. Another showed her running into Party Ark just as a man dressed in black rounded the corner.

"Ivan," I said. "He wasn't the one who broke our window."

"One of those Party Ark lunatics did it."

"And you didn't think to call the police?"

She let out a sigh. "I didn't know how dangerous they truly were, and I wanted to get the story. I had no idea they drugged and kidnapped people."

"They must have written those threatening notes," I said shaking my head. "Using text speak. I thought they had dyslexia."

"Nope. They were just extremely addicted to their cell phones, and kind of stupid. They led the local ARK chapter here, but they took it a step further than Party Ark ever intended. Rather than helping their community, they devised a slightly different agenda." She pulled a blue book out of her purse and handed it to me. "This is the manual I was talking about. Read it and feel sickened. I certainly did."

I opened it and leafed through the pages. It contained detailed descriptions of how to befriend neighbors and other members of the community until they reached a certain level of trust. It recommended going to local sporting events, plays, concerts, coffee shops, the mall, or places people were likely hang out in order to build friendships. It provided a forty-seven-point list of things to do with those new friends, ideas such as inviting them to Party Ark gatherings and bringing them small gifts. It also suggested spending extra time on those "hard-to-reach" people, the ones not immediately receptive to the Party Ark message.

"It sounds like they're grooming people to join a cult," I said.

"And you haven't even reached the good part," said

Tiffany. She turned a few pages and pointed at a section for me to read.

I frowned, reading the passage aloud. "*With regard to the delicate matter of homosexual lifestyle and practice, Party Ark believes such activities clearly not to be in accord with the purpose of creation and should therefore be shunned.*"

"They also have an issue with tattoos, the whole your-body-is-a-temple thing. And they hate witches. You know the quote on their candy corn?"

I pursed my lips. "*Have nothing to do with the fruitless seeds of darkness, but rather expose them.* Ephesians 5:11."

"Yeah, the actual verse in the Bible has nothing to do with witches or candy corn."

I raised one finger. "Harvest candy."

She laughed. "You're right. Sorry. Anyway, they took it to a whole new level, and tried to off your aunt Lucy."

"What were their plans for Sally, Ralphie, and Bubu?"

"Conversion therapy. Even for the dog. Nice, huh? They learned all about it at one of their ARK retreats. They thought by dressing Sally and Bubu as males, and teaching Ralphie the error of his ways, they could change all three of them. Part of their mission."

"As was getting rid of people who didn't fit their vision of what the South Side should look like?"

"Exactly, and Aggie ended up being an easy tool for them to use. Vulnerable, isolated, and with a definite weakness. Those monsters saw it right away and figured out how to exploit it." She shook her head. "I thought they were just vandals, and it would be a little piece in the local news."

"But it became much bigger."

She smiled, and for the first time it seemed almost genuine. "Yep. I hit the investigative reporting jackpot. When I saw Dario sniffing around the story, I knew it would be good. He got distracted by you, of course, and stopped pursuing it. A win/win for me—a great story and a way to get even with Dario for his poor taste in women." Her lips twitched, but I wasn't sure if she joked with me or not.

Anthony, who'd been listening in, stared at her in disbelief. "Is that seriously how you see this? A woman almost died today. If you'd reported this story earlier, none of this would have ever happened."

Tiffany glared at him, her blue eyes cold. "I didn't even know the truth of the whole story until I landed in the middle of that storage unit. Beforehand, I lacked anything but a few wild guesses. And, I did you a favor, Officer Belfiore." She reached into her pocket and pulled out a small black object.

"A voice activated recorder," he said, giving her the barest hint of a smile. He wore his black police uniform, his gun belt low across his narrow hips, and the muscles of his arms showing under the sleeves of his shirt. "Did you get anything we can use?"

"I did."

"Which is why she kept asking them so many questions," I said. "She recorded their answers. Nice move, Barbie."

"Thanks, Endora," she said without missing a beat.

I let out a rather unladylike snort. It was pretty funny. Tiffany started laughing too. Part stress induced, but mostly a kind of giddy relief it was finally over.

Anthony watched us, perplexed. "Who the heck is Endora?"

The expression on his face made us laugh even harder. When Dario came back from making his phone call, he heard Anthony's question. He looked back and forth between the two of us in confusion.

"Endora. The mother-in-law from *Bewitched*. You know, the witch with red hair. Why are you talking about Endora?"

Tiffany and I nearly fell off our chairs. It took us a while to settle down, and when we did, we both wiped away tears of laughter from our cheeks.

"Are you two friends now?" asked Anthony.

Tiffany studied my face. "Not exactly," she said. "But we're not enemies either."

Tiffany's story made national headlines. The day after it broke, the Party Ark on East Carson Street closed forever. We were happy to see it go, and even happier when a judge launched a federal investigation to look into Party Ark. Hopefully the Ark Angels and their horrible manual would soon be wiped off the face of the earth forever.

I spent the rest of my time in the South Side working at the magic shop and getting ready for my review board hearing. I stayed most nights with Dario, and visited Aggie every day, but I decided to spend my last night in Pittsburgh with Aunt Lucy. Dario was out of town for work, and I wanted to share some quality time with my sweet, eccentric, slightly dotty aunt.

"Thank you for helping me, dearest," she said, as we sat by the fireplace in her apartment. "You saved the shop, and you saved me, too."

"You would have done the same for me."

"You're right, but it was more than your help in the shop or taking care of me. I'd grown kind of jaded and sad. It may have had something to do with the drugs those girls gave me, but it started long before that. I doubted myself, you see. I felt like a charlatan, and, well, I hate to say it, but after my Anton died, I almost stopped believing in magic." She said the last words so softly I barely heard them. "Until I saw all the magic brimming inside of you. It made me believe again. *You* made me believe."

I took her small hand in mine. "You made me believe in magic, too."

She kissed my cheek and toddled off to bed. I curled up

on her couch to sleep with Jinx next to me. A few hours later, I jerked awake and instantly knew I was no longer alone. Ivan Trabuski sat in one of the chairs by the fire, watching me as I slept.

"I don't have the Dragon Rouge," I said.

"I know," he said softly.

"And your last name is not Rochat."

He shook his head. "No, it's Trabuski. I'm sorry I lied to you."

"You lied about more than your name. You also omitted being a thief and a scoundrel. Is there anything else? Are you going to push me down the steps, too?"

He leaned forward in his chair, frowning. "I never pushed your aunt. She fell down the steps all on her own. I reached for her, trying to stop her, but I couldn't get to her in time." He tapped the arm of the chair with one hand, a clear sign of his irritation. "And who do you think called the ambulance, made sure your aunt rested comfortably, and left the door of the shop open so the paramedics could enter? If I'd truly wanted to harm her, why would I have done any of those things?"

My brow furrowed. Although still groggy with sleep, I realized he made a good point. "You're the hero?"

He let out a soft laugh. "Definitely not. Never mistake me for a hero. As you said, I'm a thief and a scoundrel."

"Well, Sir Galahad was born a bastard, but he became the most perfect of knights. Maybe there's hope for you yet."

"A scientist who still believes in fairy tales." He sighed, his golden hair gleaming in the firelight. He did bear an uncanny resemblance to Uncle Anton, even though Uncle Anton was dark and Ivan fair. "How rare you are, Grace. How wonderful. How...magical. So magical perhaps you may even be able to redeem me."

"You should focus on redeeming yourself."

"But it would be so much more fun if you did it." He gave me a crooked smile. "I'd ask you to come away with me, but I know you won't. I wanted to say goodbye and give you this. I knew you'd appreciate it, and I'd like you to think of me fondly from time to time when I'm gone."

He handed me a small book as the clock on Aunt Lucy's mantle chimed midnight. The title read, *The Life and Untimely End of the Witch Maeve McAlroy, as Written by Her Daughter*.

"Where did you get this?" I asked, leafing through the pages, but when I looked up, he was gone. The clock on the mantle now showed a quarter after twelve, which meant fifteen minutes had passed, but I couldn't account for them. Jinx sat up and let out a giant kitten yawn, acting as perplexed as me about Ivan's sudden disappearance.

"How does he do that? It's so annoying."

Jinx provided no answers for me. He jumped off my lap, curled up on the hearth, and fell right back asleep.

I went through the apartment, checking each door and window. None were open. If not for the small book clasped in my hands, I'd have thought I'd completely imagined Ivan's entire visit.

I sat on the couch, a blanket over my shoulders and stared into the dying embers of the fire. Part of me wished I could disappear like Ivan. The idea of facing the review board terrified me. I'd leave the South Side tomorrow, this comfortable place I'd grown to love, and head off to an uncertain future.

I reached for the book Ivan gave me and read about Maeve McAlroy. Her life hadn't been so dissimilar from my own. Jealous of her talents, her husband sounded like the seventeenth century equivalent of Jonathan. And when the physicians in the town understood Maeve's skill and brilliance as a healer and a midwife, they said she owed her talents to the devil.

"Not so different from Roger," I muttered to myself.

Roger didn't accuse me of sacrificing children, but he'd insinuated what I achieved at work had more to do with my breasts and my physical appearance than my brains or my work ethic. A tale as old as time. Men being envious and afraid of smart, strong, powerful women.

I thought I'd looked like Hester Prynne in my cape. Maybe my dear ancestor Maeve and I had more in common with good old Hester than I realized. Hester wore a letter "A" emblazoned on her chest, but Maeve pretty much endured a "W" for witch on hers.

And what would my letter be? "C" for cheater, or for chemist?

I'd soon find out. The review board was only a day away.

CHAPTER 45

KEEP CALM AND BLIND THEM WITH SCIENCE.

The members of the review board sat in a row at a long table in one of the chemistry lecture halls. Sunlight gleamed through the leaded glass windows, streaming over the honey oak interior. It reminded me of a classroom in England, with its wooden floors, old-fashioned desks, and paneled walls. A beautiful room. One I'd always loved. Odd that they'd chosen such a peaceful, scholarly setting for something like this.

Dr. Lewis occupied the center chair, his glasses resting low on his nose and the hint of a scowl on his face. Two other professors flanked him, a woman named Dr. Ericka Huston whom I'd only spoken with a few times, and a man named Dr. George Bandik who'd always been kind to me. Next to the professors sat two of my fellow PhD candidates, Phillip and Karen.

The desks behind me, long heavy tables made out of the same honey oak as the walls, soon filled with people. I heard the soft murmurs of their whispered conversations but didn't turn around. It would make me more nervous to see their faces. Were they here to support me, or witness my public humiliation? I wasn't sure. I kept my face forward and my back straight.

Dr. Lewis read the charges against me. From the beauty of the room, to the serious faces of the people in front of me, this moment acquired a surreal quality. Even with weeks to prepare, I still couldn't believe this was happening.

Dr. Lewis called Roger as the first witness. He sat in front of me with a smirk on his lips and a nasty gleam in his eyes as he told lie after lie. It surprised me Dr. Lewis let him get away with it. He made serious accusations against me but supplied no proof. Only opinion and conjecture.

"She's had a reputation for cheating since we were undergrads."

"Do you have any documentation to back up these statements?" asked Dr. Bandik.

Roger glared at him. "No, but we all knew. Ask anyone."

"Which seems like a non-answer, but we'll give Ms. O'Leary a chance to speak." Dr. Huston turned to me, her dark eyes piercing. "Would you like to respond to these accusations?"

I nodded, my movements stiff and strange. "I've never cheated or allowed any of my students to cheat."

Roger's smirk widened. "You couldn't have gotten the scores you did as an undergrad without cheating. Give me a break."

My blood boiled. "What bothers you, Roger? Are you angry because I did well, or because I did better than you? You've always been jealous of my success and my position at the university. I have documentation to prove it."

"What documentation?" asked Phillip. "Can we see it, please?"

I brought up copies of group emails and texts, and screen shots of Roger's Facebook page and Twitter accounts. It wasn't hard to find proof Roger didn't like me, or that he exhibited issues with women in general. As the people on the review board read through the information I'd compiled, Roger's face reddened. "Excuse me, but I'm not the one on trial here."

"Ms. O'Leary has the right to defend herself. How do you know she gave her answer key to a student?" asked Dr. Bandik as he took notes on a yellow legal pad.

"I don't," he said. "You'll have to ask Seth Billings about that."

Seth, the next witness, slouched in his chair, like the entire process bored him. His gaze, however, kept moving to a tall man in a suit standing near one of the windows. Judging by the resemblance between the two of them, I assumed he was Seth's famous father, Silas Billings.

"When exactly did you find Ms. O'Leary's answer key?" asked Dr. Lewis, getting right to the point.

Seth straightened in his seat. "Right after I took the test."

He looked at each member of the review board, his blue eyes so sincere even I almost believed him. Almost, but not quite. Karen didn't seem to fall for it, either. "And you found it on the floor of your classroom?" she asked.

Seth's gaze rested on her, his expression morphing into one of vague annoyance. "Yes."

"Why didn't you give it to Ms. O'Leary?" she asked.

"I didn't know what it was at first." Seth's gaze shot to me, and I glimpsed the ugliness existing beneath the beautiful surface. "She's a terrible teacher. Her class was awful, and she constantly sabotaged me. Making things harder than necessary. I could never have passed her test without help. She's an evil, conniving witch."

I contained a snort of laughter. Everyone called me a witch lately. Perhaps Maeve McAlroy created a spell to take care of entitled assholes like Seth Billings. I guessed she probably had.

"Ms. O'Leary, would you care to respond?" asked Dr. Bandik.

I took a deep, calming breath. "Perhaps it's best to let Seth's work speak for itself." I took a stack of papers out of a folder. "A list of each assignment he didn't turn in, and all the labs he missed. I also documented his attendance, which was spotty at best."

Seth leaned forward in his seat. "I didn't come to class because you suck as a teacher—"

Dr. Lewis interrupted him. "Thank you, Mr. Billings. That will be enough."

Seth got up and walked back to his seat, muttering under his breath. I glanced at his father, who kept an unreadable expression on his face.

Dr. Lewis called upon several other students who spoke on my behalf. A few of my colleagues came as well, including Megan. After she spoke, saying wonderful things about me, we took a fifteen-minute recess.

Trying to calm down, I went over the elements in my head. *Hydrogen, helium, lithium, beryllium, boron, carbon, nitrogen, oxygen...*

I heard footsteps behind me, and someone put a hand on my shoulder. I turned, expecting to see one of my students, or perhaps a colleague. I hoped for a friendly face, but I got a lot more.

"Dario?" He wore a suit and carried a briefcase, and it looked like he'd worked hard to comb his hair into submission this morning.

"Hey, Grace," he said softly, kneeling next to me. "How's it going?"

"I'm not sure yet. I can't believe you're here."

He squeezed my hand. "I wouldn't miss it." He took some papers out of his briefcase and handed them to me.

"What's this?"

"It's an interview. Roger was the guy I met with in the bar, right before Tiffany showed up and put your potion in my drink."

"Wait. You met with Roger?"

"Yes," he said. "I came to Philly on three separate occasions to try to figure out the truth of the story and find a way to help you. I knew you were innocent, but each lead went nowhere. And then I realized something."

"What?"

"Not a single student or teacher said a bad word about you, except Roger and Seth. Why did Dr. Lewis believe Seth, a student with an obviously poor work ethic, and not you, his employee? There was only one possible answer." He paused, his dark eyes intense. "This is a cover up. It's the only possible explanation, and you're the one person who can figure it out."

The review board members came back into the room. "But I don't know who's behind this," I said. "I've thought about nothing else for months."

He put a hand on my shoulder. "A scientist and a reporter both ask the same questions when they're trying to find the truth. Think like a scientist. Use your intuition. Read over this interview with Roger. Something is off, but I can't figure it out. You can. You've got this."

Dario went back to his seat, but knowing he was there, right behind me, made everything so much better. And knowing what lengths he'd gone to trying to help me, made me stronger. He'd believed in me from the start. I thought, for the first time, I might win this after all.

I looked over Dario's interview with Roger, doing what he said and letting my intuition guide me. Dario interviewed Roger under the pretense of writing an article about rising stars in the scientific community. Roger took the bait and ran with it, and when he bragged about how he'd secured millions of dollars in funding for the university, bells went off in my head.

What was he talking about?

My gaze shot to Mr. Billings, still standing by the window, his expression grim, and the dots slowly connected in my head. Mr. Billings possessed millions of dollars, and a passion for his alma mater. He also had a problem. His son's incompetence in my organic chemistry class.

I could never have passed her test without help.

Dr. Lewis told me Seth failed the exam. I knew it wasn't true. I'd seen the first page of Seth's exam with my own eyes. He'd gotten each answer right.

He passed the test, with help...thanks to Roger.

When the review board reconvened, Dr. Lewis announced it was my turn to ask questions and call witnesses. I sat up straighter in my chair.

"Seth, could you please return to the witness chair?" He complied, dragging his feet and giving me a dirty look. I turned to the review board. "Is there someone here who has access to Seth's exam? The one he took on the day he said he found my answer key?"

"Why do you ask, Ms. O'Leary? Is this truly necessary?" asked Dr. Lewis. He spoke to me in the same kind, gentle, fatherly way he had since the first time I met him as an undergrad, but this time I heard a hint of condescension in his tone. Had he always spoken to me that way?

I thought he treated me like all the other students in the chemistry department, but he actually treated me like he did all the *women* in the department. He never used that cajoling, overly calm and sensitive tone on Jonathan or Roger, I was sure of it.

Thoughts tumbled through my mind as I put pieces of the puzzle together. I didn't have all the answers yet, but a theory formed, and Dario's interview with Roger led me toward a conclusion.

"I'd like to see his exam," I said. "Is there a reason you don't want me to see it, Dr. Lewis?"

"You're being ridiculous," he said. The kind and gentle note in his voice was gone. "I will not continue with this charade."

Dr. Bandik scratched his beard, watching Dr. Lewis closely. "I see no problem with Ms. O'Leary's request."

"Nor do I."

The voice came from the back of the room. Dr. Ramona Randall, the newly appointed chancellor of the university, stood up and stared daggers at Dr. Lewis. Dr. Randall took over the job a few months ago, when the old chancellor retired. She enjoyed the double recognition of being the first woman and the first African American appointed to the position. I never got to meet her, however, because my academic suspension occurred not long after she started.

Dr. Lewis shook his head. "We handed those tests back to the students weeks ago."

Jonathan raised his hand. "We scanned all written tests this semester as instructed, Dr. Lewis. I can pull up the test right now, if you like. All the TAs have access."

Dr. Lewis looked like he wanted to smack Jonathan on the head. "Why, thank you, Mr. Gottfried," he said through gritted teeth. "That's incredibly helpful of you."

Jonathan gave me a sidelong glance as he took out his laptop. I blinked in surprise. Was he helping me?

Roger paled, looking like he might throw up. "I don't know how sharing this helps anyone," he said. "The first time Seth took the test, he failed it, so he couldn't have used the answer key."

He looked to Dr. Lewis for encouragement, but now Dr. Lewis appeared to be the one on the verge of puking. I glanced at Dario, and his eyes widened. Had Roger just said what I thought he'd said?

Dr. Huston caught it as well. "Hold on a second." She leaned forward in her seat. "Are you telling us Mr. Billings took the test more than once?"

Dr. Lewis's face tightened. "In lieu of what happened, it only seemed fair."

He used the same fatherly tone on Dr. Huston he used on me. She didn't seem to like it any more than I did. She pursed her lips and looked at Chancellor Randall. "This is highly irregular," she said.

"I agree," said the chancellor. "And I'm curious to see what Mr. Gottfried pulls up for us."

Jonathan carried his laptop over to the review board and placed it directly in front of Dr. Lewis. "What do you want me to do?" asked Dr. Lewis.

Chancellor Randall walked slowly to the front of the room. "You can start by telling us what grade Seth received on his test."

Dr. Lewis grew redder still. "He passed, so this must be his second test. Not the first."

"Can you prove it?" she asked.

The solution to the problem appeared right in front of me as soon as she asked that question. "I can," I said, jumping to my feet. "If it's the first test, there should be checkmarks next to each answer on the first page. It's a habit of mine. I do it to make sure I read each answer thoroughly. The checkmarks will be in pencil, but you should be able to see them on a scan."

Chancellor Randall moved to stand directly behind Dr. Lewis and looked at the laptop. "There are definitely checkmarks on this test. You're right, Ms. O'Leary."

Dr. Lewis responded with an angry shake of his head. "It doesn't prove a single thing. Other TAs use the same system."

"Is this true, Mr. Gottfried?" asked Chancellor Randall.

Jonathan shook his head. "No one but Grace does it that way. She's OCD about double-checking answers. The entire department knows. Just ask."

"I don't think there is any need," said Chancellor Randall. "And it appears Mr. Billings passed this test, which means someone here is lying. Maybe even several people." Her gaze went to Seth. "Your academic career is on the line here, young man. I need to know the truth. If I find out you are not being honest with me, you will face serious consequences. I want to separate fact from fiction now. Did you take this test more than once?"

Seth glanced at his father. The embarrassment and disappointment radiating from Mr. Billings was almost palpable. Seth swallowed hard and looked back at Chancellor Randall. "I did not."

She folded her arms across her chest. With her salt and pepper braided hair piled high upon her head, she looked like an avenging queen. "Why did Mr. Frisk lie?"

Seth shrugged. "I don't know. He's trying to cover something up, I guess."

Chancellor Randall looked like she was getting a headache. She rubbed her temples. "Seth, did you even find the answer key on the floor of the classroom?"

"I did not," he said, his voice softer this time.

"So you lied to the review board," she said. "What else have you done, Seth?"

Things clicked into place at rapid-fire speed. The more Seth spoke, the more I understood there was only one way he could have gotten such a high grade on this test.

"Did someone give you a copy of the answer key prior to the test?" I asked, and he nodded, refusing to meet my eyes. "Who?"

He lifted his hand slowly and pointed at Dr. Lewis. "Mr.

Frisk gave me the other key, the one I was supposed to say I found on the floor of the classroom."

"Why?"

"He and Dr. Lewis offered to help me pass. Dr. Lewis gave me the original key, but when he found out I shared it with a few of my fraternity brothers, he got extremely pissed off and told me we had to cover our tracks. He said you weren't a team player and insisted we had to get you out of the way as quickly as possible so we could do damage control. He came up with the idea of having Mr. Frisk take it from your brief-case. He mentioned grabbing it in the TA room, but he worried about getting caught. Instead, he went to your apart-ment, and took it."

I stared in shock at Dr. Lewis, my former mentor. I had suspected Roger had a hand in this from the beginning, but not him. Never him.

"It was you? You did this to me?"

"Nonsense. This is nothing but lies and wild speculation." He turned to the blond man standing by the window. "Mr. Billings. We'll sort this out as soon as possible. I'm not sure why Seth is saying these things. Perhaps someone threatened him."

"Or maybe he's saying them because they're true," said Seth's father. "I've heard enough. I know what my son is like. When I asked you to help him, I didn't mean you should cheat. I was talking about tutoring."

"Dad, I can explain—"

He shook his head. "I'll speak with you later, son. We have a lot to discuss, but it's better if we do it in private. We'll have plenty of time to chat, since you won't return to school anytime soon."

Dr. Lewis grew even more agitated. He pointed at me. "You cannot prove this. Right now you're working with a hypothesis, not a factual conclusion. If you keep this up, you'll never work in this field again. I swear it. I'll destroy you."

In the last few weeks, people had poisoned me and held me at gunpoint, and I'd been psychically possessed by an evil stone. I'd made love potions, faced deranged maniacs, and danced nude at midnight. More than being just some redheaded girl in a skirt, I was the descendant of Maeve McAlroy, who'd been killed because men couldn't handle her power. The same power flowed through me. Grace O'Leary, PhD candidate, chemist, and part-time witch. And I was about to school my professor.

"You don't scare me, Dr. Lewis. You already tried to ruin me with your lies. But the truth, as well as the evidence, is on my side."

"I agree," said Dr. Bandik. "I think we can safely say Ms. O'Leary is the innocent party in all of this."

Relief washed over me, but I still wanted to know something important. "Why did you do this to me, Dr. Lewis?"

"I know why," said Mr. Billings, lifting something off the table next to him. "He did it for this."

He unrolled a poster board and held it up so we could see it. On it was a rendering of a new wing attached to the current chemistry building. In large letters above the picture it read, "The Billings/Lewis Chemistry Annex. Coming soon."

"I'd planned to make the announcement today at the university board meeting," he said. "I guess we'll have to change the name."

"This is complete and utter nonsense," said Dr. Lewis, standing up and shoving his notes into his brief case. "I will not listen to another word. Ms. O'Leary is a blot on the reputation of this fine institution, one I have spent most of my life building. I deserve to have my name on the annex. I suggest we expel her immediately, and make sure she's never able to teach or work at another university ever again."

"I don't think so," said Chancellor Randall, her mouth a tight, narrow line. "Sit, Dr. Lewis. We have a lot of questions for you, and also for Mr. Frisk. "

Dr. Lewis sat, suddenly looking much older, as if he understood no amount of bluster or bullying would get him out of this mess. Roger, who'd been trying to sneak out of the room, stopped in his tracks. He'd soon find out how it felt to be persona non grata, but I wasn't the least bit sorry for him. He'd exhibited great promise as a chemist, but he let his jealousy and ego control him and destroy his career. And he didn't even have a Dragon Rouge to blame it on.

I looked at the other members of the review board, and at the chancellor. "What happens now?"

Dr. Bandik, taking Dr. Lewis's role in the proceedings, straightened his bow tie and folded his hands on the table in front of him. "Well, because of what came to light today, you are exonerated on all charges and free to continue on as you were before any of this nastiness occurred. Are we in agreement on this?" The other members of the review board expressed their approval. Dr. Bandik picked up Dr. Lewis's gavel, and slammed it on the table. "All charges against Grace O'Leary are hereby dropped. And, when you are ready, I look forward to hearing you defend your thesis. I'm certain it will be quite interesting."

A cheer erupted from the audience. After I thanked everyone, and accepted their congratulations, I searched the room for Dario. I spotted him immediately. He stood by the door waiting for me, and, when I reached him, he hugged me so hard he lifted me off the floor.

"You did it," he said, his cheek against my hair.

"And you believed in me."

"Of course I did," he said, lowering me to the ground. "And I always will."

"Uh, excuse me," said Jonathan, clearing his throat. "I

don't mean to interrupt, but I owe you an apology, Grace. I'm so sorry."

I leaned against Dario's arm, my hand linked with his. "Thank you for saying so, and I appreciate what you did for me during the hearing. It was brave of you to stand up to Dr. Lewis and Roger."

He ducked his head, giving me a crooked smile. "I should have been brave before. I'll always regret how I acted. But I guess things worked out well. For you at least."

"They did."

I said goodbye, bearing no ill will toward Jonathan. In the end, things really had worked out well for me. I had friends in the South Side, a thesis I knew I could defend, the chance to do the job I'd always wanted, and I'd fallen madly in love with Dario Fontana. Life was pretty perfect.

As we walked out of the building hand in hand, Dario lifted his face to the bright autumn sun. "What are you thinking about?" I asked.

"Neil deGrasse Tyson," he said, and laughed at the look on my face. "You didn't see that coming, did you?"

"No, I did not. What about Neil deGrasse Tyson? He happens to be one of my very favorite astrophysicists."

"Mine, too. Dr. Tyson said, 'The good thing about science is that it's true whether you believe it or not.' And that's what happened during your hearing. A couple of scientists got a hard lesson in the truth."

"Did you suspect Dr. Lewis was behind it all along?"

He shook his head. "Nope, but I knew you were innocent."

"Stop walking," I said. "I want to kiss you."

He grinned. "You don't have to ask me twice," he said, his lips brushing against mine. "I'll kiss you anytime, Ms. O'Leary."

I wondered if a heart could burst from too much happiness. Even though I knew it wasn't scientifically possible, I thought mine was about to explode.

"You promise?" I asked, as I clung to his coat. "I might want a *lot* of kisses."

He grinned and kissed me on the steps of the chemistry building, as dry leaves swirled around us, and I knew we had it all. Love, trust, honesty, chemistry...and something else, too. Something I'd never believed in, but now recognized.

Magic.

And it didn't take a genius...or a witch...to figure it out.

CHAPTER 46

MAGIC IS SCIENCE WE DON'T UNDERSTAND YET.

Thanksgiving at Alvida Fontana's house was a crazy, chaotic, loud, and crowded affair. Tables heaped with food nearly sagged under the weight. She designated an entire room just for dessert. Unlike the traditional Thanksgiving meal of turkey and sweet potatoes we usually enjoyed at my parents' house back in Philly, the Fontanas also added ham, lasagna, ravioli, and a plethora of side dishes, each one more delicious than the last.

I sat next to Dario, his hand in mine, as I basked in the glow of great food and wonderful company. All of our friends from the South Side attended. Aunt Lucy sat with Mr. Dalca, flirting shamelessly. Aggie finally felt better and sat between Sally and Ralphie. Even Bubu came as an honored guest. We all had a lot to be thankful for this year, especially me.

Dario tapped his fork against his glass and rose to his feet. "I'd like to propose a toast," he said. "To friends, family, health, and happiness. And may I also toast Grace, who will soon be known as *Doctor* O'Leary."

"Here, here," said Aunt Lucy, a slightly drunken smile on her sweet face.

"*Ti amo,*" said Alvida, blowing me a kiss.

"Thank you," I said, my heart soaring with emotion. I'd obtained everything I'd ever wanted, but I also faced some tough decisions, and that small cloud darkened my happiness.

Dario asked me about it as we walked back to his house after dinner. "Are you okay?"

I nodded. "Dr. Bandik called me into his office before I left yesterday," I said. "He's the new head of the chemistry department. He wanted to talk with me about a job."

"Wow," said Dario, his expression neutral. "What do you want to do?"

"I don't know," I said. "It's a great opportunity. It's kind of hard to pass it up, but..."

I paused when I saw another couple approach. It was Candace, the woman from the bank who'd been one of the first to purchase a bottle of my now infamous love potion. "Hi, Grace," she said, grinning from ear to ear. "This is my boyfriend Jerry."

I sensed a tingle in the air. Chemistry and love and happiness flowed between them, just like it did between Dario and me. No longer mousy and shy, Candace exuded confidence, and Jerry couldn't seem to keep his gaze off her.

Dario and Jerry knew each other, and as they chatted, Candace pulled me aside. "I wanted to thank you," she said. "For the love potion. It worked even better than I expected."

"Candace," I said, my voice soft. "I had nothing to do with it. He loves you because you're a great girl. Not because you gave him a love potion."

"Oh, I know," she said with a giggle. "And I didn't give him the love potion. I took it. As Mrs. Periwinkle instructed. It helped me have the courage to go after what I wanted, and it opened my heart to the idea Jerry might want to be with me, too."

I stared at her. "Wait a second. Mrs. Periwinkle told you to *take* the potion?" I asked remembering the tiny dab of the stuff I'd tasted myself. It definitely felt kind of strange as soon as it hit my tongue, and right after that, my attitude toward Dario changed significantly. I'd texted him the same night.

"She told me giving it to someone you're interested in might work temporarily, but taking it yourself would change your life. And she was right," said Candace.

I frowned, wondering if we'd misunderstood Maeve McElroy's potion and her grimoire. Rather than bending others to our wills or playing tricks on unsuspecting hearts, perhaps it gave us the power we needed to make ourselves happy. And maybe it was also about breaking the rules and thinking outside the box.

It made my head spin, but Candace didn't seem to notice as she gave me a hug goodbye. "Thank you, Grace. For everything."

"You're welcome," I said, wondering how much of her happiness I could take credit for, and suspecting my love potion contributed very little to what blossomed between Candace and Jerry. Like the water in the fountain, and the discovery in my thesis, it simply acted as a catalyst for bigger and better things.

As I put my arm through Dario's and we continued walking, he cleared his throat. "About the job Dr. Bandik mentioned, you should take it. It's a great opportunity."

"I don't want to do this long distance."

"Me, neither," he said, facing me. "So, I'll move to Philly and get a job there. It would mean starting over, but it's worth it if we can be together."

I stopped walking and stared up at him, the stars in the cold night sky sparkling like a million diamonds above his head. "You'd give up your job, your family, your house, and the hockey team you're coaching, all to be with me?"

He pulled me closer and kissed the top of my head. "It's not what I'd be giving up, it's what I'd be getting. Which is *you*. I support you, Grace. If this is what you want, if this is the job you want, then let's do it."

"Well, I love you for saying so, but I've already decided it isn't the job for me."

"What do you mean?"

I bit my lip to keep from smiling at the confusion on his face. "I have a lead on a job at Carnegie Mellon," I said. "I'm going to talk with them while I'm here. As long as things go well when I defend my thesis in two weeks, they've told me the job is mine."

"You're going to turn down Dr. Bandik?"

I tucked a lock of hair behind my ear. "I'd like to have my first real job at a place with no bad memories. I'll miss my old colleagues, but there are people who resent me for what happened to Dr. Lewis, and there are others who still believe I did something wrong. It's so easy to ruin a person's reputation, but so hard to repair it. I don't want the past to hang over me. I want a clean slate. I also promised Delilah I'd help with a project or two at the community college, in my spare time, and I'm excited by the prospect. So, what do you think? Do you mind staying here? Because I'd rather not leave the South Side."

He didn't reply right away. He studied my face, a shadow of worry in his eyes. "Are you sure this is what *you* want? I don't want you to feel pressured or pushed—"

I put a finger to his lips. "This is what I want, and it's about more than my job. I've finally embraced who I am. I need to learn more about all this witchy stuff, and Eliza Dragonsong promised to teach me. She reached out to me a few days ago, and it's a great opportunity. Also, Aunt Lucy is getting older. She could use my help." The thought of my aunt made me smile. "I have family here, and friends. I have a better job with more possibilities for advancement, and a chance to learn about myself, and my heritage. And, most importantly of all, I have you. This is where I'm supposed to be. I feel it in my bones. Are you okay with staying right here?"

He let out a whoop and lifted me into the air, swinging me around. "Oh, Grace. This is the best news ever."

I laughed. "How could I take you away from here? You love the South Side. It's your home. Also, Nunny would kill me."

He put me back on the ground, his hands gently cupping my face. "Home is wherever you are, and wherever we both are, together."

He kissed me again, and I felt as if my whole life clicked into place. Much like an experiment proving my hypothesis, or an equation being solved, it hadn't been one decision or one step determining the outcome. It was a series of choices, a little something called luck, and maybe, just maybe, a touch of supernatural assistance from my old, dead witch of an ancestor.

Thank you, Maeve. I sent the thought straight up to the sky and gasped as a shooting star appeared and streaked across the heavens.

"What was that?" Dario looked up to see what I stared at, but it was already gone.

"Just some dust and space rocks falling to earth," I said. "And a message from Maeve McAlroy."

"And what did darling Maeve have to tell you?" he asked, a smile playing on his lips.

I reached up and stroked his strong jaw, loving the way he

looked at me. Loving everything about this man. "The best kind of happiness, the best kind of magic, and the best kind of future, is the kind you create for yourself," I said, and as I pulled his head down for a long, sweet, perfectly magical kiss, I knew Great Grandma Maeve had been absolutely right.

ACKNOWLEDGMENTS

Thank you to my editors, Ramona DeFelice Long and Lara Parker, and my sensitivity readers, Malissa Close, Susan Johnson, and Karen Loschiavo. Thank you also to my brave proofreaders: Suzanne Boyd, Charlene Kowalski, Sheila Mills, Rebecca Moore, Beth Spence, and Marylu Latagliata Zuk. A big thank you to the Blankie Brigade (Kathleen Shoop, Lori M. Jones, and Kim Pierson) for your unwavering support and friendship, and to my wonderful and brilliant son Devin for patiently listening to me discuss the scientific elements of the book, and actually being impressed (and a little shocked) when I got it right.

ABOUT THE AUTHOR

National award winning author Abigail Drake has spent her life traveling the world and collecting stories wherever she visited. She majored in Japanese and Economics in college and worked in import/export and as an ESL teacher before she committed herself full time to writing. Abigail is a trekkie, a book hoarder, the master of the Nespresso machine, a red wine drinker, and a chocoholic. She lives in Beaver, Pennsylvania with her husband and three sons. A Labrador named Capone is the most recent edition to her family, and she blogs about him to maintain what little sanity she has left.

ALSO BY ABIGAIL DRAKE

Women's Fiction

The Enchanted Garden Cafe

Delayed Departure

Sophie and Jake

Saying Goodbye, Special Combined Edition

Saying Goodbye, Part Two

Saying Goodbye, Part One

Traveller

Young Adult Fiction

Tiger Lily

Novellas

Can't Buy Me Love

Valentine Kisses

Short Stories

Into the Woods

CPSIA information can be obtained
at www.ICGtesting.com
Printed in the USA
LVHW090548230819
628457LV00004BA/631/P

9 781093 510874